Defending the Reaper

Book 5 in The Playmakers Series®

BY G.K. BRADY

Trefoil Publishing

ISBN 978-1-7354558-9-1

Cover design by Getcovers
Edited by Jenny Quinlan, Historical Editorial
Proofread by Word Servings

Contents

Dedication

To my readers, who not only read what I write but who inspire me to keep at it. I thank you from the bottom of my heart.

Chapter 1

One Way to Meet Hot Chicks

Dave Grimson propelled himself through the arena's corridors as though fire licked at his feet, eyes focused forward, veiled behind a curtain of vivid red, his jaw muscles bunched by fury. Christ, he was sick of the damn coaches barking out his mistakes in front of everyone! The season had just started, and he was back under the microscope, facing their recriminations, suspicions, and aspersions. Their endless drug tests. And most of his teammates were no better. He'd been their captain for ten years. *Ten years!* The *C* he wore on his sweater was a joke because he was captain of squat. One slip-up and he was persona non grata. Where the hell was the loyalty? How many of those fuckers had he gone to battle for? He'd lay odds that a good chunk of them had committed the same sin he had. They just hadn't gotten caught.

When the hell would this stop? How much more could he take before he said, *Fuck it!* and walked away?

Quit while you're still on top of your game, old man. Keep your dignity intact. Don't be that *guy*. Except he wasn't *on top* of his game, no matter that he'd kept up a grueling training schedule throughout the off-season. Never mind that he'd been forced onto the IR though he hadn't been injured—killing his perfect iron man streak—or that when they'd let him return from his bogus IR stint, he *had* been injured when he'd broken his hand in last season's finals. And by some cosmic fluke, he'd *re*-broken the hand during practice when he crashed into the boards at an awkward angle. How jacked-up was that?

Daylight brightened the end of the tunnel, and he emerged in the clear, crisp air of a late Colorado fall morning. The chill did little to cool the heat percolating in his veins.

He stalked to his gleaming midnight-blue Aston Martin DBX, barely registering slamming his gear bag in the cargo space or banging the door shut once he'd slid behind the wheel. In autopilot mode, he switched on the ignition and raced from the parking lot, his mind grinding away at everything that was wrong in his life.

The voice of reason was straining to be heard, but his pissed-off self was in control and shouted it down, ready to holler its indignations from the rooftops.

Rubbing more salt into the wound had been the team owner's douche of a son, Travis, who'd taunted him from the stands. "I hear hand-to-eye is the first thing to go, Grims." Fucker! At thirty-two, Dave might have a few years on Travis, but Travis had nothing on Dave's hockey smarts or skills. But he couldn't say a damn thing to the entitled son of a bitch, so he'd swallowed his mad—even when Travis had warbled, "And he's buying his steroids at seven," to the tune of "Stairway to Heaven." Yeah, that had pushed his self-control to the screaming limit.

An intersection came up quicker than he anticipated, and he took the corner a little too hot so he could beat a red light. A guy who'd taken a step into the crosswalk jumped back on the curb and flipped him off.

"Watch where you're going!" Dave yelled, even though no one could hear him. *What the hell is wrong with people?*

Today was supposed to have been a *good* day—a rarity lately—but only an hour in, Nicole had derailed it. One of her best talents. Dave pounded his good palm against the steering wheel as he recalled her phone call first thing this morning. She'd laid an excessive guilt trip on him about taking Benny for a few days and about everything wrong in *her* world, as if he was supposed to run and fix it. She'd lost that privilege when she'd dumped him a year ago to look for "something better"—translation: *someone* better—so why the hell did she keep jerking his leash? And why the hell did he let her? *Guilt.* A powerful emotion with the ability to obscure the solidest logic. He needed a do-over in the worst way. A clean slate.

A moment of clarity struck. Maybe he *should* walk away. Not from the game he loved, but from the city that had soured on him, along with everyone in it. He could make a clean break, start fresh with a new team.

He punched in his agent's number. After two rings, the guy picked up.

"Mr. Grimson. To what do I owe the pleasure?"

"Hi, Herb. I need you to shop me to another team."

The silence on the other end lasted several beats. Then there was a huge intake of air. "Any particular team?"

"No. I don't care. As long as I'm out of Denver."

"How about Ottawa? They're always looking for talent, but they're also an eternal cellar-dweller."

Shit. It's really cold in Ottawa. And the team does *suck.* "Maybe not my top choice—if I have a choice—but I don't care. Just get me the hell out of Denver."

Herb spent a few minutes trying to schmooze Dave off the ledge, pointing out truths, like how beloved Dave was for his tireless community work, which just pissed Dave off even more. "I'm asking—no, demanding—a trade. It's time for a change. I am done with this city."

"Are you clean?"

"Yes," Dave hissed, "and I've got a fuck ton of test results to prove it." *Damn it! Why do I keep having to defend myself?*

"All right," Herb sighed dramatically. "I'll put the feelers out. How's the hand?"

"Good as new."

Another pause, which told Dave Herb wasn't swallowing the lie. "Son, will you take a piece of advice?"

Dave let out a sarcastic chuckle. "Do I have a choice?"

"You always have a choice. But consider this: you've been a huge part of that community for a long time, and no matter what you think, people there love you. You'll be starting from scratch wherever you land. I just think it wouldn't hurt to take a few deep breaths and mull over whether a trade is really going to solve your problems."

Your problems. As if Dave had brought *all* of this on himself. "I'll do that, but in the meantime, I expect you to be looking at every single team that needs a defenseman."

Dave hung up and muttered to himself. "*Your* problems. Christ, even my agent doesn't believe in me. What the hell is wrong with everybody?"

A deafening squeal cut off his thought, the sound reminiscent of a *Jurassic Park* monster scraping its claws down a blackboard. Time slowed. He had the sense of a horn honking, a skidding car, smoke pouring from tires. Then came the sickening screech of twisting metal. His vehicle was moving, out of his control, pushing another car across an intersection.

Shit, shit, shit!

Stop, stop, please stop!

The front of his Aston Martin pile-drove the other vehicle into a light post. The impact juddered through the steering wheel, traveling up his wrists, his arms, jarring his shoulders. Everything went still. A breathless instant passed.

Stunned, he stared through his cracked windshield at the car he'd hit, now a mess of groaning gray metal. His heart threw itself against his rib cage, over and over, like a trapped animal trying to escape. His breathing came in ragged gasps, as if he'd quadrupled his shift on the ice.

Then he was moving, unbuckling, throwing his door open, racing for the other driver's door. It creaked open just as he reached it, and a woman fighting an air bag staggered out. He reached out to steady her and was met by eyes that shot flares at him.

"You just blew through a red light without even slowing down!" she screamed. "What the hell is wrong with you?"

Then she was on the attack, storming at him, shoving at his chest until his back bumped against his SUV. At least a head shorter than his six-foot-three frame, she was no physical threat, but he held his hands up in surrender.

"Are you all right?" he panted.

"Do I look all right?" Her volume skyrocketed. "You T-boned me! My van is totaled!"

Suddenly, they were swarmed by people buzzing in various tones of urgency. "I'm an EMT," one announced.

The acrid smell of burned rubber stung Dave's nose. Fluids leaked onto the pavement. The EMT was insisting the woman from the mangled car take a step back so he could check her out, then he shot Dave a cursory look over his shoulder.

He answered the EMT's unasked question. "I'm okay." The dude slid him a look, then nodded and turned back to the woman.

Hovering by the Aston's wrinkled hood, Dave took in the other car. Crushed side panel with familiar, though unreadable, lettering clung drunkenly to a metal structure that reminded him of an accordion in places. Cockeyed tires. Broken windows. Behind the vehicle's open tailgate, white flower petals decorated mounds of dark, rich soil amid a jumble of shattered pots. And boxes and boxes of … Christmas lights. The odd mixture had spilled from the back of the van onto the ground.

Yeah, he doubted anything was salvageable.

Steel bands constricted his chest, and his stomach rolled over. He raked his fingers through his thick, collar-length beard. Why hadn't he paid attention? He'd been too busy wallowing in his pathetic pit of misery, that's why.

I could have killed her!

Not much of a praying man anymore, he nonetheless broadcast a series of silent pleas that the other driver wasn't hurt. Money could solve the broken van. It couldn't, however, solve a broken body—a fact of which he was painfully too aware. While she didn't *appear* to be broken, injury might be waiting to manifest itself. Trauma could be latent.

To the EMT, he said, "Should she be standing? What if she's hurt?" But the guy ignored him—just like the other driver was ignoring the EMT's efforts to assess her. *Her* overriding concern seemed to swing between her destroyed vehicle and Dave. Epic distress when her gaze landed on her wreck, and epic venom when it returned to him. He wanted to wither up and blow away. Pull Harry Potter's invisibility cloak around himself and slink off.

Instead, he whipped out his phone and dialed 911. "I'll take care of this," he assured the woman, though exactly what he was assuring her of wasn't yet crystal clear. She glowered at him, and he kept a wary eye on her while he reported the emergency. Suddenly, she turned to her vehicle, and all emotion and color drained from her face, leaving it a blank canvas. Then her body shuddered, and she wrapped her arms around herself. Panic welled inside him.

"I think she's going into shock. Do something!" he snapped at no one and everyone.

An hour later, she was alert, having *finally* let the paramedics dispatched to the scene take a look. One of them seemed to be flirting with her, which Dave took as a good sign. The guy wouldn't be chatting her up if she was injured, right? No. She'd have been driven off in the ambulance a while ago.

Dave studied her covertly—something about her was familiar. She sported khaki cargo pants, work boots, and a green sweatshirt with a logo that also looked familiar. Her ball cap was off, revealing long reddish-blond hair pulled into a tight ponytail on the crown of her head. The style, combined with the shape of her face and her light eyes, reminded him of Nicole, and he fought to separate the two in his mind's eye. Shaking Nicky's image was hard enough without living, breathing reminders in front of him, though maybe it explained why he thought he recognized the other driver.

The police officer who'd arrived on scene and interviewed him stood back and gave him an uninterested head-to-toe sweep.

"You Blizzard players get around." Her voice was a flat monotone.

In the background, the scene had emptied. An accident investigator, who'd been measuring and photographing, packed up his gear. A tow truck driver tugged one of the straps securing the Aston Martin to the flatbed before hopping into the cab of the truck and pulling away. The pile of scrap metal that had once been the other driver's van had been hauled away a while ago.

Dave gnawed his bottom lip. What had the officer meant? "Excuse me?"

She shook her head. "Never mind."

"You a hockey fan?"

Her partner jabbed his thumb at her. "Die-hard. She wasn't born in Canada, but she bleeds Canadian. Even knows the anthem by heart. And sings it. On duty." He gave a dramatic eye-roll.

"There's a special suite set aside at every game for military and law enforcement," Dave blurted. "If you're interested in coming to a game, you let me know, and I'll make sure you and your family get in."

"Are you trying to bribe me, Mr. Grimson?"

Bolts of electricity shot through him. Shit, he didn't need to take *another* walk on the wrong side of legal. Horrified, he put up his hands in surrender for the second time that day. "No, no! I didn't mean it like that."

One corner of her mouth twitched, the only hint of emotion on her inscrutable face. "You have that kind of pull, huh?"

He shrugged, trying to calm his jumping nerves. "Sometimes." *All the time.* It was his suite after all. Eight years ago, he'd bought it on his own dime. Few people knew, and he kept it that way. No reason to grandstand, especially since he got such a kick out of it—the act bordered on selfish.

Without answering, the policewoman dipped her head and made for her patrol car with her partner. Dave took the opportunity to steal another glance at the other driver. The paramedics were gone, and she stared at her phone as though it were a foreign object that had somehow landed in her hand.

Slowed by crushing guilt, he took tentative steps toward her. "So you're okay?"

She raised her head. Slate-blue eyes narrowed and pierced his. "No thanks to you."

He heaved out a breath. "I am so, so sorry. If I—"

Her hand flipped up in a stop-right-there-buster motion. "Mr. Grimson, I *know* you're sorry. It doesn't help right now."

"You know who I am?" A modicum of pride ballooned in his chest. He didn't normally play on his celebrity, preferring to fly under the radar, so the fact she recognized him—

"Yes. I copied it from the paperwork. You're Darryl—or is it Daniel?— Grimson."

The balloon deflated. "David. Dave." Why hadn't *he* thought to discover *her* name? "And your name is?" Fuck. Could he sound any stupider? He acted like he was meeting a dance partner at a hoedown. Next he'd be asking if she wanted a cup of punch.

When she didn't respond, he said, "Is there anything I can do?"

"Yeah," she bit. "You can replace the gardenia plants and the thousands of lights you destroyed, take them to my client's, and get them arranged in the next, oh," she tilted her forearm and glanced at a rugged watch that was too big for her slender wrist, "two hours, so I don't lose this project." Before he could ask what she did for a living, an old-fashioned ringtone chimed. Her voice softened when she answered. "Hey, Finn."

Dave turned away while she gave *Finn* her location. He pulled up his Uber app with a sigh and ordered a ride.

Behind him, the other driver was ending her call. "See you in ten."

"You've got a ride to … wherever it is you need to go?"

"I'm covered," she retorted.

"Okay. Good." He stuffed his hands in the front pockets of his track pants. "Um, so pick out whatever replacement vehicle you want, and I'll pay for it."

She snorted. "I doubt the vehicle I need will be covered by what insurance pays."

He shook his head. "Doesn't matter. This is on me. I'll cover whatever insurance doesn't. In fact, keep the insurance money, and I'll pay for the whole thing."

Her arms seemed to cross her chest on their own, and her eyebrows pinched together. "Are you for real?"

"'Fraid so."

Tilting her head, she scanned him and seemed to see him for the first time. "So what are you? A trust fund Wookiee?"

"A … what?" He didn't school the bewilderment that surely commandeered his features.

"A Wookiee. You know, *Star Wars*. Big, hairy animal that growls and scares the crap out of people."

Unable to hold back, he burst out with a humorless laugh. "Is that the impression I give off?" Okay, so maybe the beard needed a trim—and the hair. And oh, that's right: he hadn't put his front teeth in before he'd stormed out of the arena. Not that he usually did anyway. Why bother? He didn't go to the trouble unless he was making an appearance at a black-tie fundraiser. Or going out with a woman he wanted to impress. Which he hadn't done since before Nicky.

"Trust me, you don't want to know my impression of you," she snarked.

You're probably right.

Chapter 2

LET'S GET IT STARTED!

Ellie Hendricks slumped against the passenger door and stared out the window at nothing in particular. Like her thoughts, the view was one big blur. "What a shit day this turned out to be," she mumbled.

From the driver's seat, Finn side-eyed her. "You *sure* you don't need to see a doctor? I mean, what if you've got a neck or back injury that won't show up for months?"

She smoothed her dirt-stained pants over her thighs. God, she needed to find some time to shop for new clothes, even if they came from Amazon and didn't fit right. But when she got the rare hour of free time, she invariably wound up vegging out, all good intentions falling to the wayside. "If it's not going to show up for months, then how will a doctor see it now? Besides, I don't have the luxury of being injured." *The curse of the self-employed.* She cut him a look, and the concern on his face made her regret it instantly. She reached out and squeezed his forearm lightly. "Finn, I'm sorry. I didn't mean to be snippy."

"It's okay. You're entitled."

Remorse took some of the iron out of the dark cloud pressing down on her head. "Thanks again for coming to get me."

"No worries. It's what we do for each other, El. God knows you've done it for me more times than I care to count. I still have a long payback road to travel before I'm caught up." He squirmed in his seat.

True.

An uncomfortable history hung between them by a thread—one he wouldn't want to be reminded of—so she ran in a different direction. "And thanks for handling Mrs. Monroe. How did she deal with the fact we won't be finished until tomorrow?" Ellie couldn't keep from cringing. She'd been walking a tightrope with Mrs. Monroe for months and had won the job decorating her mansion for her daughter's wedding by the slimmest of margins. That margin had been the promise that everything would be completed days before the wedding. Which was tomorrow.

Finn chuffed and swiped at a lock of sun-bleached blond hair that had fallen in his eyes. "After she recovered from her stroke, I explained what happened to you and reassured her all the decorations would be done in time for the wedding."

Inwardly, Ellie groaned. Finishing the job while the caterers were setting up was specifically the scenario Mrs. Monroe *didn't* want. And despite Ellie's meticulous planning, fate had decided to toss a few roadblocks in her path to trip her up. Such as Mrs. Monroe deciding at the last minute that *gardenia* plants were the perfect accent—and only choice—for the indoor venue. When Ellie's special order for said gardenias was accidentally shipped to a different customer, she and Finn had spent days scouring the planet for replacements. The last plants had been in Ellie's vintage Toyota Sienna van on their way to the Monroes. Now those plants were debris swept to the side of an intersection littered with her crushed van parts.

And that was only one of the stacks of dominoes that had cascaded from the get-go on this prestigious, highly coveted job. This doomed-to-fail job.

The white globe lights she'd ordered had arrived in time—in the form of garish color-change lights. They'd looked like something that belonged in a brothel, not Mrs. Monroe's elegant white-and-gray marble spaces. The substitutes for that screwed-up order had shipped just in the nick of time. Thousands upon thousands of white twinkle lights. And the lion's share of them had also been in the wreck.

As for the very cool curtains of LED lights Ellie had planned to hang around the venue, the supplier had lost her order and was too backed up to get her new ones.

So much for impressing the tony guests and picking up higher-end jobs. If anything, this would earn her *negative* publicity, which she did *not* need. She'd spent the better part of the last two years cleaning up the debt and countering the bad press her ex had garnered. This was not where she'd expected to be at the ripe age of twenty-eight. She'd always seen herself with kids by now—two at least, with the third and fourth coming before she turned thirty-four—working from home as a landscape architect so she could be a full-time mom while Will ran the landscaping business. When he was home, they'd go bike-riding or camping or skating. They would be the perfect family she and Will had dreamed of when they'd started dating in college.

"Just a little longer, Ellie," he'd reassured her during the mayhem of their early years launching their landscaping company. "The business is almost to a point where we can start that family we've always talked about." But he'd been living a lie. That lie had grown and compounded and splintered into a million other lies, and she'd never seen any of it coming. She'd been blindsided, her happily-ever-after shattered to smithereens.

What she'd been left with were the shards of a company on the brink of bankruptcy, the aftermath of a sham marriage, and the anger and resentment that went with it all—not to mention the same unanswered question: How had she missed every single sign?

She sighed and circled back to her current … challenge. "Did Mrs. Monroe calm down?"

"Eventually. As we speak, Felipe's picking up bloomless star jasmine from a dozen different nurseries—that's the closest they had to gardenias—along with fake blooms everyone in his family will attach tonight. He swears they'll look like the real deal."

Ellie pictured lots of hands twisting white pipe cleaners around stems laden with glossy green leaves, and her eyes almost rolled back in her head. No way would they resemble the real deal, and no way would the fakes sneak past Mrs. Monroe.

Fortitude, girl! her inner Ellie barked. Or was that her dad's voice? *What doesn't kill you will make you stronger!* Shouldn't she be strong enough to give Superman a run for his money by now? At least the imitation gardenias wouldn't *kill* her, so there was that. Besides, what choice did she have this late in the game?

"He's doing this at no charge, you know," Finn added quietly. "He feels really bad about what happened."

"As he should! Nothing like being busted by ICE for hiring workers *he* recommended, who happened to have *fake* documents." She shuddered as the memories slammed into her, stirring up a riot of terror, outrage, and humiliation that swamped her just as they'd done the day the ICE agents had raided her client's work site. She'd been appalled and utterly impotent to stop it—they'd had surprise and a federal warrant on their side. The sound of the agents barking orders, the workers shouting in fear, the metallic clink of handcuffs, and the neighbors' horrified gasps still swirled in Ellie's head. They'd hauled her team and *her* away so fast she hadn't been able to pull up all her company signs and contain the bad publicity.

I'll never get work in that subdivision again.

Other recollections from that shocking day included spending time in a cramped, dingy interrogation room seated at a shabby table with nothing but a cold cup of coffee that tasted like yesterday's bitter dregs while an unsmiling officer grilled her over and over. Ellie prided herself on holding back tears, but that day she'd been mortified by how often they had completely overrun her.

It's over. For now anyway, though ICE still suspected her of misdeeds. Still watched for her slip-ups. Still showed themselves from time to time as a *courtesy reminder* she was on their radar.

She slouched a little farther into the seat with a resentful grumble. Felipe had assured her it had come as a shock to him too and was, in his own indomitable way, trying to help. She might have fired him if she could have afforded to, but she was shorthanded. Besides, he was *Felipe*. He'd been part of the business since the beginning and was the only employee loyal enough to stick around after the Will fallout. Sure, he screwed up—who didn't?—but loyalty was worth its weight in … gardenias.

A sigh escaped her. She couldn't count on her Monroe dreams panning out. What else could she do to generate enough revenue to keep regular paychecks coming for Felipe and Finn? They both relied on her, and right now she was failing them miserably. But they never complained—which made her feel worse.

Ellie straightened. "What about replacement lights?" She braced herself for more bad news.

"Ah. Now there I have some good news. The big box stores are already selling Christmas merchandise—can you believe that?—so I've placed a shit ton of orders I'll be picking up as soon as I drop you at the car rental place."

"If Felipe and his family are doing the plants, who's doing the lights?"

He didn't answer.

"Finn?"

"You and me?" He offered her a weak smile. "It'll be fun, El. An all-nighter, like in high school. Minus the keg."

"And the fun," she snorted. "Not to mention that was ten years ago, and I don't have those kinds of energy reserves anymore." She drummed her fingers on the armrest. The thought of spending hours stringing lights … "Wait. What about your latest squeeze? What's her name? Kimmie? Kammie? Eighteen-year-olds always think stuff like this is fun." She pictured a young woman bouncing in place, holding a lit string of lights and squealing with delight.

Finn blew out a breath through flapping lips, making a motorboat sound. "Keira, and she's twenty. We're not seeing each other anymore."

"Twenty. So *only* seven years younger than you. Why did you break up? Didn't you just start up like a week ago? You're losing your touch, Finn," she tsked teasingly.

"Nah, I'm just taking a break from dating."

"Whoa! Has hell frozen over? Wait. She didn't dump you, did she?"

"She totally did." He didn't convey anything remotely close to disappointment. Probably because he'd have her replacement lined up in a day or two with a flick of his pinkie. With Nordic blue eyes, a tall, tanned hardbody, and a Colorado cowboy attitude, women couldn't resist Finn. There'd been a time when she and her other stepsiblings had entertained themselves by placing bets on how quickly he could get a woman to leave a bar with him. Over the years, Ellie had had a hard time keeping up with his cavalcade of conquests.

"So why'd she dump you?"

He cleared his throat. "Megan asked to come over a few nights ago."

Ah. Finn's *last* ex. Now it made sense. "She needed a Finn fix, and you were happy to oblige." Ellie chuckled in spite of herself. "After all, who can resist a booty call from an ex?" *Me, that's for damn sure.* Not that Ellie got them herself—she hadn't collected that many exes. And why would she when she shied away from getting into relationships in the first place? She thanked Will for that too.

"It's not like Keira and I had been together that long," Finn protested, "or that it was anything but sex with Megan. Why don't women get that?"

"You mean the 'It was only sex, she doesn't mean anything, you're the one I really want, oh baby, baby,' spiel?"

"Yeah. Why can't they understand it's not about them? Men are just wired that way."

God, I hope not all *men, or I'll be that crazy woman living with thirty cats in her dilapidated house yelling, "Get off my lawn!" at all the neighborhood kids.*

No point in arguing with Finn that being "wired that way" did not excuse the entire male side of a species—she'd already tried multiple times over multiple years to make her case. "Fidelity is so overrated," she said dryly instead.

"What happened to you is different, El."

Ignoring *that* comment, she said, "Let's put the shoe on the other foot. How would *you* feel if you found out a girl you were seeing was sleeping with another guy? Or girl?"

"Girl? Interesting." Had she been looking, she would have no doubt glimpsed a dirty flicker in his eyes.

He shrugged. "Don't know. It's never happened."

"That *you* know of."

A cocky grin crept over his face. "No, I know. It's never happened."

Can I throttle you now? She blew out a disgusted breath. The truth, she suspected, was he was killing time until the "right one" caught all his attention … and Ellie couldn't wait to meet her.

"I think that after you pick up all the lights, you should troll your favorite watering hole and kill two birds with one stone: you can get us extra *free* help tonight *and* get yourself laid afterward."

The grin spread. Of course it did. "Not a bad idea. Must be why you're in charge."

"No, I'm in charge because Will left me no choice when he took off." She could feel the black cloud moving in again, threatening to rumble and rain down bolts of lightning on her head. It had been two years; she needed to finish picking up the pieces.

"Maybe it'd be easier to let go of the past if you stopped working so hard, El. You need to cut loose once in a while."

"Easy for you to say." *You're not the one scraping to pay the bills.* But he was right: time to go on a quest and get her sunny self back again. Hadn't that been on her list of New Year's resolutions, along with finally firming up her thighs? Well, forget the thighs—they'd be back on the list next year, as they'd been the past ten years—but she still had two months to put her life with Will in the rearview mirror.

Let's get it started!

In her mind, she was rocking out in her neon-pink-and-yellow bedroom to the Black Eyed Peas. The *only* place she'd felt safe dancing because she was *that* bad—Elaine Benes from *Seinfeld* had nothing on Ellie Hendricks's dance moves. She'd barely danced at her own wedding for fear of terrifying the guests.

Weddings. Twinkling white lights. Mrs. Monroe.

She heaved out another sigh. The search for her happy place would have to wait until *after* the lights were done.

Chapter 3

No Girls Allowed in My Man Cave

Dave climbed out of the Uber in front of a luxury garage condo complex. He placed his hand on a remote keypad, a side gate clicked open, and he strode to his six-bay garage. Once he unlocked the service door and stepped inside, he flipped on lights and drew in a satisfied breath. This was *his* space, bought and paid for. And these were *his* babies. Every slot filled. Nothing disturbed. Everything as it should be. A bright note in an otherwise wholly dismal day.

Each of his six vehicles sported a cover, but he didn't need to take them off to know what hid beneath. Every detail of every piece of machinery was tattooed in his brain and his heart. He *loved* his cars. Some he'd bought new, and others he'd restored, but they were all works of art. And right now he needed to free his mind of the ping-pong balls bouncing around inside it. Being here, breathing in the oil and rubber, running his hand over steely, gleaming surfaces, was the best way he knew to ground himself.

Some of his buddies found their zen on the ice. Well, not *buddies* anymore, which caused prickles of resentment to stick in his throat as though he'd just swallowed a thistle. Maybe he'd screwed the pooch, but he'd done it for *them*. For his team. Maybe not the smartest decision he'd ever made, but he'd been paying for it this past year and then some. Not only in everything he'd lost, but in his never-ending struggle to give doping up for good—a struggle no one ever saw. And though he'd tried his damnedest to prove himself worthy of his teammates' respect, nothing he did would ever be good enough. He'd worked harder to get back in their good graces than he'd ever done to earn the *C*. Well, he hadn't actually *worked* for that. More like it had been foisted on him at a time when the team had been in turmoil, and he'd been dumbfounded they'd picked him. Was *still* dumbfounded and couldn't figure why they hadn't stripped it from him when he'd offered to give it up.

A trade would be good. God, he hoped Herb could find him a team with a shot at the Cup. Dave wasn't *that* old by NHL standards—D-men didn't hit their stride until their late twenties, and he was in the prime of his career—but it didn't take a brain surgeon to figure out he was on the downhill side of that career. And the broken hand wasn't helping. But he'd do what he had to—the legitimate way, no matter how tough that made it—to make sure it healed all the way.

A nagging little doubt poked him now that his blood pressure had tumbled a few steps. Usually, he was the last man off the ice after practice or a game. It's what good captains did, whether they were healthy or not. Today, though, he'd played the little bitch and stormed out *before* everyone. Embarrassment heated his cheeks, and his inner Yoda pointed out he hadn't done himself any favors. Tomorrow he'd be apologizing and prostrating himself, metaphorically speaking. Dancing like a monkey on a chain, groveling for peanuts.

His inner Han Solo shouted the green Jedi down. "They should be apologizing to *you*," Han railed. "For fuck's sake, give a guy a break already!"

Okay. Now I'm listening to voices in my head. Voices that belong to fictional characters. Time to get a grip, Grims. He dragged one of the covers off, revealing a cardinal-red metallic Mercedes-Benz GLS 450, and couldn't keep a grin from tugging his mouth.

His phone buzzed, and his fledgling smile crashed. Dropping the cover, he picked up the call from his attorney he'd been expecting. "Tom?"

"Yeah, Grims. Am I reading your message right about you T-boning someone?"

Tom Carlisle had been his attorney for so long that they'd forged a friendship—an amazing accomplishment, considering they were both irascible. Dave filled him in, and the first question Tom barked was whether anyone had been hurt. Tom's tongue could slice you like a newly sharpened skate blade, and his next question carried even less tenderness than the first.

"Let me see if I have this straight. You run a red light and T-bone a woman. You admit it to everyone, *including* the woman you hit. *Then* you advertise you've got assets by offering to buy her a car of her choice, carte blanche. Am I right so far?"

"Hadn't thought about it quite that way, but yeah, that's about the gist of it."

"You not thinking is why I get the big bucks. Let me tell you what else you didn't think about. She's going to call one of those ambulance chasers on TV who promise to get her what she 'deserves.' That lawyer will hand her a menu of possible latent injuries and say, 'Pick one! Hell, pick four!' Every single choice will be so debilitating that she won't be able to work for the rest of her life, and guess who will pay for that, dude?"

When Dave didn't respond, Carlisle snorted. "That's right, brainwave. You!" Then he grumbled, "For fuck's sake, why is it my clients only call when they've behaved like morons?"

"If they only called when they were acting smart, you wouldn't have any billable work, now would you, asshole?" Dave shot back in frustration.

Carlisle chuckled. "I'll give you that one, Grims. I've heard it put more eloquently, but your point is well taken. All right. Let me handle this going forward. I'll see that Ms.—what's her name? Never mind—the other driver's vehicle is replaced with something *reasonable*. In other words, it's crystal clear she doesn't get to pick a brand new, fully-loaded Maserati Levante. From now on, though, I'm the point man on this. Your job—your only job—is to keep your pie hole shut. If you can do that, I'll see about squeaking you out of this situation without exposing your ass more than you've already bared it to the world."

"Gee, thanks?"

"Trust me. You'll thank me later." Tom chuckled. "You'll even be whistling as you pay my bill."

They hung up, and Dave exhaled. The bubble of joy he'd felt admiring the Mercedes had popped. In fact, his entire car collection wouldn't be enough to stitch his frayed nerves back together. This conclusion was confirmed seconds later when his phone rang again.

He opened the driver-side door and slid behind the Mercedes's steering wheel. "Hey, Nicole."

"Did you get my text?" she snapped.

"Which one?"

"The one about taking Benny next weekend! You never answered me when we were on the phone earlier."

A doozy of a headache was building behind his eyes, and he rubbed his forehead. "I *did* answer you. You just didn't like the answer. That weekend won't work. I've got too much going on."

"Like what?" He could picture her jutting out a hip and parking a well-manicured hand on it.

"Like two home games. And like I was in a car accident today." Not that the accident had anything to do with taking the dog, but still. He wasn't above playing a sympathy card, although she hadn't been moved by the busted hand. No, it would probably take a gasping deathbed scene to pull an icy tear from Nicky's arctic heart.

"Oh." A few beats of silence passed, then, "Wait. I'm talking a week from now, and you don't need a car to have Benny stay. I'll even bring him over." Her voice lilted, which usually signaled she was trying to sell him on something he didn't want. "Besides, you have a whole fleet of other cars you can use."

He squeezed his eyes shut. "Aren't you even going to ask if I'm okay?"

"I'm guessing you are because you're taking calls. You are, right?" The lilt was gone.

His head spun, and what little energy he had seemed to drain from a hole in his soul. "Never better."

By the end of the conversation, he'd agreed to take the dog—because bottom line, he *loved* that damn Australian shepherd-boxer mix that had once been *his* dog. He shook his head, wondering how she'd managed to finagle him *again*. She'd used her usual MO, which was to use what he cared about against him and wear him down, that's how.

He started up the Mercedes and hit the garage-door opener. The thought of returning to four walls of space devoid of any living thing dragged him down further, so he detoured and, fifteen minutes later, parked in a strip mall in front of a salon. A cheerful pink-and-black sign read, "Shear Indulgence." A bell rang over the door as he opened it—an old-fashioned touch that quirked a corner of his mouth—and his eyes swept the stations as they adjusted to the darker interior.

A chorus of "Hi, Dave" greeted him, as did smiles from five hairdressers in various stages of styling clients' hair. A few added exaggerated eyelash flutters and soft giggles. Even some of their clients joined in the flirty greetings. The attention didn't faze him—he was used to it—so he nodded his hellos and focused on a mop of bright red curls emerging from the back. He shaded his eyes with one hand.

"Whoa! Now that's bright!"

She stopped and shot him a lofty look. "Always the charmer."

When he reached her, he pulled her into a bear hug and rubbed his knuckles over her curly crown.

She gave him a playful shove. "Off me, you big ape!"

He kissed the top of her head and released her. "You love it, and you know it." He scanned her hair and realized shocking pink was woven into the red. "New color?"

She fluffed her do. "Nice of you to notice."

"Christ, how could I miss it?"

"What's the occasion? Obviously nothing special since you're toothless today." She clapped her hands. "Ooh, I know! You're finally going to let me take off that rat's nest that found a home on your chin."

A set of fingernails climbed the back of his bicep, surprising him, sending chills up his arm. Next came an overpowering spicy scent. He swiveled his head and leveled his gaze at a shapely, overly made-up brunette.

"You going to introduce me to your handsome cousin, Sonoma?" The woman was talking to Sonoma while eyeing him like he was her next meal. He took a step back, but she followed him right into his personal bubble.

Sonoma rolled her big blues. "Mandy, this is Dave. Dave, this is Mandy." Before he could give the expected cordial answer, Sonoma gripped his arm, pulled him into her back office, and shut the door. He caught a vague, disappointed-sounding, "Hope to see you soon, Dave," behind him.

"New girl?" he asked.

"Obviously. God, I get tired of them doing that."

"How do you think *I* feel?"

She flicked her wrist at him. "Pfft. You're a man. You love it."

"Not so much. You realize that if I didn't play pro hockey, they'd completely ignore me. Or run the other way."

She shrugged a shoulder. "Oh, I don't know. It's been a while, but as I recall, you do clean up well. Besides, a lot of women fantasize about being dragged off to a cave somewhere, so for them, the Bigfoot thing is very appealing."

Apparently not to the woman he'd hit. He arched a skeptical eyebrow. "Yeah, especially when they think Bigfoot has deep pockets."

"Poor you. So what brings you here? Not that I'm not happy to see you."

He shoved his hands in his front pockets. "I wondered if I could buy my favorite cousin a drink?"

She studied his face. "Need to talk, huh?"

He blew out a breath. "Meh. Maybe."

Soon they were seated at a corner table in his favorite bar. The dark wood, small-tiled floor, and smoky mirrors reminded him of something from the old west—probably because it was a relic from the 1800s—and it wrapped him with a sense of comfort, like a warm blanket. *Wonder if I'll find a place I like as much in my next town?* The bartender gave him a wink and said, "The usual, big guy?" as soon as she'd spotted them walking in.

"How come she only recognizes me when I'm with you?" Sonoma grumbled.

He tweaked her hair. "Because you change your hair color all the time? You're a woman of mystery, Nome."

Sonoma preened and took a sip of her wine. "So what's got you blue, dude?"

One swallow and he'd consumed a third of his beer. Then he told her about the accident.

"Oh shit, Dave. But you're okay?"

"I'm fine. Apparently, I wasn't going as fast as it felt like. And I guess it's better to be the T-boner than the T-bonee—from a preservation-of-body-parts point of view. Fortunately, even though it was old, her van did its job safety-wise."

"And she said she was okay?"

He nodded. "Yeah, but you know how those things go. She might wake up in three months and be in pain."

Sonoma snorted. "Yeah, after being coached by a lawyer."

He twirled his pint glass. "That's not what I meant. What if she really *is* hurt but it doesn't show up for a while? That could really fuck up someone's life. I don't know what she does, but she looked fit, athletic. Say she runs marathons and suddenly can't because she's got a pain shooting down her leg. That would suck."

Sonoma gave him a sympathetic look and let out a little sigh. "What if you don't worry about it until it's an actual problem? I swear you love to punish yourself."

He straightened and wiped his palms on his thighs. "No, I don't."

Bright blue eyes appraised him. "Yeah, you do. It's why you stuck with Nicole for so damn long."

"You forget. She stuck with *me*. Until she didn't."

"Yeah, well, you know where I stand on that whole deal. You're better off without her. Or *are* you without her? Is she still roping you into doing stuff for her?"

He ducked his head before throwing back more beer.

"Oh, Dave," Sonoma tsked.

"I'm watching Benny, which isn't that big a deal. Besides, this way I get my fix."

"You don't look so happy about it, though." His cousin then had the gall to point out the pathetically obvious. "You need to stop telling her yes so she stops asking. But maybe you can't because you're hoping that if you keep doing shit for her, she'll realize what a mistake she made and come back. Is that it?" She arched a red eyebrow at him. Jesus, she'd even dyed those.

"No. It's just that … she's used to me doing things for her and Isaac, and I can't just *stop* when they both still need me."

"When was the last time you saw Isaac?"

He finished his beer and signaled the bartender for another one. When he lifted his chin at Sonoma, she placed her hand over her mostly full glass and shook her head.

"Well, that would be June-ish, before he went to stay with his grandparents." He squelched the discomfort digging into his spine like barbed wire.

"Uh-huh. So you've seen him, what, three times since you two split?"

He shrugged. "You forget he's not my kid."

"Not biologically, but damn, for a few years you were a better dad to him than his own father!"

Dave winced inside. Yeah, losing Nicky had meant losing her eight-year-old too, though the relationship between him and the boy had become strained with "Dad" in the background tugging on the poor kid's emotions. Isaac had been caught between his parents, pulled like a Stretch Armstrong toy, and Dave had been helpless to do anything about it. The few times he'd tried, Nicky had shot him down faster than a clay pigeon at a top-gun shooting tournament. Still, after innumerable relationships in his life that had gone nowhere, he'd gotten a taste for being a family with Nicky and Isaac, and he'd liked it—even if it had taken Nicky throwing down an ultimatum to move in together. Once he'd grown accustomed to living with her, he'd liked that too. Liked being needed.

His mind zipped back to when he'd first met her. It had started like all the other relationships. He'd been at a club with some teammates, and when he'd laid eyes on her, he'd been dazzled. So had his buddies. She was beautiful and sleek and flashy, like his cars. An air that screamed, "Unobtainable!" had rolled off her, and the challenge had been too tempting to resist, especially when one of the guys threatened to make the first move. Competition was a strong motivator. Just like his unexpected captaincy, though, he was perpetually amazed that girls like her—the tens, the ones who'd never given him a second glance in high school—would actually fall for him.

Confident he might actually catch her, Dave had chased her—or at least he thought he had. Now he couldn't help but wonder if she'd simply played him, pretending to run until she let him snag her.

"Can we talk about something else, please?" he pleaded. "Like that great accident I was in and the awesome car I'm going to buy for this woman?"

"Before we do … I just want to say one thing."

He puffed out a derisive breath. "Which really means six."

"Behave." She gave him a fake glower. "I've known you a long time, and from where I sit, it looks to me like Nicole is taking advantage of your protective side. You're probably still giving her money, aren't you?"

"Nome, you know I love you like a brother, but that's none of your damn business." So what if he wrote Nicky a check once in a while to get stuff for Isaac? Dave made a lot of money. And he had a lot to make up for.

"You just answered my question." Sonoma sipped her wine primly.

"It was hard on her," he muttered. He and his teammates weren't the only ones affected by his fall from grace.

That comment earned him another pointed look from Sonoma. "Guilt colors judgment, Dave. But let's put that aside. Either you're still in love with her and you want her back or your battered ego wants her back because it needs a victory right now. But you forget she put you through hell, even during the good times. The woman thrives on drama, which is the complete opposite of who *you* are. If she called you today and told you she'd changed her mind, would you *really* want her back?"

Did he want Nicky back? A little voice—Yoda, probably—piped up with a *nope*. Though lonelier, life was simpler in many ways with him not living under the same roof as Nicky, and it freed him up for the single-mindedness he needed to keep his head in the game. All training, all the time, no distractions—even more critical now that he was looking for a trade. Sometimes he'd felt like she was a rock collar suspended around his neck, pulling him under, drowning him. Admitting it, though, forced a fresh surge of guilt.

His second beer appeared, and he slugged down half before setting the glass on the tabletop. He admonished himself to slow down—alcohol was a little too easy to throw back these days. "I guess not."

"She's got you in a choke hold, and the only way you're going to break it is to get yourself unwrapped from her little finger." Sonoma peered at him, mischief dancing in her eyes. "And I know the perfect way to do that. Bonus: it could give your self-esteem points in the win column—"

"My self-esteem is dandy, thank you very much," he snorted.

Ignoring him, Sonoma kept right on going. "Let me set you up with my neighbor."

"No."

"She's cute, smart, *not* a man-eater …"

"Curls clogging your ears again, Nome? What part of *no* did you not hear?" God, she drove him crazy, but she was his best friend, and—he grudgingly admitted to himself—he loved her. A mere two years divided them, and they'd had each other's backs growing up together in Utah, the only children born to their twin-sister moms. His bond to Sonoma was like entwined steel cable, far stronger than any bond he shared with his younger half brothers, who lived with his dad and stepmom in far-flung Singapore.

Which was why he was sitting across a table from her right now, indulging her inclination to feed him a bunch of annoying bullshit, including her trying to set him up—again—with her mysterious neighbor. He didn't want to hear it, no matter how much she insisted he needed to.

Sonoma let out a sigh of defeat. "Okay. Just trying to put a smile on your face again. It's been MIA way too long." She took another sip of wine. "If you won't let me help you, how about you helping me? I have a salon chair I need to move into storage. Could you maybe bring your truck and meet me early tomorrow, Mr. Muscles?"

"That I can do."

"What about your hand?"

"Eh, I'm a hockey player." He gave her a dismissive wrist flick with his good hand, followed by an eyelash flutter. "Besides, I'd do anything for my favorite cousin."

"Except date my neighbor," she snorted.

"Except date your neighbor," he agreed.

Chapter 4

Howdy Ho, Neighbor

The next morning, Dave parked in the alleyway behind the block of buildings that housed Shear Indulgence and its neighbors, a mix of mom-and-pop businesses. No sign of Sonoma yet, and her back door was locked, so he took a moment to lower his window and look at the eastern sky streaked in pale yellows and muted corals. He popped the top off his travel mug, inhaling the aroma of fresh, rich coffee curling up his nostrils. About six car lengths behind him, headlights turned into the alleyway and swept the pavement. A gray Ford F-150 crept past, its windows too darkly tinted to reveal the occupants. But a familiar logo on the pickup's door snagged his attention and had him nearly dropping the scalding brew in his lap: the same logo on What-Was-Her-Last-Name-That-I-Crashed-Into's crushed van and polo shirt.

What the hell? His heart rate kicked up a notch or five as the vehicle came to a stop and parked several doors down. The driver's door swung open, and out stepped a big blond guy who rounded the hood. The passenger's door opened too, and a petite woman with a long strawberry-blond ponytail hopped out. Well, more like stumbled out, but the man steadied her. She looked up at him and shook her head, laughing, the sound musical as it drifted on the crisp morning air.

Her profile came into view, and Dave's mouth fell open. Not only did he recognize the logo, but he recognized the woman too. *Shit! She's stalking my ass, and she's brought her bodyguard along to kill me!*

The man leaned down and hugged the woman, and her arms wound around his neck. Broken bits of conversation told Dave the man was asking if she'd be all right, did he want her to come in, and she was reassuring him she was fine and thanking him for last night. Didn't sound or act like a woman stalking Dave. So why the hell was she *here*?

At least she's not too banged up if she was out with this guy all night getting … banged up.

A puff of relieved breath escaped him, steaming the chilly air leaking through the window, and for a beat he considered shooting a picture of them clinging to each other—in case his attorney needed proof she hadn't been hurt.

Before he could act, Blond Guy stood back, giving her room to unlock a back door she shimmied through. Once it was closed, BG trotted back to the Ford, climbed in, and drove away.

Dave wedged his mug into the cup-holder and started his engine, slow-rolling his truck past the door she'd stepped through. And there, plain as day, was the logo and "Landscaping with Altitude" painted on the back door. How often had he glimpsed it on the business's front door while entering Sonoma's salon? He'd probably seen the T-bonee a half dozen times too.

No wonder she and the logo had looked familiar.

She was Sonoma's goddamn neighbor.

He circled back around through the parking lot, looking like a creeper as he peered at the woman's business from the front. Through glass doors and windows that sported the same logo and name, a light shone in a back hallway, then flicked off. As he rounded the row of buildings and re-entered the alleyway, he spotted her darting out the back door and scurrying into a dark Dodge Grand Caravan he hadn't noticed before. On the bumper was a green Enterprise Rent-a-Car sticker.

Yup. The rental to replace her demolished van.

Sonoma still hadn't shown up, so he pulled out his smartphone and googled "Landscaping with Altitude." *Bingo!*

He stabbed at the link, and up popped the company website. He clicked on the "Who We Are" tab, and his eyes landed on a wholesome, pink-cheeked blond, her hair in soft golden-red waves cascading over her shoulders. *Ellie Hendricks, Owner.*

The name rang a bell—no doubt because he'd heard it at the accident site—and he sat back as if he'd been shoved.

Feeling a prickle of guilt as if he was doing something sinister, he scrolled down and found two more pictures. The first was of the dude in the truck—a guy who could have modeled in magazines, he was so damn pretty. The name under the picture read "Finn Callahan" but had no title. This must have been the *Finn* Ms. Hendricks had spoken to on the phone, the one who'd just dropped her off after obviously taking her home for the night.

The last picture was of Felipe Salazar—also title-less—a smiling, middle-aged man with laugh lines creasing the weathered skin around his brown eyes.

So this was Ellie, aka "T-bonee," Hendricks's "team," and she was sleeping with the help. Not that it was any of Dave's business. More power to her.

A honk had him jerking his head up. Sonoma's car dove in front of his and came to a rocking stop. She burst from the driver's door with a breathless, "Sorry I'm late!" Sonoma was *always* late. Came with the territory. Did she keep clients waiting too?

"I really appreciate you doing this, Dave," she puffed as she leaned down to his partially open window.

Releasing the seatbelt, he unfolded himself from the driver's seat. "You better. I totally gave up my beauty sleep for you, and God knows I need every minute I can get."

"If you'd let me manscape you, you wouldn't need beauty sleep."

"Maybe later."

"That's what you've been saying for the last six months," she snorted.

Hoisting the chair into the bed of his Summit White Chevrolet Silverado 2500HD High Country, he struck the most who-gives-a-fuck demeanor he could muster. "So do you know the blond lady with the landscaping business?" He lifted his chin toward Landscaping with Altitude's back door.

"Ellie?"

"Yeah, I guess that's her name."

A shit-eating grin slowly hiked Sonoma's cheeks to her ears. "Did you talk to her?"

"No. Just saw her when her boyfriend dropped her off."

The shit-eating grin dissolved into a frown. "Boyfriend? Since when does she have a boyfriend? This ruins everything." This she said quietly, as if to herself.

He secured the chair with ratchet straps. "What's the big deal if she's got a boyfriend?" Not the real question. No, the one he *wanted* to ask had everything to do with Ellie Hendricks's character—and how it would impact him and his wallet.

Sonoma parked her fists on her hips. "It matters because *she's* the neighbor I wanted to set you up with."

Wait. What? He stared at Sonoma, unsure he'd heard her right. The full impact slammed him like a body check delivered by a linebacker. Horrified, he spluttered, "I thought she lived in the apartment next to yours, not that she worked next door!"

"Does that make a difference in you going out with her?"

"Yes! No! What matters is that she's the chick I ran into yesterday."

Sonoma gaped at him, her eyes rounder than pucks. "You ran into *my* Ellie? No fucking way."

"Fucking way."

"Oh shit. She'll never go out with you now."

"Nope." *And that's okay by me.* "Nome? Invoking the bro code here. Do. Not. Tell. Her."

"She's gonna find out, Dave."

"Someday, maybe, but I don't want that someday to be now." *Better if I've been traded out of Denver when she does find out. Shit. I'm gonna miss Nome.* "Don't be too disappointed. Looks like she already set herself up with some other sucker."

"What about you? I want to set *you* up so you'll stop being so … so grumpy."

"You can always set me up with Mandy." He wiggled his eyebrows. Not that he *wanted* to date Mandy. Well, not for more than a few hours anyway. Scratch that. No Mandy. The last time he'd hooked up with someone on an impulse had left him feeling bleak and hollow. Bad idea. No, this had nothing to do with Mandy and everything to do with needling Sonoma because he got such a kick out of it. She didn't disappoint.

"Over my dead body!"

"No Mandy, then. Or *anyone*. Got it? I'm a big boy now, and I can get my own dates."

She harrumphed. "Hasn't worked out too well for you so far, has it, *Big Boy?*"

Ouch. Did she really have to state the obvious?

Fisting his second whiskey since coming home, Dave sank into a big-ass man recliner—one of the perks of living alone again—in his otherwise very modern, very sterile three-story row house. It was one of those narrow jobs with a rooftop patio and tiny, useless decks hanging off the different levels. The master and guest bedrooms were on the top floor, the kitchen, dining, and family rooms on the second floor, with another bedroom and living room he'd appropriated for a gym on the ground floor. Not his first choice in housing, but when Nicole had given him his walking papers, he'd had to rent something fast.

He clicked on the TV and surfed hundreds of garbage channels before tuning into a Pandora classic rock channel. After a sip, he let out a laugh at Sonoma's expense. She'd been talking up her "neighbor" for almost a year, and she must have been crushed to learn *he'd* literally crushed any chance of neighbor Ellie going out with him. What descriptions had Sonoma included in her sales pitches besides "strawberry-blond," "smart," and "cute?" Damned if he could remember.

Pushing a cleansing breath through his lungs, he nabbed his iPad and pulled up the landscaping company's website. Soon he was looking at Ellie Hendricks's image again but on a bigger screen. Why had he thought this woman looked like Nicky when he'd first seen her at the accident site? She didn't resemble Nicky. At all. Ellie Hendricks looked to be in her mid-twenties, and she was pretty. *Very* pretty—not that Nicky *wasn't* pretty. But where Nicky was sultry-supermodel stunning, Ellie was wholesome pretty. Girl-next-door pretty. Not a woman to get your engine revving just by looking at her, but someone you could sit down and talk to and laugh with … who'd give you the sunny smile she wore in her picture.

No doubt the beautiful smile that reached her shimmering blue eyes contributed to her appeal. The color of those eyes reminded him of a 1969 Chevy El Camino SS he'd painstakingly restored and painted Delta Blue. He'd loved that car. How had he ever let himself get talked into selling it?

One more stupid decision to toss into his junkyard collection of poor choices. That junkyard was pretty damn full at the moment despite his efforts to scrape the lot. He took another sip of whiskey while a favorite quote blared in his head: "Not to brag, but I don't need alcohol to make really bad decisions."

No more bad decisions.

Too bad he wasn't so good at heeding his inner Yoda. Which was exactly why he found himself, over the next few days, cruising through the strip mall parking lot where Shear Indulgence and Landscaping with Altitude were located. This, he told himself repeatedly, was nothing like stalking. He was merely "satisfying his curiosity" about Ellie Hendricks. Besides, the surveillance kept his mind off his tumultuous standing with his team and the fact that Herb hadn't garnered any interest in him yet.

He wouldn't need to worry about butting heads with his teammates for a few days. They'd just left to play some away games, and he'd been held back because of his damn hand. "You're close," the trainer had assured him, though it was no consolation.

As for Ms. Hendricks, what he learned was that she spent *a lot* of time in her small office alone—except for the company of a medium-sized pale mutt who didn't look like much of an attack dog. An ankle chewer, maybe, but that was the extent of the dog's superpowers. The Felipe guy waltzed in once, and Pretty Boy Finn was MIA. Shouldn't a boyfriend stop by once in a while to make sure his girl was safe? Bring takeout so she was fed those evenings when she stayed late? Massage the kinks out of shoulders cramped from hunching over a desk for hours at a time—*especially* since she'd been in an accident days before?

Not his problem. He had enough of those crowding his priority list.

Chapter 5

Wookiees Have Feelings Too

Ellie glanced up from the Habitat for Humanity house's landscape design with achy eyes. When had the sun dipped below the horizon? She'd been slaving over the plan for hours—no, days—and while it wasn't complicated, she continually second-guessed herself because the design had to be *perfect.* A pro bono project that would, hopefully, bring Landscaping with Altitude a ton of feel-good exposure and a boatload of new paying clients. Ulterior motives aside, she was doing the community a service.

Few plants would survive the fall temperatures, so she'd convinced Damian Mencher, one of Denver's Habitat directors, to let her install a xeriscape. It had appealed to his environmental sensibilities, and, selfishly, it had set her up for some sweet publicity through the slow months. By installing the rock and hardscape *now*, she could put up her bandit signs advertising the business and leave them in place until the spring, when the plants would go in the ground. And bonus: the house sat on a busy corner lot close to one of Denver's trendiest neighborhoods.

Yep, she'd scored on this one. Maybe.

Besides anally tweaking her design into excellence, her biggest challenge was manpower. She could barely pay Finn and Felipe, and Damian's team had drummed up disappointingly few volunteers to fill in the gaps. Why didn't people want to do backbreaking landscape work on these glorious, chilly weekends instead of watching bugling elk while they sipped spiked hot chocolate?

She snorted at her own stupid joke and stretched, digging her fingers into her knotted neck muscles. God, what she wouldn't give for a massage!

Headlights caught her eye. She glanced out the front window as the beams swept through the mostly empty parking lot. And froze. How many days in a row had it been now?

Ellie jumped up, Casper at her heels, and peered through a darkened corner of her window. Huh. Same gorgeous muscle car. The path the vehicle took was exactly the one it had taken before. The driver was obscured, so she had no way of knowing if it was an ICE agent—they didn't drive muscle cars, did they?—or a strip mall tenant, though she'd never noticed this particular car before. And she would have noticed.

With her inner voice telling her she was being ridiculous, that it was just coincidence, she leaned down and gave Casper a scratch. "Your mom's got a touch of paranoia, girl."

Ellie traipsed down the hall to the kitchenette in search of food and drink. "Should be some energy bars Finn didn't find and a vitamin water." Apparently, Finn *had* found everything because all she came up with were a desiccated bouillon cube, a pack of stale saltines, and tap water. "I think this means it's time to go home, girl." Casper wagged her stubby tail and barked her agreement.

As Ellie headed out of the kitchenette, a rap came on the glass door. "What the …" Back against the wall, she crept carefully, one foot in front of the other. Casper darted around her and ran—Ellie could only presume—to the front door.

"Way to guard your family," Ellie muttered.

She kept her cautious steps even, and when she peered around the corner, a large form was crouched in front of the door, feather-tapping on the glass in front of Casper's snuffling nose. The dog's tail was on high-speed auto-wag. *Sellout!*

The form stood, and shit, was it big! It nearly filled the door frame. The man—he was too big *not* to be a man—gave her an incongruous little wave.

What the hell? Do I know this guy?

She snatched her phone from her desktop and hit Finn's number. The guy shoved his hands in his front pockets, not even trying the door she'd forgotten to lock. Finn's phone rang and rang. It wasn't completely dark out yet, and she narrowed her eyes on her visitor. He looked like a … Wookiee.

Not this guy!

Now he was pointing to his left, jerking his head in the same direction.

"What do you want?" she yelled through the door. Yelling did two things: it hid the quaver her slamming heart was causing in her voice and it furthered the illusion of a locked door. Casper chose that moment to put her paws against said door, pushing it into the mountain man who'd smashed Ellie's car.

Damn it!

He grasped the door, leaving a gap the width of his huge hand—a hand that could kill and maim—and stuck his mouth in the opening. "It's okay. I'm Sonoma's cousin."

What? "Sonoma the hairdresser?" My *hairdresser—when I get it styled. Once a year.*

A little grin formed in his beard. "Yeah. The one with the flaming hair."

"El? That you?" Finn's sleepy voice crackled through the phone.

"You're sleeping?" she practically shrieked into the phone.

The Wookiee frowned. "No, I was trying to—"

"Or not sleeping," Finn groused. Ellie understood a heartbeat later when she heard a muffled female voice.

"Shit! You're having sex *now*? What time is it? Five thirty?"

The Wookiee looked so confused she almost burst out with a laugh.

"I *was*, and I think you just ruined my chance for the seven thirty and ten thirty repeats," Finn said dryly.

"You're … I don't think the dictionary *has* a word for you! Here I am, about to get attacked, and—"

"Whoa, whoa, whoa!" The Wookiee held up one hand but didn't loosen his grip on the door. Casper's tail was beating at hummingbird-wing speed now. A blur of white. Apparently, she liked the mass murderer on the other side of the glass.

"What do you mean, you're about to be attacked?" Finn had the decency to sound concerned.

"Ask Sonoma," the Wookiee pleaded. "She's got someone in her chair, but just ask her if her cousin is Dave Grimson. Wait. I'll call her."

"Did I hear *Dave Grimson* is about to attack you? The Grim Reaper?" Finn was all kinds of interested now, but not in a you-are-so-screwed way. More like a that's-so-cool way.

"Yes," Ellie shot back. "So when the police find my mangled body, you can tell them who did it. Wait. Who's the Grim Reaper?" *And where's his scythe?*

Wookiee jabbed his thumb against his chest and waggled his considerable eyebrows, but he still hadn't let go of the door. As Ellie was preparing to slam her body against the door and crush his fingers, Sonoma appeared at his side with a wave and a smile. She seemed to be catching her breath, as though she'd just run. "Hi, Ellie. This is my cousin, Dave." She placed a friendly hand on the big guy's shoulder. "I guess he ran into you the other day? Literally?"

Finn was squawking in the background about wanting to meet Reaper Man. Ellie's head was spinning.

"You are *no* help at all," she growled into the phone. "Later."

She could hear his quail-dying "Waaaait!" right before she hung up. Casper, in the meantime, wedged her nose in the gap, widening it enough to bolt through.

Sonoma pointed back toward her salon. "I need to get back to my client before she turns platinum, but I'll vouch for Dave. Of course, if you don't want to talk to him, I totally get it." She flashed him an impish smile and patted his shoulder while he scowled down at her.

Meanwhile, Casper was busy inhaling his leg. He crouched and held out his hand, palm up, and Casper, fierce protector that she was, went straight to work licking him to death.

"I think he likes me. Or the bacon I had a little while ago." He chuckled … a nice, warm, rumbly sound.

"He's a she." *Wow. Is that the best your tough self can do, El?*

The Wookiee—no, Dave Grimson Reaper Man—looked up at her from under his ball cap, a question mark scrunching his dark eyebrows. "And all this time I thought Casper was a he. It's kind of hard to tell, though, now that I think about it, with the high-pitched ghost voice and all."

"Why are you here?" Ellie blurted.

"Would it be all right if I came in? Or you stepped out? Just so we're not shouting through a door?" He rose to his feet, and she took a step back and nearly crushed her own fingers in the door.

Opening the door fully, she motioned him inside. Though he hunched his shoulders, the guy was big. And scary. But his fierce appearance wasn't lining up with his body language. No, his stance broadcast self-conscious. Nervous. Shy maybe. He offered her a semblance of a wobbly, white-toothed smile, and some of his ferociousness fell away.

She peered at him—in an embarrassingly bold way, she realized—because there was something incongruous about his face. He stared right back.

"Teeth!" she blurted. Her chest and cheeks heated with mortification. "I'm sorry. That was really rude of me."

"It's okay." His smile widened, showing off straight white teeth. "Glad you noticed, otherwise it wouldn't have been worth the trouble of putting them in." Even though it was buried inside lots of beard, it looked like a nice smile. He should probably show it more often. *Yeah, and that's how serial killers lure you in.*

She folded her arms across her chest. "So what can I do for you, Mr. Grimson?"

Hands dipped into pockets again, and he began rocking on his feet. *Nervous.* "I was worried and wanted to find out how you're doing. I also wanted to find out if you've heard anything yet about replacing your van."

"Wait. Back up a sec. How did you know where to find me?"

"I was waiting for Sonoma at her back door early the morning after the accident, and I saw your boyfriend drop you off."

"My what?"

"Tall, good-looking blond guy? You were hugging on each other?"

"Oh, Finn! God, he'll laugh when I tell him." She caught herself right before she chuckled, reminding herself she needed to maintain the tough façade, lame as it was. Dave tilted his head, and she went on. "He's my stepbrother, not my boyfriend. I have no time for boyfriends—or any interest in one, especially now that I've graduated from Masochists Anonymous."

He barked a laugh. "You too?"

An awkward silence hung between them. He raced into it. "So you're doing okay? Physically, I mean?"

Should I be talking to this guy about this? The achingly concerned look on his face loosened her tongue. "So far, so good."

His knees dipped, and something akin to relief softened his features—he was probably grateful to hear she wasn't preparing to sue his ass. Yet.

"Thank fu—that's good to hear. What about your van? Have you heard anything from either insurance company?"

"Not yet. And it's like pulling teeth to get anywhere. One automated selection sends you to a different automated selection."

"Yeah, I hate when that happens. I can call my agent and—"

"No, that's *my* insurance company." She let a sigh slip out. "At least they're covering most of my rental."

"Most?" He glanced down at Casper, propped against his leg in a sloppy sit. Very unladylike. But if Casper was giving him a thumbs-up, he couldn't be all bad, could he?

"I had to upgrade to get a van. They wanted to give me a beep-beep car, but those don't work for hauling stuff."

"So I hate to ask, but I've been wondering … how did that job turn out for you?"

"Not well. Because I couldn't deliver what I *promised* to deliver, nor could I deliver according to the timeline I agreed to. My opportunity to pick up new clients with bigger bank accounts was a spectacular bust." Anger simmered inside her with the recall of the disastrous Monroe job. Oh, they'd pulled off a good look, though it wasn't what the woman had ordered, and Ellie had given her a painfully steep discount.

Yeah, and it was your fault. Well, not all *of it, but I don't need to tell you that.* At least he had the decency to look pained.

"God, I am so sorry."

He looked *so* forlorn, in fact, that Ellie felt a pang of remorse. "She was a pain in the ass anyway," she grumbled. "I don't enjoy working with people like that." *But beggars can't be choosers.*

"So what was with the Christmas lights?"

"We were decorating her house for her daughter's wedding. I'm trying to diversify so I can keep my guys busy year-round. Like lots of landscape companies, we hang Christmas lights in the winter, but there's not a lot of work in between. I thought decorating houses for other special occasions might be a good way to fill in the gaps." *And why in God's name am I telling him all this?*

"Sounds like a great strategy to me."

"Yeah, it was. Now I'll have to start over with a new client who's never heard of Mrs.—"

He was about to apologize again, she could tell, so she held up her hand. "I know you're sorry, but honestly there's nothing you can do about it now."

A flush colored what she could see of his cheekbones. "Actually, there *is* something I can fix for you."

She cinched her arms a little tighter. "What's that?"

"I can take you car-shopping and buy you a replacement."

Her mouth dropped open.

"I'm serious," he said. "I've been looking at some vehicles that might work in place of the Sienna. There's always a new Sienna, if that's what your heart's set on, but this would be a great time to trade up if you've been wanting to." His eyes lit up like someone had flipped on a switch. "Have you checked out the Mercedes Sprinter? Ford has one called the Transit Connect, and Chevy has commercial van options too. Or would a pickup work better? Except … doesn't your company already have a pickup?"

She was frozen in place, still gaping at him, wondering if she'd dropped into a different dimension.

He shrugged, a sheepish half-smile curving his lips. "I get a little carried away when it comes to cars."

"So what kind of rental did *you* get?"

"Uh, didn't need one. I had a spare vehicle."

Suspicion narrowed her eyes. She darted them out to the parking lot. "Is that your Pontiac GTO convertible out there?"

He shot her a curious look. "Yes."

"What year?"

He gave his beard a tug. "1964."

Nice. "Stock engine?"

A quiet chuckle rumbled from him. "No. I dropped in a performance engine."

Dad would approve. Suddenly, she remembered that car had been cruising her parking lot the past few days, and she gave herself a mental shake. Alarms clanged in her head. "Did you drive by yesterday?"

"Guilty."

Fear bubbled up from her gut. "Are you *stalking* me?"

He shook his shaggy head and let out a long, tired sigh. "No. Ever since I realized you work here, I've been coming by, trying to figure out how to approach you to find out how you're doing and about replacing your van. Today I finally decided to just knock on your door."

"Why didn't you just have your cousin introduce us?"

"Sonoma? No way," he scoffed. "She's hard enough to deal with as it is. She doesn't need to know *all* my business. Think about all the secrets that get passed around in a ladies' hair salon."

"Isn't that a little sexist?"

He shrugged his big shoulders. "Not if it's true. Dudes don't gossip in barbershops."

"You sure about that?" *And when was the last time you were actually in a barbershop?*

"No."

Something about him, about the way he said what he said, had her believing his story. "Do you own other cars?"

There was that small smile again. "Yeah, I love cars. Which is why you should let me take you car-shopping." Hesitation must have shown all over her face because he raised his hands in surrender, like he'd done at the accident scene. "I'll bring Sonoma. You should bring Finn."

Not what she'd expected. "Why?"

"In case I'm a serial killer, of course. Safety first." He winked at her.

Oh! He did refer to Finn as a tall, good-looking blond, didn't he? Maybe he wants to meet him. Wait till I tell Finn! Nah, let's let him be surprised. Wait. Am I actually considering going car-shopping with this guy? And letting him buy me a car?

"So what do you say?" He tucked his massive hands under his massive shoulders. The T-shirt he was wearing stretched, displaying an equally massive chest. His posture eased. Not so nervous now. Much more relaxed, though the body language still didn't match the scary Wookiee face. *Wonder what he looks like underneath all that?*

He tilted his head. "Hello?"

"What? Oh, sorry! Um, when?"

"How about Monday? I'm off that day, and so's Sonoma. Can you take time off?"

"Pfft. I know the boss."

He gave her a funny look. At least she *thought* it was funny.

"That was a joke," she explained, suddenly feeling awkward as hell.

"Yeah, I got that."

"Then why are you giving me that look?"

"What look?" His expression said he was genuinely baffled.

"*That* look."

"I have a look?"

"Um, yeah."

"Sorry. I didn't mean to give you a look. I was just thinking I need to call my attorney and let him know what I'm doing." Her puzzlement must have been obvious because he went on in a low, conspiratorial voice. "He told me to let him handle everything, but at the rate these insurance companies go, you won't have a check for at least another month, and I hate to see you without wheels that long."

"Oh. That's … thank you." *Wow. That's really sweet. Unless you're a serial killer, of course.*

Chapter 6

Manscaping Design

Dave left Ms. Hendricks and Casper and took a jaunty stroll to Sonoma's salon. Jaunty because he'd finally dragged a semblance of a smile out of the very reluctant landscaper. *Score one for Grims. Count the dog loving me up, and that's two.* That score—and getting to buy her a new car on Monday—would lift some of the guilt weighing heavy on his shoulders.

He pushed open the door to Shear Indulgence, and its greeting bells rang out in jubilation. His eyes landed on Sonoma finishing up.

"Got time for one more?" he called.

She jerked her head toward an empty station. He took a seat and inspected himself in the mirror. Hairy and scary. Hadn't those been Ellie Hendricks's words? Shit, he hadn't meant to scare her then *or* today. She'd probably thought he was a perv or the *actual* Grim Reaper. The moniker, along with his grizzly persona, were fine for throwing the fear of God into his opponents—something he fed off of—but not so with tiny blond women.

Sonoma cashed out her client and pointed at her station in the back. "Ooh, do I finally get to shave off that bird's nest you call a beard? If so, you have to promise to find good homes for all the animals living there."

"Haha." He ambled over. "She called me a Wookiee."

"*Who* called you a Wookiee?"

"Your neighbor, Ellie What's-Her-Name."

Sonoma gave him the requisite eye-roll. "Hendricks."

He totally knew that. For some odd reason, he didn't want Sonoma knowing he knew, though.

Sonoma pumped the chair down, adjusting the height, then spun him until he faced her mirror. Placing her hands on either side of his head, she leaned in, looking at him in the reflection. "I'm surprised she didn't call you something much worse. See? Told you she was sweet."

"Sweet?" he scoffed. "If she was sweet, she'd smile more and she wouldn't be so dead set against having a boyfriend. Her words, not mine, and she offered them freely. Girl probably eats them for lunch." He didn't really believe that—actually, he had no clue—but he needed to deflect Sonoma's attempts at matchmaking.

"Words or boyfriends?"

"Men."

"So what are we doing here?"

"Trim. Cut, maybe. No shave. Not completely. I'm not ready for that."

"Got it. Baby steps."

"She called me a Wookiee," he repeated lamely. "She also mentioned 'hairy' and something about scaring the shit out of people."

Sonoma straightened and smirked. "So the woman who eats men for lunch and *isn't* sweet has motivated you to make the change I've been begging you to make for months? How does that work, exactly?"

"Oh, shut up. That's not what I meant. What I meant was I'm taking her car-shopping on Monday—I'd like you to come, by the way—and I don't want to scare the shit out of her again. That's all."

"Oh goody! Are you going to buy me a new car too?"

"I just did, like a year ago. So you'll come? I think she'd feel more comfortable. Plus, I told her to bring her stepbrother."

Sonoma shrugged. "Yeah, I'll come. Now. About what we're going to do with you. Being called a Wookiee could be good or bad. Wookiees are badass and cuddly at the same time."

Dave looked at her from under furrowed brows. "I don't think that's what she had in mind."

"Okay. So smelly and terrifying, and she wants to run every time she sees you. You *are* intimidating, even without all the hair."

"Me? I'm a teddy bear."

"More like a pissed-off grizzly." Sonoma threw a cape over him, faced him away from the mirror, and got to work. "The girl's not in the market for a boyfriend because she doesn't have time," she murmured. "Business comes first, and as a result, all she does is work. Like you. See there? You two already have something in common."

He smirked and got a head whack with Sonoma's comb. "Ouch! What was that for?"

"What's the smirk for?"

"Just thinking that whatever douchenugget goes after *that* girl better love a challenge." *Good one, Grims.* He executed an inner cheer. *Dee-fence!*

"All guys love a challenge. It's probably why she gets hit on all the time."

"She does?" The surprise in his voice belied the realization that he was not, in fact, surprised.

"Of course she does. Have you looked at her?"

Sure. Online. Where she's smiling and not sizing up my ass for a good chewing. His mind wandered to her Masochists Anonymous comment.

"So she doesn't have any steadies?"

"Not that I'm aware of, but I doubt she'd tell me anyway."

They kept talking, and he lost track of the scissors and trimmers Sonoma wielded. So when she finally whirled him back to the mirror, he almost didn't recognize himself.

"Shit, Nome. What have you done to me?"

"Made you handsome? You're welcome."

He ran his hands over his high, tight sides, then raked his fingers through the longer strands she'd left on top. The biggest shocker, though, was the beard. The huge bush was gone, and in its place was a neatly trimmed version akin to a few weeks' growth. He ran his hand over it, feeling incredibly naked. He should have thought this out. What the hell was he going to tug on? "Uh …"

"What do you think?"

He tilted his head, inspecting his face from different angles. "It's gonna take some getting used to."

"But do you like it?" Imploring eyes searched his.

No. Maybe. He gave her a reassuring nod and eased when her expression brightened. "You did an awesome job. I can see my jaw now."

"And a fine, manly jaw it is too. The ladies are gonna love it!"

He rolled his eyes. "Didn't do it to impress the ladies."

She unfastened his cape, brushing stray hairs off him as she went. "No, just one." Then she chortled, "You're manscaping for the landscaper."

The protest he was forming was interrupted by a high-pitched squeal. "Oh. My. God! Look at you!" Mandy stood off to one side, eyeballing him shamelessly. When had she sneaked in? *Shit.*

Sonoma leaned to his ear. "Not *that* one."

No kidding, he thought to himself.

"That's a great look on you, Dave." Mandy's voice was so husky he could have shucked it like a corn cob. "Can a girl buy you a drink? I'm all done for tonight."

He didn't need a degree to interpret her facial expression—he'd seen the look before. It was hungry and feral and broadcast something along the lines of "Fuck me now." His baser self should have at least given the blatant invite some due—it had been a while—but his cock didn't even stir, preferring to nap in its cozy pouch. A forceful *No, thanks* echoed in his head. Yoda would have been proud.

Mandy's reaction did do one thing for him, though. It told him Ellie Hendricks *might* not run screaming for the hills when she saw him, and *maybe* she would tolerate being with him for the time it would take to get her car. So there was that.

Sonoma was staring at him pointedly in the mirror, her lips twitching as though fighting a sneer.

He darted his gaze to Mandy. "Uh, thanks, but I've got plans." *Eating a shit ton of popcorn, parking my ass on the couch, and watching hours of hockey and cooking shows. Alone.* Her face crumpled, and guilt had him foolishly adding, "Maybe some other time?"

That lifted her expression. Probably too much. Damn. He was too rusty to play this game skillfully.

"I need to lock up, Mandy, so now would be a good time for you to finish whatever you're doing," Sonoma practically growled.

Mandy finally left—after sliding Dave a few more dirty smiles—and he stuck around to be sure Sonoma got out safely. Truth was he wasn't in a hurry to return to his empty house.

"Why'd you hire Mandy if you don't like her?" he asked.

Sonoma sighed as she dumped a final dustpan of hair into the trash. "I needed to rent the station, and she didn't show her true man-crazy colors until after I'd brought her on."

"She comes on to your male clients?"

She laughed. "Some. With *you*, though, she's way over the top. Don't let it go to your head."

"No need to worry your pretty red curls over it. She's not my type."

"Why not?"

"I don't know. Too eager? I prefer to do my own chasing."

She narrowed her eyes at him. "What *is* your type anyway?"

He blanked for a few beats. That question used to have a stock answer—any girl that looked like Nicole—but lately, things had grown surprisingly fuzzy. "I have no idea. Low maintenance?" *That would be a change.*

With a hip bump and a smile, she said, "Guess you should figure that out, huh?"

"Nah. Not planning on doing any chasing anytime soon."

After he saw Sonoma to her car, he strolled back to his GTO—in Silver Cloud Gray—glancing at Landscaping with Altitude. The interior was dark, and an unexpected breath of relief left him. Had Ellie still been inside, he would have felt compelled to hang out until she was safely away.

Why did it matter? Because he'd been raised that way, that's why. And there was nothing else to it.

Ellie was five blocks from home when she picked up Finn's incoming call. "What happened to your hot date? Your seven-thirty sesh and your whatever other time it was?" she teased.

"Jealous I *had* a date when you haven't in, what, the last twelve months?"

"Eight," she growled. Yeah, he'd hit a nerve. "So was this with someone I know?"

"Keira."

"Thought you guys broke up?"

"We did."

"Ah. A booty call, then." God, what Ellie wouldn't give for a booty call … from practically anyone. At this point, she wasn't picky, as long as he was clean and normal and smelled good and would leave her bed when they were done so she didn't have to deal with the awkward morning-after eggshell dance. She was such a bad dancer.

"Maybe. We'll see," Finn evaded. "So tell me about Dave Grimson!"

"Yeah, what's up with that? You went all fangirl on me. Is he someone you know?"

"If he's who I think he is, he's the captain of the Colorado Blizzard hockey team."

"And this is gush-worthy why?"

"Dude's a beast! That's why they call him the Grim Reaper."

Ellie quelled her fresh surge of horror. "As in the dementor who carries a scythe?" *What the hell have I gotten myself into?* Though he'd had a mouth full of teeth this evening, the image of Dave Grimson's gap-toothed face—which reminded her of a jack-o-lantern sporting a mountain man beard—was stuck in her head. Yeah, that. So *not* appealing. Maybe she wouldn't take a booty call from just *anyone*, not that she'd considered one from him in the first place. Although, Casper had recognized something likable in the guy. Then again, Casper was easy.

Ellie checked her snoozing dog in the rearview mirror. "I'm not so sure this is the same guy, Finn. He looks like he's straight out of a wilderness reality show. He probably pounds his chest and howls, spears fish with sharp sticks, and skins bears—with his teeth. If he *had* teeth, that is."

"Sounds like the Grim Reaper."

"Well, you can find out for yourself on Monday. He wants to take me car-shopping and told me to bring you along for protection." *And because he might just have a crush on you.* She stifled a snicker.

"The guy you're describing sounds like the same Dave Grimson, but I still don't know why he was there or why you felt threatened. Was it a case of stranger danger?"

"No, because he *wasn't* a stranger. He's the guy who totaled my van, thank you very much, and he's been cruising by the office the last few days."

"Say *what*? El, what've you been smoking?"

"I'm serious as a swarm of locusts, Finn! He says he feels bad about the wreck and wants to personally replace my car and that he was getting up the nerve to approach me."

Finn laughed. "Whether he's the hockey player or not—and I doubt he is, or he wouldn't be shy—this sounds too good to pass up. Yeah, I'm totally in. Just tell me when and where. I'll be there with bells on."

Something about this ridiculous situation had Ellie's lips quirking. She found herself looking forward to Monday.

A mostly full beer bottle and a jumbo bowl of popcorn propped beside him, TV tuned to hockey, Dave lounged on his leather couch, scrolling through his iPad, marking vehicles and dealerships to check out on Monday. A good couple of days were headed his way. His team would be back for a two-game homestand, the trainer declared him day-by-day for play, and he was car-shopping. What was not to like?

His phone pinged as if on cue. Nicky, confirming a time to drop off Benny. Okay, so there was one thing he wasn't looking forward to, but it would be over with quickly. And if he had a few more beers—maybe another shot of whiskey—he could dull the thought entirely tonight.

Morning came, and he was returning home from his run when a familiar Lexus SUV pulled up in front of his garage. Familiar because he'd bought it. Long, lean legs in tight jeans and spiked boots swung from the driver's side. The heels clicked when they hit the pavement. Next came a tumble of white-blond hair and a face that would have been beautiful if not for the scorn etched in its feminine features.

"I can't believe you made me bring him at the ass crack of dawn," Nicky grumbled.

Absently, his hand moved to tug a beard that wasn't there. How long before he was cured of *that* habit?

"Good morning to you too," he snorted.

She peeled off her sunglasses—it wasn't even light yet—and settled narrowed eyes on him. Those eyes widened. "What happened to you?"

"Uh, I've been running?"

"No, I mean your beard. Your hair." She swept her sunglasses up and down.

"I finally gave in to Sonoma's nagging."

One side of Nicky's mouth curled up—not in a smirk, but in a rare smile of appreciation. "Well, it's an improvement."

Really? Thought you liked the other look. "Thanks?"

Her eyes flashed. "You must be seeing someone."

"Because I got my hair and beard cut?"

Benny saved him from further uncomfortable conversation by bounding from the SUV and crashing into his leg. Dave ruffled the dog's neck and let him rub himself against him. "Good to see you too, boy. Miss me?"

Dave loved this damn dog. He had found it—or had it found him?—as a stray when he and Nicky first got together. While it had ripped his heart out to let him go, he figured Benny would be good for Isaac. Now he wasn't so sure that had been the wisest decision.

"How's Isaac?" Dave peered through the windshield, but the boy wasn't in the vehicle.

"At home, asleep."

Isn't he a little young to be left alone? None of his business anymore. Before Dave could follow up on his original question, Benny nearly took out his knees. Dave corralled his collar. "Sit." The dog did. Dave patted his head. "Good boy."

"How do you get him to do that?" Nicky let out a little puff of disgust. "He won't listen to me."

Nope, Dave wasn't going down this road. They'd argued way too many times about consistency in discipline—canine *and* human—with Nicky usually flipping him off, metaphorically speaking, and going about it whichever way suited her.

"Anytime you want to give him up …" He put it out there. Again.

She shook her head. No, of course she wouldn't give him up. He was too handy to hang over Dave's head.

"So where are you guys going?" Why was he asking? He was only setting himself up for a letdown. Nicky hadn't wasted a moment getting back out in the dating pool looking for the Mr. Right that *wasn't* Dave, and these weekend jaunts were usually with some guy. He never knew if it was the same guy or a random each time. And there was squat he could do about it. Not that he cared who the fuck she spent time with, but did she have to drag Isaac along too? The poor kid probably had whiplash, being shuttled between his dad and Nicky's man-toys. A few times she'd left Benny *and* Isaac with Dave, but she hadn't "appreciated Isaac's attitude" when she'd brought him home. Too much testosterone throwing its weight around, or some bullshit like that. Christ! Did that mean when Isaac stayed with his father, there *wasn't* testosterone? No way. Dave knew better after having been around the douche one too many times.

"Aspen—in a private jet."

"Nice." Why had she dangled the bit about the jet? So he'd know the dude had bucks, no doubt. Nicky and her head games. "Welp, have a good time. C'mon, Ben."

He began punching in his garage code and stopped cold when she said, "Don't I even get a hug?"

He turned slowly. Now she wanted a *hug*? What the hell was going on with her? "I didn't know we *hugged* anymore." She hadn't moved from the driver's side door. *If she wants a hug that damn bad, the least she can do is get her ass over here.*

She fluttered her hand at him. "Never mind." And just like that, she was behind the wheel, surging the car forward, looking madder than a cat getting a bath, and leaving him to wonder—again—what the hell he'd done wrong.

Chapter 7

Hockey Is a Contact Sport

"Sorry, Grims. You're not ready yet."

"What? You gotta fucking be kidding me! My hand's fine!" Dave's temper zoomed upward even as his hopes bottomed out.

The trainer shook his head. "No, it's not. You've *got* to rest it and let it heal."

Dave opened his mouth to argue, but Coach LeBrun walked into the room and gave the trainer a chin lift. "So?"

"Sorry, Coach. Like I was just telling Grims, the hand's not ready yet." The trainer darted rabbit eyes between Coach and Dave. "Maybe next game."

Next game, my ass! How the hell is Herb supposed to shop my ass if it's parked?

Dave rocketed to his feet, anger flowing like heat through his veins.

Coach arched his eyebrows, his eyes on Dave while he spoke to the trainer. "And practice?"

"I don't recommend it. He can skate—in fact, he *should* skate—maybe tap a few pucks, but absolutely no contact."

Coach nodded and turned to leave but stopped and glanced over his shoulder. "Go ahead and suit up for morning skate, maybe help out on a few drills. Tonight you're watching from the suite."

Dave gritted his teeth and gave Coach a curt head bob before heading for the locker room. *Damn pussy trainers!* Two years ago, his trainer, Bobby, would have cleared him for play—*after* giving him the juice and painkillers he needed—and he wouldn't have missed a beat. *And* the hand would've healed up in no time, unlike now, when it was taking for-fucking-ever. But Bobby had been canned, and now they were *overly* cautious. Like he was some fucking piece of glass that would break with a sneeze. Christ, he really missed Bobby.

By the time Dave hit the ice, he was so fired up that he flew around its slick surface as if someone had added wings to his skates.

"Watch out! Grim Reaper thinks he's got wheels. He's a collision waiting to happen," yelled Quinn Hadley, their first-line left winger. Quinn was one of a handful of guys who treated Dave as if he weren't a leper, or worse, the team outcast. In other words, he treated him normally.

"It's because he finally molted and isn't carrying around a fuck ton of fur," chortled Wyatt Tompkins, the team's number-one goalie and reigning manwhore. Quinn had turned in his manwhore crown when he'd fallen for Sarah, Gage Nelson's "off-limits" sister. The team's only other overachieving womanizer, Hunter McMurphy, had been traded during the off-season. And thank God because, while he'd been a good player, his presence in the locker room had been pure poison. Sometimes guys fit in and gelled, and sometimes they didn't. Hunter had been in the latter category from day one. It occurred to Dave that maybe that role had shifted to him, but he stuffed the disturbing thought away.

"Or maybe he *finally* got lucky and doesn't have to haul around balls that weigh twenty pounds apiece. Even the Grim Reaper has to score once in a while." Quinn barked a laugh at his own stupid joke. A puck whacked his shin pad, and he told his soon-to-be brother-in-law, Gage Nelson, what he could do with himself, followed by, "Stop fucking firing pucks at me, asshole!"

"Stop sleeping with my sister," Gage shot back, a shit-eating grin plastered on his face, his words punctuated by another zinging puck. This had been an ongoing joke—mostly—since Quinn had snagged Sarah. A ballsy move, and if Nelson, who was also one of the alternate captains, would give Dave more than a passing grunt, Dave might have a better handle on what Nelson really thought and whether a potential clash was looming between the two that would fuck up team chemistry.

Dave slowed his skating, picking up bits and pieces of conversations as guys stretched, skated, or lobbed pucks at the net. The easy banter between the boys buoyed and saddened him at the same time. Buoyed because a club in sync was not only crucial to winning it all, but it was a beautiful thing, and this club meshed. Mostly. And that's what saddened him. He was an outsider looking in, the one puzzle piece that no longer snapped into place, and he needed to find that fit again. Until he got his trade, he'd have to figure out how to make it work with this bunch. Putting on a captain's swagger wasn't his style, and it sure as shit wouldn't get him anywhere anyway. Quinn and Wyatt poking fun at him felt *good*, felt like he was one of them. Damn, but he missed that.

He glided up to the other alternate captain, T.J. Shanstrom, and tapped his boot with his stick. T.J. turned and gave him a chin-jerk greeting. Shanny was a bruising right-winger, and while Dave matched him pound for pound and inch for inch, he lacked T.J.'s nasty streak—which was why T.J. was the team's enforcer. Since being traded to the team, though, T.J. was racking up points instead of penalty minutes.

Unlike Nelson, T.J. hadn't been part of the "inner circle" that had witnessed Dave's humiliating downfall firsthand, so things had remained cordial between them. Not exactly buddy-buddy, but T.J. usually didn't shut him out. Dave would take whatever scraps he could get.

"Nice road wins by you and the boys," Dave threw out. "Can't beat that."

"Yeah, it was a sweet trip," T.J. agreed. "So you suiting up tonight?"

Dave shook his head and groused. "No. Trainer thinks my hand 'needs to rest,' like it's some decrepit grandma. I think *he* needs glasses."

"Too bad. We could use you out there, but the medical staff knows its shit." With that, T.J. skated away.

Had there been an undercurrent of something in T.J.'s tone? Dave shoved away the prickly thought and pushed off for more laps.

When he came off the ice, he was surprised to see a text from his old trainer, Bobby. *Hear the hand's been giving you trouble. Let me know if I can help with that.*

Dave stared at the screen. Was the guy fucking serious? They'd been friends, so Bobby understood how much an injury like the hand was gnawing at Dave. He also understood how far his "help" could go in turning that injury around. They'd shared a hell of a lot of drinks blasting the NHL's policy on the banned substances.

"If this shit can help an athlete, why do they ban them? It's not like the stuff makes you crazy," Dave had argued, and Bobby had agreed.

Except Dave's withdrawals had made him "edgy," as Nicky liked to describe it, but Bobby had told him it was all psychological. Yeah, they'd stayed in touch, though Dave had cut off the communication these last six months. Now as he looked at his phone, he was sorely tempted to ramp up that friendship again. The drug tests had been cut back after the first year, and Bobby's shit would mean the difference between playing and not playing. With a sigh, he replied, *No thanks, I'm good.* But he cracked the door open with, *How've you been doing?*

Hours later, he watched from the team's suite in a different kind of suit, his stomach in one massive knot, his parched throat aching for a shot of whiskey and a beer chaser to slide down and soothe it. What he wouldn't give to trade the coat and tie for his jersey and skates! Didn't matter that he was surrounded by luxury and people waiting on him hand and foot. He wanted to be on the ice, helping out his team.

After fielding Herb's call this afternoon, though, he was screwed six ways to Sunday.

"So they're sitting you tonight? Are you a healthy scratch, or is this about the hand?" Herb had asked.

"We have a new mother-hen trainer who's afraid of his own fucking shadow. He's trying to look like he's doing a good job, so I have to sit," Dave had fired back, his mind wandering back to Bobby's text. *I can help with that.*

"Either way, you sitting doesn't help our cause. I'm going to hold off on shopping you until you've been back on the ice for a few games. That way, interested teams can see you're a hundred percent. No use trying to float it out there right now."

"Did you get a chance to float it out there *at all*? Was *anyone* interested?"

"A few teams. Arizona, for one."

Shit. Arizona's a good team. And it's not in the fucking frozen north. "I guess that's *some* good news, then." *And I'll take any I can get right about now because things aren't looking so good.*

At least he had car-shopping to look forward to in two days.

Chapter 8

Have I Got a Beauty for You!

Ellie rocked on her heels as she peered out the front window of her office, waiting for Finn so they could all go "car-shopping." How weird was that? "The guy that hit me wants to take me car-shopping—with his cousin and Finn," she'd told her mom during their weekly call. "He sounds like a very considerate—and contrite—person," her mother had said. Of course she had. Mom never took off her rose-colored glasses, which gave Ellie hope she might see the world through a less gloomy lens. After all, they shared the same DNA.

A gleaming burgundy Porsche Cayenne Turbo pulled into the parking lot. Eyes roaming over the lines of the gorgeous SUV, she didn't notice the driver until he unfolded his big frame from behind the steering wheel and stepped out. He was a well-built man sporting jeans, leather Oxford sneakers, and a long-sleeved black T-shirt that hugged his square shoulders. With well-groomed chestnut-brown hair and a dark trimmed beard over a square jaw, he presented an appealing package. Like she had his vehicle, Ellie appreciated his lines. Broad, muscular, chiseled. He looked thirty-ish and had a way of moving that exuded easy masculine confidence. Not a swagger, but an air that said, "This is who I am. Take it or leave it."

She tucked herself into a corner, keeping him in her line of sight, watching as he stood beside the Porsche, scrolling through his phone, his head down. Though she hadn't gotten a close look at his face, she could tell it was nice enough that she wouldn't kick him out of bed for eating crackers. *Wonder if* he'd *be interested in a booty call?*

He looked up, and she ducked back, but not before registering something familiar about him. Gears aligned in her head. Tall guy, nice car, hanging out in her parking lot. And she was appalled. She'd been ogling "The Grim Reaper Wookiee"! Where had his Wookiee suit gone? She told herself she had it wrong, that this smooth stranger was different from the one who looked as if he'd just stepped out of the back woods for the first time in a decade.

A moment later, another car pulled up, and out hopped Sonoma. The last cog slid home when the man bent down to hug her. *That* is *him!* Realization smacked Ellie in the forehead like a piñata stick that had missed its target. "Oh. My. God. He must have spiffed himself up to meet Finn," she said aloud, followed by an incredulous chuckle. "Definitely noooo booty call for you, El." Even if she'd *wanted* to sleep with the dolt who'd hit her … which she certainly did not.

The back door crashed open, about launching Ellie from her suede ankle boots.

"Hi, El."

She whirled, hand on her chest, and gulped in a breath. "Jesus, Finn, you scared the shit out of me! Maybe go easy on the door next time?"

"Sorry." His eyes popped. "Holy fuck, look at you!" He gave her a cursory eye-sweep. "Nice to see you out of uniform and looking like a … a … *female* of the species." He sniffed the air dramatically. "You even wore your hair down and used shampoo."

He stood too far away for the shove she *wanted* to give him, so she had to settle for the eye-roll he so richly deserved.

A slow smirk formed on his face. "Did you get dressed up to impress the captain of the hockey team?"

"We don't even know if he's the same guy." Heat raced up her neck and burned her cheeks like a blazing beacon—not because Finn was right, which he wasn't, but because she'd just been salivating over said captain of the hockey team, who would probably pick Finn over her anyway. "And no, I only wore this because everything else was dirty." Not true, but she'd merely donned skinny jeans and a form-fitting pink sweater under an ivory vest. No big deal.

Finn joined her at the window. "Yeah, right. So are they here?"

"Looks like. At least I recognize Sonoma."

Finn's eyebrows pinched together. "That's not Grimson with the cute redhead. Or is it?"

"Let's go find out, shall we?" Ellie locked the back door, picked up her purse, and perched her sunglasses on her head.

"She his girlfriend?" Finn asked with a casualness she recognized as fake.

"No, his cousin, whose salon is four doors down. I can't believe you've never noticed her."

"Me neither."

Ellie didn't miss Finn's eyebrows inching up his forehead as he locked the front door behind them. "Please don't hit on her. I *like* how she styles my hair. After you dump her, I have no idea who will cut it."

Finn rolled his eyes. "I'm not going to hit on her, El. But if *she* hits on *me*? I might not be able to fight her off."

Ellie sent a death glare his way, and he returned a cocky grin.

It was an unseasonably warm, gorgeous fall day—the mini heatwave that usually preceded a clobbering snowstorm. "Finn, we need to send out an email blast to our clients reminding them to protect their plants and disconnect their hoses."

He whacked her arm. "Give the work brain a rest, El."

"But—"

"Don't worry. I'll take care of it. Now relax, for fuck's sake!"

Sonoma and Dave glanced their way as they approached. Ellie zeroed in on Dave, waiting for any telltale looks he might send Finn's way, but she was caught flat-footed when instead his eyes darted from Finn and landed on her—and stayed there. For a breathless moment, she was caught in an intense beam she couldn't escape. His eyes were dark green or blue—she couldn't tell—but something flared in them before they drilled deeper. She finally broke the uncomfortable stare, the heat in her cheeks intensifying, but *he* didn't look away until Finn stuck out his hand.

"Finn Callahan, Ellie's stepbrother."

"Pleasure. I'm Dave Grimson, and this is my cousin, Sonoma Hartley."

Finn beamed Sonoma a white-toothed Finn special.

"Hey, Ellie," Dave greeted her, his voice all low and soft and *not* scary.

She gave him a head bob, trying to swallow past her dry throat.

"Are you *the* Dave Grimson?" Finn blared.

"I don't know about *the*. There are lots of Dave Grimsons."

"But they don't play D for the Blizzard. That's you, right?"

A nod.

"Shit, I didn't recognize you without the beard! How's the hand, man? I miss seeing you play."

Dave flexed his right hand. "It's great. I'll be back playing any day."

Sonoma elbowed Ellie. "What do you think of Dave's new look, Ellie? Big improvement, huh?"

Dave's expectant gaze shifted to Ellie, and she squirmed inside. *Way to put me on the spot, Sonoma. No tip for you next time!* "Well, it definitely cuts down on the scare factor." Her failed attempt at diplomacy made her cringe inside. *God, could I sound any lamer?*

But Dave broke into a smirk that flashed white. *Yeah, with what he makes, he can afford the best dental care money can buy.* "Less scary was the whole idea. I didn't want to give you nightmares."

"See?" Sonoma cried triumphantly and patted Dave's shoulder, then ran on to explain how she'd been after him to clean up his act, and how he'd finally gotten motivated. She shot Ellie a sly glance.

Is this about impressing Finn?

"You weren't giving me nightmares," Ellie told him, "but I have to admit you're easier on the eye now." She could have sworn a blush colored his angled cheekbones.

They piled into the Cayenne, Dave insisting she ride in front, where he handed her a stack of papers. "I took the liberty of printing some specs for you. That way you can look them over and jot down any questions before we hit the dealerships." He handed her a pen. "I ranked them in order of best features first, focusing on their keyless entry systems and hands-free liftgates. Thought that might be important in your line of work."

She turned her head and gawked at him.

He didn't seem to notice. "We're starting with Chrysler first. From there, Honda, Kia, and Toyota." He gave her a sidelong glance as he drove. "I really hoped Mercedes would be a good option, but when it comes to keyless entry, their vans don't stack up against the others. I'm totally down to go there, but it's your call."

In the backseat, Sonoma and Finn buzzed with conversation. Ellie slid a look at Dave maneuvering the Porsche. His motions were practiced and smooth, and her eyes zoomed in on his hands commanding the steering wheel—hands that looked as though they could turn a piece of rebar into a pretzel. Rough. Rugged. An image of them on her bare skin popped into her head, and she recoiled inside. *What is wrong with me?* She yanked her gaze away and shook her head to get rid of the torrid vision, reminding herself Finn might be more Dave's type.

A frown knotted Dave's eyebrows. "Does that mean Mercedes is out?"

"What? Oh. No. I was just … You put a lot of time and effort into this."

He grinned like a little kid about to get a Dairy Queen double-dipped cone. "I enjoyed it. Cars are fun."

You should smile like that more often, Mr. Reaper.

Sonoma seemed to tune in from the backseat. "Dave's a total motor head. Don't get him going, or he'll quote you every spec on every car ever built." She paused a beat. "And if he *does* get going, just tell him to shut up."

"I'll keep that in mind." Ellie fought the quirking at the corners of her mouth. Her father was a motor head, and she saw nothing wrong with it.

Dave glared at the rearview mirror. "Gee, thanks, Nome." He side-eyed Ellie and dropped his voice conspiratorially. "All she cares about is the color."

Ellie held up the stack of papers. "What colors *do* they come in?"

He let out a gust of air. "You did *not* just say that." The twitch in his lips told her he was joking.

"She so did," Finn threw in. "But don't let her fool you. She knows her way around cars."

"Only the oldies without all the complicated onboard computer crap," she added.

Dave's eyebrows inched up his forehead. "That's how you knew about the GTO. Where did you learn?"

"My dad. He used to fix up cars for a hobby, and he let me tag along. I guess I pestered him with lots of questions, so I ended up learning a few things." *Before* he married Finn's mom and became a father to her passel of kids. After that, not only did he stop tinkering with cars but alone time with him grew scarce, making those early years that much more precious. Ellie stifled a wistful sigh.

They pulled into the Chrysler dealership, and Dave killed the engine. "I'd like to know more about that sometime." The grin was back in place, and she felt an inappropriate flutter in her belly.

As they headed inside, he spouted details about power trains, brakes, suspension, and safety ratings. "They also have a hybrid version we need to check out."

And so they did.

Three dealerships later, Ellie's head was swimming, and her belly was growling so loudly that Dave shot it a look. "Either someone has a lion living in her stomach, or she needs to be fed." As if on cue, a roll of thunder rumbled from *his* stomach, and he chuckled. "Maybe we should stop for lunch?"

"God, yes!" Sonoma called from the backseat. "What about you, Finn?"

"I could eat," Finn agreed cheerfully.

"Finn, you could eat twenty-four-seven," Ellie teased. Sonoma let out a giggle, and it occurred to Ellie she'd never heard the hairdresser giggle before—not that they were besties or anything, but they'd known each other for years. Ellie turned to Dave. "I'd like the break. Then I can take a minute to breathe and go over some of these choices. They're all mushing together in my head at the moment."

He kept his eyes focused on the road. "I'll help. Sushi okay?"

"Sushi would be great." How long had it been since she'd had sushi that didn't come prepackaged from the grocery store? Worse, the discounted stuff that had sat in the case too long because she'd been too busy to get there sooner?

When they walked into the restaurant, Dave asked for a booth. "It's sacrilege not to eat at the bar, but it'll be easier to look over your notes if we can spread out a little."

In a surprise move, he placed his fingers at the small of her back, guiding her as they followed the server, then pulled them away an instant later. While her first reaction had been to flinch, his fingers were gone before she could do *anything*. And now she realized the touch had felt kind of nice. Protective, almost. Someone had taught him some manners.

At the booth, he motioned for her to slide in, and he joined her, his hip knocking hers. The closeness—warm and solid—radiated up her side, and she felt its loss as soon as he mumbled an apology and moved away. *It's been way too long if I'm enjoying this guy bumping my hip and prodding my back.*

Across from them, Sonoma wore a fangirl look Ellie had seen before on women in close proximity to Finn. *Oh, this is no good.* She felt the urge to warn Sonoma that Finn was a bad bet if she was hoping for more than a fling. But Finn had a goofy smile plastered on his face, as if he were equally infatuated. *Oh no!*

Ellie snuck a look at Dave, who studied the sushi menu, his pencil poised, seemingly oblivious or uninterested in the chemistry crackling on the opposite side of the booth. She didn't know what she'd expected—for him to be jealous that he wasn't having the same kind of connection with Finn?

Before she could ponder it too long, four women sidled up to the table. Dave jerked his head up. Eight eyes were trained on him, wide smiles to match. Fans wanting his autograph. Or something else from him.

"So you recognized him?" Finn asked the girls, sounding incredulous. The silly grin he'd directed at Sonoma was gone, replaced by a genuinely curious look. He didn't seem to be checking them out, which was weird because they were all pretty.

"I'd recognize the captain of the Blizzard *anywhere*," one gushed as she thrust a pen and paper place mat at Dave. "Would you mind signing?"

Dave's entire demeanor shifted. Whereas his big shoulders had been loose a second ago, he straightened as if a hockey stick had been shoved up the back of his jersey. With an automatic nod and a strained half-smile, he rattled off, "Of course not. Be happy to," as if he'd said it a thousand times before. He probably *had.*

"Oh. And make it out to Tiffany?" she added with a bat of her eyelashes—totally wasted on Dave because he was bent to the place mat, busily scrawling. Without missing a beat, he added her name and handed it back to her.

Ellie watched in silent fascination as the next woman elbowed *Tiffany* out of the way, and the process repeated itself until the last fan's turn arrived. She was wearing a Blizzard jersey with the number ninety-two on its sleeve and a big *C* on the left side of her chest. Tugging on the jersey so it tightened across her boobs, she boldly leaned into him and asked him to sign the letter.

A subtle flinch traveled between his shoulder blades. "I'm happy to sign the back." Though his voice wasn't gruff, his it's-not-happening tone was unmistakable. *Must be why he's the captain.* The girl spun, and with an audacity completely foreign to Ellie, stuck her ass out. Wordlessly, he rose and, without any of his body managing to touch hers, penned his name between "Grimson" and his number.

After he sat back down, she pivoted toward him. With a wicked gleam in her eyes, she offered to sign something for *him*—and add her phone number. He declined politely, though he consented to a few selfies with them. They lingered several beats, and with an astonishing amount of grace, he asked if they'd give him time with his "friends he hadn't seen in a while." How could they say no? His shoulders flexed under the T-shirt fabric and dropped an inch as an exhale left his body.

"Impressive," Ellie said. "If you ever decide to give up hockey, you should think of becoming a diplomat."

Dave turned, one side of his mouth curving up. "No, thanks. I've had my fill of it in *this* career."

Finn focused on the women as they walked away. "So that must happen all the time. Tough life, bruh."

"Dave's on hiatus after his last disastrous relationship," Sonoma threw in with a smirk, pulling Finn's attention back to her. Dave shot her a glare only siblings or close cousins could exchange without torching each other. She shrugged sans apology. "It's true, Dave. You know I love you, but you've got way better taste in cars than you do women." Her eyes darted between Finn and Ellie. "*Unfortunate* taste might be a better description."

Oh! Guess Finn's not his type after all. A quick, inexplicable pulse of warmth in her chest left Ellie light-headed.

"Take the last one," Sonoma drawled. "Nicole."

Ellie's momentary dizziness evaporated, knocking against her rib cage.

Dave gave Sonoma a warning glare and growled, "Nome? 'Nuff said."

"Right. Sorry. You seem to be enjoying yourself today, and I don't want to ruin it."

"No," he huffed. "You don't."

With fortunate timing, the server appeared at their table, and when he left with their orders, his departure took some of the building tension between the cousins with him.

Dave grunted, took a sip of water, and turned to Ellie. "Are you going to be putting your new van to work right away?"

Smooth segue. Except the spotlight settled on her. "Well," she coughed, "we're sort of between projects at the moment, so if I get the van—"

"Not if. When. I fully expect to see you driving off in something when we're done today."

She suppressed the ridiculous "uh" that wanted to slip from her mouth as she ordered her thoughts. Getting a new van today hadn't occurred to her. In fact, she was still wrestling with the whole notion of having him buy her a van outright. Was it legal? The idea both made her uncomfortable and sent a thrill through her. Had she ever had a brand-new car before? No. And totally paid for? What were the tax consequences? Why hadn't she thought of this beforehand? Maybe her brainpower had been compromised in the accident.

Finn rushed into the pause. "Ellie's been working really hard on a project for Denver Habitat for Humanity. It won't pay much—"

"It won't pay *anything*," she corrected, "but it should give our company good exposure that will hopefully pay off in the near future."

"What she said," Finn directed at Dave, who leaned forward on the table with his beefy arms crossed. "And the plan she designed is amazing."

Ellie rolled her eyes to mask her embarrassment.

"It's true," Finn continued. "But she keeps telling herself it's not good enough, even though Habitat gave her their rubber stamp a while ago." He tore wooden chopsticks out of their wrapper and pointed them at her. "I see you messing with the plan, El, thinking it's not good enough." To Dave and Sonoma, he said, "The fact of the matter is, it's a damn good plan, and these guys are wetting themselves over it. What she doesn't understand is that they're grateful and would be happy with just about anything as long as it doesn't come out of their pockets. Ellie's a landscape architect, and a damn good one. If it weren't for all the time she has to put into running the business, she'd be back doing that exclusively."

"Finn—"

Wooden platters of sushi suddenly hovered before them, held by three servers. Ellie laughed as Dave and Sonoma rearranged the items on the table to accommodate the overflowing trays. "Who's eating all of this?"

Sonoma cut her a look. "This is your first time eating with Dave, but have no doubt, nothing will go to waste. And it's not unusual for him to order *more*."

"I'm a growing boy," he mumbled as the servers slid the platters onto the table, arranging them like a jigsaw puzzle. He waited until everyone had filled their small plates before serving himself. "So you'd be *back* to landscape design," he said. "Sounds like that's what you really love and not running the landscape company. What changed?"

Ellie popped a piece of fresh salmon in her mouth to keep from answering.

Finn smirked as he loaded up his soy sauce boat with wasabi. "Dave's not the only one with unfortunate taste in relationships."

An urge to choke Finn welled inside her, but she hoped an extra dollop of wasabi would do the deed for her. Or maybe she and Dave could tag team—he could strangle Sonoma while Ellie strangled Finn.

"I wouldn't be talking if I were you, Romeo," she retorted instead.

Sonoma whipped her head toward him. *Ha! At least now she knows who she's dealing with—if she even* wanted *to deal with him in the first place.* To Ellie's disappointment, her cocky stepbrother seemed unfazed. Of course he did.

Dave, who'd been silently shoveling sushi into his mouth, put his chopsticks down and finished chewing. "Tell me about the Habitat project, Ellie. Sounds really interesting." He twisted his body so he faced her.

She sent him a mental thanks for diverting the conversation away from her failed love life, and for asking about the project in the first place.

While he gave her his undivided attention—no food passed his lips—she filled him in. "Unfortunately, the event isn't getting anywhere near the publicity I'd hoped for. It looks like I'll be donating labor for a good cause, but not much advertising beyond the little signs they let me put up." An extended sigh escaped her lungs. It hurt to say it out loud.

He stared at her with an intensity that was as intriguing as it was unnerving. What thoughts were streaming behind his bright eyes? Eyes a color she'd never seen before: deep mossy-green with amber starbursts around the pupils and dark blue flecks that matched an ultramarine ring around his irises. They reflected light like a pool of clear Rocky Mountain water—like something she could dive into and drown in. Stunning.

She looked away abruptly for fear of getting swallowed up in their depths—and to hide the blush creeping over her cheeks.

"What if," he began, snapping her out of his electrifying gaze, "I can help?"

Finn and Sonoma leaned in.

Ellie's gaze dashed back to his. "How? I can't imagine having you do manual labor. Besides, we have volunteers for that."

"Not so much, El," Finn chirped. "Remember what Damian said? His volunteers are spread thin the day of the project."

Damn you, Finn! Of course she remembered—it was one more obstacle in a course more challenging than the one aspiring athletes tackled in *American Ninja Warrior.* But no way would she let a hockey player—a celebrity, no less—do grunt work on her project. Especially if he was nursing a hurt hand. Hockey was a foreign language to her, but among other useless bits of trivia stored in her brain was the knowledge that hockey players were tough as nails. They would play through injuries that would bring someone like her to their knees. Broken legs, torn up ankles, busted collarbones. But didn't they need healthy hands in order to play? Like a concert pianist. On ice.

"I can think of a couple ways to help," Dave said. "What if this were a joint PR event? Your good deed plus some guys from the team there to help out and do a meet-and-greet at the end? If potential volunteers are fans, it could boost your recruits." He paused and stroked his bearded chin. "The Blizzard has a dynamo PR team that knows how to play this stuff up and get lots of splash. It'd be good for Habitat, good for the Blizzard, and good for you. A triple-crown win."

Finn threw himself against the back of the booth. "Oh wow, El. Think what that would do."

Her eyes searched Dave's. Was the man serious? From what she could tell, he was *always* serious. *Wonder what it takes to make him laugh?* "You'd actually do that?"

"Absolutely. Let me talk to the PR folks and to the boys, and you talk to Habitat. If it's cool with everyone, then we've got a date."

Ellie's mouth dropped open. She didn't want to find anything likable about Dave—male magnetism and forest-green eyes with gold starbursts aside—though the exact reason why escaped her at the moment.

Chapter 9

WHY WON'T YODA STOP TALKING?

Dave bit back the laugh threatening to erupt from his chest as the Toyota saleswoman gave Ellie a crash course on her new Sienna's features. Those expressive blue eyes bounced from focused to bright and back again, depending on what the woman was showing her, and he nearly forgot the throbbing in his hand as he basked in his double victory. Not only had he finagled his way into helping Ellie with her project, but he was enjoying the satisfaction of finally wrangling the stubborn woman into a vehicle. His chest ballooned.

She'd protested most of the day about him buying the van, but when they'd hit the Toyota dealership, she seemed to fall in love and make a snap decision. He got it. He felt the same way when he found that perfect vehicle, and if the Sienna was the right one for her, fine by him. It was reliable, easy to maintain, and she was used to driving one. Plus, of all the vans they'd looked at today, the Sienna was the most fun to drive. How did he know? Because she'd insisted he test-drive every single vehicle she did.

The saleswoman stepped away, and Ellie shot him a glance. "Are you listening? You should know what you're getting."

"I'm not planning to repossess it," he countered.

"I'm going to will it to you, so if I get bumped off by a roving pack of Ents tomorrow, it's yours." The corners of her pretty mouth tipped up.

"Ents rove? I thought they … lumbered. Trudged. And why would they want to bump you off?"

"Because I'm responsible for ripping up their relatives and moving them to new holes?" she offered with a twinkle in her deep blues.

He let go the laugh. Damn, that felt good! "So you're a granola-crunching tree hugger?"

"Hmm. Not exactly. I don't like granola—I'm a Lucky Charms kind of girl—and I don't exactly *hug* trees, but I've been known to talk to them and stroke their trunks."

Breath halted in his throat because his brain was blowing a circuit over her stroking trunks. Things twitched south of his belt.

She visibly winced. "That sounded bad, didn't it?" Then she bit her lower lip in a way that had the twitch in his pants swelling into a bigger problem. He managed a bland half-smile and was rescued when the saleslady returned.

With Ellie once again occupied, he studied her, reminding himself that while her looks might have struck him dumb when he first saw her this morning—and were still having a disturbing effect on him—he was *not* interested in her. He wasn't interested in *anyone*. *Especially* if he was getting traded and moving to a different city. A different country.

He was already flirting with trouble enough by buying her a car. His attorney was going to blow a gasket over that alone, and Dave didn't need to add to the verbal drubbing he'd just set himself up for. Besides, she broadcast an aloofness that said she was even less interested in him than he was in her. Even if a moment of weakness prevailed and made him contemplate taking a run at her, his ego didn't have the spare parts.

"Are you sure about this?" she hissed at him when the saleswoman beckoned him toward her office to sign paperwork. "I'm just as happy with the white one, and I don't need a tow package."

But I'm not getting you the white one. Of course she'd pick the stripped-down model over this flashier high-end hybrid version *he* insisted on. An all-wheel-drive, dark burgundy Limited Premium with black-out wheels and every bell and whistle imaginable.

"Yes. I'm positive," he whispered back, adding a wink. "Besides, you never know when you might have to pull a trailer full of garden gnomes."

"But this one's twenty thousand more than the white one!" she protested, keeping her voice hushed.

"It's just money," he tossed back and got a Delta Blue glare for his trouble.

Maybe he'd been overbearing with his car knowledge and money today, throwing them around like he threw his weight around on the ice, but she'd given as good as she got, throwing her own weight around—what little she had to throw. Small but mighty. Hadn't there been a cartoon mouse that fit that description? Ellie was like that, minus the superhero beefcake chest. Which was a good thing because her chest was perfect as it was. Not that he'd noticed.

He gave himself an inner slap and fell in behind the saleswoman.

In the locker room after another lame practice the following day—for him, not his teammates—Dave shucked his jersey, chest protector, and elbow pads while the room buzzed with players talking, laughing, razzing each other. He turned his back to his stall and whistled. "Can I have your attention for a sec?"

The droning died down, and he swept the room with his eyes. "I've got an opportunity for those looking to do some extra work in the community. Some of you need to up your PR game"—he gave Wyatt a pointed look, and to his credit, Wyatt flinched—"and this one should get lots of attention. It's a Habitat for Humanity gig. We put in a few hours of work, then stick around for a fan meet-and-greet."

Players started buzzing again. Damn, he was losing them already.

"Shut the fuck up and listen to your captain!" a voice barked. Dave swiveled his head toward the voice. T.J. stood with his arms crossed and a do-not-fuck-with-me expression. He gave Dave a chin jerk. "You have the floor."

Dave wanted to hug him but dipped his head in appreciation instead. "I only need a few guys, so if you're interested, speak up." To his relief, half the boys threw up their hands. Some were the regulars—they always chipped in—so he zeroed in on the slackers. "Wyatt, you're in. Hadley, you too. Rookie," he directed at Viktor, a fresh-faced Czech center who had made the roster this season.

"The rest of you, I thank you." Dave executed a goofy curtsy, plucking at his breezers like a skirt. What possessed him, he had little idea, but it garnered numerous chuckles.

Soon he was surrounded by his three recruits. "So what are we doing and when, Cap?" said Hadley.

Dave filled them in, including what Serena, head of Blizzard PR, had laid out.

"Hads will get all the female attention, and he's not even single anymore," Wyatt whined.

To which Hadley replied, "That's right, dickhead, because I'm way better looking than you. Besides, everyone knows gingers have no soul. But I'm bringing Sarah with me for protection. She'll push the talent your way."

This made everyone within earshot laugh, except Wyatt. Sarah feared no one, as far as Dave could tell. How Hadley had pulled off catching that girl, Dave had no idea. For that matter, he had no clue how T.J. had bagged his wife, Natalie, or Nelson had wrangled Lily. Dave found himself envying his teammates, all younger than he. He'd once thought he had what they had with Nicky, but he'd been dead wrong—just like every other relationship he'd tried. Maybe Sonoma had been right and he really was clueless about picking the right ones because, in the end, they all seemed the same. Then again, he probably didn't deserve a woman like those the guys had won. Those ladies were bright, independent, and couldn't have cared less about the celebrity. In fact, the spotlight that usually drew women like wasps to syrup had gotten in his teammates' ways when it came to their SOs, but somehow they'd persevered.

Perseverance. What every hockey player needed to make it to the Big League and stay there. Dave had it too, which was why he was still in the NHL *in spite* of his screw-ups. That had to count for something.

Now all he had to do was try to get healthy, stay healthy, and get himself traded. If he couldn't get traded, he needed to find a way to make his teammates respect him again because the current situation was downright intolerable. *Might as well add finding a girl I don't deserve and making her fall for me to the* Mission Impossible *list.*

He yanked off his Under Armour shirt with a mirthless laugh. *Yeah, right. Piece of cake.* His mind once again meandered to Bobby and the performance-enhancing drugs he offered, how easy it would be, how much better his hand would feel and how soon—

"Once you start down the dark path, consume you, it will," damn Yoda huffed at him.

Shut up, Yoda. Give me back Han.

Chapter 10
Of Nefarious Soccer Mom Vans

Ellie climbed into the van and carefully shut the door. Though it was parked in the alley behind her office, she looked out the windows and checked the rearview mirror, reassuring herself she was alone. With a long, satisfying inhale, she closed her eyes, pulled in that new-car smell, and smiled. *Nothing else like it.* She'd only had it a week, but she wanted to savor that smell for as long it lasted. Should she be enjoying something she'd fought against accepting? Something so extravagant? Sure she should. Besides, she was going to pay Dave Grimson back. He didn't know it yet, but when she finally got her insurance check, she was signing it over to him—and she'd continue paying him until she'd given him back every penny.

A knock on her window jolted her from her amble along Grimson Lane. A man who resembled a shorter version of Dwayne "The Rock" Johnson stood outside. As she was debating the wisdom of opening her door, he held up a badge. The word "ICE" flashed its bright gold, and Ellie's heart plummeted to the fancy new car mats.

She hit the power window button, but nothing happened. *Shit! Key!* She reached for the ignition, forgetting it was a push button start. *Shit! Shit!* Another knock came as she fumbled for the button. Finally, she stabbed the right spot, and the engine purred to life. With a deep inhale, she located the power button and lowered the window.

"Miss Eleanor Hendricks?" he rumbled.

The name made her cringe. Loved the late grandmother she'd been named for but hated the old-fashioned name. It always brought to mind fussy lace doilies covering every surface.

"Um, I'm Ellie Hendricks."

"Miss Hendricks, would you please step out of the vehicle?"

Panic rushed from her gut and constricted her throat such that, "Am I under arrest?" came out in a squeak.

"Just step out of the vehicle, please."

Her legs wobbled as she complied, and she leaned against the van to keep herself steady, square, and tall—well, as tall as one could be at five-three. "What is it?"

His eyes flicked over the van. "Nice wheels. Hybrid?"

"Yes."

"Looks new."

What does that have to do with anything?

When she didn't answer him, he continued. "And judging by the temporary tags, it's *brand* new. What did it set you back? Fifty-five, sixty grand?"

Ellie crossed her arms. "Is that why you're here? To look over my company's new van because you're thinking of one for yourself?"

Seemingly ignoring her snarky question, his eyes traveled back to the Sienna. "It's interesting that your company's been on its financial deathbed the last two years, yet suddenly you're able to pay cash for the wheels."

Alarm bells clanged in her head. "How would you know about my company's finances and how I paid for the van?"

He simply smirked.

Her heart slammed against her rib cage so hard she worried he might hear it and mistake her fear for guilt. She slowed her breathing. "Well, Mr. … I'd like to see that badge again, please."

He pulled it from a pocket and held it inches from her nose.

She cleared her throat. "Thank you, Mr. Clemente."

He slid it back into his pocket. "*Agent* Clemente."

Scrunching her brows, she gave him her fiercest glower. "As it happens, *Agent Clemente*, the vehicle was purchased on my behalf by the party who wrecked my other van."

If he was surprised, his calculating brown eyes didn't show it. "And this other party's name?"

"What's going on here?"

Finn. Ellie's shoulders slumped in relief but tightened all over again as her mind leapt forward. If these guys knew about the van, they knew about Finn's past record. *Drug user. Drug dealer. Shit! Guilt by association?*

She wasn't mistrustful of law enforcement, but it dawned on her how bad things looked from a law-enforcement point of view. Beads of sweat formed along her hairline. No doubt she was broadcasting all the signs of misconduct, even though she'd done nothing wrong.

"Ms. Hendricks and I were having a friendly discussion about her new van."

Finn leaned his arm casually against said van. Ellie wanted to tell him not to touch, that she'd have to buff that spot, then she realized how ridiculous she sounded in her own head.

"It's a beaut, huh? Especially for a soccer mom minivan," Finn drawled.

"Should be, for what it cost. Which leads me to wonder how she afforded it?" Agent Clemente tapped his chin thoughtfully.

"She got T-boned by a hotshot hockey player. Dave Grimson, captain of the Blizzard. Know him? Dude felt so guilty he bought her a new one. Needed to pacify his conscience." Finn jabbed a thumb at Ellie. "*She* couldn't afford it, but guys who make more in a year than the three of us will ever see in our lifetimes *combined* can afford it."

Clemente blinked. Ha! *You didn't find* that *out in your snooping, Mr. Ice, did you?* Still, why was ICE here again?

"Everything okay?" Sonoma was advancing cautiously from her back door, and Ellie turned toward her. Finn jerked at the redhead's voice, then flashed her a goofy grin. Sonoma returned a subtle eyelash flutter, but Ellie let the mystery of their nonverbal exchange go. She needed to focus on Agent Clemente's nonverbal cues.

"Hey," Finn said to Sonoma. "Tell this guy about our day with Dave last week."

Sonoma frowned in bewilderment. "You mean when he bought Ellie her new van? Why? What's going on?"

The officer glanced at Sonoma. "And you are?"

"I'm Sonoma Hartley. I own the beauty salon a few doors down. Who are you?" She smiled sweetly, and he hauled out his badge again. Sonoma pulled her phone from her back pocket. "You don't mind, do you?" He held the badge flat so she could take a picture. *Why didn't* I *think of that? Because I was too busy panicking to think straight.*

Felipe stepped out of the back door, and when his eyes landed on Clemente, they went wide. "Boss lady," he said as he kept his gaze fixed on the agent, "everything okay?"

"Yes, Felipe, we're enjoying an impromptu coffee klatch in the back alley," Ellie said dryly. Felipe shot her a look that said he had no idea what she was talking about.

Clemente rattled off something in Spanish, and Felipe rattled right back. Ellie had a limited grasp of the language—mostly landscaping phrases like, "Put that plant there," along with the usual necessities such as, "Where's the bathroom?" and a handy collection of curse words. She listened carefully, straining her vocabulary to interpret the exchange.

"What're they saying, El?" Finn asked her.

"I think Agent Clemente is asking Felipe if he's seen his 'illegal friends' lately and if he knows how I was able to afford the van." Fire ignited in her belly. "*Now* he's asking how I acquired a large pile of cash—"

Sonoma cut her off. "My cousin is David Grimson," she announced. "He's the captain of the Colorado Blizzard, he makes a gazillion dollars, and *he* bought her the van because he destroyed her last one. I'm sure if you contact him, he'll collaborate … um …"

"Corroborate," Ellie offered. *Oh shit! Now Clemente thinks I'm looking for corroboration, like I really* am *guilty.*

Agent Clemente gave Ellie a bemused sweep from head to toe, and the insinuation in his eyes caused the flames inside her to bloom and flare. "With all your Big Brother intel, did you not see an accident report?" *Oh shit! Will you also find out that Dave told me to cash the insurance check? Wait. Is that illegal? Even if I repay him with it?* She told herself to keep her mouth shut, that her rising temper would only make matters worse.

Clemente's inscrutable expression gave nothing away.

"Mister Officer," Felipe interjected, "Miss Ellie do nothing wrong. Maybe you wish to speak to me?"

Ellie had almost forgotten Felipe flanked her right. The four of them—Felipe, Ellie, Finn, and Sonoma—were lined up in a wall of solidarity opposite the agent. Or looking like they were ready to be cuffed.

Finally, his gaze landed squarely on Ellie. "No, I got what I came for. Have a nice day."

Ellie's stomach bottomed out.

"What did he mean by *that*?" she said to no one in particular as Agent Clemente pulled away in a black car she hadn't noticed before … because, like all other unmarked cop cars, it was nondescript. She expelled a gust of air that about doubled her over.

Her three companions started talking at once. Felipe was apologizing, Finn was telling Ellie, "We got this," and Sonoma was assuring her Dave would straighten everything out. But Ellie didn't want Dave straightening anything out. It was *her* mess, even though she wished it would go away so she could get on with pulling her company off its "financial deathbed."

Chapter 11

Queen of Glam

Days after Agent Clemente's unfortunate appearance in the alleyway, Ellie received a jarring email from him, where he said something about contacting Dave Grimson, who "corroborated" her story. He'd added a winking emoji face. The message went on to say he hoped she understood he was doing his job, and asked if he could buy her a coffee so he could explain further. Not exactly an apology, though she wasn't sure exactly *what* the purpose of the email was. She'd brushed him off politely. With luck, she'd never hear from or see Agent Clemente again, but somehow she doubted such a happy eventuality was in her future. Instead a sword labeled "ICE" hung over her head.

Now, nearly a week after the alleyway confrontation, Ellie tucked the incident into a back corner of her mind. Habitat day had finally arrived.

As she gathered up copies of her design, her phone chimed with a text from an unknown number. *It's Dave Grimson. The boys and I have practice, so we'll be there about a half hour after you start, but we're looking forward to it.*

She couldn't remember giving him her phone number. A second later, another text pinged. From Sonoma. *Dave wanted me to relay a message, so I gave him your # and told him to contact you directly. Hope I didn't overstep.*

"Yes, Sonoma, you did overstep," Ellie said aloud to her empty office. *But it's okay.* Especially since Sonoma had rearranged her Saturday to help out at the Habitat site. Saturdays had to be a hairdresser's busiest day, so she must have doubled up her workload elsewhere on her schedule.

No problem, Ellie texted her, then sent Dave a message.

Looking forward to having you guys there. Thanks for taking Agent Clemente's call.

He texted her back with three question marks.

Ellie: *Didn't an ICE agent contact you?*

Dave: *Not that I know of. What for?*

Ellie: *Never mind. See you soon.*

She gathered up the rest of her stuff, turning over Clemente's email before she buried it again. An hour later, she parked across the street from the corner lot, her blood fizzing with excitement. Rocks in varying colors and dimensions were arranged in neat hills along one side of the street beside a pile of coffee-colored dirt and pallets of garden wall blocks. Staked Habitat signs waved in the wind beside Landscaping with Altitude signs. Cars already lined the street, and a group gathered on the sidewalk, though the start of the event was an hour away. Once people found out Blizzard players would be there, the response from volunteers had overwhelmed the Habitat office. Damian had had to limit their numbers, but judging by the growing buzz before her, Ellie suspected she'd have more cooks than kitchen space today. A good problem to have.

Felipe and Finn were scheduled to meet her here, but she texted them and told them not to come. They'd offered to work for free, but now that she didn't need them, she wanted to cut them loose so they could enjoy some time off. Felipe thanked her, but Finn insisted he was still coming.

A Habitat truck pulled onto the lot, and Damian and another employee hopped out. He waved and cracked a boyish smile. Yeah, he was excited too. She trotted across the street and unshouldered her bag to help them unload shovels, wheel barrows, tables, chairs, and tents.

"This is great, Ellie. Did I tell you we've had a boatload of donations from people who said they couldn't be here but wanted to help?"

"And they're not expecting Blizzard autographs in exchange?" Ellie laughed.

"Nope. They heard about it and wanted to contribute in some way." Dark-haired and brown-eyed, Damian was good-looking—the type she was usually attracted to. But lately he was toeing the line between professional and personal, making Ellie more uncomfortable every time she saw him. At least she'd be surrounded by lots of people today, and they would keep it all business.

Some of those people were already on-site, raring to be put to work, so she got down to handing out copies of the plan, explaining what was needed, and assigning each person to a team.

More folks drifted in, and soon Ellie was swimming in volunteers, trying to come up for air. Giddy didn't even begin to describe her state of mind. All these people, and the players hadn't even arrived yet!

But when they did arrive sometime later, there was no mistaking the shift among the volunteers. A woman gasped, and everyone turned their heads. So did Ellie, who stifled a gasp of her own. The buzzing crowd quieted as four broad men—and one woman—strolled across the street. Dressed in jeans and ball caps and hoodies in varying shades of the male navy-black-gray clothing spectrum, they weren't flashy, but they had an air about them that made people notice. The way they moved—heads up, shoulders straight, self-assured, smooth—made her breath catch in her throat. And leading the athlete alpha pack? Dave Grimson, all growly bear business until his eyes landed on her. Then his whole face seemed to light up, and she felt a blush invading her cheeks. He strode straight for her while people clustered around and gaped. Wow, he had a beautiful smile!

"Hey." He grinned down at her. "Looks like a great turnout." His fern-green eyes—or were they gold?—swept the crowd, and he gave an approving nod. He pulled on a jersey bunched in his large fist, his last name and the number ninety-two emblazoned on the back, while the others pulled on their own jerseys.

"Hi," he called to the crowd. "Nice to see everyone." Someone yelled, "Grim Reaper!" in response.

He clamped a meaty hand on his teammate's shoulder, and to Ellie he said, "This is Viktor Havelka. Make sure you work him extra hard." Viktor rolled his eyes and chuckled. Pointing to the others, Dave said, "Wyatt Tompkins, Quinn Hadley, and his fiancée, Sarah Nelson." Sarah wore number eighteen, Quinn's jersey, but cut for her body. She looked adorable in it.

The men grunted greetings, and Sarah gave her a wave and a sunny smile. "Reporting for work. Where do you want us?"

"Over here." Ellie liked her right away, and they fell into step, Dave flanking Ellie's other side as she rattled off her plan. The other three men trailed after, and the volunteers seemed to funnel in behind them.

When they reached the spot she'd mapped out, Dave began issuing orders to his companions in spite of the swelling crowd pressing in around them. Not in a pushy way, but in a reassuring, take-charge, I-know-what-I'm-doing way. Confident. Calm. Commanding.

Quinn, dark-haired and handsome, draped his arm across Sarah's shoulders. "Keep me with her so nobody hits on her."

Sarah gave him a smirk. "Isn't it the other way around, Sparky?"

An unexpected pang of envy jabbed Ellie, but she couldn't keep from smiling. Quinn was obviously smitten with Sarah and didn't mind if the whole world knew it. And right now the entire crew of volunteers knew it because work was at a standstill while the worker bees admired the Blizzard players. Ellie would have to remind everyone that autographs and exchanges came *after* the work was done. Turned out she didn't have to.

"Hey, everyone," Dave spoke up in that same masterful voice that was hard to ignore. "We're really happy to be here today helping out Habitat for Humanity and Landscaping with Altitude. If you haven't met her yet, Ellie Hendricks is the talent behind this project and the one running it, so direct questions to her." He paused a beat while folks applauded. "Serena"—he pointed toward a pretty, dark-haired woman waving beside the check-in booth—"is in charge of anything Blizzard-related. Her crew will be taking pictures and shooting video, so be sure to get with her and sign a waiver so we can show those pictures on TV or in the team's promotional material. Those of you who'd like to hang out with us when we're done turning this yard into Ellie's masterpiece, you're welcome to bring whatever you want us to sign, or we have pucks to hand out. But *that* fun can't start until we get *this* fun out of the way. So let's do it!" He clapped. "Everybody got what they need? Know your assignments?"

A cheer rose up, punctuated with shouts of, "You bet, Grims!" and "Thanks, Reaper!"

Ellie chuckled.

"What?" Dave turned his grin on her.

"Nothing. You just did my job for me, only much more effectively. So thank you for that. And thank you, again, for being here and bringing your friends." Tears unexpectedly pricked her eyes, and she had to clear her clogged throat before meeting his gaze squarely. "It really means a lot."

Surprise flared in his eyes, and he leaned down to her, his voice dropping to a low, intimate tone seemingly meant only for her, as if he were trying to soothe her sudden display of emotion. A simple masculine scent, like man shampoo or body wash mixed with skin, rippled over her. He smelled oh-so-manly and really, really good. "Hey, it's okay. We enjoy doing stuff like this. Gets us closer to the community and our fans, you know? So thank *you* for making the opportunity available."

"Of course." If she stood beside him any longer, she'd either snuffle at him like Casper or burst into tears, so she turned and scurried away, wondering why what he said and how he said it had stirred up a maelstrom of emotions inside her.

Ellie soon recovered and got lost in the project while she went from one cadre of volunteers to the next, making sure they had what they needed, making sure the work was coming together as she'd envisioned. It was always a thrill to get a plan just right on paper, but seeing it spring to life? Positively exhilarating. She'd never been disappointed, and it gave her confidence a healthy boost. Of course, it wasn't just her. It was all the amazing people donating their time and muscle, including the four Blizzard players working and talking among those people.

While Ellie didn't outright gawk like some did, she did sneak peeks at Dave and his teammates. Truth be told, her glances were mostly directed at Dave, and she got a zing in her boots every time she caught him looking at *her*. It was silly. *So* silly. So middle school. What was this anyway? Attraction? No. It was probably just fangirl curiosity on her part and PR training on his part. With his rugged good looks and a heady blend of mystery and confidence oozing from every pore, he could have anyone he wanted, and that anyone wouldn't be a worn-out landscaper in dirt-covered clothing. *The queen of glam I am. Not.*

Ellie had always been attracted to leaner men closer to her height. Never the big guys. Not tall guys. Not guys who could turn into mountain men by skipping a few haircuts and beard trims. But something about *him* intrigued her. Was it his quiet command? The way he just dug in—literally—and got to work? A solid, down-to-earth guy despite his celebrity.

People continually interrupted him, but he never acted bothered. Gave them polite half-smiles while he worked and finessed them back to their own jobs without them knowing he was doing it. With the children, he spent extra time. Unlike the adults, whom he gave his practiced public persona face, he flashed genuine smiles at the kids, and it made her insides flutter to glimpse the warmth beneath the gruff exterior. The kids all seemed to be hockey players, and Ellie overheard him asking them questions about their teams, what positions they played, how their seasons were going. Sometimes he'd crouch down so he was eye-level with the littler ones, and she thought about what a good dad he'd make.

If the youngsters were unabashed admirers, so were some of their moms, along with an abundance of starry-eyed young women who approached. He gave them all the same treatment, striking a certain look that straddled the line between friendly and a Wookiee glower, and it broadcast that he was all business—without offending them. *Probably has lots of practice. And a girlfriend or five. No, Sonoma insists he's single.* Really *single.*

"Hey, thanks for coming out today," Ellie overheard him say more than once, along with, "Glad you're enjoying the product we're putting on the ice." Not "Hey, wanna hook up?" or "How about giving me a blow job in the port-o-let?" No personal information was exchanged, though she watched as one determined woman pulled out her phone and offered it to him. In all fairness, the other guys got similar treatment—less so with Quinn, who kept Sarah glued to his side—but Dave was the most popular target of the bunch. Probably because he had that whole leader thing going on. But he had to, didn't he? He *was* in charge of his team after all.

And she could understand what women were attracted to. He was broad and chiseled, and she was fascinated by the way his powerful shoulders and forearms flexed as he picked up a handful of blocks or shoveled a pile of dirt. Now that he wasn't buried beneath his Wookiee cover, his angular jaw and strong cheekbones really stood out. The shorter hairstyle highlighted the golden strands woven with the nut-brown ones, catching and reflecting sunlight. Put the whole package together, and the man was walking sex appeal.

Her contemplations were jolted off their rails when one of the players—Viktor?—sidled up beside her and told her she was pretty. *What?* Between his accent and his startling stealth, she *must* have misheard. "Excuse me?"

"I say you are very pretty." He smiled shyly and ran his fingers through his tousled curls. Yeah, he was cute—cute like a stray puppy, and she had no desire to house-train a puppy.

She barely got a chance to thank him for the compliment when his eyes widened and the smile fell. Someone whispered in her ear, and she nearly yelped.

"How's it going?"

Damian. A few steps and she was almost out of arm's reach. "It's going well. What do you think? Is this everything you hoped for?" She couldn't corral her babbling. Maybe if she grabbed Viktor's arm, Damian would take the hint and leave her alone … but Viktor was nowhere to be found.

Damian gave her a smile that bordered on a leer. "I was wondering … when we're done here, would you be interested in grabbing a coffee or a cocktail?"

"Um, well," she stuttered, "I'll be tied up for a while, so I don't think that'll work." *Am I suddenly smeared in eau de bacon? What's with these guys coming around? The moon's aligned with the planets. My zodiac house is in the seventh sky. The nine realms are in convergence. Thor will appear with his magic hammer. And if he asks, I'll totally date him.*

"I'd love to ask you out for dinner, but I already have a date tonight." He—Damian, not Thor—paused to smirk or sneer, she wasn't sure, but it wasn't a good look. Was this his way of showing her how desirable he was? *Not working, buddy.*

"Maybe tomorrow night?" he had the audacity to ask.

Dude! Get a clue! The scary thing was that Damian *was* her type—and not just physically. He was also intelligent, well-read, and carried a certain air of superiority. With his expressive eyes and devilish smile, he probably got a lot of female hearts racing. Maybe *she* was finally getting a clue because he was doing absolutely nothing beyond making her recoil inside.

She took a step back and slammed into a brick wall that grunted.

Chapter 12

Aliens Hijacked My Brain

Wyatt paused, planted his shovel tip in a pile of rock, and rested his forearm on the butt end of the implement. His gaze wandered across the lot and stayed there.

Dave wedged his transfer shovel under another load of rock and grunted, "What do you see?"

"Admiring the scenery."

Dave paused and followed Wyatt's gaze. The only *scenery* was Ellie Hendricks. The sun played on her hair, making the pale red strands shimmer with gold, and they whispered to him. *Silk. Touch.*

"Something about that girl in those boots is really, really hot." Wyatt had a look in his eye Dave had seen before. It was the one he got right before he pounced. "You dating her, Cap?"

"What? No." *She's just a woman I crashed my car into. And that I've been staring at since I got here.*

Wyatt looked him in the eye. "Then you don't mind if I ask her out?"

Yes.

Whoa! Where did that come from? "She's no bunny, Bro."

"I know that," Wyatt scoffed. "Maybe I'm sick of bunnies." His face split into a wolfish grin. "Besides, she doesn't have to be a bunny for me to rock her world."

Something surprisingly green and toothy deep in Dave's gut sent a surge of energy through his bloodstream, and he bent back to work, forcing the shovel so hard he nearly snapped the haft. He looked up at Wyatt, who continued his ogling.

"You gonna work or just stand around with your thumb up your ass?" Dave bit.

"In a sec, Cap. Fuck!"

Dave straightened. "Now what?"

Wyatt's gaze was still pointed in Ellie's direction. "Fucking Viktor. *He's* making a play for her. Asshole! Rookie's not respecting the seniority code."

Dave pivoted and watched as Viktor raked his fingers through his long curly hair. That gesture, along with his accent, was part of his aw-gee-shucks routine that women found "adorable"—for some unfathomable reason—and made them trip all over themselves to hop in the sack with him. Judging by Ellie's body language, she wasn't one of those women, and Dave's heart lifted.

"What the hell's the seniority code?" he asked absentmindedly.

"You know. The oldest guy or the one who's been on the squad the longest gets first crack. I out-senior fucking Viktor."

"I don't think he's making any headway," Dave remarked blandly. He handed Wyatt his shovel.

"What's this for?" Wyatt protested.

Dave pushed up his jersey sleeve and wiped his forehead on his Henley. "Seniority code in action. I out-senior *and* outrank both your asses."

"But you said you weren't dating her," Wyatt spluttered.

"That's about to change."

As Dave walked toward the pair, he had abso-fucking-lutely no clue what had spurred him or what he would do once he reached them. He wasn't about to ask Ellie Hendricks out; she'd probably shut him down anyway. That lady wasn't like the usual women he mingled with who were bowled over by a player's celebrity or the flash of bills in his money clip. No, she'd only be swayed by behavior that came from the heart because she was *real*–which put her out of his reach. He'd just corral the rookie and make sure he didn't make a pest of himself.

An errant thought streaked through Dave's mind as he locked on his target. Ellie was rocking her work boots again, and yeah, she *was* hot in them. In everything. Visions of her in the tight pink sweater she'd worn when they car-shopped pranced in his head and damn if his horndog brain didn't detour to her minus the work boots—along with the rest of her clothes. The sudden twitch in his pants had him admonishing himself. *Down, boy.*

When he was about fifteen feet away, the Habitat dude stepped beside her and gave Viktor a silent signal that sent the rookie packing—something along the lines of "Back off, I was here first."

Dave's heart dropped an elevator floor. Habitat Guy was smooth *and* classy—and looked like he had designs on Ellie. Dave might have seniority and rank over his teammates, but he had nothing on this guy. Probably a product of some Ivy League school. Probably spoke a bunch of foreign languages. Probably had manicured nails he never got dirty or greasy under the hood of a car.

They hadn't noticed him yet, and he argued with himself about doing a one-eighty and leaving them alone. Ellie pivoted so her back was to him, and he couldn't help himself. His gaze dipped to her ass of its own volition. Even in her baggy cargo pants, the contours were easy to make out. She had a very fine ass, and his twitch grew a little more enthusiastic. He was so distracted he didn't see her take a giant step back until she stomped on his toe and slammed against his chest.

"Oof!" His forearms instinctively hinged up and cradled hers. She gasped and craned her head, and his hands automatically slid to her tiny waist. That felt nice. So did her back leaning against him. Thank God there was still daylight between his crotch and her butt, but he did catch a whiff of her rain-fresh fragrance and had to stifle the urge to bury his nose in her satiny ponytail.

She spun from his grasp with an apology, putting distance between herself, him, and Habitat. Her cheeks were bright pink. Mad or embarrassed? Dave couldn't tell, but her eyes kept darting to Habitat as though she were a mouse looking for an escape route around a determined cat.

Dave eyed the dude, whose lips formed a hard, straight line that communicated he was none too happy Dave had crashed the party.

Try me, fucker.

Habitat hooded his eyes and seemed to shrink back. Dave took the opening and turned to Ellie. "We still going out after we're done here?" *Who the hell is running my mouth at the moment?* The guy inside him who hated seeing women harassed by jerks they obviously didn't want harassing them. He was being chivalrous. Right. That was it.

His presumed damsel in distress gave him a blue-eyed, bewildered, "What?"

No surprise. He was bewildered himself. "Dinner. You and me. Remember?" *What the fuck?*

To his astonishment, she beamed at him. "Oh, that's right. With all the craziness today, I nearly forgot." Her eyes flashed as though the sun had just lit the sea, and his breath caught. He sure as hell hoped her unspoken message was "Thank you, Dave" and not "I'm calling the nutso wagon to haul your crazy ass away."

"Can't wait." He stuffed his hands in his front pockets and winced when his injury reminded him he had gone too hard at practice and the Habitat project. *Ow, ow! Don't be a wuss.*

"Well, I'll check in with you in a few," Habitat cooed at Ellie before shooting Dave a death glare.

"Thanks, Damian." She offered *Damian* a half-smile, and Dave took comfort in its lack of wattage, especially when he compared it to the brilliant one she'd turned on him, even though he'd made a complete idiot of himself.

She folded her arms across her chest. "Dinner? What was that all about?"

He flexed his sore hand. "You looked like you needed rescuing. And I'm holding you to that dinner."

Her lips tipped up. "I can handle myself."

"I'm sure you can—it appears you get a lot of practice at it—but it doesn't hurt to have a pissed-off Wookiee on your side, does it?" He grinned despite the needles of pain shooting up his wrist. "Shit. Maybe I misread. Wouldn't be the first time. Did you *want* those guys coming on to you?"

"Who says they were coming on to me?"

"Someone who understands what's going through their minds."

She seemed to appraise him. "First you buy me a van, and now you chase away unwanted attention. How lucky can a girl get? I have my own personal superhero." Her pretty lips formed a cute little smirk.

Hearing her call him her superhero messed with his insides. He'd never been anyone's superhero before. Unless that was sarcasm lurking in her sparkling blues. "Me?" He jabbed his thumb against his chest, and a groan got away from him.

"What's wrong?" Her expression morphed into unadulterated concern.

He cradled the hand against his chest. Something was locking up and cramping. "Nothing. Just … my hand's healing, and sometimes I do something stupid and … Mmph!" *Ow! Fuck!*

She sprinted away. Yeah, he'd run away in her shoes too. *Boots.* She wasn't gone long, though, and when she returned, she came bearing gifts: an ice pack and a bottled water.

He rolled his eyes. "I'm fine."

"Yeah, I can see that," she replied dryly. "Hold these." She shoved the water and ice at him and gently took his sore hand in both of hers, turning it palm up.

He stared down at the top of her head. "What are you doing?"

"Playing nurse."

A wholly inappropriate comeback about playing doctor nearly tumbled off the tip of his tongue.

"What's your hand healing from?" She kept her head down and ran her small thumb lightly over his palm, sending shivers chattering up his spine. Hard to believe something so little and soft could cause such a powerful reaction.

"I, uh, re-broke it at the start of the season."

She tilted her head and narrowed her eyes. "And you're out here *shoveling*? Are you a masochist?"

"No." He shrugged. "I thought I was a superhero."

"A superhero who needs his hard head examined, maybe. I'm guessing your doctor didn't prescribe shoveling for your physical therapy." She shook her head, and her ponytail swished, the strands reflecting different shades of yellow and rose gold. "You have to sit down and keep this ice pack on for at least ten minutes." She pointed to a vacant chair by the check-in tent being repurposed by Serena and another young woman. They were stacking boxes of Sharpies, pucks, and cards, reminding him his hand still had some work to do.

"You're going to need that hand to sign lots of paraphernalia, so best ice it while you can," Ellie said.

"Memorabilia," he corrected her.

"Right. I knew that."

"I can't sit and do nothing when my teammates are all working," he balked. He glanced over at his teammates, whom he'd totally forgotten until this moment. Wyatt, Vik, and Hadley, with Sarah beside him, stood in a semicircle yukking it up.

Ellie followed his gaze. "Pretty sure they're all done. And so are you, Superman."

Bossy little thing. Of course she was bossy. She was used to running crews of men—some of them probably pretty rough—just like she'd been running the show all day. And running it well. "Yes, ma'am. I'll just go tell them to pick up their tools and—"

"Sit. *Down.*" The tone of her voice reminded him of a teacher ready to let her ruler fly on his ass, and he grinned.

She perched her fists on her hips and glowered. Well, tried to. She might *be* tough, but she was too pretty to put on a very convincing tough face. "Don't mess with me, Captain. For years, I worked summer camps filled with pubescent boys, and I'm used to dealing with troublemakers like you." Her eyes held an unmistakable twinkle that made him chuckle. With a snappy pivot, she marched away from him, and he took in the view until Serena called him over. Fans were lining up, but he didn't mind—he had dinner to look forward to. All in all, losing his mind was turning out well. For a change.

Chapter 13

A Quiet Dinner for Seven

Dinner was not what Dave expected, though he should have because little went his way anymore. His biggest complaint? The table they shared was far more crowded than he would have liked. When the project had finally ended and they'd all stood in a cluster, he and Ellie going to dinner had become a topic of conversation. How that had happened, he had no idea because *he* hadn't offered up their plans. The end result was that they were surrounded at the table by Quinn, Sarah, Viktor, Sonoma, and Finn, who had decided they had nothing better to do tonight than crash Dave's date. Well, it wasn't exactly a *date*, but it had had the potential of developing into one. Not that he'd planned on anything beyond spending time with a pretty lady over a meal. Why make his already complicated life even more complicated when he was preparing to leave Denver behind, along with everyone in it?

At least he sat beside Ellie—the only win he'd scored, and he'd had to politely nudge Sarah out of the way to claim the privilege. On Ellie's other side sat Viktor, who seemed to be trying to win a score of his own with her.

Which brought to mind his second complaint: Viktor was monopolizing Ellie's attention. While Dave hadn't expected a good-night kiss at the end of this non-date—she'd insisted on driving on her own—he sure as hell didn't want Viktor angling for one either.

And now for his third complaint. Besides vying for the portion of Ellie's attention *not* devoted to Viktor, Dave was competing with everyone else at the table for the remainder. As he'd showered off the day's sweat and grime, he'd indulged pleasant images of getting Ellie alone, heads together across a dark, cozy table for two while sipping wine. Because, even though the practical side of him warned him away, he liked her—enough to want to get to know her a little more. He *was* getting to know her, but only because he overheard her answers to the questions she was fielding from everyone else. Finn didn't participate in twenty questions, but he tossed in the occasional Ellie factoid. Which was *another* complaint Dave had. Dude was getting awfully friendly with Nome, but she glared at Dave every time he gave her a look that said, "I *will* beat his ass if he goes too far."

Ellie jerked his attention to the here and now when she leaned across him to share a conversation with Sarah. He sat back to give her line of sight, and her warmth and her sweet feminine fragrance invaded his senses. Maybe not the dinner he'd envisioned, but this was certainly a highlight.

"Do you know Paige Miller," Sarah was saying, "of Anderson Homes? They do a lot of rehabs and some new builds too."

"Yeah, I've seen the signs around town, but I've never met her."

"I think you need to. I work for her part-time, so I know she needs someone she can count on. She's been going through landscapers like hockey players go through sticks. The fact that you do design is a huge plus. She has a great eye for what goes *inside* a house, but the outside, not so much."

Ellie's blue eyes brightened. "Would you pass on my contact info?" She reached into her back pocket and pulled out a few business cards, passing one to Sarah.

Dave held out two fingers like a pair scissors. "Can I have one?"

Ellie blinked at him.

"In case I come across someone who needs landscaping work," he added. "In fact, maybe I'd better have a few more." He snagged the rest of her cards and quickly stowed them in his wallet before Vik could get his hands on one.

"I'll text you so you have my number too," Sarah told Ellie. "We're having a girls' luncheon soon—just the P-team—and it would be great to have you join us and meet the other girls."

Dave's brows knitted together. "What's a 'P-team'?"

Sarah laughed. "Paige's Powerhouse Playmakers, or something along those lines."

"I'm not a playmaker like Quinn, but do I get an invite?" he blurted, only half kidding.

Sarah tapped him playfully. "Girls only. No men allowed. Besides, what do you know about house construction?"

"I know how to disassemble a motor and put it back together. Does that count?"

"Sorry, no. Skill set aside, you've got the Y chromosome, so you're an automatic out."

He opened his mouth—to say *what*, he wasn't sure—when Quinn gave him a chin bob and a smirk. "Don't even try." Ellie giggled, and Quinn threw an arm around Sarah's shoulders and pulled her close, which left Ellie still leaning across Dave's space with no one to talk to.

He looked down at her. "There's something I've been meaning to ask you."

She straightened and moved away—*damn!*—taking a sip of her water. "And that would be?"

"In your text earlier today, you said something about an agent contacting me? What was that about?"

Ellie filled him in about this ICE agent, a guy named Clemente, who had questioned her about her new van. "Sonoma told him to contact you to verify the story, and he sent me an email saying he had done just that, so I was in the clear."

"Clear from what? You didn't do anything wrong to begin with."

"Tell Agent Clemente that," she huffed. "I think he subscribes to the 'guilty until proven innocent' motto."

Dave's pissed-off-o-meter climbed for reasons as yet unclear, and he acknowledged his *next* complaint. Why the hell was this dude fucking with Ellie? "Sounds like he's harassing you."

"I think he felt bad about it, and the email was his way of saying sorry."

"Did he actually apologize?"

Her eyes traveled to the ceiling. When they landed back on him, she gave a little shoulder shrug. "No, but he asked me out for coffee to explain"—air quotes on the last word—"so I assume he was planning to apologize in person."

He wants to get in her pants. Fucker! "If he gives you any more shit"—he stabbed at his chest—"tell him you have a big, bad Wookiee on speed dial."

"But I don't have a Wookiee on speed dial." She laughed, and the melody of that laugh lifted his stormy mood.

He pointed at her phone. "Yeah, you do. Check your texts. My cell number's there."

"Oh, that's right! Sonoma handed out my number, didn't she?" Pretty blue eyes sparkled with mischief.

"Is it okay that I have it?"

She flicked her wrist. "It's fine. I just don't want her writing it on bathroom walls." Before he could respond with, "She wouldn't, and if she did, I'd take care of it," Ellie zeroed in on his hand. "How's the hand doing?"

He flexed it and lied. "Feels great."

Her soft pink mouth parted to say something, but her head jerked to the side when Viktor tapped her forearm. Dave fired him a special Grims glower, but the rookie didn't acknowledge it. Across the table, Sonoma's eyes darted between him and Ellie, and a knowing smile tipped her lips, as if she were saying, "See? I *told* you you'd like her." *Too late. I'll be traded before the all-star break.* A needle of regret pierced him.

No, he didn't need to get caught up in anyone right now—not beyond a one-night stand anyway, and Ellie was definitely *not* on his one-night stand radar. Not that anyone else was either. Or that his one-night stand radar was operational these days. Maybe he needed to fire that puppy up so he could ignore the traitorous tug in his chest toward the woman beside him.

Finally, they went from seven to four at the table. Viktor would have made it five if Quinn, Viktor's ride tonight, hadn't dragged his ass away. Vik had had the Hulk balls to ask Dave to give him a ride instead, his eyebrows bouncing in Ellie's general direction, which gave Dave the pleasure of shaking his head and saying, "Not tonight, rookie."

Then Vik had tapped Ellie's arm and appeared to be on the verge of asking *her* to give him a ride. A totally different ride that didn't include four wheels, Dave was damn sure. The rookie wised up and caught the look Dave sent him this time. When Dave answered for Ellie, repeating, "Not tonight, rookie," Vik said his good nights and trailed Quinn and Sarah. *I'm gonna have to clue that kid in on Wyatt's seniority code. Except I'm not trying to date this girl. But I don't want him dating her either. Shit. What's wrong with me?*

Sonoma pinched Finn's sleeve, motioning him to slide beside her as she settled herself across from Dave. "So did you hear?" She raced on, not waiting for his answer. "Uncle Stan's coming to Denver."

Oh no. He was afraid to ask his next question. "What for?"

"Some old buddy is hosting a big box social at his spread in Sterling, and Stan's going to be the caller." A grin Dave didn't like was spreading across her face. It signaled trouble. "He's asked us to be there to help him out and because he wants to see us."

A look of confusion scrunched Ellie's features. "What's a box social? And what's a caller?"

Dave opened and closed his mouth, afraid to say something that would either incriminate him or have him stepping into whatever trap his cousin was laying.

Sonoma darted her gaze to Ellie, and before he could stop her, she said, "A box social is a get-together where women bring boxes they've decorated and packed with a meal, and men bid on the boxes. The idea is the man doesn't know which box belongs to which woman, and he wins the box and the woman that goes with it for the meal. They're really fun." Sonoma seemed to wiggle in her seat, as though she was just getting down to the good stuff. "A caller is the person who gives direction at a square dance, who sings out things like 'Swing your partner.' Our Uncle Stan is a famous singing caller, which means he actually sings while he tells the dancers what steps to take. He lives in Oklahoma now, but he's traveled all over the country." Sonoma's grin widened. "When Dave and I were kids, our families used to take us along. We got to watch Uncle Stan and dance at the same time."

Ellie's head whipped toward Dave, her expression a study in astonishment. "You square-dance?"

He winced. "Not since I was a kid." *And had no choice.*

Sonoma fluttered her eyelashes "Oh, but you still know how, Dave." With a conspiratorial tone, she leaned toward Ellie. "We haven't seen our Uncle Stan in forever, and he's getting up there in years, so you need to help me convince Dave to go."

"No way, Nome," Dave growled. "I'll go see Uncle Stan, but we can catch breakfast with him or something instead."

Acting as though Dave weren't in the same room—let alone seated at the same table—Sonoma added, "And the way we convince him is you come too."

Ellie's gaping mouth telegraphed her stun factor. "I don't dance."

Finn busted out with a laugh. "Because we won't let her. It's a disaster of epic proportion. She embarrasses the whole family."

Ellie narrowed her eyes. "Are you *trying* to get fired?"

"No, just speaking the truth, El." He turned to Sonoma. "She's been known to stomp and maim small children who get in the way."

Surprise flashed through Sonoma's eyes. "On *purpose*?"

"No, not on purpose. She's just an incredibly klutzy dancer."

Dave felt Ellie squirming beside him, and two forces collided inside him at once. He felt a powerful pull to make her discomfort disappear, and another part of him heard the siren's call of a solid challenge. She was stirring up emotions inside he didn't want stirred. He peered at her, biting back a smile. "You stomp?" Somehow it didn't come out with the humor he'd intended.

She dropped her face in her hands. "I stomp," came her muffled voice. When she raised her head, her cheeks glowed bright pink, giving her a look that was part-Bambi and part … he didn't have a word for it, but it was tantalizing AF. His mind took a fleeting detour to leaning down and kissing that cheek, then trailing his lips to her mouth. His dick perked up and cheered. *Chill the fuck out!*

"Don't worry, Ellie. Dave's a very good lead. He'll teach you the steps, and he won't let you stomp on anyone. Will you, Dave?" She gave him a syrupy smile.

I swear, when I get my hands on you, Sonoma …

"Oh. And did I tell you?" she continued singing. "All the money raised by the box social goes to Heifer International." She patted Dave's arm. "A few hours of dancing for a worthy cause, and getting to see Uncle Stan, what's not to love?"

"Uh, wearing a western shirt and cowboy boots?"

"Cowboy boots are sexy! You didn't get rid of all that stuff, did you?" She added a huge dose of drama to her tone.

Now he felt *his* cheeks blazing. He had way more country clothing than he'd ever want to fess up to, and Nicky had always given him crap about it. But it wasn't because he liked the stuff. It was simply because he seemed to move houses every few years, and with hockey eating up all his time, he'd never gotten around to purging.

"Doesn't matter if you did. We'll get you new stuff." Sonoma's bright eyes gave her a slightly unhinged look. "And, Ellie, I'll take you shopping to get what you need. C'mon. It'll be fun! Finn already said he's in."

Finn's eyes popped. "I did?"

Sonoma shot him a look that said, "I have a voodoo doll with your name on it, and I'm not afraid to use it."

He gave her a wide grin. "What the hell? You only live once, right?" He reached over and gave Ellie's arm a soft punch. "C'mon, Sis. This'll make a great story for this year's Callahan Christmas. Might even prevent a fight or two."

Ellie turned pleading eyes to Dave. "Get me out of this," that plea said.

His inner Yoda picked just that moment to take command of his mouth. "Finn's right. It's always good to try new things."

"I'm clearing you for the road trip." The trainer spoke the sweetest words Dave had ever heard. The icing-and-ibuprofen routine for the past week, combined with the hand-rest regimen, had paid off, though the pain was still there. Exchanging texts with Ellie hadn't hurt either because she'd invariably scolded him about his hand. Truth be told, he wanted it to get better so he could play again, but he had extra motivation: if he was being forced into square-dancing, and he was going to dance with *that* girl, he wanted to do it with both hands functioning properly.

Once more, he thought about the quicker, easier route. He and Bobby had been exchanging texts, but neither one had mentioned hooking Dave up. Which was a good thing because Dave wasn't sure he would have been able to say no.

After practice, he called his agent. "Herb? I'm going on the road trip. You can put the feelers out there again."

"Not so fast, Dave. Like I said before, let's see how it goes your first few games."

He grudgingly agreed. At least he was headed in the right direction—for now.

An extra spring in his step had him bounding onto the team bus headed for the airport, and he was able to overlook Nelson and the guys who barely acknowledged him. So what if they treated him like the Invisible Man? Their loss, not his. He plunked into an isolated seat in the back and stared out the window at a few of his teammates in the parking lot hugging on their girls and kissing them good-bye.

T.J. was one of those guys, and when he finally let Natalie go and lumbered onto the bus, he parked his big frame in the seat across from Dave. "Glad to see you're coming with us, Cap. Bet you're glad too."

"You have no fucking idea."

T.J.'s eyes flared. "Actually, I do."

"Oh shit. Yeah, you do, don't you? Sorry, man. Didn't mean to bring up a sore subject." When T.J. had been acquired by the Blizzard, he'd been serving a twenty-plus-games suspension for sucker-punching another team's player. If anyone knew about self-inflicted downfalls, it was this guy. After a beat, curiosity had Dave asking, "How did you come back?"

T.J. shrugged. "I stopped blaming everyone else and feeling sorry for myself. Then I worked my ass off."

"I remember. Turned out so well I'd forgotten it happened." Dave recalled T.J. being the hardest-working guy at practice, staying behind to sharpen his shooting skills on his own, even though he couldn't be in the lineup. And he hadn't limited his efforts to the ice. In his spare time, he volunteered, coaching a sled hockey team.

"That's the whole idea. And from where I sit, you're crushing the whole working-your-ass-off part of the equation. But the other? Something to think about, Cap." T.J. plugged in his earbuds and leaned his head back.

Wait. Does he mean I'm blaming everyone else and feeling sorry for myself? What the hell? Dave's blood heated to a slow simmer. Those two situations were totally different.

Weren't they?

Chapter 14

Wookiees on Ice

"Ouch! What did you do that for?" Finn rubbed his head.

"Sorry," Ellie sang. *Not sorry.* She'd just tossed a fully loaded walnut at his head and wished she had a bag full. Though more than a week had passed since she'd been roped into a hokey square dance, she was still steaming. The date was coming fast, and she pictured herself in some rancher's field, stuck on a scratchy hay bale eating a box dinner with some bowlegged stranger. Finn was the closest target for her frustration.

Cross-legged on her couch with a big bowl of popcorn, she stuffed a few kernels in her mouth and flicked a few at him too.

"Knock it off, El! I thought you *liked* Captain Dave and wanted to go to the dance with him." Finn snickered. "High school déja vu all over again."

"I don't like him like *that*, and don't call him Captain Dave! You make him sound like some goof wearing white pants and a navy blazer in an Old Spice commercial." Exactly why was she protesting on Dave's behalf? No idea. "And by the way, I don't know what's going on between you and Sonoma—"

He cut her off—a little too quickly. "We're just friends."

Wait. Finn's never "just friends" with women. "Whatever. Just don't … sleep with her. And if you *do* sleep with her, do not toss her away like you do everyone else."

He looked affronted. "What's it to you who I do—or *don't*—go out with?"

"I've known her a long time. She's sweet, and she's … she's my friend. I don't want to see her get hurt. She's also my stylist, and she'll take her revenge out on *my* hair, which means I'll have to kill you. And no one will ever find out because I will scatter your body parts in every landfill along the Front Range."

"Right. I think I'm in way more danger from her cousin, who actually *could* tear me limb from limb. Nome says he's uber protective."

Nome? Oh, this might be serious.

"Heard from Keira lately? Or the other one? What was her name?" Yeah, that was mean, but Ellie couldn't help herself.

"We're done, over," Finn mumbled.

Ellie turned to him. "Seriously?"

He leaned over and snatched a handful of popcorn from the bowl. "Dead serious. She called the other night, and I brushed her off."

"Just like that? No booty-call reprisal?" Ellie feigned a gawp. "Are you sick?"

He gave her an eye-roll. "No. I just don't want to hang out with her anymore. She's too young. Besides being annoying, she doesn't have a lot to say that's worth listening to."

"I didn't know conversation figured on your priority list."

"Haha. You're a laugh riot. Seriously, El, I told her and 'the other one' I'm not interested anymore."

"Because why? You're interested in someone else whose name starts with *S*?"

"El," he huffed. "We're not in high school anymore."

Ellie turned toward him, a quip forming in her brain. The wistful expression on his face as he stared straight ahead caught her by surprise, and she veered in a different direction. "I can't believe we're actually going to a square dance."

"We've lived in Colorado our whole lives, and neither of us has ever been to anything like it. Middle school PE class doesn't count. I can't wait to see what it's all about. Besides, it's only for a few hours."

"Not exactly, since we're staying overnight in the host's ranch house slash mansion, remember? So we'll hang out with these people for at least twelve hours." A light bulb winked on in her head. "And *these people* have money and may need landscaping help. I can turn this into a business opportunity."

He picked up the walnut Casper was pushing around with her nose. The popcorn that had hit the floor was long gone. "Christ, El, when did you get so boring? Business, business. Cut loose and live a little, for fuck's sake. Get outside your uncomfortable comfort zone. You're a ninety-year-old woman in a twenty-eight-year-old's body, wasting away. Hell, I know ninety-somethings more fun than you are."

The words clobbered Ellie, and she gaped at him, trying to come up with a retort. But then realization struck her like Colorado dry lightning. *Shit! He's right. When did I become so damn serious? After Will left me with a mountain of debt, that's when. Thanks again, douchebag.* After a beat, another brainwave struck her. *Does that mean I let what he did control who I am?*

She shimmied in place, as though it would shake off some of her grumblies. "Casper!" Ellie tossed a kernel that the dog caught like a champ. Then a few more.

Finn pressed the remote. "This oughta cheer you up, El. Grown men beating each other up."

"Are we watching boxing?"

"Better. We're watching the Blizzard play the Flyers."

"Oh." Ellie didn't know much about hockey beyond a general idea that skates and ice were involved, but it occurred to her she should learn. If she was going to an overnight hoedown with a hockey player—who had bought her a van!—she should at least understand a little about what he did for a living. Not only did he know what *she* did, he'd seen her at work.

Such an odd concept. Skating around with a stick and chasing a puck was his *job.*

"I'll explain as we go, El, but with each shift, pick out one player on the ice—could be from either team—and follow him. Watch what he does," Finn said.

After he explained what a shift was, Ellie tried to focus on individual players but only seemed to keep her eye on big number ninety-two. Halfway into the period, she realized there was a whole heck of a lot more to his *job* than skating. His main role was defending, and every time he was on the ice, he was *doing* something. Moving. Passing. Skating fast. Barking out orders. Taking shots at the net. Muscling the puck away from an opponent. Clearing guys out of his goalie's way with his stick, his hands, his entire body. Sacrificing himself, as Finn put it, by getting in the way of wicked, lightning-swift shots—which made Ellie cringe. *That's how they lose their teeth!* And the look on his face? Burning intensity. Pure, unadulterated determination verging on hunger … as if he was *hungry* for the puck. *Lordy, that's all kinds of hawt!*

Watching him, watching the game, was mesmerizing. The speed! And how could such big men move as though made of liquid?

Finn was good as his word, filling in details and answering questions so she had an overall idea of how the game worked. An elaborate game of keep-away so one team could control the puck and shoot it past the goalie to score a point. Er, goal. They were allowed to hit each other, but within limits. A fine line she didn't yet understand. And if they committed an infraction, they sat in the penalty box while their team was down one player. The Blizzard had taken one penalty, and Dave had been on the ice for the "kill." He also "quarterbacked" the power play when the other team got sent to the sin bin, which meant he was on the ice a lot.

A hulking hockey player from the other team clobbered a Blizzard player against the boards as they battled—literally *battled*—for the small puck. Dave skated in and shoved the bad guy out of the way while his teammate coaxed the puck onto his stick. The same hulk ran at two other Blizzard players on his way to his team's bench.

"He's not very nice," Ellie declared. "I don't think I like him."

"Who?"

"The stupid Flyer guy who keeps knocking our guys down."

Finn laughed. "That's his job. Besides, he's a beast and hits everything out there. Haven't you been watching Grims? He's doing the same thing, only I'd put my money on him over the other dude *any* day. Grims is stronger and way smarter with the puck. He rarely turns it over. When he's out there, watch his body position, his feet, his stick, how his head's on a swivel. He's an awesome D-man because he's got great vision that allows him to keep track of the puck, his guys, their guys, while they're all going at hyperspeed."

After the game ended, Finn left and Ellie let Casper out one last time. She climbed into bed, wide awake. Hockey players skated through her mind at blazing speed, and she replayed different scenes—each one starring ninety-two—trying to puzzle out what happened and why. Then her thoughts leapt to him standing in front of a cubby-looking thing on TV. The helmet was gone, and so was every other piece of upper body armor, leaving him in a tight, long-sleeved black shirt that molded to his well-cut body. Sweat slicked his forehead and cheeks, and he swiped at it whenever he shoved his thick hair back. Microphones and cell phones were clustered around him, and reporters asked him questions, which he answered with the same ease and confidence she'd witnessed during the project. Nothing rattled him. Any credit for their win tonight he bestowed on his teammates, even though he'd scored a goal of his own. He was plus-four for the game, whatever *that* meant. Finn had told her it was all good.

The only time she saw a flinch was when one female voice asked about team chemistry. He'd given a wooden answer about what a great group of guys his club was and how everyone on the team skated for one another. When she tried asking the question a different way, he flicked his eyes elsewhere and fielded a question from a different reporter. What was *that* all about?

Her mind roamed back to how he'd looked, all hot and sweaty, his sculpted muscles showing with every movement. While she'd listened to what he said, she'd also focused on his mouth as he talked, easy now that he'd lost that whole Wookiee thing he'd had going on. He had a beautiful mouth that hinted at what a great job it would do kissing and nibbling. *Oh Lord.* Just like she'd never been into big guys, she'd never been into hot and sweaty, but on him? He wore it well. Testosterone seemed to wave off of him and leak right through her TV screen, and a tickle down low confirmed her lady parts were checking the box marked "Hot!" And not just sweaty hot.

If he hadn't slammed his car into her, she'd never have given him a second glance. Maybe she'd been drawn to the *wrong* type all these years. What had drawn her to Will, and the occasional boyfriend before and after him, was that they were … unobtrusive. She knew she'd be able to take her landscape design career to any height she wanted without them telling her what to do. Maybe a little more testosterone in her life would have been an improvement.

With that thought, she *really* couldn't sleep, so she popped out of bed, flipped on her office light, and waited while her computer whirred to life. Her fingers danced a tippy-tap across her keyboard, and soon she was staring at pictures of Dave in hospitals with kids and adults, in nursing homes with seniors, and in shelters with pets. He was active in community giving and had been for the ten years he'd been with the Blizzard. No wonder he'd offered to help with her Habitat project—that kind of thing was right up his alley. Who knew a once-terrifying Wookiee could be so magnanimous?

Why was a guy like him single?

Sonoma said he had "unfortunate" taste in women. Sprinkled among the many images were a few of him all dolled up for charity events with women on his arm who were anything but "unfortunate." Blessed with bountiful beauty was a more apt description. And no wonder—he was a sought-after bachelor who made ten mil a year. Whether he sported the mountain man look or not, he had his pick of the stunners, though one particular woman seemed to be his exclusive, for all the times she was with him. A model named Nicole Something-or-Other. Statuesque, breathtakingly beautiful—a dead ringer for Charlize Theron. They had broken up a year ago, and his name hadn't been linked with anyone since.

Instead of giving Ellie a boost—as if she'd ever stood a chance with him, not that she'd wanted one—the realization made her sag inside. She hadn't measured up for Will, an everyday guy. How could she even *compete* for a local celebrity who was the walking, talking embodiment of masculine perfection?

Dejectedly, she allowed that she might, just might, be crushing a little on Dave Grimson. Even if she *wanted* to date him—which she didn't—he'd never ask. He was so far out of her league that he might as well have been playing hockey on one of Jupiter's moons.

The team barely eked out a win the next night, no thanks to Dave mishandling the puck. Repeatedly. And it bit him in the butt when he turned it over in his own zone and the Penguins pounced on it and fired one past Wyatt. The mistakes weren't going to help his marketability score. But damn! Despite it being the second game of a back-to-back, it had felt good to be playing again, even if he was totally gassed and his hand throbbed like the red goal lamp. No better way to get his timing back than being in a real game, and there was no place he'd rather be than on the ice. He fucking loved this game, and he'd missed being out there.

That night, after Quinn, his road roomie, fell asleep, Dave covertly iced his hand and stared at the hotel room ceiling. Something T.J. had said bobbed in the stew bubbling in his brain. *I stopped blaming everyone else.* Dave had resented the hell out of hearing it, which made him wonder if there was a nugget of truth in there for *him.* He'd let that one simmer a while longer.

Two nights later, he couldn't wait to get on the ice. He was pumped to beat Columbus—so pumped that his testosterone levels had to be off the charts. Lack of sex *might* have contributed to the elevated T-factor, and he told himself there was a bright side to his dismal dry spell before shoving it from his mind. Whatever was pushing him, he flew across the ice on his first shift and didn't let up the gas pedal. All game, he shadowed their best players, making a six-foot-three nuisance out of himself as he flattened opponents, blocked shots, took away pucks. He could feel his rhythm coming back.

The whole team, in fact, was firing on all cylinders, and it was a thing of a beauty. They shut Columbus down, frustrating the hell out of them. Going into the third period, the Blizzard were up by two goals.

"Let's keep playing smart, boys," he said to the room as the second intermission was winding down. Coach had already come and gone, and no one else was talking, so Dave stepped into the quiet—something he hadn't done in a long while. Adrenalin was crackling in his veins. "Defense first, but we take advantage of our opportunities. We've been beating these fuckers all night, and they're gonna open up and take chances. We're the better team out there, so let's go show 'em how it's done."

He yelled the last words, and twenty-something pairs of wide eyes stared at him. A handful of guys grunted their agreement, and then it was crickets. Without another word, he turned to his stall and pulled on his gear. A puck could have rolled over thick carpet and the trainers in the next room would have heard it. *Never was good at speeches anyway.* He locked it out and got his gladiator on. He'd make any potential teams watching his play drool over the chance to bring him aboard—*especially* Arizona.

Chapter 15

Brain Scramble

"Thanksgiving's next week, Dave. Have you thought about what you want to do?" Sonoma was bent to the side, examining Dave's head before taking a few more snips. Today her hair was a shade of purple that probably had some food name to describe it. Plum or eggplant or—

"Next week? Already? Shit! No, hadn't given it a thought."

"Mm-hmm." She turned on the clippers, and they buzzed against the back of his neck. "What would you think of adding Finn and Ellie to our sad little twosome?"

Sad was right. In the past, she'd flown to Florida and spent the holiday with family, and he'd been with Nicky, Isaac, and his teammates, eating way too much, watching football, enjoying the hell out of himself. But their moms and the rest of the family had decided to take a seven-day Caribbean cruise, and neither he nor Sonoma had the luxury of a week off. Dave hadn't gotten an invite from any teammates.

After being on the road for the past week, getting in at 2:00 a.m. this morning following a frustrating loss to Chicago, hearing Ellie's name perked him up, though he told himself it shouldn't. Pondering the possibility of spending turkey day with her fired up and lightened his stomach at the same time.

"We're not sad, Nome, and they're probably spending it with family or friends."

"Nope. I asked. Ellie usually hosts a dinner for Finn and the other guy who works there—Felipe, I think. I guess he has a big extended family, and they all come. But for some reason, that's not happening this year, so they're a sad little twosome too. Maybe we could all crash your place and you could whip something up that you learned on one of your cooking shows? Then we'd be a fat, happy foursome." Sonoma spun him so he faced the mirror. "There. Better?"

For the first time in as long as he could remember, Dave had actually *itched* for his cousin to clean up his appearance, going so far as arranging an appointment from the road. "This'll do. Thanks, Nome." Smoothing one side of his head and raking his fingers through the top, he was poised to rip off the cape and push up from the seat.

She whacked him with her comb. "I'm not done!"

"Then hurry up!" He re-settled himself.

"Why are you in such a rush?"

Because I want to say "Hi" to Ellie before she leaves her office. "Who says I'm in a rush?"

"You've been twitchy since you sat down. Honestly, you're acting like Finn."

"Are you serious about the guy, Nome?" Dave couldn't help himself. Sonoma was usually guarded when it came to relationships, but she seemed to have a thing for the dude. While Dave tried to stay out of her business—just as he expected her to stay out of his—he didn't want to see her heart strewn over a debris field, and he wasn't sure Finn could be trusted not to do just that.

"What? No. We're just friends," she fired back. Which told Dave volumes. *She's totally into him. Maybe Thanksgiving dinner is a good idea. I can suss the guy out.*

She brushed his neck and unfastened the cape. "Well, I still think it would be more fun to share Thanksgiving dinner with them than be bored with just the two of us."

"Gee, thanks." He stood from her chair. "But you're probably right. And it'd be easier to cook for four than two."

She patted his chest. "Good. Go talk to her."

"What do you mean, 'Go talk to her'?"

"I mean, with the holiday right around the corner, I'm swamped today. Everyone wants their hair done." She turned and waved to a woman at the front of the shop as if to demonstrate *how* swamped. "I'll be right there, Mrs. F." To Dave she said, "I saw Ellie's van, so I know she's in her office right now. All you have to do is poke your head in and say, 'Ellie, would you and Finn like to join Sonoma and me at my place for Thanksgiving dinner?'" Sonoma shrugged. "Easy peasy." She turned her back on him and went to work sweeping her station.

He blew out a breath. He *had* planned to stick his head in, but only for a casual "How's it going?" Not an invitation to Thanksgiving dinner. Ellie was gonna think he was stalking her. Again.

"It's your idea. *You* ask her."

Sonoma wore a sly smile. "Is the big, bad hockey player afraid of a little landscaper?"

"Ha! You're hilarious, Nome. Maybe we should keep it just us. I could nuke a couple of chicken pot pies—"

"Think how much more fun it'll be having them over. Maybe you can teach Ellie some basic steps before the big dance so she doesn't *stomp* all over your feet."

He scoffed. "I doubt that girl weighs enough to damage a bug, much less my feet."

She pushed him toward the door. "It's *your* place. *You* ask her."

"All right." He checked himself in Sonoma's mirror one last time and strode through her salon, ignoring Mandy, who was giving him big eyes.

At Ellie's office door, he paused a beat, practicing what to say. Suddenly, all he could remember from Sonoma's script was "Thanksgiving." Before he had time to ponder further, his attention caught on a white barrel on four legs hurtling toward the door, stubby little tail going a hundred miles an hour. Motion in a shadowy corner became a lithe blond with a brilliant smile motioning him inside. Whoa! Had he seen *that* smile before? And could he make her do more of that?

He cracked the door, and Casper wiggled through, burying her nose in his shoes. Snuffling and panting, she followed him as he stepped inside.

"Looks like you've got a dog attached to your leg." Ellie chuckled, crossed her arms, and leaned against a desk. Today her hair was in a thick braid that hung down the front of a dark hoodie. This one was fitted, not her usual baggy style, and it was paired with running tights that showed off toned thighs and calves. His gaze skidded down her body of its own accord, landing on her running shoes, where he tried to ground his focus before lifting back up to her bright blue eyes.

"Ha! Guess I do." Hoping he didn't sound as off balance as he felt, he crouched and scratched Casper's fuzzy chin. *Get yourself under control, dumbass!*

"Keep that up, and she'll attach herself permanently."

"That wouldn't be so bad." One last ruffle of Casper's neck, and he stood and stuffed his hands in his front pockets.

"You seem to like dogs. Do you have one yourself?"

"I did. Now I only have visitation rights." His bad hand shot to the back of his head and smoothed. "Actually, not even those. I get to see him when no one else can take care of him, so it's a sporadic thing." Why, exactly, was he spewing? Anything related to Benny—and therefore Nicole—was on a need-to-know basis, and Ellie didn't need to know. Probably didn't *want* to know.

She cocked a shapely eyebrow. "That sounds … I'm sorry. You're welcome to love on Casper anytime you want. She certainly won't object."

Wonder if her owner would object to me loving on her*? Christ! Where the hell did that come from?*

As his mind tried to unknot why he was here and what he was *supposed* to say, she looked at his hand. "How's your hand?"

He stared at the hand in question. "What?"

"Your hand. You played as though it wasn't bothering you on the road, especially when you slapped, er, shot, er, hit the puck really hard from the red line—or is it blue?—and got a goal against the Blackhawks."

He tried to mask his delight, barely registering her stumbling over the terms. "You watched our away games?"

She gave a nonchalant shrug, but her cheeks tinged in telltale pink told a different story. The whole time he'd been gone, anytime he wasn't in game mode, he hadn't been able to get this girl out of his head, and it made his insides dance to think she had been watching *him*.

"Finn made me." There was that mischievous gleam in her eyes. "He also tried to teach me, but obviously I'm not a good student."

"I'm happy to teach you." Why did that come out sounding dirty? Probably because assorted dirty thoughts were lurking at the back of his mind. It occurred to him he needed to shut down this … this … whatever the hell was scrambling his brain.

An awkward pause hung between them, and she rushed in with, "So your hand's good?"

Her question brought him out of his stupor. "Yeah, fine." It had hurt like a mother on the road. Coach had debated playing him, but then he'd had an unbelievable game against the Flyers and had convinced Coach he was good for the rest of the trip.

And now his brain zigged when it should have zagged. "Next time I have Benny—that's my dog—maybe we could take him and Casper running together?"

"Oh, I don't run. I barely walk."

Huh? "Not sure I follow."

She let out an embarrassed laugh. "What I meant was, with my schedule, I hardly have time to take Casper for a walk."

"Oh." *Smooth, Dave.* He stood there like an idiot, trying to figure out how, exactly, to work in a Thanksgiving invite. The painful pause had him opening his mouth and blurting, "But you don't work holidays, like Thanksgiving, right?"

"No, usually not." Her lips tipped up in amusement. "So I guess I'll have no problems walking her that day."

"Yeah, about that. Thanksgiving, I mean." The hurt hand dove back into his pocket. "Sonoma said you and Finn aren't doing anything, and … well, Sonoma and I aren't doing anything either—not that we usually *do* Thanksgiving together—but she thought … we both thought it might be nice for the four of us to spend it together. At my place. I'll cook." Now one of her eyebrows quirked. Yeah, he was totally blowing this. "You could bring Casper," he tossed in.

"And walk her at *your* place?"

"Absolutely. If you want to. Totally up to you where you walk her, of course. Your place, my place. There's a park right around the corner where I run with Benny … when I have him. I won't have him at Thanksgiving, though, so Casper would be on her own. In the canine department, that is." Either he was a complete and utter moron, or he was doing a damn fine job imitating one.

Ellie must have agreed because her lips quivered like she was holding back a laugh. He couldn't blame her. *Should have texted instead.* He braced himself for the shutdown that was inevitably coming any second now.

"I can't speak for Finn, but Casper and I would like to come. What can I bring?"

Stupefied, he stammered, "N-nothing."

"Do you have time to get everything? Aren't you playing a bunch of games between now and then? In fact, I think you play the night before, right?"

She's paying attention! A grin broke free. "Well, yeah, but it'll be no big deal to get what I need." *I hope.*

"How about this, then? I have a greenhouse in my backyard where I grow herbs. Can I at least contribute those and some wine? Maybe something for the dessert table?"

It was just sinking in that she'd accepted, and something cartwheeled through his stomach. "Yes!" he said a little *too* enthusiastically. He got himself under control. "In fact, I've been watching these cooking shows, and there are a bunch of recipes I've been wanting to try. Just didn't have the audience to try them on."

Her eyes seemed to spark with interest. "Which shows?"

"Pretty much anything on Food Network. I really like *Beat Bobby Flay.*"

"I used to watch him. Not lately, though. Too busy to cook, but I do like to eat. Text me what you need, and I'll raid my herb garden."

"I can do that."

It took an hour for his stupid grin to wear off.

Chapter 16

Of Turkeys and Spangles

Ellie let out an inner groan. It was the Monday before Thanksgiving, and with the box social only weeks away, Sonoma had convinced her it was a good time to get outfitted for the dancing portion of the event. Now she was at Sonoma's mercy. When Ellie had told herself to shop for new clothes, she'd never imagined the first store she'd step into would be a … a … she wasn't sure how to classify it. Maybe it stood in a class of its own. Spangly, shiny, poofy things adorned the walls. She was surrounded by figure skaters' costumes on steroids. Bigger, brighter.

"Ya'll come in. Don't be shy," said a platinum-blond bombshell who reminded her of a slighter version of Beth Chapman. "What can I help you ladies with today?"

"My friend here is attending her first square dance, and she needs a prairie skirt and maybe some shoes?" Sonoma announced cheerfully. "And I'm in the market for something new myself."

Ellie's eyes fastened on the vivid, satiny fabrics embellished with yards of lace. "Nothing too, uh, fancy for me, please."

Bounty Hunter Beth swept Ellie with appraising eyes. "Size six, I'd say." The woman didn't wait for her answer, instead making a beeline for a round packed with skirts in every color and pattern imaginable. "First square dance, huh? Got you a fella?"

"No, I—"

"She's going with my cousin," a grinning Sonoma offered as she riffled through the clothing.

Because you strong-armed us! "But I don't even know how to dance," Ellie grumbled.

"Doesn't matter if you're in the right man's arms," the shopkeeper declared with a flick of her hand. "He'll take you where you need to go and have you thinking about the foreplay, not your steps." She gave Ellie a sly wink.

What the hell does that *mean?*

Ellie didn't get the chance to ask because the woman was busy plucking a dozen hangered skirts. She tossed them over her sturdy arm and maneuvered her way toward a back corner, pausing to snatch a few more from a different round. "A pretty thing like you won't have any trouble finding a different partner if you don't like the one you're with."

Foreplay? Switching partners? Ellie kept her mouth from dropping open. What had she gotten herself into? Dave might not be her first choice—hell, the dance wasn't her first choice!—but what a crappy thing to do to someone. Hopefully, *he* wasn't the type to swap *her* for a different date. *Except this isn't a date!*

"Dressing room's back here, hon," Beth sang over her shoulder.

Ellie stumbled after, feeling as though she'd fallen through a trap door into the twilight zone of square dancing. She stepped into the dressing room as Beth was arranging different skirts and colorful petticoats on pegs. Some were showy, like the other stuff in the shop, but others were muted. Ellie fingered the drabber fabrics, picturing Laura Ingalls Wilder tumbling through tall grasses.

"Holler if you need anything. My name's Beth," the woman announced as she closed the door. Ellie nearly laughed out loud. *Is her last name Chapman?*

She dropped trou and tried one skirt after another, disappointment growing with each one. The bright ones were positively *loud.* The petticoats that went with them added a puffiness that made her look like an overgrown baby doll. But the calicoes washed her out and hung on her hips like her cargo pants. "If you're going to blow a wad, at least pick something that looks good," Ellie's reflection told her.

Beth peered into the room, Sonoma right behind, decked out in an emerald-green-and-white-lace number that looked spectacular on her. Ellie let out a long-suffering sigh as she inspected herself in the mirror in blue-gray blah. "These just aren't me. Well, they are, but they're ..."

"Boring," Sonoma chirped.

"Are you dead set on a prairie skirt?" Beth said.

"I guess not, but I wanted to get something I could use for other occasions too." *Can't afford to dump a lot of cash on a dress I'll use once in my life. Can't afford to blow a lot of cash on anything right now.*

With a snap of her fingers, Beth pivoted and rushed off.

"You can totally pull off that look, Sonoma. That dress looks great on you! Especially with the burgundy hair. I'm envious."

Sonoma inspected herself before raising her blue eyes to meet Ellie's in the mirror. "Thanks. I really love it. And don't worry. We'll find something you love too."

Ellie pinched her own skirt on either side and held it up skeptically. "This was the best of the bunch. What do you think? I mean, does it really matter since I'm only going to wear it once?"

Sonoma crossed her arms. "Of course it matters. This is your first square dance, and you want to feel pretty."

Beth reappeared with several dresses, and Sonoma hopped out of her way, announcing, "I'm getting this one. I'm just gonna change."

After Beth had hung up the dresses and swished out, Ellie's eye was drawn to an ivory one covered in bright red roses. Not her style, and nothing she would have ever picked for herself, but something about it made her smile. She wiggled out of her clothes and pulled the dress over her head. It was lightweight, flowy, and floral, and she twirled in front of the mirror. With a square neckline, smocked bodice, and fluttery short sleeves, it hugged her in the right places. A two-tiered ruffled skirt fell from a snug waist and floated around her calves. She stared at herself in the mirror and saw not a bedraggled landscaper, but a young woman dressed up for a party. How long had it been since she'd felt this feminine? Too long.

Beth stuck her head in. "Oh, honey, you do wonders for that dress! Just got that one in, and I haven't seen it on anyone, but it looks like it was made for you."

"Let me see." Sonoma barged in holding her green outfit and came to a grinding halt. "Oh, Ellie!" she gasped. "It's beautiful on you! It really brings out the creamy color of your skin."

Ellie took another spin, letting the skirt swirl around her as she looked over her shoulder and admired the square back with a tie at the top. "I'm not into floral, but I think I could get used to this one." *I am rocking this! Wait. Is this outfit gonna say "ready for foreplay"? Shit.*

Sonoma dumped her dress in Beth's arms. "Well, we found the dress. Now let's find some shoes to match." She tugged Ellie from the dressing room.

"You want something comfortable. They have some cute flats, but it'd be fun if we could find something colorful for you." Sonoma's eyes scanned a wall of shoes, and Ellie's gaze followed. Soon that gaze wandered from the Mary Jane, T-strap, and crossover styles that were so *not* Ellie to a different wall that held cowboy boots in an explosion of colors.

Ellie's eyes wandered from turquoise to magenta to cobalt, resting squarely on a pair of cherry-red suede boots with a fringe cuff. These weren't Ellie's style either, but something about them called to her. "Sonoma, can you square-dance in cowboy boots?" Ellie had always wanted a pair of cowboy boots, and though she'd lived in Colorado her whole life, she'd never tried on a pair, much less owned one.

"Sure, as long as they're comfortable." Sonoma turned just as Ellie plucked the sample boot from its shelf.

Beth swooped in. "Love, love that boot with the dress," she crooned. "Let me see if I have your size."

When Beth returned and Ellie pulled them on, she spun in front of a full-length mirror and nearly laughed and cried aloud at the same time. The look was perfect! Even better, they were comfortable, and she'd wear them *and* the dress more than once. It had been a long time since clothes had given her a lift, and her stomach was all aflutter—until she looked at the three-hundred-dollar price tag on the boots box. *Oh shit! Why didn't I check that* before *falling in love?* Now her stomach settled below its starting point, and she sagged into her seat to tug them off.

"These are out of my price range. Maybe I'd better stick with something less expensive?" As it was, the dress was already stretching her budget at a hundred and fifty.

She settled on a boring pair of faux leather black Mary Janes that pinched her heels, but at fifty bucks, they were the cheapest option. With a sigh, she turned her purchases over to Beth and got dressed. Oh well. At least she had the pretty dress. When she exited the fitting room, Sonoma handed her one of two shopping bags.

"What's this?" asked Ellie.

"It's your new outfit."

"Oh. I didn't expect it be bagged up already." She set it on the floor to wrangle her wallet from her purse, and as she did so, she glimpsed the box of red boots inside the bag. "Wait. I was getting the Mary Janes."

Sonoma pushed at her hand holding the wallet. "Put that away. It's all paid for. Dave's treat."

Wait. "What?"

"Dave told me to buy whatever you and I needed." Sonoma grinned. "And no arguing."

Ellie's gaze bounced between Sonoma and Beth. Beth gave her a knowing smile. "Honey, just relax and enjoy. Your man wants to spoil you."

"He's not my man," she started to protest, but Beth barreled ahead. "Trust me, you're gonna have yourself a grand time. And if he's as generous in bed as he is with his wallet …" She paused to fan herself dramatically. "My man's that way, and I've been happily married for forty years. I knew the first time he took me in his arms on that dance floor that he was the one." Then she winked salaciously. "You can learn a lot about the way a man moves in bed by watching his hips on the dance floor. I'm sixty-five and he's sixty-seven, and we still make whoopee twice a week."

Ellie's mouth dropped open and snapped closed before she croaked out a "Thank you." Honestly, what else was there *to* say?

Ellie parked in one of the designated visitor slots Dave had told her about. As she gathered Casper's leash and a box filled with herbs, wine, and pumpkin-cream cheese cupcakes, she looked around for Finn's truck and Sonoma's SUV. *Not here yet.* She walked to the row house marked 3625, and before she could ring the bell, the door whipped open.

"Hey, let me help you with that," Dave said as he liberated the heavy box from her grasp. Then he propped the door open with his shoulder and motioned her in with a jerk of his head. She tugged Casper inside, though the dog was more interested in sniffing Dave's bare feet than in following Ellie. Of course she was. Ellie bent to remove her booties, taking in the living room furnished with … gym contraptions. Such a guy way of decorating.

He closed the door behind them. "You can leave your shoes on if you want."

"Is it okay to let Casper off her leash?"

"Absolutely. Sorry for the tight space. This was supposed to be a living room, which is a total waste, so I turned it into my gym. Follow me. The actual living area is up here." He headed up a staircase lining one wall, Casper right on his heels. "Any trouble finding the place or using the gate combo to get in?"

"No, your instructions made it really easy."

The staircase opened onto a wide rectangular great room with a sleek kitchen at one end, and a large living space at the other. In between were a dining table and chairs for six, festooned with fall decor between place settings and a variety of glasses. By contrast to the festive table, the living area was stark, dominated by blank white walls, a humongous muted TV with a football game on, and an equally humongous black leather sectional. A heavy wood-and-iron coffee table with matching side tables and a navy-blue recliner filled the rest of the space. It looked as though someone had just moved in and hadn't gotten around to decorating yet. In the background, the soft sound of a Spanish guitar played. *Interesting blend of styles.*

Dave set the box on the kitchen island and returned to help her off with her coat.

"Oh! Thank you." *Not used to gentlemen, though I'd like to be.* She shimmied out of it.

"I'll just toss this in my room. Want me to get your purse out of the way too?" He held out his hand.

"Um, sure."

"If you need it, it'll be in the master bedroom. Just take a hard left at the top of the stairs." With that, he jogged up yet another set of stairs, followed by his new ghostly white shadow on her four stubby legs. Wrapping her arms around herself, Ellie ambled toward the kitchen, where colorful foods were in various stages of preparation. Funny, she didn't smell a roasting turkey.

Dave brushed past her, startling her. She hadn't heard him return nor felt him come up behind her. Her nose did pick up his scent, however: a wonderful combination of citrus, spice, and fresh woods. She suppressed the urge to follow the drift.

"Can I pour you a glass of wine? Get you a beer? Make you a cocktail? I have flavored sparkling waters and some blood orange juice too."

She nearly coughed out a laugh. Was there such a thing as the "Sophisticated Wookiee"? Not that she'd thought of him as a Wookiee in a while. "A glass of red wine sounds good." She heard a lapping sound and realized Casper was drinking out of a ceramic bowl beside the island. "Oh. Would you rather she didn't—"

"No, she's fine. I set it out specially for her. Can I give her some dog biscuits?"

"Sure. She'll love you even more than she does now."

"Good. I need my dog fix."

He tossed a few Casper-sized biscuits, which the dog easily caught, before uncorking a bottle of red he poured into two goblets. Raising his glass in a toast, he said, "Happy Thanksgiving. I'm glad you're here."

Ellie felt a blush rushing up her neck. "I'm glad I'm here too … um, we're here. Casper and me." *What a dork!* She took a quick sip. "I expected to see either Sonoma or Finn by now, though."

"Nome said Finn was gonna pick her up, but he had an errand to run and they'd be a little late."

"Oh! I didn't realize they were coming together."

Dave's eyebrows slowly raised. "Yeah, I think those two have something going on, but damned if Nome will spill anything."

"Same thing with Finn."

"Which means it's serious," they both said at the same time.

With a deep, warm chuckle, Dave raised his glass again. "Here's to fledgling love affairs. Not my thing, but more power to them. Let's hope no one gets hurt."

Her glass kissed his, and she downed another sip, unsure what to make of what he'd just said. She put it aside and switched gears. "I have a bone to pick with you, Mr. Grim Reaper."

Now his eyebrows shot to his hairline, and his eyes went wide. "What did I do?"

"You had Sonoma buy my clothes for the social square box dance thing."

His face relaxed, and a devilish grin formed. Oooh, it was a good look on him. "Box social. Square dance. And it was the least I could do after my cousin roped you into coming."

She started to protest, but he held up his hand in a stop-right-there motion. "No take-backs, and absolutely no paybacks."

I was afraid he'd say something like that. "I can't take your charity."

He guffawed "What makes you think it was charity? I might've done it for my own selfish reasons."

"Such as?" She couldn't hold back a smile.

"Such as it makes me happy, so don't shit all over my gesture or you'll make me cry. Ever seen a Wookiee cry? It's not a pretty sight." The grin was still firmly in place.

A laugh burst from her. "I expect it isn't, what with the tears and snot and all that fur."

He laughed too, and the corners of his eyes crinkled. "Takes forever to clean up."

"You should do that more often."

"What? Clean up?"

"No, laugh."

A subtle bob of his head, and he added, "So should you."

"I *do* laugh."

"You're pretty damn serious when I'm around."

"Oh, look at the pot calling the kettle black!"

"Touché." He dipped his head.

"Anyway, thank you for the clothes. It was unexpected and a very lovely gesture."

"Unexpected because you didn't think I was capable of a lovely gesture?" He winked.

Flustered, she spurted, "That's not what I meant at all."

"Sonoma told me all about the dress and boots. I'm looking forward to seeing you in them." Now he wiggled his eyebrows.

Heat rose from her chest, spreading over her neck, racing up to her cheeks. It seemed to happen whenever she was around him. When was the last time a guy had made her blush so much? *God, I hope you end up with my social dinner box!*

She rose on her toes and bounced to disguise how her firing nerve endings were making her jittery. "Looks like you've been prepping all day. What can I do to help?"

"Nothing. Just keep me company while I prepare the stuffing." His fingers snaked around an amber-liquid-filled shot glass that had been tucked away. He took a healthy sip and set it back down.

She peered at a mixture in a bowl. "I don't think I've ever had turkey stuffed with wild rice."

"And you're not going to today either. We're having Cornish game hens with savory wild rice, roasted in white wine." He let out a puff of air. "By the time I hit the store, the turkeys were wiped out. I hope you don't mind."

Ellie's mouth watered. "God, no. They sound delicious. Besides, if someone's willing to cook for me, I'm happy to eat whatever they put in front of me."

"I'll remember that."

Is he planning on cooking for me in the future? Despite telling herself not to get carried away, tentative tendrils of warmth encircled her heart.

He picked up the bag of herbs she'd brought, opened it, and inhaled. "Oh wow. These will be great." As he pulled them out and lined them up on a cutting board, he softly asked, "No one ever cooks for you?"

Not anymore. "Not lately, no. When I hang out with Finn, we either order pizza or do takeout."

"Sounds like he's your best friend."

"Yeah, I guess he is." She took another gulp of wine. "And speaking of best friends, what happened with yours?"

Hazel eyes raised to hers. "What best friend?"

"Your dog, Benny. I've been wondering why you didn't get to keep him." She'd been tempted to quiz Sonoma about Dave's "unfortunate" choices in women when they'd gone shopping but had held herself in check. Too middle school.

He rinsed a bunch of parsley and shook it out, then arranged it on the cutting board and started chopping. "Well," he coughed, "I got Benny about the same time my girlfriend … uh, ex-girlfriend … moved in." He paused to sip from the shot glass.

Wineglass in hand, Ellie leaned her hip against a counter.

"She has a son, Isaac, who lived with us part-time," Dave continued. "Isaac's kind of shy, kind of awkward, and he bonded with Benny. So when Nicole and I broke up, she asked if she could keep Benny." He met Ellie's gaze. "How could I say no?"

Nicole. The beautiful blond in all the pictures with the legs twice as long as mine. And huh. The Grim Reaper's not grim at all. In fact, he might be a big softie. A stitch of insecurity gave Ellie a swift jab. "How long ago did you break up, if you don't mind my asking?"

He paused and stared up at the ceiling. "A little over a year now." The knife rose and fell as he diced the parsley. "It was rough at first—things ended on a sour note—but I think it's smoothed out since."

"Are you close to Isaac? Do you still see him? Them?" Ellie held her breath, though she wasn't sure why.

A wry chuckle. "Not really. Unless Nicky wants something from me. Otherwise, I don't hear from her. As for Isaac, I've seen him a couple of times since we split, but it sounds like he and his dad are closer, and that's good." She didn't miss the sad note in his voice, and her heart tugged. He blinked, seeming to put it aside. "More wine?"

"I'll get it." She topped off both their wineglasses, embarrassed that hers needed more "topping off" than his, until she remembered the nearly empty shot glass. At least her fidgeting was mellowing. "Must be tough on a relationship when you're on the road a lot."

He paused, picked up his wineglass, and, peering over its rim, pierced her with those intense eyes of his. "It shouldn't be. Other guys in the league do it, and it works for them. The sudden moving can be hard, especially if the woman's got a career or a business that's rooted, but I've only ever played for one team, and Nicky didn't work." He shrugged.

Whoa! He supported her? Cripes, no wonder she looks so good. With all that time on her hands, she could afford every spa treatment, every … Okay. Not fair, El.

Ellie pulled in a lung-filling breath and quietly let it back out again. "What happened? If I'm being too nosy, just tell me to mind my own business."

Scraping the parsley into the rice mix, he shook his head. "I did something really stupid and got caught."

Chapter 17

ATTACK OF THE WARM FUZZIES

Ellie whooshed out a fractured gasp, and Dave's eyes darted to her startled ones. *Oh shit. She thinks* … "No, no, it's not like that. I didn't cheat on her. I'm not that guy."

She let out a scoffing noise that had him shooting her a pointed, arched-eyebrow look.

Her eyes became big blue rounds. "Oh, that wasn't directed at *you*. It's just that … Well, I've been with *that* guy." She raked slender fingers through her wavy strawberry locks, causing Dave's brain to take a hard right from who *that* guy was, like a roller-coaster car yanking its passengers around its track. Did her hair feel as silky as it looked?

"So what did she catch you at?" she said.

What? Taking his time, he rinsed a few sprigs of rosemary, held them to his nose—*so fragrant!*—and began stripping them, sorting his thoughts after they'd jumped the track. She sipped her wine in the awkward pause, eyes pinned on him.

"She didn't catch me at anything," he finally said. "I got caught by a few teammates using, uh, PEDs." Holding his breath, he glanced up at her. Her features were scrunched in a question mark. "Performance-enhancing drugs. HGH, steroids, plus painkillers I hadn't been prescribed," he explained. "Not recreational drugs, like cocaine or Molly or—"

"For hockey," she blurted, light suddenly playing in her expressive eyes. "Because you were hurt, and those helped you heal."

He must have looked all kinds of stunned as he stared at her and mumbled, "Mm-hmm." She got it, but she wasn't passing judgment. Not from the little he knew of her expressions anyway, and he felt a lift of relief. Why he was telling her any of this shit, he had no idea, but something about the way she asked and her thoughtful expressions made him want to talk. It had been bottled up inside him for so long. He'd barely talked to Sonoma about it because he'd been so embarrassed, but this girl … she had a way of probing gently, cautiously, like a surgeon looking for the source of an infection—as though she genuinely gave a shit—and it made him spill like Niagara Falls. And now he'd just confessed the very thing that had sent Nicky sprinting out of his life like he was damaged goods, or worse, diseased and contagious. Did it really matter what Ellie thought of him? After all, it wasn't as if they were anything to each other. But the fact that she was still there—*not* looking utterly horrified while relief washed over him—told him it was, in fact, important to him on some level. Maybe just as some small reinforcement that he wasn't scummier than the scum of the earth.

Not only did she not show a flicker of disgust, but she slid onto one of the barstools across from him and offered him a half-smile. Setting her glass down, she settled in, lacing her fingers under her chin, looking like she belonged there. Like she *wanted* to belong there.

Her eyebrows pinched together over those big, sparkling blue eyes that broadcast they were unraveling a mystery. "Let me see if I have this straight. Your teammates busted you doping, your girlfriend found out, and she took off?"

Surprisingly, hearing it didn't send spikes into his chest like it usually did. Maybe a few needle pricks, but no more. "That about sums it up."

"No offense, but I don't get it. Why wouldn't she stick by you while you were going through all that turmoil? You must have been at a really low point when this all went down."

Understatement of the century. He pushed a breath through his lungs. "She was worried about Isaac being exposed to the shit-show."

"What shit-show?"

"I'm not exactly sure. I was a little … moody. I didn't yell or take it out on them, but I was tough to be around, I guess."

"But it's not like you were injecting heroine or snorting coke!"

"No, but I *was* injecting."

He kept wary eyes on her, looking for a shift in her open expression, but instead, with a voice filled with curiosity, she said, "It must be a slippery slope. How did it start?"

To say he was astonished was akin to saying a trip to the Stanley Cup Finals was exciting. Way too obvious.

He released a sigh. "It started when I tweaked a shoulder, and a trainer said he had a 'little something' that would fix it right up. And it did." Dave had known Bobby was offering him banned substances, and Dave had taken a hard moral line—at first. They were banned for a reason, and using them was unethical. He'd played through the pain, but his performance had suffered, and as a result, so had his team. When it happened again, that hard moral line had fuzzed. After researching the substances in question and arguing with Bobby over the wisdom of the NHL's stance, that moral line had blurred even further. After all, if something like HGH could actually help a player heal faster without screwing him up, why was the league so dead set against it? Maybe *they* were in the wrong.

Dave had been skeptical about the banned substances' effectiveness, but he'd decided to try them anyway—more research, he'd told himself. Once couldn't hurt, could it? Yeah, he'd bent the rules, but didn't guys bend all kinds of rules all the time? On the ice? Off the ice? When his healing time had been cut nearly in half, his moral line had moved, flipped, and he'd climbed aboard the enhancement train, convincing himself that *not* using what was at his disposal was wrong. How could he behave in a way that hindered his team? That was downright selfish.

And just like that, treating injuries with PEDs became the *right* thing to do. With each injury, it got easier to stretch the truth. Not only did they help him overcome injuries in record time, but they made him feel more powerful, more on his game, and he'd never considered he might have punched a one-way ticket. Stopping had been harder than he'd ever imagined. Maybe they weren't physically addictive, but mental addiction, at least for him, was a different story. He'd kidded himself he was in control, but he'd found out how wrong he was when he'd been forced to quit. If he hadn't been busted by Gage and the freshly traded Hunter McMurphy, would he have found the willpower to do it on his own? To this day, the temptation was strong, especially as his aches and pains prevented him from being the force he *knew* he was.

"I had an iron man streak going," he explained, "and I wasn't ready for it to end. Besides, I thought I was helping my team. It was a viable explanation at the time." But hearing himself now? It sounded like what it was—a lame excuse for cheating.

"What's an iron man streak?" She tipped her wineglass to her lips.

"It means I'd played five hundred consecutive games. In my case, it was over six hundred. I was out to beat some records, get myself in the nine hundreds." He shrugged. "Ironically, the streak ended when they sat me and I wasn't even injured."

"They sat you for using steroids? But lots of people do it!"

She's defending me? Her fierceness surprised and warmed him. He cocked his head, letting an indulgent half-smile tug at the corners of his mouth. "But it doesn't make it right. I broke the NHL's rules, Ellie."

She blinked. "How did your teammates react when they found out?"

Now the needle pricks intensified. He cleared his throat. "Most of them didn't know at first, but let's just say socializing isn't what it used to be." *Which is why I need to get traded.*

The pleats between Ellie's brows deepened. "But you did it so you could recover quicker, get back on the ice, and help your team out, right?"

"Yeah, which, according to the league, right or wrong, doesn't matter because it gives me an unfair advantage. That's why they're called 'performance-enhancing drugs.' What I did was wrong, plain and simple. Exposing my teammates was wrong. Not only did I put *my* career on the line, but worse, I jeopardized my entire club. I'm surprised more guys didn't write me off." Hearing it took him aback. Had he ever admitted any of this aloud before—and meant it?

"Do they *all* know?"

A mirthless chuckle escaped him. "Oh yeah. Didn't start out that way, but Nicky made sure all the SOs knew and—"

"What's an 'SO'?"

He kept forgetting she wasn't part of the world he'd lived in for so long, and his smile grew a little wider. How refreshing to talk to a woman who knew little about the game or the players, and who didn't seem to care about either. Who wasn't angling for anything. "Significant other."

Ellie rocked backward. *Now* horror was etched in her delicate features. "She told your teammates' wives and girlfriends? Why would she do that?"

"Revenge? Because she was humiliated by what I did? I upset her perfect world." And here he was, making excuses for Nicky—again—though he'd been grappling with her betrayal ever since Quinn had told him what she'd done months ago. Why? Maybe because he didn't want to admit the hard, hurtful truth in Nicky's parting words. She'd left him to find "something better." His interpretation? A guy with *more* money, *more* prestige, although it wasn't as if his paychecks or his standing had suffered that much with his team suspension. Huh. Maybe in the end he hadn't been enough for her, and this had been her way out.

"But she humiliated herself by telling everyone!" Ellie exclaimed, yanking him back to the present. "They wouldn't have known otherwise."

"Maybe. With the team sitting me, guys might have figured it out on their own anyway."

"I get being upset, maybe even disappointed, but … I don't know. I guess I'm being naive, but it seems like your heart was in the right place. You used steroids for the inflammation. I assume they were catabolic—is that the right word?—and not the kind that turn muscles into mountains."

"Because it's so obvious my muscles aren't the size of mountains?" he quipped. "Damn!"

A pretty blush colored her cheeks, providing the perfect distraction. "That's not what I meant."

"What *did* you mean?" he prodded, biting back his amusement as he refilled her wineglass.

"I meant … well, your … your muscles look … they're … You're in really good shape."

He found himself buoyed by the fact she'd noticed, and he stifled the ridiculous urge to scratch the back of his head and flex.

Her blush deepened, and before he realized what he was doing, he reached over and tugged a soft wave of strawberry-blond hair where it cascaded over her shoulder. *Even silkier than it looks.* "I'm just teasing you."

"So … and … um, the growth hormone speeds the healing process," she continued haltingly, "and painkillers make it all tolerable while you're healing. Which is why you did it."

Is this girl for real? She's doing a better job justifying than I ever did. And that's just what he'd done, hadn't he? Justified. Somehow it didn't sound so just when someone else made the argument on his behalf. "I'm guessing you've spent time around athletes. Finn?"

"No. It's … I read a lot. And watching you play hockey … I mean, watching hockey on TV, it's staggering how beat up you guys get, yet you hop right back to it and skate full-out, like a freight train *didn't* just hit you. Well, I guess in your case, *you're* the freight train. But still. It has to take its toll." A warm chuckle bubbled out of her. "If we mere mortals took that kind of punishment … Well, I know I'd just curl up in a ball until someone scraped me off the ice. You must be one big walking bruise all the time."

He wasn't sure which blew him away more: that she'd registered the effort players put in out there, that she'd noticed *his* physical play, or that she'd watched him on TV in the first place. Whatever it was, it shifted something deep in his chest and made his insides a little squishy. Way squishier than he wanted. She was tearing down his carefully erected façade and taking a peek behind.

"I know it doesn't make it right," she clarified, "but I get it. And we all make mistakes."

He found himself staring at her again. "Yeah, some of us more than others. Thanks for the support, though."

He broke eye contact just as she tucked a strand behind her ear. "May I have some water?"

After snagging her a cold bottle from the fridge, he began stirring the rice mixture. Soft snuffling came from under the dining table, and he glimpsed Casper curled up on the room's lone rug. The cold, drab walls of his townhouse suddenly felt … cozier. "Would you like to come to a game sometime? Watch it live? You could bring Finn or a girlfriend." Something surprisingly foreign and possessive jolted him. *No Habitat dudes. Or any other dudes unless they're family.*

Her pretty blues popped, and she paused mid-gulp. "Are you serious? I'd love to come. And I know Finn would die for the chance."

"Consider it done. We have a homestand coming up, so we'll take a look at the schedule and see what works for you."

"So how's the hand these days? Fully recovered after the Habitat workday?" she ventured.

"It's getting there." It wasn't a lie this time. His hand *had* been feeling better, but it still wasn't a hundred percent—not that he was about to let anyone know. "And don't worry. I haven't been using anything to help it get there." Though, once again, he couldn't help but think how much quicker recovery would have been.

"I wasn't worried—I have confidence in you—and I'm glad to hear it's healing."

As the warm fuzzies over her declaration of confidence drifted into the general area of his heart and started settling in, he was jerked back to reality, recalling her comment about *that* guy. Who had he been, what had he meant to Ellie, and why had he let her go? How had he wronged her? Dave didn't get the chance to find out because she reached into her back pocket and pulled out a folded envelope.

"Before Finn and Sonoma get here, I want to give you something." She carefully extracted a slip of paper and thrust it at him.

He took the paper and stared at what appeared to be a check. "What's this?"

The corners of her mouth curled up in an impish smile. "The insurance money finally came through."

Shock had him exclaiming, "That's *all* they gave you? And why are you handing it to me?"

"It's my first installment on the Sienna."

"*What?* Oh no, you don't." He shoved it back at her, but she raised her hands, palms out, and the check fluttered to the floor. He gave her the don't-fuck-with-me stare-down he normally saved for the ice. When he detected a flinch, he instantly regretted the hard look, but she still didn't pick up the damn check. "I'm not taking any money from you, Ellie. End of discussion." Suppressing a headshake and a smile, he stepped away and washed his hands, returning to scoop up a handful of the rice mixture and fill the hollowed hens.

"Well, you'll just have to because I'm not taking it back." Arms cinching over her chest, she tipped her cute nose in the air.

Bossy. He opened his mouth to argue—he was *not* going to back down—when someone came tromping up the stairs.

"We finally made it," Sonoma sang as she unwound a scarf from around her neck. Finn was on her heels, loaded down with a box and a few bags. He called out a "Hey!" and Dave pointed to some open counter space where he could unload.

"So. What are we doing?" Sonoma crooned. "Ooh … drinking wine, it looks like."

Ellie hopped up. "Dave's got his hands full. Can I pour you a glass?"

Sonoma waved her off. "I got it." Then her eyes traveled to the floor. "What's that?" She stooped and picked up the check.

"It's my insurance check, which Dave refuses to accept," Ellie huffed cheerfully.

Sonoma side-eyed him and smirked. "Yeah, you're fighting a losing battle, Ellie. Trust me on this one, unless you *enjoy* beating your head against the brick wall of 'Dave.'"

"Hey! I resent that," he chirped.

"Well, it's true." Sonoma pulled down a wineglass and snagged a beer from the fridge, which she uncapped and handed to Finn, like it was the most natural move in the world.

Dave's gaze collided with Ellie's, and they seemed to share the same thought. *Oh yeah, something's* definitely *going on between these two.*

Sonoma seemed oblivious. Filling her wineglass, she prattled on. "If you're dead set on paying him back, then I suggest taking the money and donating it to his favorite charity instead. Trying to foist it on him will be an epic waste of time."

Ellie's face lit with a mischievous grin as she watched him stuff the last of the hens. "What's your favorite charity?"

"Don't think I have a favorite. How about you donate to *your* favorite charity—namely yourself?" Christ, he *knew* she could use the cash for her business. Why didn't she just take it? *Bossy* and *stubborn.* Oddly, he found the combination kinda sexy. Or maybe it was just her. *No, don't go there. You're moving soon.* The trade deadline was three months away.

Her eyes narrowed. "How about I donate it to Habitat in your name?"

For some reason, his mind leapt to her personally handing the check to the douchenugget schmoozemeister from the landscaping project who wanted in her pants. "How about not? Or if it goes to Humanity, we do it jointly?" *That didn't come out right. Now it sounds like I want credit, damn it.*

Sonoma's eyes had been bouncing between the two of them, and now she thrust her full wineglass in the air. "I think we have a winner! Let's drink to Habitat getting a big, fat check."

"Not *that* big," Ellie said.

"Or that fat," Dave agreed.

One side of Sonoma's mouth curved up in a knowing smirk. *What?* he wanted to say. *Nothing to see here. Just move along and leave me alone.*

He put aside the stuffed hens and pulled out the sage Ellie had brought. Sonoma peered over his shoulder as he began blending the drizzle for the butternut squash he'd baked and cubed.

"Is this from one of your shows?" she asked.

"Yep. Looked simple, and I wanted to experiment on all of you. In fact, this whole dinner is one big experiment."

Finn held up a hand. "I, for one, have no qualms about being a guinea pig."

Ellie raised her glass. "I second that!"

"Hear, hear!" Sonoma chimed.

As Dave worked on the food, cheerful chitchat, music, and wonderful aromas filled the air, and he smiled to himself. He couldn't remember being this relaxed in … forever. *This is what it's* supposed *to be like. Too bad I'll be leaving it behind.*

Chapter 18

Hidden Agendas

Dave dropped his bag in the room he was sharing with Quinn. They'd just arrived in Edmonton after beating Calgary in a matinee game, and he was anxious to ditch the suit jacket and tie and grab a cold one in the hotel bar. His phone rang, but when he saw who it was, he let it go to voicemail. He didn't need the aggravation, and he had a more important call to return anyway.

Quinn was already in shirtsleeves, rolling his cuffs to his elbows. Dave loosened his tie. "Why don't you head on down, Hads? I have to take care of a few things, and I'll be right behind you."

Quinn left the room, and Dave shucked the coat and pulled the tie over his head, then parked on the edge of the bed and tapped his agent's number. "Herb?"

Herb had sent him a few encouraging messages about teams he'd been talking to, including Arizona, who'd perked up at hearing Dave's name in a possible trade, and Dave couldn't wait for what he hoped was a positive update.

"There you are. Thought you might still be making your way to Edmonton. Nice game today."

"Thanks. So what's going on?"

Herb cleared his throat. Never a good sign. "Well, the teams that were interested in a trade went dark."

An invisible fist punched Dave in his solar plexus. "All of them? Even Arizona?"

"Says they're waiting until after Christmas before they seriously entertain anything from anyone."

"That doesn't sound right."

"I think they're holding back because they're still not convinced your hand's where it needs to be, though no one's come out and said that."

Dave's pulse kicked up a notch. "Haven't they been watching? I'm playing the best hockey I've played all season."

"Don't get your panties in a wad, buttercup. I know that, you know that. They're just being extra cautious. Any team that brings you aboard is facing a hit to their salary cap, and they have to be sure it's worth the spend."

Dave raised his eyes to the ceiling and gusted out a breath. "Fuck."

"Things getting any better with your team?"

"Not really. I'm still the Invisible Man."

"Can't lead a club that way, and that's one of those intangibles GMs will be looking at. Yeah, they're looking to pick up a solid defenseman, but they're also looking for leadership in the locker room. If I were you, I'd hedge my bets and figure out how to make it work in Colorado. It'll increase your marketability and … well, just in case you wind up staying put."

Herb wasn't telling Dave anything he didn't already know, and part of him was pissed he was hearing it again. Pissed *and* disappointed. But a small part of him had been turning over the possibility of staying in Denver a while longer, and that part was thawing—slightly—to the idea. Probably because it was buying into the stupid Yoda voice that kept repeating, "Make it work, you can."

Could he find a way back, find a way to fit in once more? He needed cooperation from his teammates, though, and damn it, it just wasn't happening. Didn't help that he was still butting heads with Gage Nelson. Guys looked up to their alternate captain, cared what he thought, followed his lead. So if Nelson wanted to shun him, they would too.

He hung up and pinched the bridge of his nose, debating whether to go to the bar or just say, "Fuck it!" and watch a movie. Play a video game. Watch hockey highlights. Instead, he picked up his phone and stared at his last text exchange with Ellie. All benign crap that started with her thanking him for Thanksgiving—again—and him teasing her about the "social box" she had to prepare for their upcoming weekend. No lie, thinking about that weekend gave him a lift, but he told himself not to get too carried away. Maybe a trade wasn't coming this month, but after the holidays, chances would improve, especially if his hand continued its slow grind toward healthy. He could not, would not, start anything with this girl. Even if she *was* taking up a chunk of his idle thoughts. Like how good it had been having her in his house, how comfortable, and how incredibly hollow he'd felt when she'd left.

"Who says she'd want to start anything with *you* anyway, dumbass?" he muttered aloud. One fact was becoming painfully obvious the more time he spent with her: she deserved someone who had his emotional shit together. Someone smarter, more sophisticated, more than the sum of his salary and celebrity … just more. Keeping it in the friend zone was the right thing to do. The only option.

A few minutes later, he strolled into the hotel bar and spotted his teammates. Puck bunnies swarmed their tables like wasps swarmed picnics on hot summer days, and Dave looked each one over. They were all attractive and all there for one reason. A few looked his way and gave him wily smiles. If he wanted, he could lose his bad mood for a while with one. *If* he wanted. But he didn't want, and maybe it was because a certain strawberry blond was front and center in his mind, and though she was only a bright mist, she looked better than anything else he was seeing. Better than anything he'd *ever* seen.

The realization surprised him.

Ignoring the ladies, he zeroed in on Quinn, seated beside Nelson. They seemed to be sitting in a bunny-free zone, which was a phenomenon Dave *still* hadn't gotten used to—at least where Hadley was concerned, not that Hads spent much time in bars anymore. But when he did, he barricaded himself behind some kind of invisible force field that telegraphed "Not interested!" loud and clear. Nelson was even less likely to hang in the bar and had a force field of his own. Dave hadn't expected to see him and debated whether to do a one-eighty back to his room, park his ass in the bunny-infested section, or suck it up and join Nelson and Hads.

Yoda chose that moment to growl out a gravelly command to suck it up, and Dave's feet seemed to take charge and propel him in that direction.

"Hey. Okay if I join you guys?" he said when he reached them.

"Sure," said Hads.

Dave took Nelson's grunt and shrug as a yes, and, uncomfortable as it was, sat down. "Hope I didn't interrupt anything."

Nelson raised his eyebrows.

Quinn shook his head. "Nah. We were just shooting the shit."

A waitress appeared, and Dave pointed at his two teammates before ordering a beer. Quinn said, "Why not?" while Nelson said he was done. Of course he was. Any minute, he'd down the rest of his brew and hustle off to his room.

Shit. Dave hadn't meant to shorten the guy's stay by joining them. He rummaged around for common ground and started talking about their game. "Wyatt saved our bacon today."

"Guy stood on his head. Looks like he's celebrating." Quinn sat back and laughed, and Dave glanced over his shoulder at Wyatt, who was chatting up the bunnies, a big grin splitting his face. Dave was reminded of how the dude had leered at Ellie, and his blood heated a few degrees higher. The contrast between these girls and her—well, it was stark. Did Wyatt actually put them on an equal plane?

Dave swung his gaze back in time to witness Nelson living up to his prediction. Dude polished off the contents of his pint glass and stood. "I'm beat. I'm gonna head up to my room."

Asshole.

Before Dave could open his mouth and call him on it, his phone rang again. He glanced at the caller ID and hissed out a curse before picking it up. He hadn't even listened to her voicemail yet.

"Hey, Nicky." Dave didn't miss the surprise on Hads's face, or the fact that Nelson chose that moment to make himself scarce.

"I tried calling you just a little while ago." Her tone was part-pout, part-accusation.

"Yeah, I was just getting settled in my hotel room." He said a silent thank-you to the waitress as she deposited his beer.

"You're in Edmonton." A statement, not a question. "You looked great in today's game."

"Uh, thanks?" After an awkward pause, he said, "What's going on?" That was more polite than what he really wanted to say, which was, "What do you want?"

"Nothing. I just wanted to call and say hello and let you know I was thinking about you."

This confused the hell out of him. "So you're okay? Isaac's okay?"

"We're okay."

"Benny's okay?"

He could practically *hear* her eyes roll. "Yes, Dave, Benny's fine. We're *all* fine. Can I not just call to say hello? And to say I miss you?"

WTF? "Do you need money?" he blurted. Across from him, Hads was scrolling through his phone, looking all kinds of uncomfortable. Probably as uncomfortable as Dave felt at this moment.

"For God's sake, Dave, I don't need money!" She paused a beat. "What I needed was to hear your voice."

He was too dumbfounded to reply.

"So, um, sounds like you're sitting in a bar," she ventured.

"Yeah, and I'm with some buddies, so I really should go."

She let out a mirthless laugh. "You sure you don't mean 'bunnies'?"

Seriously? Now she was just pissing him off. He'd never cheated on her—hadn't even considered it, not once—yet she had always given him flak about hookups that hadn't happened. Just because a guy liked to grab a beer with his teammates didn't mean he was fucking every female in sight. Yeah, he talked to them on occasion—no need to be a jerk—but he never touched. In Nicky's world, he was supposed to hole up in his hotel room and stay put while he was on the road. Apparently, he wasn't trustworthy. His mind suddenly turned a sharp angle. What if *she'd* been fucking other guys behind his back? People who threw accusations around were often guilty of the same sins. If *that* wasn't a Yoda-ism, he didn't know what was.

His inner Han stepped to the forefront and cut her off.

"Will you call me later?" she asked as he was about to hang up.

"Doubtful." Okay. So he *was* more than capable of being a jerk when the situation called for it. He stowed the phone, shot Quinn an apologetic look, and took a big swallow of his beer.

"She's still calling you?"

"Not still. She just started recently, and I can't figure out what she wants."

Quinn tipped his glass at him. "They always want what they think they can't have. Now that you're seeing someone—"

"I'm *not* seeing someone."

Quinn's eyebrows did a crazy crawl up his forehead. "Oh. Wyatt said you were dating the cute landscaper."

"Ellie. And no, I'm not dating her. I just told him that because he was about to go all horndog on her."

"Jesus." Quinn laughed. "Yeah, best to protect the girls who aren't hip to the Wyatts of the world."

Dave doubted Ellie had much experience with said "Wyatts of the world"—something Quinn used to be, Dave refrained from adding. But who knew? There was so much about this girl Dave *didn't* know, and he had to admit he was intrigued. For instance, what had happened in her past with *that* guy? He'd tried some subtle prodding at Thanksgiving, but she'd skillfully dodged and redirected.

"Things good with Sarah? The new house?" he asked.

Quinn sprouted a goofy grin—just like the one Nelson wore whenever he talked about Lily. *Did* I *look that stupid when I talked about Nicky? No way.* "It's going good. Couldn't ask for better."

"I'm happy for you, man. How's her brother taking it?"

"He's fine with it. He just likes to give me crap, and mostly I let him."

"Sorry if I broke up your party. Didn't mean to chase the guy off."

"Don't worry about it." Quinn sipped his beer and leaned his forearms on the table. "I just hope one of these days you two can patch things up."

I'm trying, for fuck's sake! But that stubborn jerk-off won't stop being a jerk-off. Yoda piped up with his asinine quote about doing over trying, which caused a question to zoom through Dave's head: How much effort had he *really* put out—with *any* of them? He merely replied, "Me too," and gulped his beer.

Now that Thanksgiving was over, the demand for Christmas decorations had skyrocketed, and Landscaping with Altitude was busy stringing Denver in lights. A good problem to have, though the boom would be short-lived, and Ellie was feeling more than a little guilty about her and Finn taking off for the better part of a weekend and leaving Felipe on his own. Plus, she was fitting in an impromptu cut and highlight with Sonoma. Another hour and a half where she'd be away from the office.

She'd considered maneuvering their busy time into a plausible excuse to bow out of the box social—she still didn't know what she was going to make! But she couldn't leave Dave high and dry at the last minute—

especially after he'd bought her the clothes—and no way would Finn let her get away with it. He was actually *looking forward* to the event.

"Don't worry, Boss Lady. My brothers help. We hold your back," Felipe had assured her with a big grin. She couldn't bring herself to correct his twisted idiom, especially after he really *had* had her back on one of the job sites where Agent Clemente had paid an impromptu visit. Ellie had arrived just as the agent had, and when she'd questioned his reason for being there, he'd shrugged and said, "Just looking for tips for my place." Technically, he hadn't done anything wrong. He'd simply observed Felipe and the crew from the sidewalk. But it hadn't kept her alarm at bay, nor had it kept Felipe from tossing a few anger-laced Spanish phrases at the agent. What little Ellie had understood included choice words about leaving the boss lady alone. So yeah, Felipe had wormed his way back into her good graces.

But today she was putting it all aside because she was excited about joining Sarah Nelson, Paige Miller, and a few other ladies for a business luncheon.

As she was getting ready to shut down her computer, she checked emails one last time. A new message sat in her in-box, and when she saw who it was from, a cold shiver raced through her, raising the hairs on her arms and neck. Worry settled right back in her chest like a twenty-pound dumbbell.

A quick tap—as if the key might explode—and the email from Agent Clemente filled her screen.

I trust you had a pleasant Thanksgiving and were able to take some much deserved time off. I think you're the only other person I know who puts in as many hours as I do. And speaking of putting in hours and taking breaks, I was wondering when we could grab that coffee together. Let me know when you have an opening in your schedule—sooner rather than later, I hope.

Another winky emoji that struck her as the slightest bit creepy. Was he up to something sinister, and if so, what? Another shiver chattered up her spine.

"Don't think I'm going to have a spare minute for months, *Agent* Clemente," she told the computer as she shut it down. She huffed out a breath. As she stepped into the gloomy gray day, her pulse ramped up. Her head on a swivel, keeping an eye out for a dark government-issued car, she swiftly climbed into her van and drove off. The farther she got from her office, the easier her breaths came.

Chapter 19

Elvis Says It Best

The rolling rumble of an engine that came to an abrupt halt alerted Ellie it was time to go. Within seconds, a soft rap sounded. Casper was already there, her nose snuffling at the bottom of the front door. Assessing herself in the hall mirror, Ellie twisted one last spiral of hair and smoothed her jeans before whipping open the door.

Dave backpedaled, which took him down a step. Even so, he stood taller and more rugged than she recalled—rugged in every good sense of the word. Broad-shouldered, square-jawed, hard-planed, a dash of handsome mixed with confidence that broadcast he could handle anything, or anyone, that came at him with ease. A capable mountain man who was so well groomed he didn't *look* like a mountain man. Had he just spent time in Sonoma's chair too? There was something to be said for a big, powerful man who could protect you. From other big men. Like Agent Clemente.

Am I even thinking straight right now? Probably not.

Mr. Rugged shoved his hands in the front pockets of his jeans, the look on his face shifting from intensely masculine to achingly uncomfortable until Casper charged him, and he dropped into a crouch to pet her. Ellie took a quick appraising sweep, liking what she saw. A spruce sweater open at the collar, revealing a white T-shirt. The jeans hugged his broad thighs, the hems resting on a pair of thick-soled hiking boots. Pretty manly stuff that put an extra flutter in her tummy and did little to tamp down her anxiety about the evening ahead. Although, whereas the anxiety had been over the dance and her boxed dinner, now that anxiety—or was it excitement?—was all about the man in front of her whose thick head of golden-brown hair she was staring at. It looked so soft and touchable and …

"Amber waves of grain" blared in her head for some ridiculous reason. In a bid to distract herself, she glanced over his shoulder at a really big, really white Chevy Silverado. "Is that yours too?"

With a glance over his shoulder, he said, "Yep. We'll be on some dirt roads, and I thought it'd be the best option for getting us there."

Instead of asking him if he owned a fleet of cars, she said, "No GTO today?"

He peered up at her through thick, dark lashes she hadn't taken stock of before, giving her a crestfallen look. "Ah damn, I wish you'd said something."

She laughed—more to blow off steam than because she found his reaction funny. "No, it's fine. The truck makes perfect sense, but I might need a step stool to get inside."

He rose while Casper capered around his ankles. "I can give you a boost." One side of his mouth hitched. "And next time I'll take you for a ride in the GTO."

Are we going to have a next time? The thought warmed her—maybe a little too much. She waved him in. "I just need to fill Casper's water bowl and lock up. Come in."

"Thanks." He closed the door behind him, and his eyes started tracking around the small space.

"Want the nickel tour?" she blurted.

"Sure. So what are you doing with Casper while you're gone?"

"My neighbors will help out. Plus, I just met Natalie, your teammate T.J.'s wife, the other day and found out she dog-sits. She agreed to stop by a few times, make sure Casper has what she needs, and take her for a walk. I'm really happy the timing worked out so well."

"Yeah, Natalie's the best. She used to watch Benny for us—me, I mean. She's great."

Ellie brushed off the slip. *It's hard going from a "we" to a "me." Apparently, he hasn't made the full adjustment yet. Or is he hoping to go back to …* She pushed aside the startlingly unsettling thought.

It took less than five minutes to show him the living and dining rooms, kitchen, two bedrooms, and one bath. "There's another bedroom and laundry down in the basement, but it's kind of a mess, so we'll skip it."

He peered out the windowed kitchen door to the backyard and pointed. "Is that the greenhouse where you grow the herbs?"

"Yeah. Want to see?"

He was already reaching for the knob. "I'd love to." He stepped off the back stoop and landed on the gravel with a soft crunch. "I thought a landscaper would have grass everywhere," he laughed. "It's mostly rock back here."

"Low maintenance and takes less water. The beds fill in during the spring and summer, so it doesn't feel quite so stark."

"It's not stark. It's really nice. Homey." His gaze ran over her Adirondack chairs surrounding a fire pit table she never used.

She walked into the cramped greenhouse, and he followed. The space tightened, and as she faced him and looked up, he was looking down with that laser-beam intensity of his. The breath nearly whooshed from her lungs. She waved her hand over the plants as though she were Vanna White presenting a prize. "So here are the herbs." She suppressed an eye-roll at her own lameness.

"Smells really, really good in here," he said without taking his eyes off of her. Was he talking about the plants or …? His gaze moved from her eyes to her mouth and slowly swept back up again. The subtle scent of cologne and man wreathed her and, with the fresh herbs, made a heady combination. Her pulse jumped.

Whew! Getting hot in here. She tried to take a step back, but with no room to maneuver, she crossed her arms as if barricading herself against—what, she wasn't sure. "Guess we should get on the road, huh?"

He seemed to snap back from wherever his mind had traveled—a mystery visit that intrigued her. "Yep. Let's do it." He swung his arms to the side and clapped his hands, toppling over one of her plants. "Oh Jesus! Sorry."

She waved him off. "No big deal." When his big body moved out of the greenhouse, she caught her breath and righted the plant. What was wrong with her, and how on earth was she going to keep her wits about her for the next two hours in the confines of his truck cab?

Christ, get a grip! Something charged had played between them in that greenhouse, making it hard for him to breathe, pulling him toward her. Was it because the tiny space had forced them closer and she'd smelled so fucking good? Whatever it was, he'd been on the verge of moving in to kiss her. *Han, not Yoda, in charge.* Thank God she'd yanked him out of his fog. Damn, if he was having this much trouble standing *next* to her, what was dancing with her going to do to him? At least he'd be in a big crowd, and that would keep him honest. Thank God they had separate rooms.

He stowed her stuff in the backseat while she got settled in front, taking extra care with her boxed supper. It was in a plain brown container with some kind of bow that looked like hay tied around sprigs of flowers and herbs. Simple, natural, pretty. Like her. He placed it in a cooler, then climbed behind the wheel and got on the road.

"We may not be in the GTO, but I'll put on some Elvis, and we can pretend." Right on cue, "Let Yourself Go" drifted through the speakers.

She clapped. "Perfect. We might have to listen to some country and western too to warm up."

"I don't really listen to it. Do you?"

She wagged her head from side to side. "I've been known to on occasion."

"All right, then. You're in charge of that part of today's musical entertainment."

"You trust me?" She wiggled her eyebrows.

"Implicitly." And he realized he did, and not just in the music department. She was different from any woman he'd ever met, and the fleeting thought he'd been hanging with Ms. Wrong all these years skittered through his underperforming brain.

As he drove, they talked about his road trip—she'd watched every game, which sent the odd tingle rippling through him—her busy season, and her business luncheon with Paige and the rest of the "P-team."

"I really enjoyed meeting her. She's already talking about projects that need landscaping, and she's asked me to draw up some preliminary plans. And it's the kind of thing we can work on during the cold months because she's totally into xeriscaping. Plus, that woman is really well connected, and she asked if she could give my name out to her clients. I've already had one call! Omigosh, my mouth just ran away from me."

He enjoyed this animated side of her. Something that felt ridiculously like pride that she showed it to him welled inside, and he smiled. "It's all good. I'm glad to hear it. You deserve something like this after all the hard work you've put in." *And I like hearing the sound of your voice and your laugh. Soft. Musical.* "So what did you end up packing in your 'social box'?"

She gave him a sly sidelong glance. "You mean my boxed supper? I think I'm finally getting the hang of the terms."

"Phew! And not a moment too soon," he teased. Which made her laugh again. God, her laugh fired him up, especially knowing it was because of what *he* was saying. It had been way too long since he'd been responsible for bringing out the humor in a woman—besides Sonoma, who didn't count. Then again, when was the last time he'd been inspired to make a woman laugh?

"Well," Ellie's voice took on her usual seriousness, "I did some research, and it seems fried chicken is the traditional way to go, sooooo … I went the opposite direction and improvised. Because how was I going to fry chicken? And I didn't want to buy it at the store or the Colonel's."

"No, I can see how that would be bad form. But now you've got me *really* curious." Outside, yellowed farmers' fields whizzed by under a bright blue sky dotted with white cotton puffs. A perfect fall day.

She wiggled in her seat until she partly faced him. "I sliced up chicken breast and marinated it in this Thai concoction. Then I grilled it—"

"Grilled, as in barbecued?"

"Yes."

"Like, on a real outdoor grill?" He couldn't keep his astonishment from making him sound like a complete and utter asshat.

Little pleats formed between her brows, and she let out a cute snort. "Yes, with flames and everything. Contrary to popular belief, barbecuing is *not* exclusively in the male domain."

"I always thought it was, so I stand corrected … and impressed. What else did you make?" He smiled in spite of the lowered-brow look she leveled at him—or maybe because of it. She was doing the stern thing again, which looked completely out of place on her heart-shaped face. Today her strawberry-blond hair was down, twisted into long spirals that fell over her shoulders and lay glossy against the deep royal blue of her fitted shirt.

"I whipped up some peanut dipping sauce—for the satay, of course."

"Of course," he agreed solemnly.

"Are you teasing me?"

"Absolutely not. I take food very seriously."

She let out a little hmph. "I guess I should have known that after Thanksgiving."

"Exactly. Now what else did you make? I might want to bid on this box."

Even though his focus was on the road, he didn't miss how wide her eyes grew. "You can't do that, can you?"

"Why not? I've got to bid on *someone's* box. Yours is sounding pretty good."

"Oh! I never thought … Well, I just figured I was eating with someone I didn't know."

Not if I can help it. "So what else you got?"

She absentmindedly twirled a thick spiral around her finger, then seemed to cringe. "It's kind of an eclectic mix because I was going for quick and easy. I made Asian cucumber slaw with vinegar dressing, a wild-rice-with-feta-and-cranberries thing, and corn salsa—with *grilled* corn—and tortilla chips."

He glanced over at her, noting how she was biting her lower lip. He almost laughed out loud at the worried look on her face, though he couldn't tell if she was more concerned about eating with a stranger or what that stranger would think of her dinner.

"I'd call that more international than eclectic. Either way, it sounds delicious. Is there dessert?"

"Of course," she scoffed. "Dessert's the best part of the meal. I made chocolate-coconut bars with walnuts."

He made a sloppy slurping noise. "I might have to bid on your box for those alone."

The Denver skyline faded in the rearview mirror, and conversation rolled easily like the wheat-colored plains stretching before them. So easily, in fact, that the more they talked, the more questions bubbled up in his brain. Like about her family and all those stepsiblings. Her car knowledge. Her landscape designs.

"So you're a landscape architect by training. Did you go to college in Colorado?"

"I did," she declared. "I graduated from CSU."

"You stayed local, huh?"

"Yep. How about you? Where did you grow up? And did you go to college or skate straight into professional hockey?"

He chuckled. "I grew up in Utah and attended Colorado College in Colorado Springs, but I quit so I could enter the draft early. Feels like a lifetime ago."

"What were you majoring in?"

He side-eyed her and grinned. "Teaching." Because he'd had no idea what else to pick at the time. The end game had always been hockey.

"Wow! I'm trying to picture you as a teacher. I bet your students would have behaved." She let out a little laugh.

"Maybe. If I'd done the scary Wookiee thing."

Another giggle, then her tone grew more serious. "Your parents must be proud. Are they close by?"

He shook his head. "My dad was a workaholic, and my parents divorced when I was six. My mom lives in Florida near Sonoma's mom—they're twins—and I see her a couple times a year. My dad remarried and started a new family; I have two half brothers. He works in oil and gas, and they live in Singapore, so it's been years since I've seen them. We stay in touch through email, but we're not close."

She shot him an assessing look. "So the overachieving apple doesn't fall far from the overachieving tree?"

"Me? I never looked at it that way, but you might be right. Enough about that, though. Where does someone find a job doing what you do?"

Her eyes slid to the window, and she seemed to go into a dream state. "I didn't. I … opened my own business instead."

"Landscaping with Altitude?"

"Mm-hmm."

Why did he get the feeling there was a lot more to the story? "How did you manage all that?" He couldn't hide the awe in his voice. "I mean, starting out on your own, trying to get clients. You must have put in more hours than you do now. Did you ever sleep?" A chuckle rumbled inside him, but he cut it off when he glanced over at her … because … the look on her face. He was stricken by the sadness in her eyes as she turned toward him. Suddenly, all that *easy* seemed to get sucked out of the truck's interior.

She cast her gaze down to her lap, where her palms were running over her already-smooth jeans. "Now's probably a good time to tell you a few other things about me you don't know. After all, you told me about Nicole and about using the banned meds."

He held his breath.

Eyes back on him now. "I got married right out of college. Will and I … He did the nursery and landscaping side of things, and I did the design work. For a while, it all worked."

Gobsmacked. Was that a real word? If not, it should be because nothing else could describe Dave's shock in that moment. She'd never let on, never mentioned … Shit, she'd been married.

He shifted in his seat. "So what happened?" And now he was prying, but damn, he wanted to know because it didn't sit well with him for some reason.

She shook her head. "Long story short, I surprised him and … one of our employees in the office one day when I was supposed to be on a job site. Needless to say, things fell apart after that."

Jesus! He couldn't think what to say. Mumbling an "I'm sorry" was not only inadequate, it did squat to help her. "How long ago?" he asked instead.

Fingers in her hair, she raked them through her tresses. "A little over two years now, and I'm still trying to fix it. Not only did I catch my husband screwing someone else, but he'd been screwing up the business too. Making commitments to clients he didn't keep, blowing off vendors we owed money, taking money out of our business account to lavish on his, um, dalliance. And I was so … so blind. I didn't see any of it coming."

Dave scrubbed his hand over his jaw. "You're not actually blaming *yourself* for what *he* did, are you?" *Not your fault the guy was a douche of epic proportions.*

Another headshake. "It was my business too. I should have paid more attention. Should have tuned into these little nagging doubts I was having—that's what responsible people do—but I was caught up in my designs and I … didn't. So yeah, I'm partly to blame."

Something twisted inside him to hear her beating herself up over not being "responsible." Hell, she was one of the most responsible people he knew. Work first, fun later, though she never seemed to get around to the fun part. And now maybe he understood why. She'd had a husband, the same partner in all facets of her life. She should have been able to trust the asshole. How was not following up on her "nagging doubts" her fault?

"Not for the affair," he said firmly. He hadn't earned the right to wade in on the business end of her life—not that he was looking for that right.

She wagged her head from side to side as if considering what he said. "Maybe. It turns out I wasn't what he wanted or needed. I should've seen the signs there too, but I missed them."

Dave tried not to gape at her. What she said was so wrong on so many levels. That she could think she was responsible for the guy's wandering dick … He couldn't see it. Who would wander on a girl like this? A light blazed on in his head. "Is this why you're not doing as much design work as you'd like? You're too busy doing the other stuff to keep the business viable?"

"Yep."

"Finn must be a big help?"

Her mouth opened and closed.

"Or not," he quickly added.

"No, he is. I don't want to give you the wrong impression because he's a good guy. He's been helping me pick up the pieces since Will took off, but it was really rough at first. And Finn's had a few wild hairs that have, shall we say, gotten him into trouble." She turned bright eyes to Dave's. "But that's in the past."

A little ball of unease that had been tightening in his gut loosened. "I guess we all have skeletons rattling around in our closets. Some more than others."

"Yes, some definitely more than others." As she said this, she broke eye contact, turning to look at the radio. "Time to find a country station?"

"Sure." The discussion died on the twanging chords of "There Was This Girl" as Riley Green's voice drifted over the speakers. But it didn't kill the feeling Ellie Hendricks was one big Rubik's Cube waiting to be solved. Dave had never been good at geometry, though he found himself wanting to take a crash course.

Chapter 20

Carrie Underwood, Eat Your Heart Out

They'd been bouncing over a rutted, twisting, packed dirt road ever since driving through the ranch entrance fifteen minutes ago. Just as Ellie was convinced there was no home, they turned a hilly corner and a jaw-dropping spread came into view, complete with an iconic red barn, rolling wheat-colored pastures that climbed gentle rises, and miles of crisp white rail fencing. In the midst of it all sprawled a house that was more lodge than it was residence, surrounded by a half dozen smaller-scale replicas. The sun was slung low in the sky, and it gilded the scene in gold. A gasp escaped her.

"Oh my gosh! This is … this is gorgeous!"

She snapped her gaping mouth shut and side-eyed Dave, who sported a frozen frown as he focused on steering the truck into a huge dirt-and-gravel parking area already lined with pickups and SUVs. The slower he went, the louder Rascal Flatts's "Powerful Stuff" blared.

Mumbling, "Nice little place," he hit the volume button on his steering wheel, and the sound of crunching tires replaced the chorus singing how so, so sweet it was.

The lodge, er, *house*, had a deep wraparound porch, and several figures stood under its roof, lost in the long afternoon shadows. Dave parked, and as he helped her climb out of the truck, two of those shadows broke free and headed toward them.

"Hey! You guys finally made it," Sonoma called, Finn ambling behind her.

After she hugged Ellie, she sidled up to Dave, who leaned down for a one-armed hug. "Are we late?"

"No, I was just looking forward to seeing you guys. Uncle Stan's on his way." She fisted her skirt repeatedly as Finn gave Ellie a light punch in the arm and exchanged a gripping manshake thing with Dave.

In the background, guys dressed as cowboys—they probably *were* cowboys—swarmed the barn, and Ellie craned her head, glimpsing an open space inside surrounded by hay bales.

Dave opened the back door of the crew cab and started unloading. In silent man language for "We're big strong men, and we got this, so back off," Finn grabbed whatever Dave handed to him, leaving Ellie in charge of only her purse. She chuckled inside at Finn stepping up to the "gentleman" plate. Usually, she was doing her own schlepping. *Nice change.*

Dave turned, a bag and the cooler in his hands. "You guys get your rooms yet?"

"Yep, we're all set. We're in the main house in the 'lesser rooms.'" Sonoma air-quoted the last two words. "I'll show you yours."

They greeted the people they passed on the porch and stepped into a huge entry. Beyond the entry was an immense vaulted common area done in logs that surrounded a massive stone fireplace. Had she just stepped into the Yellowstone lodge? No, this space was modern, lighter, and someone's actual *living room.* Head on a swivel, she stumbled behind the rest of her party as she took in enormous beams and hand-carved wood scenes. There was even a gigantic tree trunk that seemed to sprout from a stone floor and soar up, up, through the ceiling towering twenty feet above.

By comparison, their rooms were … well, just as Sonoma had described. Lesser. Ellie's was cramped with a full-size, quilt-covered bed. A chair and a small side table sat beside the room's only window. What she gave up in luxury, though, was more than offset by a private bath. Dave's room was next to hers and only a little wider to accommodate a queen-size bed he'd probably have to sleep in diagonally to fit.

But she wasn't complaining. No, she was in a world far different from the one she normally spent time in, and suddenly her heart lifted, feeling more and more like a helium balloon bumping along the clouds. She'd escaped the "usual" for a little while and was on the verge of maybe, possibly, having fun.

"Do you have your box dinner, Ellie?" Sonoma asked from the hall outside both rooms. "I'll take it and put it with the others."

Dave bent down to the cooler and retrieved Ellie's box, which he handed to Sonoma. Now that she saw it in someone's else's hands, Ellie realized how drab it looked. She was going for country elegance, but she'd missed by a mile. Hopefully, it didn't get stuck next to anything colorful, or the thing would get lost.

"Careful with how you handle that." Dave threw Ellie a wink. "We have a very eclectic meal in there."

Prize in hand, Sonoma nodded, and soon she and Finn were headed down the hall, their heads together as though they were hatching a diabolical plan.

Ellie leaned against her door frame. "What do you think those two are up to?"

Dave rearranged his bag and cooler on the floor, then glanced around. "No good, I'm sure. Looks like you get the only bathroom."

"Feel free to use it when you need to."

He stared at her a moment, thoughts seeming to whir behind those hawk-intense eyes.

"Like, if you want to shower before the dance, for instance," she clarified, then embarrassingly added, "But be aware there's a strict no-toilet-seats-up rule in effect." *Epic humor fail, El. Why did I just say that?*

A slow smile spread. "I might just do that. And don't worry. I'm well aware of the 'leave-no-toilet-seat-up' regulations."

Right. Because you lived with a drop-dead-gorgeous model once. Way to kill the fun, El. Sheesh. I need a drink because … ugh … no matter how pretty the dress and boots, I still *can't do clever banter or dance!*

"Why don't we head downstairs, find Nome and Finn, and check this place out? I could use a beer. You?"

"I think I need a whole six-pack," she muttered.

His dark brows crashed together. "Everything okay?"

"Yes," she chirped a little too boisterously. "I'm just … I'm a little nervous about the whole dancing thing."

Now those brows inched up his forehead. "Don't be. Half the people here have never square-danced. Besides, it's not that complicated, *and* I'm betting lots of folks will be liquored up, so they won't notice someone else's moves."

She raised her hand as though she were answering a question in class. "I think I'd like to be one of those liquored-up people. Then maybe I won't notice my *own* dance moves … um, non-moves."

He threw his head back, and a deep laugh rolled through his chest, reminding her of thunder. "Then we'd better hurry and find the alcohol, although I suspect that in your case it won't take much."

She stuck her chin in the air. "Are you calling me a lightweight?"

"No, ma'am. Just saying you're light in weight, so it probably doesn't take as much as it would, say, for someone like me or Finn."

She hooked her thumbs in her belt loops. All she needed to complete the look was a piece of straw dangling from her teeth. "I'll have you know I've bent elbows with the men folk sitting around in the garage talking cars."

"When you were *ten*?" He coughed out a laugh as he led them down the stairs and onto the porch.

Wow. He *had* been paying attention when she'd told him about her dad marrying Finn's mom. Before she could muster a clever comeback, Finn and Sonoma waved at them. They stood beside a galvanized water trough filled with iced adult beverages, talking with a tall, middle-aged, birdlike man with a bad comb-over. On his other side was a plump, mahogany-haired woman about his vintage.

Dave placed his fingers in the small of Ellie's back and propelled her toward the foursome. "Uncle Stan," he called, his hand shooting out for a shake. The gawky man—Uncle Stan—grinned and clasped Dave's hand. They did the man-hug-pat thing before Dave stooped to embrace the woman and plant a kiss on her cheek. "Aunt Viv, it's great to see you."

Just as Ellie was contemplating ducking away from the family reunion, Dave introduced her. His Aunt Viv had a way of smiling that made her cheeks pull up and her eyes squint, like every muscle in her face was playing a part in that smile. It radiated happiness. "Looking forward to the box social, Ellie?"

"Um, yes."

"Ellie doesn't dance, so I think she's a little nervous," Dave explained.

Aunt Viv's fingers brushed Ellie's arms. "Don't you worry. Dave will have you dancing as though you've been doing it your whole life."

Ellie tilted her head and smiled. "That's what I keep hearing. Hopefully, I don't break his toes."

They all laughed at this, except Finn, who smirked. She recognized that look. It said, "They don't know how bad you really are, El."

Soon they all had beers, and Ellie chugged half of hers down to soothe her parched throat. If Dave noticed, he didn't say a word. In fact, he was already going for his second.

"So it sounds like they might have some trouble with the room situation," Stan said. "You kids have yours already, right?"

Everyone nodded.

"What kind of trouble, Uncle Stan?" Sonoma asked.

"Seems a passel of unexpected relatives showed up, and our hosts are scrambling to find them someplace to sleep."

They caught up on family and small-talked. Ellie had polished off her second beer when the conversation broke up, and everyone retreated to their rooms. Dave walked her upstairs, telling her he'd shower in Finn's bathroom so she'd have plenty of time to get ready.

Right. Get ready.

Ellie showered, pulled on a lacy panty-and-bra set she'd bought as a last-minute splurge, and tugged the new dress over her head. Stopped and stared in the battered mirror above the bathroom sink. Sighed and plopped on the edge of the mattress. Why had it looked so much better in the store than it did in this room?

A soft knock and a feminine voice on the other side had her flinging open the door to Sonoma, whose blue eyes sparkled with mischief. "Brought a little makeup and a curling wand in case your spirals need extra twists. And most importantly, this." She waved an open bottle of rosé under Ellie's nose.

"I don't know if you have enough magic to transform this pumpkin, Sonoma, but the wine will be good for blurring my vision so I can't see. And blurring my brain so I don't care." She laughed as she took the bottle from Sonoma and waved her in.

Sonoma pulled wineglasses from a big pouch she'd tucked under her arm and began laying out beauty supplies on the quilt. "What are you talking about? I'm starting with a beautiful canvas. Not too many brushstrokes needed to make it a masterpiece."

Something about what Sonoma said and the way she said it soothed Ellie's ragged nerves. Ellie splashed a generous amount of wine in each glass, then sat back to let Sonoma work her magic.

After fifteen minutes, they were on their second glass of wine, and Sonoma was hovering her own mirror in front of Ellie's face. "I didn't need to touch your hair. As for the makeup, you don't wear much, so I kept it light. A little blush, a silvery-gray shadow to pop your eyes, and some mascara to plump those long lashes. What do you think?"

Ellie blinked at herself. "I can't believe that's me! I looked horrible in the bathroom mirror just a few minutes ago."

"Yeah, well, that's the *bathroom* mirror, and it's not going to make *anyone* look good." She downed a sip of wine and wiggled her eyebrows. "But *this*. Dave's gonna have a hard time keeping his eyes off you."

A laugh punched from Ellie's chest. "I'm sure he'll have no problem, especially with the women he's *used* to looking at." *Shit. I busted myself.* The talk about Will's rejection on the way here had stirred up Ellie's feelings of inadequacy that always swam just below the surface, nibbling away at her confidence in herself. Being a killer landscaper was one thing, but an attractive woman? Not so much.

Sonoma's eyes narrowed, and Ellie gave her a sheepish look. "I *might* have seen pictures of him on the Internet with supermodel women. And his last girlfriend was … wow."

One side of Sonoma's mouth curled up. "You like my cousin, don't you? God, please say you do."

Now Ellie squirmed. "I'll admit I like him more than I did at first. He's sort of … grown on me."

"He does that. Grows on people like toe fungus," Sonoma snorted. "But yeah, he cleans up pretty well. He refused to do that until he met you, you know."

Ellie masked her surprise with a hefty gulp of her own. "Anyway, I see pictures of him with women like Nicole, and I get it. He could have anyone he wants. And next to their star-power, two-thousand-lumens-halogen-floodlight looks, I'm a dim seven-watt landscape bulb."

Sonoma caught Ellie's hand in hers. "Listen to me. First of all, no one's comparing you to her, except you. And yeah, she was a stunner … on the outside. Inside, she's as shallow as a kiddie pool."

"You didn't like her," Ellie said matter-of-factly.

Sonoma released her hand and emptied the rest of the wine into their glasses. "I didn't like her. She wouldn't give me the time of day unless she was working Dave over for something, and then she was so syrupy I wanted to gag. But I could see through her games, and I called her on it. She didn't like that. Unfortunately, he was blind to it all. Probably still is."

"But there had to be something there besides her looks. I don't know him that well, but he doesn't strike me as the type of guy who goes strictly for arm candy." Ellie's heart sank under the weight of the possibility that maybe he *was* the kind of guy who wanted the trophy girl.

A sigh dropped Sonoma's shoulders an inch. "I've been telling him for years to look beyond the flash before letting himself get hooked. He's been more interested in style over substance. Nicky was also really good at playing hard-to-get, and he fell for it. By the time he figured it out, she had him wound so tight he didn't know how to *unwind* himself." Sonoma finished off her wine and began gathering her stuff into her pouch. "A couple things to know about Dave. First, he needs very little feeding and watering to make him happy. He comes across as this tough, gruff, grumpy bear, but deep down, he's the marshmallow man. What he really wants is someone he can look after, someone he can shower with attention.

"Second, he protects people he cares about. To. A. Fault. He makes excuses for them and turns a blind eye. Sticks his head in the sand and holds out until he can't breathe anymore. He'd make a really good ostrich." She paused to tee-hee, and Ellie giggled with her. "I was so happy when Nicky broke up with him. It sounds mean, but he's so much better off without her. And I don't think he would've walked away, so she did him a huge favor. I just worry …"

Ellie rocked her mostly empty wineglass on a side table and fished out some hoop earrings. "You worry about what?"

"Oh, just that she'll realize how good she had it and try to reel him back in."

One of the hoops slipped from Ellie's fingers and bounced on the floor. She turned wide eyes to Sonoma. "You think he'd go back to her after everything that happened?"

"I hope not, but there's always a chance he hasn't learned his lesson. Plus, I think she still has the power to yank his chain. Of course, if he were seeing someone else …" There was that gleam in Sonoma's eyes again.

"You can't possibly mean me," Ellie blurted.

Sonoma tucked her pouch of goodies under her arm, cracked the door open, and pivoted. "Why not? You're flash *and* substance." Then she slipped into the hall. "See you downstairs."

Ellie stuck her head out and sang after her. "Thank you!" She swiveled her head to Dave's door, relieved it was closed.

Stomach churning, she retreated into her room, where she expelled a wine-laden breath. Sonoma had just been trying to boost her ego. It was in her hairdresser nature. Beyond that, Ellie couldn't decide which of Sonoma's comments had unsettled her more. And she didn't want to consider *why* any of them had bugged her in the first place, so she shoved them to a back corner of her brain.

He's not interested. Just get over yourself.

As she dabbed perfume behind her ears and between her breasts, she pondered the night ahead. Were the fluttery sensations in her tummy from beating butterfly wings? The wine? Or were they snails coiling tighter and tighter? And what was making her more nervous? *Dancing* with Dave, or dancing *with* Dave?

She eyed the rest of her wine and downed it. *Liquid courage.* Then she sat on the edge of the bed and pulled on her cowboy boots. One last smoothing of her hair and dress, one last glimpse in the mirror that had her waving herself off, and she took a deep breath and sailed out her door before she could change her mind.

The burble of people grew louder the closer she came to the rail overlooking the great room below. It was filled with a sea of cowboy hats and women in brightly colored outfits. Most held a drink of some kind, and she recognized none of them. *Why didn't I wait for Sonoma?* A tentative step on the landing, then down to the first step. A few sets of eyes turned her way, and she suddenly felt like *that* girl sweeping into the ball after everyone else has arrived. The grand entrance. Not at all what she'd intended. Maybe if she ran back to her room on the pretext of—

Below, a cowboy doffed his hat and gave her a white-toothed smile accented by a dimple. Ooh, he was cute. Beside him, a bigger, broader guy dressed in a western shirt looked up and winked. *Oh hell! Nothing like being on display. But hey, it's pretty good for the old ego.* The first cowboy placed his hat over his heart, cocked his head, and kept his eyes trained on her. She couldn't turn and run now, so she took another step down. A warm, rough hand circling her upper arm possessively startled her.

"Sonoma didn't lie about that dress," Dave whispered beside her, his warm breath washing over her ear and down her neck. Goose bumps she prayed he couldn't feel erupted beneath his fingers.

She craned her neck and looked up. His eyes were focused somewhere below, and he sported a spectacular scowl totally at odds with the warm notes of his voice. Nonetheless, breath stalled in her chest because Lordy! He was all hot man and hard muscle decked out in a fitted black western shirt embroidered in silver on the shoulders and cuffs. On top of his head perched a black felt cowboy hat adorned with a small silver buckle on one side. Completing the outfit were black leather cowboy boots and a pair of low-riding jeans held up by a simple western belt.

Ellie had never been into cowboys, but it occurred to her she should reconsider because this tower of male perfection beside her was positively delectable. Bite-worthy.

She'd been so shamelessly ogling him that she didn't notice his stare had shifted to *her*. The scowl was gone, but his eyes held an unmistakable intensity as they blatantly blazed a trail up and down her body. Next came an expression she could only label as ravenous. Heat rose from her chest, up her neck, threatening to set fire to her cheeks.

Suddenly, the hungry look vanished, masked by a cough and a polite half-smile. "You look really nice," he said.

Oh man, so did he. Dancing was just about to become more difficult.

Keeping hold of her arm, he began walking her down the stairs. When she looked to where the cute cowboy and his buddy had been standing, they were nowhere in sight.

Chapter 21

Courtesy Turn

Dancing was going to be damn hard if he had to deal with a boner all night. *Jesuuuuus!* Dave had a firm grip of Ellie's arm—*yeah, that's right, assholes, she's with me*—making it awkward to gawk at her more than he already had. Which was a good thing.

He squelched an inner groan. Where had this girl been all his life, and why did he have to crash into her to meet her?

Questions for another time because right now they were heading into the barn to check out the display of boxed dinners, and he needed to focus on keeping distance between her and the two pervs who'd been eye-fucking her. And if he could help it, keeping them far away from *her* dinner because damn it, it was his. The only other guy he'd let buy it was Finn, and that was only on the condition Dave bought Sonoma's.

"Hey, you two," came Sonoma's cheerful voice from behind them. She was decked out in bright green, and beside her, Finn looked a little uptight in his starchy white western shirt with sharp creases from its packaged fold lines.

While the girls oohed and aahed over their outfits, Finn cooed in a high singsong, "Oh, Dave, I just *lurve* your hat. Can I borrow it sometime?"

Dave pinched Finn's sleeve and falsettoed, "And I just *adore* your new shirt. Bargain Barn special?" In his straight voice, he added, "Looks like you put it on straight out of the package, man."

Finn shrugged good-naturedly and gave Dave a pointed look. "Yeah, well, some of us don't spend all our time pretending to be cowboys."

"Hey," Dave protested, "I already had these. Just needed to liberate them from the mothballs." *Yeah, not really.* The shirt and hat were new, but he wasn't about to fess up to *anyone.*

Sonoma tilted her head toward the stage. "Looks like Uncle Stan's running the auction."

Dave glanced over, and, sure enough, his aunt was helping his uncle get ready on stage. *Yes!* Dave would use that family connection to his unfair advantage if he had to. Whatever it took.

"Oh, there they are!" Ellie squealed beside him and pointed at her boxed dinner along with, he presumed, Sonoma's. A few eyes swung Ellie's way, including the ones belonging to the dimpled, pretty-boy cowboy Dave wanted to use as a punching bag.

So much for keeping her dinner on the down-low.

The four of them ambled toward the boxes, neatly numbered and nestled among other containers, and Dave glanced around himself like a super-secret boxed-supper spy. No one seemed to be watching them.

"Oh, Sonoma, yours is so pretty." Ellie's wistful tone tugged a protective chord inside him. The girls inspected Sonoma's splashy fluorescent-pink-and-black box bedecked in bows and shiny studs. Ellie let out a laugh. "Can I borrow one of your bows? My box is waaaaay too plain."

"It's perfect the way it is," Dave scoffed, hopeful its very plainness meant no one else would notice it.

"Yeah?" Ellie looked up at Dave, a bright smile curving her lips and lighting her eyes. He sucked in a breath before he knew what he was doing, and those big blue eyes got even bigger. "Is everything okay? Did you forget something?" Her hand flew nervously to her hair. "Or maybe it's me? Do I look okay?"

Shit! Does she think there's something wrong with the way she looks? Not a chance. "You look more than okay. In fact, you look *so* okay I'm wondering how many guys I'm going to have to fight off."

Behind Ellie, Sonoma threw him an epic eye-roll and a sarcastic, silent hand clap. He ignored her, focusing instead on the pretty blush pinking Ellie's cheeks that made him want to kiss them. God, he wished he was smoother with his words. If he were, he'd tell her just what seeing her in that pretty, flowery dress and those smoking-hot red boots did to him. Hell, if he were to slide from smooth to crude—and crude was much closer to the side of the fence he was currently standing on—he'd just put her hand on his crotch so she could tell for herself. Thank fuck Uncle Stan's voice boomed over the speakers and saved him from making an even bigger dumbass of himself.

"We have some attractive dinner boxes to auction off tonight, but the real prize is the lovely woman who goes with each one, so prepare to dig deep, gentlemen!" A round of applause, and then he got down to it with the bang of his gavel. He called out box number one, a fancy little number that Aunt Viv brought on stage to show off to prospective bidders. And so the competition began.

About halfway through, the pretty cowboy and his buddy had yet to bid on a box, but now as Sonoma's box came up for its turn, both men seemed to take interest. Oblivious, she exchanged a look with Finn, and the bidding started. After a few moments of back-and-forth between Finn and Pretty Cowboy's buddy, Dave leaned in to Finn's ear. "I'll cover you if you need—"

"I got this," Finn assured him, "but thanks, man."

Okay. So maybe Finn was a righteous dude after all. Dave would cut him some slack, especially after the guy shelled out a whopping grand for Sonoma's dinner. And the look on her face when he did it? Priceless.

Several boxes later, Ellie's brown one made it on stage. Aunt Viv's hand gestures were as animated as Dave had seen them. Was she doing a hard sell, compensating for what she perceived as lack of glitz? Beside him, he was pretty sure Ellie flinched. He *definitely* heard the sharp breath she drew in.

"And here we have this box that's beautiful in its simplicity," Uncle Stan crooned into the microphone. "You know what they say about plain brown wrappers. They hide the most gorgeous secrets." He waggled his eyebrows and got laughs from the crowd. "What am I bid?"

Surprisingly—and disappointingly—a number of hands went up, including those belonging to Cowboy Pretty and his friend. They elbowed each other and grinned. *WTF?* Didn't take long for the price to climb into the mid-hundreds. Beside Dave, Ellie bounced on her heels, her head on a swivel, a happy little smile on her face. Damn! He wasn't the one putting it there. Worse, Pretty Boy might have been the responsible party. Dave had glimpsed the douchenugget stealing glances at her, winking at her once when he'd caught her eye. The guy was pissing Dave off—and apparently messing with his head because before Dave had had a chance to put his hand up, the damn dinner was pushing a thousand.

Uncle Stan practically cackled with glee. "That's it! Keep up the bidding, boys. I think I know which girl goes with this box, and you will *not* be disappointed. Remember, not only do you get the dinner *and* the pretty girl, but it's for a good cause!"

Uncle Stan, so not helping.

Pretty Cowboy cut Dave a look and smirked like the entitled rich kid Dave was pretty sure he was. *Oh hell no!* He leaned down to Ellie's ear, and her fragrance invaded his senses and made him more determined than he already was. "I'll be right back. You'll be okay here with Finn and Sonoma?"

"Yes," she giggled back. "Isn't this great?"

No, it really isn't. But I'm about to change that.

He strode—no, strutted like a damn rooster—up to the stage and pulled a check from his wallet, which he waved at his uncle. "I have an insurance check here that I've been instructed to use for my favorite charity. In exchange for that dinner"—he pointed at Ellie's brown box—"I'll sign it over to Heifer International."

Aunt Viv bent down and plucked the check from his fingers, her eyes going saucer-wide. She flapped it at Stan. "It's over five thousand dollars!" she gasped.

"And," Dave bellowed, spinning slowly until he locked on Pretty Boy with his best don't-fuck-with-me glare, "I'm personally tripling that amount." Pretty Boy's eyes widened, then narrowed, and he gave Dave the immense satisfaction of a fuming scowl. Dave turned his glower back to Stan, who swiftly brought the gavel down with a "Sold!"

When the applause died down, Stan shook his head, grinned, and pointed the gavel at Dave. "Viv, give the box to the crazy cowboy right there."

Dave winked at her as she handed it over. "Thanks, Aunt Viv," he said in a low voice no one else could hear.

She beamed back at him. "Have fun."

He strode back to Ellie, who stood frozen in the spot where he'd left her. Sonoma hugged his arm, Finn clapped him on the back, but Ellie just looked dazed. Box in one hand, he pointed at it with the other. "This yours?"

A dazzling smile broke out on her face. "You know it is! And what a way to use the insurance check." God, the way she was looking at him made him feel like fucking Superman *despite* the silly cowboy clothes.

"So you approve?"

She wagged her head from side to side, her glossy curls moving with her. "A little over the top, but yes, I approve."

"Well, good, because I wanted to eat with the prettiest girl here. Let's go."

This time the smile Sonoma gave him was genuine and broadcast her thumbs-up, which he shouldn't have needed, but it sure felt good to have nonetheless.

He snagged a bottle of wine from a bartender's station, and Finn grabbed glasses. The four of them meandered to an out-of-the-way flagstone patio beside an outdoor fireplace, and Dave made a big show of opening Ellie's boxed dinner.

"Oh wow," he enthused. "Chicken satay. And grilled corn salsa. *Exactly* what I was hoping for."

She smacked his arm playfully. He could get used to this.

The bars were excellent, and the rest of the meal was decent—he thought of a few things he'd do differently had he prepared it himself—but he really didn't care. It wasn't about the food. All he wanted was to see the smile on Ellie's face every time he looked at her and know *he'd* put it there. *That* was more than worth the price tag.

They polished off their meals and the wine as music began playing in the barn. He stood, pulling Ellie up with him. Her happy face dissolved into sheer panic. "I don't think I've had enough to drink yet," she whispered harshly.

He stifled a laugh. "Then let's get you some more to drink." He could use a few stiff belts himself. "But honestly? There's nothing to worry about. Look, Stan asked Sonoma and me to dance with a few folks in the beginning to get everyone warmed up. You and Finn can watch from the side. You'll see the steps are a piece of cake." A thought struck him. "Unless you really don't want to dance, and then we'll find something else to do." A clip of him kissing her behind a haystack zoomed through his mind, and he quickly added, "Like go for a hayride." *With a boatload of people so I don't do anything stupid.*

Another stop at the bartender's, where Ellie got a vodka and tonic this time—because it was refreshing, she said—and he reluctantly left her behind with Finn while he beelined for an older lady clapping on the sidelines. She had a pleasant look about her, like his mom or Aunt Viv. *She looks like she wants to dance.* A quick look around for the pretty cowboy, and he relaxed and led the giggling lady onto the dance floor. From the stage, Uncle Stan gave him an approving nod. Yep, Dave was racking up all kinds of points tonight.

He and Sonoma completed two reels with different people, the rhythm and steps coming as though they'd done this just last week. He kept his eye on Ellie, who waved and smiled from the sidelines. At least she didn't look like a rabbit ready to bolt anymore. When the dance floor filled and their duties were over, he sent Sonoma toward Finn and Ellie, then detoured to the bar.

While he waited for their drinks, a hand clapped his shoulder, and he spun to see Pretty Cowboy's buddy grinning at him. The guy stuck his hand out. "You're the Grim Reaper! I thought there was something familiar about you. At first, I didn't recognize you without—"

"The beard and the hair," Dave finished for him dryly.

"Yeah, plus you're sporting a full set of teeth." The guy put his hands up as if surrendering. "Which I totally get. I mean, there's hockey, and then there's social time with your girl. And speaking of your girl, I wanted to apologize on behalf of my friend. I only bid because he wanted to drive the price up to where no one else would bid." Then the guy chortled. "Man, he never saw you coming! You sure pissed him off with your stunt."

Yeah, well, your buddy pissed me *off.* "Maybe he shouldn't try to horn in on another man's girl. Life will be much less disappointing—and safer—for him that way, if you catch my drift."

"Totally. I think he's off somewhere licking his wounds, but if I find him, I'll be sure he steers clear of your girl if he wants to see tomorrow."

Not my girl, but he doesn't need to know that. The guy seemed about to ask for an autograph or a selfie or something fan-related, so Dave grabbed up the drinks as soon as the bartender slid them over. He gave Cowboy's friend a grim nod. "You do that." Sometimes life was a little easier when people believed you were badass.

Chapter 22

Do Not Watch His Hips

"Hey, party girl, how you holding up?" Finn grinned down at Ellie as they watched the dancing from where they stood beside hay bales surrounding the dance floor. Her boots were tapping, and her body was rocking in time with the music. But her real focus was on Dave promenading a perpetually smiling fifty-ish lady on the hay-strewn barn floor. On a raised platform, Stan half sang, half called, accompanied by Viv on drums and two guys on the fiddle and bass. Ellie tried not to think about the way Dave's hips moved. She tried to lock out the wicked thoughts Beth "Square Dance Store" Not-Chapman had planted in her brain. Sadly, it wasn't working, and soon she'd have to take a check-for-drool break.

God, she was still tingling from his forceful purchase of her dinner box. Lordy, the way he'd taken command of the entire place had left her breathless! All because he wanted *her* supper, and he'd put a gob of money smack where his mouth was. It was enough to make a girl's head spin right off her neck. *My hero*, she thought sappily to herself. Not to mention how during dinner he'd praised her less-than-stellar "eclectic" meal and told her the real reason he'd bought her the clothes was because he wanted to show off the "prettiest girl here." *Prettiest girl here?* Hardly. In the past, a comment like that would have made her eyes roll or caused her to break out in a skeptical smirk before running away. But his compliments didn't sound like lines. Instead, ribbons of warmth had woven themselves around her heart and had yet to loosen their hold. He was different, this Grim Reaper. All male and not shy about owning it. No apologies. Knowing what he wanted and going after it. A man of action. She found herself intoxicated by his blend of raw power and tenderness, irretrievably drawn to him like she'd never been drawn to anyone before. And the way he moved his hips had her thinking all kinds of naughty things she shouldn't be thinking. *Yeah, I bet he owns it in the bedroom too.*

"Great! I'm great," she announced a little too cheerfully.

"Okay," Finn laughed. "As long as you're *great*! Seriously, El, you look like you're having fun, and that's really good to see."

She took another sip of her V and T. It was almost empty. No doubt the alcohol she'd consumed had something to do with the *great* time she was having, but she suspected it was more than that. The good-looking hockey captain cowboy in front of her might be playing a part. No, absolutely *was* playing a part. A quick look around the place told her she wasn't the only one admiring him. In fact, right after he escorted the first lady off the dance floor, a younger, prettier one asked him to dance with *her*, and he obliged. And sheesh, this one could actually dance. *I wonder if I'll get him back sometime tonight?*

Not a moment later, it seemed, he was there, eyebrow cocked and hand extended toward her in invitation. Oh no! If getting him back meant having to dance … She rose up on tiptoe and pretended to look over his shoulder. "I think I see someone else who'd like to dance with you."

He shook his head. "Too bad. I'm not dancing with her."

In Ellie's peripheral vision, Finn let Sonoma lead him off—hell, he practically *ran* after her—so Ellie gulped a breath, set her drink down, and took Dave's hand. *Oh God! Here we go.*

"Do what I do," he instructed.

"Not what your uncle says to do?"

"Listen to him in the background to get a feel for the steps, but until you know what those are, follow my lead."

Right. And try not to stomp on his feet, El. Dave led her toward three other couples who were forming into a square. When he squeezed her hand and grinned down at her, some of her nervousness dissolved away, replaced by a different sort of tummy flutter.

The first move wasn't so bad because they merely walked around the invisible square, him guiding her with one hand around her waist and the other holding her hand. *Easy peasy.* Not to mention it felt really good. But then things sped up, and there was a moment when he was pulling her past him—or trying to—and rather than sliding to his side, she crashed right into him, and yes—*oh God!*—managed to step on his foot. He laughed, and on the next pull by manhandled her so she had no doubt which way she was supposed to go. Ooh, she liked that! But then he handed her off to a different partner, and oh God! She did it again. In fact, she ended up turning in a circle and somehow backing into the guy. And stepping on his foot.

The man cradled her lightly in his arms for a split second before setting her straight with a chuckle. "Your first time?" he asked as he promenaded her.

"It's obvious, huh?"

"We've all been there. Just relax and enjoy yourself. No one's judging you. In fact, look around. This is the first time for plenty of people here."

Same thing Dave keeps telling me. With that, the man handed her off to the next one. This time she heard Stan sing something about a "right pull by," and the man's right hand grasped her right hand as he pulled her past to her next dance partner. *Oh! Got it.* Except *this* guy was almost as inexperienced as she was, and they ended up flubbing whatever the next part was supposed to be and bumping into each other. She didn't step on him, though, so … progress!

"And here I was counting on you to show *me* what to do," he said with a smile. She fizzed with laughter, and before she knew it, she was beside Dave again. *Thank God!* A moment of reprieve while the couples faced each other in the square, and she darted a look to Finn in the next square. He rolled his eyes at her and shook his head. *Oh, shut up!*

"You're doing great," Dave reassured her right before they launched into the next steps. She stepped on his foot *again*, causing her to stumble and land against his hard chest. Without missing a beat, he propped her up and propelled her to where she was supposed to be. "I think you did that on purpose." His whisper was low, but she could hear the smile in it. Before she could protest, he was handing her off to someone else. Soon she was hurtling toward him again, and he gave her the universal V sign with his middle and index fingers, pointing at her eyes first, then at his. "Eyes up here." Then his arm was back around her waist, her hand nestled in his. "You're getting the hang of it. You didn't step on me that time."

Before she knew it, she was twirling and pulling by and nailing courtesy turns and ladies' chains without getting her two feet tangled with anyone else's. Self-consciousness flitted away, cut loose, and she let herself go, utterly lost in the joy and the music and the fun. And the best part? Feeling Dave's big hand on her waist, or grabbing his iron-muscled forearm, or resting her hand on his impossibly square shoulder. He was all hard, hot man, and the woman in her—the one she thought she'd lost—sparked to life.

By the time they'd run through more dances, her sides ached from laughing, her cheeks from smiling, and her lungs from the workout. Tingles raced through her bloodstream. Was this foreplay? Every time Dave's eyes landed on hers, she could almost believe it was. And that hip flexing action? She tried not to look, she really did. Tried not to notice how sure and fluid his movements were because they made her more hot and bothered than the dancing did.

Stan announced the band was taking a short break and put on some recorded music for a *line dance*. What the hell was a line dance? Before she could ask—or bolt—she was next to Dave in a row of people that included Finn and Sonoma on her other side while "Boot Scootin' Boogie" blared through the speakers. And oh my God! It took her more than halfway through the song to get the sequence of the steps, but she didn't care because … it was a blast! When Alan Jackson's "Good Time" came on, Dave cocked her an eyebrow, and she let him know in no uncertain terms she was staying on the dance floor. He shrugged, dropped his hat on her head, and gave her a face-splitting grin that shot more shivers straight to her toes. She grabbed the brim with both hands and watched his moves unabashedly while falling in line.

Another song, and Stan was back. Ellie excused herself to find the little cowgirls' room, grabbing her jean jacket on her way out of the barn. With her business out of the way and after she'd slicked on a little more gloss, she wobbled back toward the barn along a dimly lit path in the crisp night air. A warm hand closed around her arm, and she turned, all kinds of happy when she realized the hand belonged to Dave.

"Where did you come from?"

"Just keeping an eye on you." His mouth curved up, and the look in those intense eyes of his … A series of shivers that had nothing to do with the temperature raced from her toes to her crown.

"Cold? We can go inside or head back to the house," he offered.

"No, I'm good. Maybe if we walked for a minute …" Lordy, her head started a sudden spin she hoped would stop with some fresh air.

Dave swept his hand in front of him in an "after-you" gesture, and they angled onto a pavestone path illuminated by landscape fixtures made of hammered bronze. Her uneven steps had her walking right into him and bouncing off.

He put an arm around her shoulders and steadied her. "Still trying to stomp on my toes?"

"Sorry. Just lost my balance for a sec."

He kept that wonderfully warm, strong arm on her shoulders and guided her to a clump of leafless trees beside a chiminea glowing with gentle flames. She held her hands out to warm them.

"So what do you think of square dancing now?" he asked.

"I love it!" She paused when a warm chuckle rumbled through his chest. "Maybe that's because I'm dancing with a real cowboy."

"I'm no cowboy." He flicked the brim of the hat she'd forgotten she was wearing.

She arched a brow. "No? Maybe a cowboy without the cow, then."

He let a laugh slip out. "Which would make me a boy."

"No! That's not what I meant." Hopefully, he couldn't see the blazing blush speeding across her face.

The timbre of his voice dropped into husky-and-deep territory. "Then what *did* you mean?" The firelight lit his face enough that the gleam in his eyes was unmistakable. He was enjoying making her squirm. For some unfathomable reason, her mind leapt to him all hot and sweaty during the after-game interview. From there, it bounded to him making her squirm in a wholly inappropriate way.

"I meant, um … Actually, I'm not sure *what* I meant, but you're the farthest thing from a boy I've ever seen." *Ellie, you dork!* God, she must have been the darkest shade of boiled lobster by now.

He stared at her a moment, the humor in his expression replaced by something altogether different. The odd notion that she was the puck and he was skating right at her crossed her muddled mind, and her heart did a quiver-bump thing. *So* many images flooded her brain at once.

He jarred her from her ridiculous thoughts by adjusting the hat. "Better," he said softly. "Although *without* the hat …" He whisked it off her head and plopped it on his, then smoothed her hair and tucked a few strands behind her ear. She closed her eyes, relishing the brush of his warm fingers. Unexpected chills cascaded down her neck and spine, spilling over her shoulders and arms. Somehow, her hand was in his, and when her eyelids fluttered open, he was *there*, eyes locked on hers, his lips one warm breath away.

His gaze dipped to her mouth. Then he cupped her head and whispered, "Ellie," right before his lips landed on hers, gentle, warm, a slow yet determined slide.

Her hands glided up his chest, skimming over the hard planes beneath his shirt before she fisted the fabric, rose on tiptoe, and pulled herself closer. The hand at the back of her head tangled in her hair while his other hand released hers and coasted over her waist to the small of her back. His fingers splayed wide, leaving a heat print through the thin fabric of her dress.

He pulled back, a little breathless. "I've wanted to do that for a while."

Dazed though she was, she couldn't mask her incredulity as she stared up at him. "You have?"

He didn't answer—not with words anyway. His lips quirked in a half-smile before they were back on hers with a softness she could sink into. A nudge against her lips, and she opened for him, welcoming his languid exploration of her mouth as he held her, practically cradling her body to his. Like his dancing, every careful caress of his tongue and hands was measured, fluid, thorough. And mind-meltingly sensual. She'd never been kissed like this before—as if he were mapping her mouth, making love to it—and heat pooled deep inside her like a magma lake threatening to expand and overflow.

She fought the urge to climb him, instead snaking her hands to his shoulders, up the back of his neck, until her fingers found purchase in his soft, silky hair. His hold on her tightened, and a humming growl came from deep in his throat. She was engulfed in his warmth, in his smoky whiskey taste, and his woods-and-spice man scent. Her knees turned watery, and she vaguely wondered if they would give out, sending her slithering down the length of his body.

"Dave? You out here?"

Untangling his mouth from hers, he let out a sigh and placed a soft kiss on her forehead. As he pivoted away, he swore under his breath. "Over here, Nome."

Oh God, had Sonoma seen them? No, because she was peering into the darkness. "Oh! There you are." Then she called over her shoulder, "Finn, they're over here," and Finn loped out of the shadows.

Ellie whooshed out a silent breath as disappointment settled on her shoulders. Telling herself Sonoma's appearance was probably for the best because … that smokin' hot kiss! How on earth would Ellie ever cool down and fall asleep tonight?

Sonoma had the worst fucking timing. Or maybe the best. Dave *knew* better than to do what he'd just done, but he hadn't been able to stop himself. Especially after Ellie told him he was the farthest thing from a boy she'd ever seen in that shy-sexy voice she occasionally let loose—the one that turned his brain to melted butter and pulled his insides out. The thought she'd meant he was more Wookiee than human had streaked through his brain, but he'd opted for a more flattering interpretation and run with it. Then he'd pulled his hat off her head. Between the tousled strawberry waves that had him wondering if that's what she looked like in bed and those great big blue eyes staring up at him, it had been game over. Electricity had rocketed through him, and he couldn't resist a taste of that full, moist mouth he'd been looking at and thinking about all night. Just one taste. One nibble. One.

Yeah, good thing Sonoma showed up when she did.

"We've been looking all over for you guys," Sonoma exclaimed as she joined them beside the chiminea.

"We were inspecting the chiminea." Ellie grinned up at him, and damn if he didn't grin right back like his idiotic lovestruck teammates.

One of Sonoma's burgundy eyebrows arched. Now Finn joined them, his eyes bouncing between him and Sonoma. Sonoma glanced at Finn before she plowed ahead. "So here's the thing. Remember those unexpected relatives Uncle Stan mentioned? Well, the hosts finally found them some rooms." She sucked in a breath. "Yours and mine."

Dave shook his head. "I don't follow."

"They moved you out of your room and me out of mine and gave them to a great-grandma and a couple of Aunt Ednas."

"Wait. *What?*"

"I guess the host thought we could either bunk together or drive home."

Well, shit. "I've had too much to drink. I can't drive," he squawked.

Sonoma shook her head solemnly. "And neither can Finn or I. But we came up with a solution." She darted her eyes at Finn again.

Uh-oh. Not a good sign.

But instead of Sonoma continuing, Finn stepped in. "Sonoma's staying in my room with me."

Never mind that Dave needed to wrap his head around *that* announcement, where the hell was *he* supposed to stay? He looked down at Ellie. "Can *you* drive?"

"What? No. I can barely walk." She hiccupped. "Why can't Sonoma and I share, and you and Finn share?" Funny. She didn't *sound* drunk; she sounded pretty damn logical. Except she kept swaying.

Sonoma shook her head. "Each room has nothing bigger than a full bed. I can't see the guys sharing something that small."

"I can't see us sharing a bed *at all*," Finn said.

"I second that. What if I take the bed, and Finn takes the floor?" Dave posed, but Sonoma shot him daggers. "Fine. Finn can have the bed, and I'll take the floor."

Her hands went to her hips. "First of all, there's hardly any floor space. Second of all, Finn and I—"

Finn draped an arm over Sonoma's shoulders protectively. "We've been seeing each other for a little while now, and we'd prefer staying together."

In a teeny-tiny cutesy voice that had Dave grinding his molars, Sonoma said, "Why can't you and Ellie share her room?"

"No!" he and Ellie exploded at the same time. Dave snapped his head toward Ellie, his jaw swinging open. *Ouch! And the ego takes one for the team.* Her eyes were wide, and he bit back the laughable urge to ask her if the thought of spending the night with him was *that* unappealing. *Guess the kiss didn't rock her like it rocked me.*

Ellie rushed into the void of their mutual astonishment. "The great room has some comfy-looking couches. I could curl up on one of those with a blanket."

"Oh hell no!" Dave bellowed. Front and center in his mind loomed an image of Cowboy Douchenugget pawing at her while she was asleep and vulnerable.

Now they *all* stared at him with owl eyes.

He puffed out a breath. "What I meant was, you keep your room and I'll figure something out."

Ellie blinked. "Such as?"

"Such as *I'll* take one of those comfy couches. Or sleep in my truck. Or a hay bale in the barn."

Sonoma giggled. "Maybe you can stay with Uncle Stan … or Great-Grandma and the Aunt Ednas."

The good feels from the evening went up in a wisp of smoke. Han—or was it Darth Vader?—whispered that he was in for a very long, very uncomfortable night.

Chapter 23

I Think You're on My Side

Oh Lordy! Ellie's fuzzed-up brain spiraled in her tornado of thoughts as she stumbled amid their little group toward the main house. The kiss still wreaking havoc inside her, she pictured Dave sacked out in his truck. Dave sacked out with her. More kissing. Her sacking Dave. Or was it "bagging"? Dave on the couch. Her on Dave on the couch. *Her* in his truck, straddling him. That kiss! Wookiee love. *Making whoopee.*

"We're gonna head on up." Sonoma's announcement jarred Ellie to the here and now at the bottom of the stairs. The dance was over, and people had been drifting into the great room, some heading to their rooms while others filled the space with talk and laughter. "Your stuff's in Ellie's room, Dave." When he shot her a quizzical look, she added, "Maybe because your room was next to hers, and they assumed … Or they thought it was a convenient spot to put it?" She shrugged, then pulled Ellie in for a squeeze while Finn, looking completely unapologetic, wished them good night. They jogged up the stairs hand in hand.

All righty, then.

She and Dave looked up at the newly minted couple, then at each other. She was pretty sure the bemused look on his face mirrored her own. He blew out a breath. "What just happened?"

"No idea, but I think it's safe to say we know what's going on with those two now." She paused a beat, trying to gauge his mood. "Are you okay with that?"

His gaze sweeping up the now-empty staircase, Dave rolled his big, broad shoulders. "It's not my call. But she likes him, and he's related to you, and *you* like him, so …"

"Meaning?"

He turned to her with a wide grin. "Meaning we should forget about them and go check out the hot tub."

She blinked. Three times. "Excuse me?"

"You didn't bring a suit?"

"No. I thought this was a square dance, not a swimming party. They have a hot tub?" *Of course they do!*

"Several, I'm told." Where there had been amusement in his eyes, there was now something far deeper, more intense. Verging on hungry. Suddenly, she was the puck on the ice once more, and he the determined defenseman trying to corral her. Why couldn't she get that picture out of her head? Because the look he was giving her pulsed fire through her bloodstream, waking up parts of her that had been dormant far too long. As if he realized where he was and who he was with, the look shifted, like a cloud being torn from the sun. "Well, no one says you *have* to have a suit to get in the water," he said on a wink.

She shoved her hands in her jacket pockets and gave him her most scandalized look. "Maybe Wookiees don't. They're already covered in fur."

He tilted his head and gave her that tummy-fluttering, devilish grin. Whatever thoughts lurked behind those twinkling hazel orbs stayed locked away.

Laughter—or was it a case of nerves?—bubbled up inside her. "But I'll give you an *A* for trying."

"So this means you *will* get in the hot tub with me?"

She shook her head.

Hands covering his heart, he rocked backward as if he'd taken a blow. "You're killing me here."

She struck a hands-on-waist pose, cocking a hip to the side. "You shock me, Mr. Reaper. Here I thought you were sooo serious, but I'm beginning to suspect you're just a big flirt."

"No"—he shook his head, the smile still plastered on his chiseled face—"just human and hopeful."

His eyes glazed over with yet another look that struck a chord deep inside her. Hopeful was an apt description … and tender … and so full of promise and regret at the same time that seeing it made her heart ache.

With the very lightest of touches, he turned her toward the stairs and rested his fingers on the small of her back. "C'mon. I'll walk you to your room, and I'll get my stuff *and* myself out of your way."

Though her head nodded agreement, the rest of her couldn't help but be disappointed.

One bad idea after another. Dave was deflecting them all, or trying to, as he walked Ellie upstairs. They bombarded him relentlessly, every single one involving a replay of the kiss that had ended way too soon. His imagination had since added a shit ton more to the mix—and that was only the beginning. Kissing Ellie had been like trying to eat a single potato chip. He couldn't stop at one.

She opened the door to her room and stepped through, flipping on a table lamp. Though it didn't cast much light, a quick sweep of the small space revealed his bag at the foot of her bed. He stood frozen in the door frame, unsure what to do next. He couldn't stay, but he didn't want to go, especially as his gaze was captivated by the way her dress swung around her legs and clung to the curves he'd had his hands on just a short while ago. Curves he wanted to touch again. Explore. See. Taste.

"The bed's big enough for both of us," she said in a quiet voice, startling him from his lustful thoughts into new, even lustier thoughts. Her eyebrows were arched, her hand sweeping toward said bed as if she were a game show hostess presenting it to him. With her in it, apparently.

Yes! I'll take what's behind door number one as long as she *comes with it!* Wait. Different game. Just like *this* was a different game, and he couldn't quite decide how to play it. He knew what he *wanted* to do. But that stupid Yoda voice was sighing at the wrongness of it. Dave was leaving Denver, and all he had to offer was casual, but nothing about Ellie was casual.

He eyed the bed skeptically. Could he sleep beside her without touching her? It couldn't have been bigger than a wide twin, and while he suspected she intended the offer as a chaste one, all he could picture was her on top of him. Him on top of her. Every inch of her bare skin against his. No way was this a good plan. He shook his head to get his tongue working and blurted, "I don't think it's a good idea. I snore." *WTF?* He didn't snore—that he knew of—so why was he telling her he did? Right. Yoda was in charge, damn it!

Her mouth wobbled, and a tiny "Oh" squeaked out.

Christ, he was doing a piss-poor job reading her cues and responding accordingly, not that he *should* be responding the way his body begged him to. With no finesse whatsoever, his dick stood up and hollered, "You're killing us here!" *God, I'm out of practice.* His mind zoomed to lying beside her, and his dick throbbed in encouragement.

"Uh, what I meant was, you may be small, but I'm a big guy, and being squished together in that bed probably involves some touching." Fuck! Could he have sounded any more like a dumbass? No.

She peeled off her jacket and crossed her arms over her chest. "Who said anything about *not* touching? We'll sleep on our sides, back to back. No doubt parts of us will touch, but it'll be minimal."

Now his imagination—active little bastard that it was—leapt to just which parts would be touching. *Yeah. No.* "I'll be fine on the couch." Somewhere inside him, Han was weeping.

Before she could talk him out of his noble plan—which would have taken pathetically little—he snatched up his bag, scooted out the door, and ran down the stairs. The party had broken up, and the great room was dark and still—with the exception of one couple on *his* couch, doing what *he* wanted to do upstairs in that small bed. *Shit!* They hadn't seen him yet, but they would if he made a break for the front door. With that escape route blocked, he wheeled for a different exit. Maybe he could flee through a back door and get to his truck. Yep, it was going to be one long, uncomfortable night, but no more so than sharing a bed with Ellie and not being able to touch her. Except *certain parts.*

When he reached a back door, he patted his pockets. Next, his jacket. No keys. He smacked his forehead. *Because I left them in my room.* Which room were they in now? Either one was off limits. With a sigh, he picked up his bag and marched back upstairs. Leaned against Ellie's door and listened. No sound. He knocked quietly. The door whipped open so fast he nearly fell in. Hand on the knob, Ellie stood in the doorway in a cute pair of short PJs. Pink PJs. They were modest, the shorts not too short, but they were made out of shiny fabric that made him want to run his hands all over it. Not to mention the fabric clung and draped in a way that showcased her contours beautifully.

Turn and run!

"So?" She snapped him out of his lustful appraisal.

"Um, so the couch is occupied. I was going to sleep in the truck, but I left my keys in my original room. I was hoping they'd moved those too and I could—"

"You can't sleep in your truck," she clucked. "It's cold, and the seats are stiff."

"I thought you said the seats were comfortable." The affront came out in his voice.

She waved him off and whisper-yelled, "If you're too big for this bed, then you're ten times too big for that truck."

"You don't like my truck?" *Ladies, meet Dave Grimson, one incredibly smooth operator. Not.*

A smile twitched her lips, and she stuffed her tongue in her cheek—probably to stifle a laugh. Yeah, he was being utterly ridiculous.

"Yes, Dave, I like your truck. It's perfect for taking rides, but for sleeping? Not so much."

Just take the damn bed, his cock blared.

"So you like my truck, but you don't think I should sleep there?"

She two-fisted his shirt front, pulled him inside, and closed the door. And there she was, Miss Bossy, setting him ablaze like a campfire doused with lighter fluid. She pointed at the bed, which seemed to have shrunk since the last time he'd eyeballed it. "I'm going to bed," she huffed. "I suggest you do the same." With that, she slid under the covers, and turned on her side. Her cute ass faced the middle of the bed. *That will be the part of her touching part of me.* He groaned inside.

Maybe he could do this honorably. He unsnapped his shirt and sank onto the opposite side of the mattress. Pulling off his boots and socks, he deliberated how much more to strip off. She had on a top, shorts, and probably panties. If he left on his jeans and undershirt, his items of clothing would match hers. Why this mattered, he had no fucking clue, but it sounded like a solid plan. He tugged off his shirt and flung it, landing it on his bag, then heaved himself under the covers. The tiny mattress dipped drunkenly, and—*Oh fuck!*—pitched her on top of him. In a mad scramble, he shoved her off him, and she emitted a little squeak as she rolled over.

"Sorry," he mumbled, repositioning himself so he took up as little room as possible … except now his front was right up against her back. His dick hoisted itself up and cheered. He gingerly rolled to his other side, inevitably rubbing her warm ass with his. He stilled. She scooted away, but there was no escaping it. There might have been an inch of space to spare, and it wasn't enough to keep her heat from sinking into his skin despite the jeans and boxers he wore.

And her fragrance! Jesus, no escaping that either. Not that he wanted to. It surrounded him, laced its fresh-flower tendrils around him until it filled his nose and tickled his senses. Easing himself to very edge of the mattress, he threw one leg over its side. How long he lay like a log stuck in mud, he had no idea. Behind him, she seemed to ease, and soon she let out cute little sighing sleeping noises. She'd fallen asleep, and he finally relaxed and urged his mind to wander *away* from the kiss that had electricity forking through him.

Coming to the event hadn't been high on his priority list. Hell, it hadn't even made it to the *bottom* of his priority list. But surprisingly, he was having a damn good time reliving some of the fun from his childhood. But the real reason? Ellie. *She* was the difference-maker. He'd never been attracted to shy, reserved women before, but this one was changing all that. And honestly? She was neither shy nor reserved. More like alluringly mysterious. A woman with many layers he wanted to strip off, literally *and* figuratively. He'd caught a glimpse tonight of what was underneath that protective shell of hers when she'd let herself go. When she'd gotten caught up in the adventure, her joy had overflowed and been infectious. Enticing. Intoxicating.

Nicky wouldn't have been caught dead at an event like this. No, he would have come alone. And if by some minor miracle she *had* come, she'd have spent the evening pouting until he'd been so miserable he would have caved and taken her home.

Such different women. What if he'd met Ellie before Nicole? Would he have been smart enough to recognize how rare she was and chase her? What would his life look like now if he'd caught her? He heaved out a sigh. No point in thinking about a life that wasn't in his future. Denver would soon be in his rearview mirror.

His stream of consciousness detoured to his injuries and the doping. His sore hand healing at a glacial pace and how easily he could get himself sideways again. How complicated everything, including hockey, had become. Too much noise in his life covered up the music. How could he get back to where he'd been? Just happy to be playing. Happy hanging with friends and family. This career had a shelf life, and he was approaching the end of it. What would take its place?

Despite the philosophical musings running rampant, he somehow dropped off because when he regained consciousness, he was curled around Ellie, his hand resting on her hip and his thumb brushing the skin above the waistband of her PJs. He froze. *Oh shit!* She seemed fast asleep, her back rising and falling in long, even rhythms. *One more touch. Just one.* His thumb twitched back into action as if by itself, and his fingers decided to come aboard because … Jesus! Her skin was silk and velvet. In his pants, his cock grew fuller, ready to rally.

Her breathing stopped, and her entire body stiffened. "What are you doing?"

Thumb, fingers, and cock shrank back. He slid his hand off her and rolled to his other side, pretending he was asleep. At least his cock wouldn't be prodding her and begging to come out and play. He'd explain in the morning. *My hands always go wandering in the middle of the night, even when I'm not sleeping with anyone, and my fingers automatically stroke soft things … like sheets. Mom never could break me of the habit, though she tried. I wore out lots of sheets.*

Behind him, he could feel her flip over too. "I know you're not asleep," she murmured.

"Sure I am."

"Obviously." A soft giggle escaped her.

He rolled back over, keeping his body on the edge of the mattress without somehow falling off. Moonlight through the window illuminated the smile curving her lips. Her elbow was propped up, holding her head, and her wavy hair draped her arm and pooled on her pillow. He grew even harder.

"Sorry," he croaked. "I didn't mean to touch you. I woke up just before you did and realized what I was doing. It was a mistake."

One eyebrow dipped. "Touching me was a mistake?" Everything about her suddenly whispered in seductive, dulcet tones—soft, feminine, touchable. Difficult to resist. So yeah, touching her was a mistake, but not the kind of mistake she implied.

"Well, no. I mean, yes," he rasped. "I mean, I didn't mean to, but I was asleep."

Her eyes darted to the dark ceiling. "So if you *weren't* sleeping and you were touching me, would it feel different?" Her eyes found his and locked on.

Two beats went by. "Well, yeah, because I wouldn't start at your stomach."

Unmistakable heat shimmered in her eyes now. He was pretty damn sure the look in his own eyes mirrored hers but with more intensity. He wanted her. But stepping over the line was a bad, bad, bad idea.

Touch, you must not, Yoda warned.

"Where *would* you start?" she breathed.

Shut up, Yoda.

His body and mind warred as he traced the side of her face with his fingers, then glided his hand into her hair. "I'd start here." He twined his fingers in her tresses, relishing the feel of the soft spirals twisted in his grasp.

She closed her eyes and let out a little moan that made his dick tap-dance. "That does feel different," she whispered.

"Good different or bad different?"

Her eyes fluttered open. "It's all good. What would you touch next?"

Oh my fucking God. And that's when his body hip-checked good intentions out of the way and took over. Han had locked Yoda in a back compartment and was at the helm.

Unable to talk, he maneuvered instead until he cradled her face in both hands. It was so small that the tips of his fingers could stroke her hair. She watched intently from beneath her long lashes.

"Next"—his voice finally came back on board—"I'd use something besides my hands." He brought his lips down to hers, gently, telling himself to go slow. But when she opened her mouth and invited him in, he didn't hesitate. Angling his head, he deepened the kiss, sweeping inside her warm, soft mouth with his tongue, savoring mint and wine and something indescribably delicious—her. She tasted even better than she had by the chiminea. Better than anything he'd ever tasted before.

Her tongue rolled over his languidly, as though trying to taste every bud, and a groan rose up in his throat. Smoldering kisses ignited and caught fire, and she let out a series of mewling noises. Soon his hands were moving down her back, under her slick satin top, over her silky skin. He dug his fingers into her shoulder blades and crushed her against him while their mouths dueled. Her arms wrapped around his shoulders, her fingers plowing through his hair. Then she draped her leg over his hip, pulling herself closer, and he gripped her thigh, holding on as he began a slow grind against her.

Suddenly, she broke the kiss and peered at him.

Panic rose inside him. *Please don't make me stop.* "Did I hurt you?"

She shook her head and smiled. His chest heaved against hers, and only the sound of their rapid, uneven breathing could be heard. His mind blanked, not knowing what to do next. That was, he *knew* what he wanted to do—and how to do it—but how far could he or should he go? He knew that answer too. *Stop now before it's too late.*

Ellie tugged up the hem of his T-shirt, exploding his analysis paralysis into shards.

"Oh, right. Your turn to touch." For fuck's sake, could he sound any more idiotic? *No, you couldn't*, his disgusted cock pulsed. *At least we're moving in the right direction now*, it threw in as a grudging afterthought.

He helped her out by grabbing the back of his T-shirt and yanking it off the rest of the way. With aching tenderness, her fingers traced his lips, his jaw, his temple, outlining his shoulders, continuing her exploration of his collarbones and every spot on his chest. He closed his eyes and let the sensations wash over him, let the goose bumps peak on his skin. When her hand glided to his abs, he opened his eyes and sucked in a breath.

She stopped. "Does that tickle?"

"Fuck no. Feels … really good," he exhaled. "Keep going."

And she did. With tortuous slowness, she first ran her fingers, then the flat of her palm over every muscle as if drawing them. He was so fascinated watching what she was doing, especially as she dipped dangerously close to his waistband, that he was caught off guard when her mouth landed softly at the base of his neck and followed the same languid path her fingers had just blazed. A groan rumbled through his chest, and he flopped onto his back, taking in every sweet thrill her mouth and hands bestowed on him. Throwing one hand over his eyes, he kept the other anchored in her hair. Her mouth kissed, nibbled, and licked, and her hand dropped to his crotch, where his cock rose to meet her touch. She skimmed over his erection, back and forth, the friction through his fly growing more intense. *Fuuuuck!*

She coaxed his belt open and began unzipping his fly slowly, slowly. His body and mind fused and collapsed on one narrow pinpoint of focus: to be inside her. In one movement, he sat up, hauled her level with him, and flipped her on her back. Her eyes were wide with surprise as his mouth crashed down on hers, taking it hard. Then his fingers were making short work of her buttons, laying her top open so at last her hot skin slid against his.

So fucking good.

Breaking a messy kiss, she wriggled out of her top. Before she was done and had a chance to lie back down, need and hunger overwhelmed him and his mouth latched on to a nipple, his tongue teasing it into a tight little bead. One arm behind her with her hand planted on the mattress, she arched her back, pressing his mouth closer with her free hand.

"Oh God, oh God, oh God. Feels so good," she hissed, her back sinking slowly into the mattress.

His cue to keep going. While he explored one breast with his mouth, his hand did the same with the other one and then switched. And again. He nibbled and tugged, massaged and stroked, nipped and suckled, adjusting his touch as she told him with her body what she wanted. He was burning up from wanting to be inside her, but this was about learning what gave her pleasure before taking his own.

His hand slid down over her flat belly and slipped under her waistband. When he sank a finger inside her, her warm wetness made him want to pound his chest. *He'd* done that to her. Her hips lifted off the mattress, surprising him, and he pushed her down gently and added a second finger. She rocked against his hand, little moans and incoherent sounds coming from her. He dared a look, enthralled by what he saw: her mouth open, eyes closed, head turning from side to side, a blissful frown on her face. As he manipulated his fingers, his mouth continued working on her breasts. She bit down on her bottom lip. Her hands gripped the quilt, and she bucked beneath him.

Fuck, she was driving him out of his mind by not holding back, by showing him he was driving her out of hers. And then her body seized, and she came hard on his fingers, clutching them. Her lips were moving, something that sounded like "Dave" escaping as she fought for breath. He felt like a fucking god!

With gentle strokes, he watched her float back down to him. He'd never seen a more beautiful sight. Her eyes fluttered open. "That was … that was … I'm not sure I have the words." She smiled at him and spread her arms wide, and he covered her body with his and let himself relax into her embrace. As she held him, he kissed her with a tenderness he'd never felt before—as if she were all his to cherish. Except she wasn't, and he'd have been wise to not start down this path in the first place, but it was too late. And it wouldn't come as any surprise to anyone, especially him, that he wasn't wise.

Chapter 24

Is That a T-Bone or Are You Just Happy to See Me?

Starbursts danced behind Ellie's eyes. Drifting back down from the stratosphere where Dave had sent her, the comforting weight of his heavy body sinking atop her was a different sort of heaven she'd never known. She was oh-so safe here, and she didn't want to ever leave the security of his warm hold. He was trailing moist, soft kisses along her neck, brushing the tip of his nose against her jaw, pressing his lips against her eyelids, her hair. The tenderness was a contradiction, a polar opposite to his frighteningly imposing, growly self, and something inside her soared with the knowledge he trusted her with this surprisingly softer side.

As awareness of her surroundings took hold, she realized his belt buckle was digging into her hip. Below that, and equally hard, his length nestled between her legs. She shifted beneath him, and he rose up on his forearms, letting cool air rush into the gap between them.

His eyes mined hers. "I must be crushing you," he murmured.

"No, it's just that your belt buckle is—"

"Oh shit! Sorry." He adjusted his weight and slid beside her, ending up chest down, eyes still locked on hers, his big hand cradling one side of her face.

She followed after, chasing his warmth, molding herself to his side. "No, you're fine." Her fingers traced the hard planes of his shoulders and ran down the channel of his forever spine. Smooth skin over hard muscle invited her to explore, making him twitch, puckering his skin into goose bumps. "But maybe if you lost the buckle …"

One side of his mouth hitched up. "Is this your subtle way of asking me to take off my pants?"

She scooted lower until her fingers finally found his waistband, and she tugged at the belt trapped by the loops of his jeans. "Nothing subtle about it."

He flipped onto his back and sat up, never taking his eyes from hers. "Then let me help you."

Shy and a little awkward—how long had it been since she'd been naked in front of a man?—she propped her head in her hand and draped her other arm across her bare chest. As he shuffled out of his pants, his boxers got caught and he started to haul them back up.

"No, those can go too." She bit back a giggle at his exaggerated wide-eyed expression.

His grin broadened, that devilish curve electrifying her body until it practically sizzled. "So bossy." Now his eyes drifted down her body to her PJ shorts, and he gave her a slow chin lift. "I can help with those too."

She slid her arm from her chest and hooked a thumb in her bottoms where they hugged her hip. "You mean these?"

His heated gaze scorched a path as it traveled back up to her exposed breasts, and she fought the urge to cover herself again, painfully aware of how inadequate she must look when stacked up against his usual perfect bedmates.

Jeans, belt, and underwear hit the floor with a clink and a thud, and he wasted no time rolling toward her, taking her face in his hands as he took possession of her mouth. *Oh Lordy, the man can kiss!* She threw her arms around his neck, anchoring herself to him as she lost herself in the feel of his lips consuming hers, his tongue plundering and plunging deeper. Soft and gentle was nice, but the promise of the beast inside him was firing up every nerve ending in her body. Her pulse took off at a gallop, and her breathing grew more ragged, matching his. She couldn't contain the desperate mewling noises in her throat.

His rough hand skidded down her side, arrowed under her waistband, pulling her shorts and panties down her legs, adding to the urgency crackling in the air. She raised her hips off the mattress and lifted her knees, and the rest of her clothes slid off her ankles and joined his on the floor.

Acres of hot skin slid across hot skin, and she melted against him. *So good.* Heavy and thick, his solid shaft lay trapped against her pubic bone, jutting up to her navel.

His hands were everywhere at once, so big they covered large swaths of skin, fingers flexing and digging one moment, then exploring and caressing the next. But she was on fire, and it wasn't enough. God, she wanted him inside her! Emboldened and impatient, she surged into him, and he fell onto his back, taking her with him so she sprawled across him. The tip of his cock prodded her entrance, and she slithered over it shamelessly. She sat up, tenting her fingertips on abs that were warm, chiseled slabs beneath her touch.

Those calloused man hands coasted over her sides, to her breasts, where they cupped and kneaded and teased. Dark with lust, his gaze took a leisurely tour of her body once, twice, before landing back with fascination on his own busy hands making her body sing. "Beautiful," he whispered.

She rocked against his steely length, oh-so tempted to slide onto it. "Cowboy up," she teased. "I get to play cowgirl." *Oh my God, who's is charge of my body and my mouth right now? Evil Ellie.*

He cocked an eyebrow, and his lips curved up in a sexy smile. "Yes, ma'am. You're the boss."

"Please tell me you brought protection."

"I brought protection." His voice was dusky and seemed to roll from deep within his chest. God, he was *so* damn hot! One hand grasping her thigh, he leaned over the edge of the bed. After some rustling, he tossed a few foil packets on the bed beside them.

Her eyes widened. "Are you using all those at once?" She'd heard about guys who doubled up, but triple?

He tore open a packet with his teeth. "No, one at a time." He scooted her back, and his cock sprang forward in its colossal glory. Her eyes grew wider still. As he rolled it on, he shot her a sly look. "I did say I was hopeful."

"I guess that makes two of us," she blurted. *Ellie! Shut. Up!*

With a sexy chuckle, he lay back down and gripped her hips, lifting her so she hovered just above his tip. "All yours, cowgirl."

She lowered herself slowly, taking first one inch, then another. They both gasped.

Panic rose up inside her. "Am I hurting you?"

He gritted out through clenched teeth, "No way. Just … Fuck, this is good." His face was a study in fierce concentration, but a smile quirked one corner of his mouth. "But I think you just stole *my* line."

She folded over with a laugh, and her hair sprawled over his chest and got stuck in his mouth, making him sputter. "I'm *so* bad at this," she moaned. *Ellie Hendricks, the great seductress.*

He stroked her hair and planted a kiss on her head. "You're not bad at anything," he murmured. "And damn, woman, you feel fucking incredible!"

His words spread a different sort of warmth through her, and she brought herself upright and let her body go, taking in all of him, impaling herself until he was seated to the hilt. The feel of his girth stretching her punched her square in the chest, wrenching the air from her lungs, leaving her no breath to gasp out.

Oh my God!

Dave's eyes locked on hers, filled with blazing intensity that caused her heart to slam harder against her rib cage. She began to move, and his features transformed with a blend of agony and unbridled pleasure. He hissed out an incoherent curse. Fingers digging into her hips, her thighs, he squeezed his eyes shut and groaned. Maybe she wasn't so bad at this after all.

Soon she was lost in the carnal sensations as she rode him, moans and mewls tumbling from her. Dave thrust up into her harder, faster, letting out noisy grunts of his own. In the background, the bed squeaked a telltale rhythm. A vague thought waved through her brain that Great-Grandma and the Aunt Ednas could hear them, but she didn't care.

With an abruptness that stole what little breath she had, Dave stopped, sat up, and, wrapping his arms around her, kissed her hard. In the blink of an eye, she was on her back and he'd gathered her knees to either side of him. With a flex of his hips, he plunged back inside her. Cowgirl playtime was obviously over and the bronc-busting cowboy was in charge … which sent more tingles rippling through her body. Clutching at his hair, his back, she gave herself over to him, letting him drive the accelerating pace as their heated bodies fused together in one smooth, slick, grinding machine.

And oh dear God, she reveled in it, spiraling upward into the clouds again, where she lost all sense of space and time before her body jolted and shuddered and fractured into infinite fragments even as he drove into her one last time, coming with her in a rocking simultaneous release.

He collapsed on top of her, burying his face in the crook of her neck, their chests heaving together in synchronized labor. Her hands flitted over his back and shoulders until he captured them and brought them above her head, lacing her fingers with his. As his panting quieted, he sprinkled kisses over the column of her neck. God, it felt so right.

"I should go take care of the condom," he breathed against her skin. But he lingered, still buried inside her, and she didn't encourage him to pull out. Finally, he hoisted himself off her and retreated into the bathroom. She ran her hand over her belly and breasts, touching every inch of flushed, sensitive skin. *He'd* done that to her. The man definitely knew how to treat a woman in bed, how to make her *feel* like a woman. Better than anyone she'd ever been with, yet she barely knew him.

She flung her arm over her head and tracked him when he emerged from the bathroom. Oh Lordy, was he a sight! Like some rugged model on the cover of a romance novel, only *better* because he was real and he was hers—at least for tonight—and she was going to enjoy him while she could.

Dave was still reeling when he approached the bed, where the most gorgeous sight in the whole damn world awaited him. Ellie's hair was fanned across the pillow, one arm folded over the crown of her head, while the other arm rested on her pale stomach. All her mouthwatering curves were exposed, and he couldn't keep from letting his eyes roam over every single one. She bit her lower lip, looking incredibly self-conscious, and he had to mentally slap himself to stop ogling her. But Jesus Christ! The girl had no idea how fucking beautiful she was, or how much he wanted to stare … and touch … and taste. Or what she'd done to him, how she'd hit every trigger inside him, making him come too soon and in powerful bursts, each stronger than the last as they'd rocked his body. He'd never felt anything like it before.

Fuck! That wasn't good.

He dropped on the edge of the mattress and looked some more, running his fingertips up her arm and into all that strawberry-blond silk. She giggled.

He couldn't corral his smile. "Does that tickle?"

"No, it feels good." She shifted to make room for him, amusement playing over her face and in her big eyes. "I was thinking how you just T-boned me again, but this time I enjoyed it."

He let out a guffaw. "I'm not sure I'll ever look at a T-bone the same way." Damn, she was cute! Too cute. Too beautiful. Too perfect. He should get dressed and run the hell away. She was waking up way too many emotions in him—some he never knew existed before—dangerous emotions he didn't want awakened. Maybe it was already too late.

Giving in to his want, he lay down beside her and gathered her up in his arms. How else could they fit in this ridiculously tiny bed? The bed's size hadn't registered at *all*, however, when he'd been deep inside her trying to rein in his climax.

His hands drifted down her back, over her ass, her thighs, and back up into her hair again. With a sigh that shot straight to his already rousing cock, she snuggled against him, her breasts heavy and warm against his chest. Fuck, she felt so damn good, and though she must've been a foot shorter, she fit him perfectly. Just like he fit her. In *every* way.

Another giggle escaped her, tickling his chest.

"More T-bone jokes?" he murmured into her hair. She smelled like soap and rain and flowers, and he breathed her in deeply.

"No. This time I was thinking about something the saleslady in the western clothing shop said."

His "Hmm?" came out in a grunt because the primal sound was suddenly about all he could manage with her pressed against him. Every drop of blood in his body seemed to be rushing south again. Christ, when was the last time he'd gotten it up so soon after sex *that* intense? Since he couldn't remember *having* sex that intense, he pitched the question. No brain power anyway.

Ellie pulled back and grinned at him. He smoothed her hair from her face—the sensation more for him than for her, selfish bastard that he was. "She said you could tell how a man is in bed by how he dances."

Uh-oh. This can't be good. Hang on, ego. You're headed for a fall.

Before he could deflect—or come up with a coherent sentence—she added in a breathy voice that drained his brain of even *more* blood, "You really do move those hips of yours nicely on the dance floor, so I'd say she hit the nail on the head."

Something warm and fuzzy bloomed in his stomach and oozed into his chest, filling it. He pulled her closer. "It has everything to do with you. I was inspired." That's what he'd call it, rather than what it truly was: that she'd driven him out of his friggin' mind, and he'd chucked self-control like he'd discarded the rubber wrapper. And he needed to double down if he hoped to wrestle that self-control back.

Chapter 25

Yoda Has Left the Building

Dave doubled down all right. And the evidence was in the trash can up in Ellie's bathroom, where all three empty condom wrappers had been tossed. If he'd brought a fourth one with him, it would no doubt be up there too. He'd done a spectacular job blanking out the Yoda voice of reason, partying with Han instead. Han was proud. Dave, not so much. As he ran his eyes longingly over Ellie at breakfast the next morning, he admonished himself for his selfishness. His recklessness. His idiocy. But then his mind U-turned to how perfect she'd felt under him when he'd been buried inside her, beside him as he'd held her close, and suddenly he was hard again and not so sorry anymore.

Christ! He wasn't a fucking nineteen-year-old, so why was he having so much trouble reining in his libido? His struggle lay in those deep blue eyes, all that soft hair, and that fragrance uniquely hers that washed over him and made him lose his mind and his way. *Don't look at her, don't touch her, and you'll be fine. You can do this.*

But it was too late. Kissing her last night had crossed the line, and he'd totally fucked up because he'd gone too far. How was he going to cut her loose? Forget if *she* was on board with sliding back into the friend zone. He wasn't. But what choice did he have? He'd taken a bite—or three—of the forbidden fruit, which had only made him ravenous for more, and he needed to stop this runaway locomotive *now* before he got so carried away he couldn't find his way back, or worse, he hurt her.

They were seated at a huge banquet table, where Ellie and Sonoma chattered with Aunt Viv and Uncle Stan over their eggs and bacon. The pure comfort of the scene reminded him of a Hallmark commercial, and he squirmed because *this*. This is what he wanted but couldn't have. In that moment, it struck him that maybe what he'd done in his professional life wasn't so different because damn if self-control hadn't been MIA then too.

He felt a pair of eyes on him and looked up to find Finn drilling into him with the same look *he'd* been giving Finn since they'd met. It said, "Don't fuck with her, or I will carve you up with a spoon and feed you to the coyotes." And shit, suddenly he was *that* guy. The user. And he was making a mess of everything.

As he glanced at Ellie, bands tightened around his chest. She glowed from inside this morning, making her even more beautiful than ever. He'd have crowed and told himself *he* was the reason behind that look, but even if that were true, it made him a *bigger* douche because last night he'd taken and taken, and damn the consequences. Consequences now staring him in the face.

After saying their thank-yous and good-byes, Dave jogged upstairs to get their bags. Sonoma appeared in the doorway and crossed her arms with a smirk. "I heard the older ladies talking about the racket that kept them up all night. Judging by the condition of that bed and how tired you look, it doesn't take a genius to figure out what the 'racket' was. You two really burned up the sheets."

He picked up the bags and turned slowly, plastering on his best deadpan face. "No clue what you're talking about, Nome. And the reason I look tired is because I slept in my truck."

"Liar."

He shrugged and nudged her out of his way.

"Okay. Play it your way, Dave." She pointed at herself. "But when your wedding day rolls around, *this* girl wants the credit she deserves for getting you two together."

He stopped and sighed. "Nome. There's nothing to give credit for. No cupids stringing arrows, no wedding plans. Just your dirty mind playing tricks on you."

"So *you* say."

He headed for the stairs. "Yeah, I *do* say."

"We'll just see," she chortled behind him.

He was still shaking his head when he reached the truck. The sight of Ellie leaning against it like she *belonged* there, her eyes closed and face upturned to the sun, gave him a jolt he shouldn't have felt. When he dropped the bags, her eyes flew open, and a wide smile lit them up.

Damn, she's gorgeous! "Hey, didn't mean to disturb your communing with the sun. Ready to get on the road?"

Sliding her hands into her coat pockets, she looked around and sighed. "I guess so."

He unlocked the doors and opened hers for her. "You like it here?"

She nodded. "It's so pretty and peaceful. No traffic, no sirens. Just nature everywhere you look."

He followed her gaze. It *was* pretty. "Yeah, I can see how someone could get used to this."

"And now that I have the boots, I can move right in!" The music in her laughter lifted on the morning breeze, tugging a reluctant smile from him.

They'd been driving for about a half hour—him brooding while she hummed along with the music—when she turned to him. "Is everything okay this morning? You seem a little, um, preoccupied."

Shifting in his seat, he kept his eyes focused on the road. "Just tired, I guess."

From the corner of his eye, he saw Ellie nod and slouch in her seat, her eyes fixed on the world outside her window. Shit, she was killing him. He turned and tugged on a curl. "Someone wouldn't let me sleep last night."

She side-eyed him and smirked. "Funny. I was thinking the same thing."

"What? That you wouldn't let me sleep last night?"

"No," she laughed. "The other way around. I—"

His phone rang over the car speakers, and caller ID flashed on the dashboard screen. No missing Nicky's name glaring at them both. Worse, he'd never changed what she'd entered in his phone when they'd first started dating. "Naughty Nicky" blazed proud and bright before he could hit the off button—which, in his erratic fumbling, turned out to be the on button.

"You there, Dave?" her voice blared across the speakers.

He punched "Off" and threw himself against the driver's seat with an inner groan, not daring a look at Ellie, who had gone stone still. The phone rang again, and this time he hit the correct button and let the call go to voicemail.

"Wonder what she wanted," he muttered lamely.

"If you'd answered, you wouldn't need to wonder," Ellie said in a voice so quiet he barely heard her.

He blew out a breath. "She doesn't usually call me. Or get in touch with me at all. It's not like we're—"

Ellie held up a hand. "It's okay. You don't owe me any explanations."

True, but why did that make him feel worse?

They rode in charged silence, emotions boiling and frothing inside him. There was so much he wanted to say, to explain, but he didn't dare for fear he'd beg her to come home with him and bring color to his four stark walls. To smile for him and make his fucked-up world right again. To climb into bed and love him and never leave.

Could he have fallen for this girl *this* hard? *This* fast? He was so screwed.

When he pulled up in front of her house, she practically vaulted out the door. Before he could kill the engine and round the truck to help her, she had the back door to his truck open and was tugging at her bag.

"Hey, wait. Let me help you with—"

"Nope, I got it. I'm good." She yanked so hard that when the bag finally came free, she nearly toppled backward. He reached out to steady her, but she shrugged off his hold as if he were some sleazeball. A quick dash of her eyes to his. "I had a great time. Thanks." Then she spun and practically ran for her front door.

A coil of barbed wire twisted in his gut. He took faltering steps toward her, but she unlocked her front door, slipped inside, and closed it before he'd made it halfway up her walkway.

Cut her loose before you hurt her. This is what you wanted. Except it *wasn't* what he wanted. And he was *already* hurting her. He was hurting them both. Last night had been incredible. Stars going supernova kind of incredible. How often did that happen in a lifetime? He lumbered into the driver's seat, where he sat for a minute, trying to gather his thoughts, but they kept scattering like paper-dry leaves being pushed around by a relentless wind. Beside him, his phone buzzed with Nicky's voicemail. He picked it up and changed Nicky's moniker to a simple "Nicole." Then he tossed it in the console without listening to her message, fired up his engine, and pulled away from Ellie's curb. Chasing him was the feeling he'd just thrown away one of the best things to ever happen to him—just like he'd nearly thrown away his hockey career.

What the fuck was the matter with him?

The answer still eluded him when he turned into his complex, rounded the corner, and hit his garage-door opener. He came to a screeching halt. Parked broadside was Nicky's black Lexus, blocking his entry into the garage.

"Fuuuuck! Can this day get any better?" He pushed a breath through his lungs.

The SUV lurched forward, leaving him a gap big enough to pull his truck inside. Before he was out of the door, she was standing in the garage bay, high-heeled boot toe tapping on the concrete floor. Without acknowledging her, he opened the back door and grabbed his overnight bag and the cooler.

"Just coming back from an overnight somewhere?" she snipped.

He finally leveled his gaze with hers. "Hi, Nicole. What brings you here?"

"Did you get my message?"

"Nope. Haven't had a chance to listen to it yet."

"Interesting. Too busy with *her*, I suppose."

Was she making this shit up? Was she following him? No clue. "Look, I'm tired, it's cold, and I've got a lot to do. Why did you call? For that matter, why are you here?" He put his stuff down and crossed his arms over his chest.

Her eyes turned glossy. "Can we go inside and talk?"

That misty-eyed look that used to rip him up was doing nothing right now except irritating the hell out of him. He picked up his stuff and told her to go inside while he closed the garage door. Jesus. What was she going to hit him with now? Whatever he *might* have speculated it was, he wasn't prepared for what came after they reached the kitchen and he'd put aside the cooler and bag.

"What if I told you Benny was dead?" she sniffed.

Glacial shards needled through his veins. *"What?"*

"Well, if you'd pick up your fucking phone when I call!" Now her watery eyes flashed fire.

He held up his hands, palms out, in a calm-down gesture. "Hold up. *Is* Benny dead?" Just saying the words caused a knot to form in his throat.

She swiped at her eyes. "No, but he could have been."

Dave ground his back molars. Temper, when it rose in him, usually went in stages, and it took time and whole lot of mad to hit each of those stages. A simmer climbed to a slow boil which, if provoked, climbed to a less slow boil. As he gaped at her, his temper shot from simmer to rolling boil. "What the hell is going on with Benny, and what the hell kind of game are you playing, Nicky?"

"He got sick, okay? I tried calling you two days ago and a bunch of times yesterday, but you didn't call me back!"

"You didn't leave me any messages! I didn't see any texts."

"Because you should have picked up, Dave!"

His head was about to explode. Had she always been like this and he'd conditioned himself to play along like a monkey on a chain? He let out a sigh of defeat. "Tell me about Benny."

"He got into some mouse poison, and the vet had to pump his stomach."

WTF? "Where did he get the poison?"

"I found a mouse in the garage, so I bought some and put it out. I thought only mice ate it! You always used to take care of these things. You need to come back, Dave."

He jerked or recoiled, he wasn't sure which. Maybe both. Was she serious? Suddenly, an old familiar feeling—one he'd shoved to the far recesses of his memory banks—wrapped itself around his throat. It was one thing to feel needed, but another entirely to be choked with the heavy chain of a boat anchor. "Where's Benny now? And where's Isaac?"

Her waterworks were full on; real or fake, he'd never been able to tell. "Isaac's with his dad," she said, "so he doesn't know what happened, thank God! Benny's home, and the vet says he'll be all right, but that visit cost a small fortune."

And there it was. She'd struck out at finding another sap with a bank account big enough to keep her happy, and she was trying to reel *him* back in to fill the void. No, she was trying to reel his wallet back in. "Tell me who the vet is, and I'll pay the bill."

"I already put it on my Visa, and now it's maxed out."

The Visa with a forty-grand limit. "Then send me the Visa bill, and I'll pay that portion."

"Why don't you just come back and make it easier for everyone?" she whimpered.

Not easier for me. He glanced around at his four walls to ground himself in reality, to double-check that he wasn't dreaming. "Nicky, what we had is in the past. You and I both know that going back would never work."

She plucked a paper towel and blew her nose. "This new girl must be a lot prettier than me. You used to say I was the most beautiful woman you'd ever seen."

He had said that, and though she'd prodded him, he really had meant it at the time. In that moment, it struck him that sometime recently, he'd wised up and realized beauty was about the whole package, not just the veneer. Right now Nicky's veneer was wearing thin. Maybe spending time with Ellie had crystallized it for him because the woman he'd once thought was the most beautiful couldn't hold a candle to the woman he'd just pushed away.

"You're still beautiful, Nick," he managed. "But I've moved on. You have too. Right now you're a little shaken up and you're looking for familiar ground. I'm not what you need. You'll recognize it in time." *Dave Grimson, Psych 101.*

He waited a few more minutes while she sniffled and wiped, anxious for her to go because he had some serious apologizing to do. "So, Nick, don't you need to get home so you can give Benny some medicine or something?" Shit. *He* used to be the one to do that kind of crap.

She waved a dismissive hand at him. "You're not very subtle, Dave. Don't worry. I'll go so you can get back to … Never mind." In the past, he'd have spent hours trying to reassure her, but those days were done, so he watched her sad figure walk out the front door, climb into the Lexus, and drive off. Relief left his lungs in a *whoosh.*

Before he'd shut the front door, he had his phone out and thumbed a text to Ellie.

I was a dick. Can I come over and explain? Or take you to dinner?

Chapter 26

THE CASUAL PLAYER AND OTHER DELUSIONS

Ellie stared at Dave's text. *I was a dick.* Maybe a little. And certainly confusing. The signals he'd sent this morning had been as jumbled as a bag full of peat moss, but she'd wanted to believe him when he'd said he was tired because it was better than the alternative: that whole morning-after weirdness when one of you was sober enough to regret the night before.

She let out a shoulder-shuddering sigh. She was a big girl, and she'd known what she was getting herself into. He was a hunky hockey player, and he'd gotten to her just like he probably got to every woman he threw a second glance. A teeny-weeny too much to drink, and she'd given in to her hot-and-bothered horny side, utterly forgetting that he *was* a hunky hockey player. But he had treated her like a princess last night, all night—*as generous in bed as he was with his wallet*—and she'd had an amazing time she wouldn't trade for all the landscape design projects in Denver. Did she want more of him? Of course she did. Which was why she'd acted like a stupid, jealous beeotch when Naughty Nicky called.

Trying not to think about what the future might hold for him and Naughty Nicky, she reread his questions, struggling to keep a cool head while she composed her answer. Her hammering heart was making it hard to concentrate, what with the blood whooshing in and out of her ears like waves hitting the shore. One thing she did know, however, was she'd rather be comfy at home, especially if what he had to explain was going to hurt. No point in showing distress to a bunch of strangers in a restaurant.

At that thought, she gulped in a breath and thumbed, *How about dinner here? I'll show off my mad BBQ skills.*

He replied immediately: *Perfect. Maybe you can teach me a thing or two. What can I bring?*

Whimsical Ellie—or was it *Wanton* Ellie?—answered: *Your cowboy hat.*

If she was lucky, maybe he'd wear that and nothing else. The vivid image zinged her in all the very best parts of her body, the ones a little sore from last night.

Dave: *Lol. If I do, will you wear it for me?*

"Ooh, Mr. Reaper," she said aloud, hope making her suddenly giddy over what *felt* like them exchanging flirty texts. "Are you having the same sinful thoughts I am?" Still, he had something to explain, which sounded serious. Could have been good or bad. *That'll depend on you*, she tapped right before pulling on her coat and grabbing her wallet on her way to the grocery store.

Several hours later, after showering, shampooing, and pulling on a pair of old jeans and a favorite black blouse, Ellie was seasoning asparagus spears and zucchini planks. These would join her marinated chicken breasts on the grill—if the weather held up. Outside her window, deep russets and brilliant golds stretched upward, their contrast stark against an iron fall sky. A storm was coming, and she and Dave had agreed on an early dinner for that reason. He had a morning skate and team meeting after, and he needed his "beauty sleep," so he'd said. In the background, the Revivalists sang "Wish I Knew You." Ellie sang along, the words striking sad chords deep inside her. What had she been doing with her life these last many years?

A knock on her front door had Casper slipping and sliding over the hardwood floor and had hummingbird wings blurring in Ellie's stomach. She checked the time on her phone. Ten minutes before Dave was supposed to be here, so who was at her front door? As if in answer, her phone chirped with a text.

Dave: *I'm a little early. Is that okay?*

Ellie let loose some pent-up steam with a nervous giggle and replied, *No. You have to wait 10 mins before I open the door.*

When she threw the door open, his cowboy-hatted head was bent over his phone. Several things happened at once. He raised wide eyes to her, Casper tried to climb his leg, and Dan + Shay started singing about being speechless.

Dave thrust a huge bouquet of mixed roses at her, a tentative smile playing on his face. "Appropriate song. Is my ten minutes up?"

She opened and closed her mouth. What had he just said? When he cocked his head, she waved him in. "I was teasing. Come in."

He stepped inside, arm still extended, his hand holding the colorful flowers. She went to take them from him, and he bent down—to kiss her, she assumed—but the brim of his hat hit her smack on the forehead, knocking it from his head. He burst out with a laugh. "If you hadn't already figured it out, my lack of hat etiquette is further proof I am definitely *not* a cowboy." He ducked, picked up the hat, and peered at her. His face fell. "Did I get you in the eye?"

"No. Yes. No. Just the forehead. I'm good. You just surprised me." *Deep breaths, El.* Seeing him, being so close, having those intense hazel eyes drilling into her—the sensory overload was lighting multiple tongue-twisting blazes inside her. *Oh Lordy!* Fortunately, she found her grin. "But I'm glad you brought the hat. Are the flowers for me?" As she took them from him, she did an inner face-palm. *I'm such a dork!*

He shucked his jacket and tossed it and the hat on her armchair. "No, they're for Casper. Just don't let her eat them all at once." He sent Ellie a wink before dropping into a crouch and scratching Casper's ears. The dog shamelessly rolled onto her back, exposing her belly, and kicked one of her back legs.

Can't blame you, girl. I'd be doing the same thing if that hunk of a man scratched my ears. Ellie strolled into the kitchen and placed the flowers in the sink. As she was reaching for a pair of shears, something big and warm snuggled up to her back. Strong arms bracketed her body, a familiar man scent filled her nose, and a pair of soft lips landed at the base of her neck and started working their way north. She tilted her head to give those lips better access. "Mmm, what are you doing?" *And please don't stop.*

"I never got a chance to kiss you good-bye when I brought you home," he mumbled against her skin, "and I totally blew my hello with the hat incident, so I figure I have some makeup work to do."

Abandoning the flowers, she leaned against him and closed her eyes. *Oh yes, please!*

He sucked a sensual path up her neck to her ear, where he lingered and nibbled. Warm breath and tongue turned her into a mass of quivering goo, and she nearly collapsed when he turned her and caught her mouth with his in a slow, probing kiss. A kiss that flashed hot and urgent seconds later. A kiss that had their tongues sliding and rolling over one another, hot and wet and hungry. That had her clawing at his back, had him hiking up her legs and wrapping them around his waist. That had him grinding the hard length restrained in his jeans into her, rocking her against the sink. That had her fingers bunched in his shirt, his hair. That fractured and stole the breath from her lungs.

Suddenly, he pulled back and stared at her, his mouth open as he gasped for air. "I didn't mean to do that."

Confusion bloomed in her foggy brain. "Do what? Kiss me?"

He rested his forehead against hers. One hand still supporting her leg, he traced his fingers along the side of her face with his other hand. "I meant to kiss you. I just didn't mean to lose my mind."

Self-satisfaction streaked through her, flushing her chest and neck with heat. She loosened her grip on his hair, toying with his strands instead, then released his shirt and rested her hand against the rock wall of his chest. "I'm sorry. Except I'm not."

Chuckling, he stepped away from the sink, sliding her down his body until she stood precariously on rickety legs. He laced his fingers together and rested them on the small of her back. "I came over here to explain about this morning."

"Oh." She pulled in a steadying breath and broke his hold. *I need alcohol.* "Can I get you a drink?"

"Yeah. I could use a whiskey if you have it. A double."

Now her stomach bottomed out, and her heart pounded for a wholly different reason. She hastily arranged the three dozen roses in a vase of water, measured out a hefty pour from the just-bought Stranahan's Whiskey bottle—it had been his go-to drink last night—and filled a wine goblet halfway with a red blend for herself. She led them to her slipcovered couch and curled up in one corner while he sank into the opposite corner. Casper had followed them—*him*—from the kitchen and now leaned against his leg. He gave her a few pats. After a long, quiet sip of whiskey, he cradled his glass and stared blankly at the coffee table.

"So … about this morning?" Ellie prodded. *Let's just get it over with.*

He cleared his throat. "I really was tired, but don't get me wrong. I'm not complaining." He shot her that sexy grin that probably got him out of all kinds of trouble. Another sip. "But I was also … a little freaked out, I guess."

Now *she* took a giant gulp. "Freaked out about what?"

"You."

That didn't sound good. "Me? Did I do something wrong?"

He set his drink on the coffee table, ate up the gap between them on the couch, and lifted her wineglass from her hand. This he placed on the table before grasping her arms and pulling her toward him. "Stop. You didn't do *anything* wrong. And that was part of my problem. You're so damn perfect that I got a little spooked, I guess."

"Spooked about what?" Yep, she was being a dork again, but honestly, she didn't get it. This big, bad Wookiee hockey player—

"Lots of reasons. I don't have a great track record when it comes to relationships, for one. For another, I may not be in Denver much longer." His eyes scanned hers as though he were trying to telegraph something he couldn't say out loud.

"Why do you say that?"

Releasing her, he sat back with a shrug that contradicted his intensity mere seconds before. "Players get traded all the time."

"But you've been with the Blizzard forever. And you're their captain! Do you really think they'd trade you?"

He shook his head. "Life's unpredictable, Ellie."

She frowned, trying to figure out what he *wasn't* telling her because what he *was* telling her sounded like a mix of excuses and gobbledygook. After all, he'd been with Nicole for years despite the fact that "players get traded all the time." The threat of a trade apparently hadn't been an issue when he'd been with her, and Ellie felt an old familiar tug. She was *that* girl. The perennial bridesmaid. The one guys were interested in at first but who didn't inspire them for the long haul.

"So did you ever find out what Nicole wanted?"

His body jerked. "I'm not really sure I know."

"Did you talk to her?" *None of your damn business, El.* But still, she wanted to know. And maybe it was better to know.

He scrubbed a hand over his jaw, and she couldn't help but follow the motion with her eyes because … God, she loved his hands! Especially when they were on her. He picked up his drink and sipped, then leaned forward, elbows on his thighs, the drink suspended between his knees. "Yeah, we talked."

Ellie reached over and plucked her glass from the table, holding it in front of her like a shield. "Are you still in love with her, Dave? Is that what's going on here?"

Slowly, he turned his head toward her. "No. Unequivocally, I am not in love with her." One corner of his mouth hitched up. "What I *am*, though, is hungry. Aren't you supposed to be grilling food right now instead of grilling me?"

"Oh believe me, I'm being gentle with you. If I *were* grilling you, you'd feel just like the chicken I'm about to char."

"Ouch! Duly noted."

She swung her legs out from under her and stood with little or no idea where she stood with *him*. He liked her; that much she recognized. Maybe he was only interested in a physical thing. Until the next better thing came along. Could she go with that? Keep it casual and not get hurt? She'd done casual before. In fact, she'd been the one to insist on it. But she was a little *too* gone for the Grim Guy already without comprehending the reasons why he affected her the way he did. *Enjoy what he has to offer while he offers it, El.* Her head hurt. And if she were being completely honest, so did her heart.

He rose and pulled her into a one-armed hug, kissing the top of her head. "Are we okay here?"

"I don't know. Have you explained what you came to explain?"

"Uh … yeah, I guess I have."

Was she going to let him skate with that flimsy "explanation"? Give him a pass? *Casual, El. Casual all the way.* "Then I guess so. Yes." She gave him a halfhearted smile and headed for the kitchen.

"You don't sound very convincing." He fell in right behind her. "Do you want me to go?" Melancholy laced his words. How did he do that anyway?

"No, I really don't. Besides, I have lots of food to get rid of." She spun and poked him in the chest. Surprise streaming through his eyes, he clutched his whiskey in one hand and her wine in the other and backpedaled. She stepped into his personal bubble. "And you're just the man for the job."

A chuckle rumbled through his chest. "Okay, Bossy Britches. I'll eat your food and help you clean up. *Then* I'll go and leave you in peace."

Chapter 27

Save a Horse, Ride a Cowboy

Ellie struggled to compartmentalize the uncomfortable conversation and all the doubts it brought with it. She was loath to admit how much she cared already, and an undercurrent of tension—hers—buzzed during dinner. Dave teased her mercilessly about her grilling techniques, among other things—though it didn't prevent him from scarfing down his portion and then some—and they fell into a laid-back, laughter-filled back-and-forth where she got in her own digs and was finally able to let go of her apprehension. He was easy to talk to, easy to be around, and though she'd spent the last twenty-four hours with him, she was ready for twenty-four more. Maybe even forty-eight. Seventy-two.

Dinner cleanup was soon done, but Dave didn't so much as twitch a muscle toward the front door, and she wasn't inclined to remind him of his promise to leave after the meal. The storm had arrived with a vengeance, and snow was falling in fat flakes that left the outside world covered with plush white carpet. He had commandeered the remote, and his body sprawled across her too-small couch like he owned it. His bare feet were propped on the coffee table, and Casper snored in his lap. They looked so darn cute together that Ellie simply couldn't tell him the dog wasn't allowed on the furniture. He seemed to need the canine fix.

She plopped beside them, and Dave draped his heavy arm over her shoulders and tucked her against him as if he'd been doing it for years. She nuzzled into him and rested her hand over his steadily thumping heart. "What are we watching?"

"*NHL Tonight*. I'm trying to get some scores."

On TV, a player carried the puck up the ice with blazing speed, executed some kind of stutter-stop spin move, and fired the puck up and over the goalie's shoulder. The announcer hooted, and so did Dave. "Did you see that sick move? That guy's amazing!"

"Which team is he on?"

"Arizona."

"Weren't you watching Arizona about a half hour ago? In fact, I thought I heard the announcer say exactly the same thing."

"Yeah, well, the highlights are on a loop."

"And how many times have you seen this loop tonight?"

"Three." He tweaked her hair. "Shut up. Don't you have landscaping shows you watch over and over?"

"Not three times." She giggled and stared up at his chiseled, bearded face. "You really love the game, don't you?"

He stroked the top of her head, and a sigh escaped his lungs. "Yeah, I really do."

"More than cars?"

His eyes took a tour of the ceiling. "That's a close one, but yeah, more than cars. Speaking of cars, sometime I'd like to take you to see mine. If you're interested, that is. I have a Chevy Nomad you might like."

"A Tri-Five?"

He chuckled. "Yep. A '56, as a matter of fact."

Hmm … making plans now. That sounds nice. "Ooh, I'd like that."

A few quiet, comfortable beats went by, and Ellie remembered an email she'd received today. "Paige Miller sent me an invitation to a holiday cocktail party at her house two weeks from now. She said to bring a plus-one. Wanna be my date? I think some of your teammates might be there." When Ellie had opened the invite, her mind had leapt to the business opportunities, and she'd contemplated going on her own for serious schmoozing. Maybe bringing Finn with her so he could help sell their services. But for the first time in a long time, she wanted to mix business *and* pleasure. "What do you say, Mr. Grim Reaper?"

Dave's body seemed to stiffen. Pulling himself upright, he lifted Casper onto the floor while at the same time unceremoniously removing himself as Ellie's body pillow, leaving her flailing on the couch. "Bathroom's that way?" He pointed toward the hallway.

"Um, yes." Ellie hauled herself up and watched him trot away. Casper gave her a dozy look. "Guess I said something wrong?" she said to the dog, utterly flummoxed.

When Dave returned, he didn't sit. Just hovered by the couch, hands stuffed in his front pockets, while he devoted his attention to a stupid commercial featuring an emu selling insurance. Ellie gave his jeans a tug and looked up at him. "Did I say something wrong?"

He gave her a pained look. She returned a confused one. "Okaaaaay. So I'm guessing you'd rather not do the social thing with me. I'm sorry if I overstepped. I just thought it would be fun and a comfortable—"

"It's not that." He sank beside her and puffed out a huge breath. "It's … When everything went south, a bunch of people were really pissed off at me."

"Yeah? And?" Hadn't they already gone over this before? "Is this about Nicole again?"

He ran a finger up her arm, and shivers skittered along her spine. "No, this is about my teammates not wanting anything to do with me, which makes getting together socially really awkward. Gage Nelson is a special thorn in my side."

Ellie gaped at him. "Lily's husband?"

"Yep. Guy won't talk to me."

"Wait. You're telling me he won't talk to you, even though everything happened over a year ago and you've been clean ever since?"

He wagged his head back and forth and stared up at the ceiling before returning his gaze to her. "The not-talking part might be mutual."

She blinked. "But isn't he your assistant captain?"

"Alternate. He's an alternate captain."

"Okay. Alternate. But I don't get it. How can you both be leaders on the same team and not talk?"

"Uh, because he's got a hockey stick up his ass?"

As soon as the words left his mouth, Dave realized how stupid they sounded. Ellie rolled her eyes. "No offense, but that sounds a little … juvenile."

Smart lady, and she's got a good point. "It sorta does when I say it out loud." He twirled a lock of her silky hair around his forefinger. He loved the feel of it. "I hadn't considered this before, but you and I have similar jobs. You're in charge of landscaping teams, and I'm in charge of my hockey club. Right now, though, you're doing a much better job with your team than I'm doing with mine. So do you have any words of advice, oh wise boss woman?"

Pursing her lips, she frowned and slanted her eyes to the side as if calculations were grinding through her head. "My dad used to tell us, 'Leaders lead, and loyalty's earned,'" she said. "Leaders step into a void and do what needs doing. Might not be easy, might not be comfortable, but they get it done. Maybe they're more determined or motivated, or just a little bit more *everything*. And those they lead notice—that's where the respect comes from.

"I've watched you, and you're one of those people who steps into the fray because someone *has* to. Leaders put everyone else first, then they put them on their shoulders. That's what you do, Dave. Just keep doing what comes naturally, and it'll work itself out, as long as your heart's in the right place."

He sifted her hair through his fingers, his mind turning over the fact Ellie was the kind of person who had your back, and what a good feeling that was. Kinda like Sonoma had his back, but on crack.

"I think it's why you step up to the plate whenever Nicole tells you she needs something, whether it's watching the dog or taking care of her kid."

Uh-oh. Boiling rapids up ahead. Nicky was a prickly subject better left undisturbed because he *knew* Ellie knew Nicky still clung to the outer fringes of his life, where she didn't belong. A shadow who wouldn't fade away.

"I guess that leadership philosophy doesn't translate the same way in relationships because loyalty wasn't one of Nicky's strong suits." The bitterness in his tone shocked even him.

"This is just my opinion, and stop me if I overstep, but I think Nicole was on Team Nicole, and you thought you were both on the family team. I've thought about it a lot, and I can't fathom abandoning someone you love when their world implodes. That's just … wrong."

"But what if I brought it on myself?"

"You were injured, and you were trying to heal yourself as best you could. It's not like you went out and killed someone. People who love each other are there for each other, good times and bad. They don't turn tail and swim away when the waters get choppy. They should put each other first, not because they're *supposed* to—it's not forced—but because they *want* to. You were there for her *and* Isaac when her ex was giving her shit, right? Because you *wanted* to be." Her voice dropped to a whisper. "You still are."

And then it hit him. Nicky hadn't had his back, ever. He had been pulling for a team that had never existed.

He tugged Ellie's curl. "That's how it was for you too, wasn't it? With Will. You thought you were on the same team, but he was a selfish player."

She shook her head. "We started out on the same team, but then he got himself traded to a new team."

"I never thought about it that way, but I guess that fits."

"No, I mean …" She pulled in a sharp breath. "Dave, he didn't have an affair with another woman."

A breathless moment passed before what she said smacked him like a puck between the eyes. *Thunk!*

"Jesus, El, you caught him with a dude?"

"Yep." She made a popping noise on the *p*.

"Christ. That had to be … I can't imagine. How did you handle it?"

She let out a mirthless laugh. "Not well." A few beats of silence charged the air, then she cleared her throat. "I was shocked and hurt and so damn confused. You think you know someone … To this day, I don't understand how I never saw it coming. I mean, when we met in college, he was dating all kinds of girls. And we had a good sex life, an active sex life. At least *I* thought it was good, so when I found them together, I was utterly blindsided."

The thought of her having a *good, active* sex life with another man—even if that man was no longer part of her life—rankled. Made the possessive side of him feel as though he sat on pins and needles. He didn't like the pictures playing on his mind's jumbotron, and he tried to shove them into a vault. "I'm sorry, El. I can't fathom how much that sucked. And then he stuck you with all the debt on top of it? Did you ever hash it out with him?"

"Not really. I felt like I was in a game of tug-of-war with Arturo, his lover. Then I was just so sick and heartbroken and worn out that I wanted it to be over with. I wanted him gone, out of my life. It wasn't until after he and Arturo left that I realized how big a financial mess they'd left me with. Turns out Will had turned over the bank account to Arturo, and Arturo took full advantage."

What? "Couldn't you turn him in or bring charges?"

Her eyes found his, and they were wet and filled with heartbreaking sadness. Then she seemed to shake herself out of it, letting out another humorless laugh. "He didn't do anything illegal because Will was an owner, and he'd given Arturo carte blanche."

Dave took her hand in his. It was small and pale, and he wrapped it up like he might an injured bird. "I'm so sorry, Ellie. Have you spoken to Will since it all happened?"

"Funny you should ask. One day not too long ago, he called to apologize when Arturo wasn't around. Not to pay me back for the money they stole, which would have been nice," she chuckled wryly. "He said he'd been feeling bad about what he'd done for the longest time and finally worked up the nerve to call. We ended up talking for an hour, and I think it gave us both closure. I doubt our paths will ever cross again, but I'm glad he's happy. I never realized how tortured he was. He and Arturo live in Texas, and they started a family." Another pained look flashed in her blue eyes. "Having kids was something we'd always talked about doing together."

Dave's chest constricted, and twin wants rose up inside him. The first was to fix her world so she didn't hurt, and, following close behind, was a startling desire to help her get those kids. She'd make a great mom.

Elbowing the thoughts aside, he swallowed hard. Unsure what to say, he caressed her hand and sighed instead. Casper whimpered at his feet, and he automatically reached down with his free hand and rubbed her ears.

Ellie shook her head again as if shaking away the bad memories, and he pulled her against him and held her while he stared blankly at the flickering TV. Her stiff body uncoiled, and she snuggled into him. While her soft, warm weight might have been firing up things south of his belt, it occurred to him that what he really wanted was to be the guy who made her face light up like the sun had just crested the horizon. He wanted to be the guy who took care of her, who took away her tears and frowns, who gave her all his affection. The one who earned her secret smiles. She stirred emotions in him that had never been stirred, and he wondered if he could ever go back to where he'd been before he'd met her. And it terrified him.

The next night, Dave was back on Ellie's couch, watching his hockey show as she sat beside him. An amazing feat, really, considering it was still snowing outside and he'd braved the blizzard to bring her Chinese takeout. Tonight she wore black jeans and a mulberry sweater with an asymmetrical zipper that Will had given her. Coincidence? Maybe not, considering how much she'd been thinking of him since her reveal to Dave the night before.

At first, the familiar stabs of anger, humiliation, and incomprehension had twisted into a knot of hurt as the vivid scene replayed itself in her mind's eye, and the same old question had tumbled inside her brain. How could she not have recognized the signs in a man she loved and thought she knew so well? "Don't be so hard on yourself, El," Will had said during their cathartic phone call. "I had it well buried, and I'd fought against it for so long that I had myself fooled. Arturo helped me understand who I really was, and I was only just coming to terms myself, so how could *you* have known? I wasn't rejecting *you*." Maybe not, but it stung like rejection nonetheless. Hearing *Arturo* had helped Will discover who he really was still made Ellie bristle. On some level, she couldn't help thinking Arturo was the supreme thief: he'd stolen her husband and her money. On calmer reflection, though, she understood Will would have eventually left her, and she hadn't lied when she'd told Dave she was happy for him.

And honestly? While she and Dave might be nursing a "fledgling affair" that would eventually crash and burn, he'd shown her how different a "good sex life" could be. Sex with him was insane, mind-blowing, and she'd never felt so feminine and alive, like some primal part of the man in him was speaking directly to the primal woman in her. You couldn't fake that stuff, and that's just what Will had done. She could see it now.

Dave side-eyed her. "I can practically hear your gears grinding. What are you thinking about?"

Startled back to the couch, she recovered quickly. "I've been thinking about last night."

"You mean when I woke you up with—"

Tickles erupted in her tummy. Yep, his *man* definitely had a straight line of communication to her *woman*. "No, no. Well, yeah, I've been thinking about that too." *Kinda hard not to with that wicked tongue of yours.* She bounced her eyebrows and grinned. "But seriously, I've thought about your dilemma with Gage Nelson. What if you just acted like you would if he were willing to meet you halfway?"

"Kinda hard when the guy won't—"

"Hear me out. What if you used the same determination you used to get my boxed dinner? From what I've seen, you're the kind of guy who, when he decides he wants something, goes after it. Period."

His eyes lit with amusement. "Oh yeah?"

"Yeah. It's this scary look you get in your eyes that says, 'Get out of my way!'" She narrowed her eyes for effect.

He craned his head and peered at her. "When have you seen me get this look? Besides at the auction?"

"Um, afterward, when we were in bed?" Her cheeks heated.

His lips quirked as if he were fighting a grin. "My *look* says 'Get out of my way'? Shit, I'll have to work on that. That's definitely *not* the message I'm trying to broadcast. It's more like, 'Get *in* my way, please.' Or are you saying I'm scary in bed now?"

She let fly a laugh, and sweet relief went with it. Just like that, Will and some of her self-doubts were in the rearview mirror, where they belonged. "No, that didn't come out right. And I meant scary good, not scary."

He let out a guffaw. "Damn, what can I say to that?"

"How about, 'My male ego and I thank you for the lovely compliment, Ellie, and yes, we'd love to escort you to Paige Miller's cocktail party.'" She tilted her head to one side.

Now he frowned. "I have to look at my calendar. There might be a game that night."

"And if there is, you can join me after." She flashed him her brightest smile.

"All right. I'll think about it. And speaking of games—"

"We were?"

He dropped his head and gave her a charging-bull look. He was good at those. "And speaking of games," he repeated loudly, "do you want to come to my game tomorrow night? I know it's last minute, but it'd be fun to have you there. I should be able to get tickets for you and Finn."

"Better include Sonoma in that. I have a feeling they're going to be joined at the hip. Have you heard from her since the big event, by the way?"

"Just a quick text saying she got home okay. You?"

"About the same from Finn."

"Joined at the hip," they both said at once and laughed.

Dave relaxed back into the cushions, and Casper stood on her hind legs, her front paws on his knee, a hopeful look in her big brown eyes. Her entire body quivered as she whimpered. "Aw, come here, pretty girl," he crooned in his baritone timbre. Then he hooked an arm around Ellie's neck and dragged her on top of him.

She started laughing and couldn't stop. "Casper thinks you were talking to her!"

"Nope. Not this time. You were whimpering louder than she was."

Ellie arranged herself on his lap. "I was *not* whimpering. I don't whimper."

"Were too. And you know what?" He tweaked her hair. "It's really sexy." His eyes landed on her zipper. "I've been wondering all night what's under this." A quick tug and her sweater fell open, exposing her bra. He sucked in a breath. "Ooh, nice."

"Stop it!" she laughed and quickly zipped herself back up. "Aren't you supposed to be going home so you can get some beauty sleep?"

"What? You going to send me off into the cold, dark night and let my poor body get battered by the storm of the century? On an empty stomach? Cruel," he tsked and teased her zipper again, sliding it up and down an inch or two.

She held on to the zipper tab. "How can you be hungry?"

His tongue darted out and swiped his lips as he contemplated her. Then he shrugged. "I'm a growing boy."

Yeah, *something* was growing … in his lap. Under her butt. She scrambled off him before she could throw herself at him. "Popcorn?"

"Love popcorn. And I'll change from hockey. What do you want to watch?" he called after her as she retreated to the kitchen.

"Hallmark Channel," she called back.

"God no, pleeaaase!" he cried.

She chuckled to herself as she melted butter and threw two bags of popcorn in the microwave. Lordy, she could have melted the butter on her skin. Between last night's fun and games in bed and him acting all hot and man-adorable just now, he'd set her nerves on fire and heated her blood so it was like a running river of lava. She wet a paper towel and pressed it to her face and neck to cool herself down. *Phew! Get yourself under control, El.* Yep, *no one* had ever made her feel this way.

When she returned, she set the bowl of popcorn on the table, where Dave had propped his feet again. He reclined on the couch, hands clasped behind his head, and frowned at the TV where, yes, the Hallmark Channel was on. "So these two are in a cook-off and they're gonna somehow go all gushy on each other and live happily ever after?"

"Where's your romantic side?"

"Come a little closer, and I'll show you my romantic side." He waggled his eyebrows. Of course he did.

"We don't have to watch this. I was kidding," she said. He ignored her, not budging, so she began clambering over his legs. He lifted a knee, trapping her, and she paused and put her hands on her hips. "Excuse me."

A gleam lit his eyes. "You're excused."

She waved her hand over his body. "Uh, could you maybe move?"

Lightning quick, he pulled her down so she straddled his lap again, and she let out a squeal. His hands anchored her hips, and his eyes raked her. His lips curled in a wolfish smile. "You're cute when you boss me around."

She feigned outrage. "*Cute?* And I'm not bossy."

"Yeah, you are. *And* you whimper."

She folded her arms across her chest and hmphed. He peeled them away. "C'mon, cutie. Boss me around."

"No," she laughed. "I thought you were hungry."

"I am." With another swift move, he flipped her on her back and pinned her hands above her head with one big hand. Then he sank his heavy body on top of hers and started a slow assault on her collarbone with his moist mouth. "If you won't boss me around, then I'm going to boss *you* around … and make you whimper," he whispered.

Tingles of anticipation down low fanned out and raced over her belly, up her chest to her scalp, puckering her skin. "Ooh … uh … um …" God, that felt good. Relishing the feel of his warm, soft lips moving over her skin, the weight of him on top of her, she closed her eyes and let out a little moan.

"You were saying?" he mumbled against her throat. His free hand returned to her zipper, and he pulled it down, slowly, slowly, until he worked it free and opened the sweater. He feathered his fingers along her side, over her ribs, causing goose bumps to erupt.

"Can't … say … much …" She bit her lower lip. "Mmm …"

Despite the thick fabric of his denim fly, she could feel the outline of his heavy erection pressing against her. "God, you drive me nuts when you make those noises," he said all low and gravelly, his breathing growing shallower.

She wanted to get her hands on him, feel his solid strength through his shirt, but he clamped down harder when she tried to wiggle her hands free. Arching into him, she wrapped a leg around his hip, digging her heel into his ass. "Thought you were going to boss me around," she breathed.

His soft hair brushed her neck, her cheek, as he worked his way across her jaw to her ear. Suddenly, he lifted his torso and braced his weight on one arm. His eyes darkened and glittered like deep mountain pools, and that sly smile curved his full mouth. "Since you insist … Take everything off from your waist up."

The heat in his eyes shot straight to her core, stoking the fire there into a conflagration. She giggled nervously. "How am I supposed to do that when I can't move my hands?"

He released her and sat up, hauling her up with him. Kneeling on the couch beside him, she grew emboldened by the hunger and intensity in his eyes. She was the puck again, and he was coming after her, no holds barred, but she was determined to torment him for a little while. Still on her knees, she scooted back and languidly pulled her sweater off her shoulder as if she were in slow-mo. His heated gaze dipped to the bare skin she was revealing one tortuous inch at a time. She repeated the striptease with the other shoulder, finally pulling the sweater off her arms and dropping it on the floor. He reached out, grazing his fingertips over her ribs as he traced them.

She shimmied away and wagged her finger. "You can look, but you can't touch. Yet." *Guess I am bossy.* With a pained expression, he thudded the back of his head against the couch, though he kept his eyes pinned on her. Slowly, she slid a strap down her arm. His eyes followed her movement then cut back to her sheer bra. She could have sworn his pupils dilated. He let out a gratifyingly low groan that seemed to rumble through him. She'd never done anything like this in her life, and she was enjoying the hell out of herself.

Down came the other strap. She paused a moment before reaching back and unfastening the clasp. The bra hung there, and she didn't move. Just let gravity pull the straps another tantalizing inch down her arms. He sat up abruptly, eyes still locked on her reveal. As she let the bra fall, she said in a throaty whisper, "Is this what you wanted?"

"Fuck!" he growled. "You are … a work of art." His voice was rough, strained. He swallowed, his Adam's apple bobbing. "Touching now."

She lifted her hair and crossed her arms over her head like an old-time pinup model, bowing her back and practically offering her bare breasts to him on a platter. She hooded her eyes and gave him a smile she *hoped* was seductive.

Calloused fingers skimmed over her flesh, lightly, reverently, spreading chills over her bare skin. His gaze darted between her tautening nipples and her face. He explored her with his fingers and eyes. "So gorgeous, Ellie," he murmured. "Like nothing I've ever seen."

He teased her nipples with his thumbs, ran the tips of his fingers along the underside of her breasts, then palmed them, shooting more shivers over her chest, her shoulders, and down her back. Her eyes fluttered closed for an instant, and a whimper rose up in her throat. God, she *did* sound like Casper! His hand glided over her abdomen and wrapped around her waist to pull her closer. He dipped his head and traced a slow circle around one nipple with the tip of his tongue, then the other. He clamped down softly and sucked her flesh into his hot mouth. *Omigod.* Her head dropped back, and she wrapped her hands around his head and plowed her fingers through his hair, lost in the sensations.

His talented mouth kept up its slow torment while his strong fingers held her exactly where he wanted her. Licking, nipping, suckling, grazing over her sensitive skin. Then he latched on and drew her into his mouth hard, the pressure making her gasp. "Oh yes, like that. More." The words tumbled from her, sounding far away, as though someone else was moaning out the plea. She braced her hands against his shoulders as he continued his intensifying assault. He brushed one hand down her side and popped the button on her jeans, then snaked his fingers under her waistband. She sucked in her stomach to give him more room, but he retreated. His mouth blazed a trail up her chest to her mouth, where he locked on possessively. Meanwhile, his hands made quick work of her fly. She wound her arms around his neck while he continued to own her mouth. A warm, rough hand slipped into her jeans, under her panties, and his finger arrowed to her soaked entrance.

He groaned into her mouth as first one finger, then another tunneled inside her, and she gasped when they hit home. "So fucking wet," he hissed against her lips. Suddenly frustrated by the fabric keeping her from feeling his skin against hers, she unbuttoned his shirt, laying it open so she could run her hands over smooth skin stretched taut over bands of hard muscle. Their tongues danced and dueled as his fingers moved in and out of her. She wanted to climb him, get closer, and she clung to his shoulders while remaining on her knees. They turned watery and buckled when he increased the friction. Arms twined around his back, tongue probing his mouth, she plastered herself to him and let out an "Oh!" when her orgasm took her by surprise.

He eased his fingers out and cupped her while he trailed a line of hot, wet kisses down her neck. When he bit her shoulder softly, she let out a strangled giggle. His mouth returned to hers, his kisses becoming ravenous, and he pulled off his shirt, pulled her pants down, and laid her back on the couch while he wrestled with his belt and zipper. Soon they were both naked, and he was stretched out on top of her, skin kissing skin, his swollen shaft trapped between their bodies. God, she wanted him inside her, but he seemed intent on making love to her mouth slowly while his hands twined in her hair, then trailed down and tortured her breasts, driving her out of her ever-loving mind.

She wiggled and writhed underneath him, shifting to line up her entrance with the head of his cock. He pulled back and peered at her, an amused twinkle lighting his eyes. "You're trying to boss me around again."

She let out a frustrated groan. "I want you inside me."

"I thought we agreed *I* was in charge. You gonna throw me that bone and let me at least *believe* I'm the boss of you for a change, Ms. Britches?"

She choked out a laugh. "Yes, Captain, my captain, Your Highness, sir."

"That's more like it. But I think I'm going to have to punish you for your insubordination." He wiggled his eyebrows.

Her eyes widened. "Um …"

Then his mouth was back on her, moving down her body, making her squirm even more. His big hands gripped her thighs and slid them over his square shoulders, spreading her wide.

"This," he whispered, then clamped his mouth on her. The onslaught he'd unleashed on her mouth he now unleashed between her legs, starting with the feathery touch of his tongue that soon turned to licking and lashing, sucking and stroking and probing, an exquisite mix of tender and ruthless and gentle and relentless. She tried to buck and escape his mouth, but he held her fast. Her fists balled and pressed into the couch, and she let out a series of sharp cries as one orgasm, then another, crashed over her.

Casper dashed over and whined, turning in circles, and Dave lifted his head, his eyes round. "What the …?"

"She … thinks … you're hurting … me," Ellie gasped. Her chest heaved, pushing air in and out of her lungs, and everything south of her belly button twitched and tingled.

Poised between her legs, he hoisted his weight onto his forearms, eyes even rounder. "I'm not, am I?"

Ellie tossed her head from side to side, trying to catch her breath. "No," she managed to huff out.

"Well, this calls for desperate measures," he rumbled.

Extricating himself from between Ellie's knees, he sat on the edge of the couch and scratched Casper's chin. "It's okay, sweetheart. Mommy and I were just fooling around. She likes it … I think … and I'm not hurting her. I would *never* hurt her." He lifted Casper's ear, leaned down, and whispered, "I don't hurt people I love."

Ellie glanced at Dave—*did he really just say what I think he said?*—but he was still petting Casper, who sat on her haunches and wagged. Something warm oozed inside Ellie's chest and wrapped a warm quilt around her heart.

Dave continued talking to the dog. "But she and I still have unfinished business, so you'll excuse us …" He riffled through his jeans and extracted some condoms. Then he grabbed Ellie's ankles and yanked her toward him, scooped her up like she was a rag doll, tossed her over his shoulder, and stood as though he didn't have a hundred-and-ten-pound woman slung over his shoulder.

"Where are you taking me, caveman?" she squeaked.

"To a cave," he grunted. "I know there's one around here somewhere."

Dangling over his shoulder, she pinched his ass and laughed as he marched purposefully to her bedroom.

Oh God, please hurry!

Chapter 28

DISTRACTIONS

Dave could lecture himself all day long about needing to stay away from Ellie and convince himself that his only reason for seeing her tonight was to tell her *why* he needed to stay away. And then go home. No touching, no kissing, no getting all cozy on the couch. No getting naked. But as soon as he'd seen her, spent time with her, he'd grown so relaxed that his brain blanked and he lost track of any good intentions he'd brought with him. In the end, it was a lost cause. Who the fuck was he kidding? This was *totally* what his scheming mind—and one notoriously single-purposed part of him—intended. As he marched down the hall to her bedroom, her silky hair swinging against his back and tickling his skin, he wondered how long he could hold out once he was finally inside her. This woman had a stranglehold on him, one that drove him out of his effing mind. A danger to his heart's health, that vague inner voice reminded him. Probably Yoda.

He paused in the doorway to her bedroom and looked around, taking stock because he hadn't last night—only the bed had registered. Now he was in no hurry to put her on it because all that smooth skin draped over him felt too fucking good. He took advantage and ran his hands up the backs of her legs and kneaded her ass, dragged a finger through her slickness and made her giggle and gasp. *So fucking perfect.*

Now his gaze swept the cozy room again. A bedside lamp illuminated light greens and creams and lavenders, like one would find in a natural landscape. The style was all her. Plus, it smelled like her. Yeah, he could spend time here. A *lot* of time.

Ellie squeaked over his shoulder, and he closed the door behind him. His plans included making her scream a whole lot louder, and he didn't need to upset the poor dog more than he had, for Christ's sake! A few steps brought him to the edge of the bed, and he slid his naked load from his shoulder and laid her on her back so her head sank into soft pillows. Propping herself up on an elbow, she twirled a spiral of hair around her index finger, seeming to invite him to roam his eyes all over her—which he took full advantage of. If her hot-as-fuck little striptease in the living room hadn't been proof enough, her current sex-kitten look broadcast that her shyness from last night had completely vanished.

"You just gonna stand there and stare?" the bold little kitten taunted.

Holding himself back, he wagged a finger at her and smirked, faking a coolness that was nowhere inside him. He was likely to break out in beads of sweat any second. "Who's in charge here?" He walked around to the nightstand, eyes glued to the gorgeous creature on the bed, and dropped the condoms while *her* eyes roved over *him*. Sexiest damn thing he'd ever seen, and his cock, already rock hard, grew even steelier under her appreciative scrutiny. Or it was showing off.

He crawled onto the bed and up her body, growling, trying not to laugh, "I said, Who's. In. Charge?"

"You are." Her words came out in a breathless rush, dripping with desire and sucking any humor out of the moment, replacing it with something sinful and lusty.

"Hands above your head," he ordered. She complied, and he brushed a few strands from her face and ran his fingertips along her cheek, tracing her cheekbones, her jaw, eventually reaching her mouth, where he outlined her lips. Her tongue darted out and licked. He slid his finger into her mouth, and she closed around it and sucked while her eyes held his. Jesus Christ! He thought he'd come right then and there.

"Taste yourself?" he near-croaked.

"Mmm." Now her tongue was swirling around his finger, and her cheeks hollowed.

"You taste so fucking sweet." He added the other finger, and she closed around that one with a moan, fluttering her eyes closed. He was definitely *not* in charge. No, he was on the verge of losing it, so he slipped his fingers from her mouth and slithered them down her body, sinking them inside her while his mouth sank into a tongue-filled kiss. Her body writhed beneath him, arched into him, and she moaned into his mouth.

He added a third finger, increasing the friction and tempo, breaking the kiss long enough to say, "Come for me, Ellie. I want to feel you come on my fingers."

Her moans grew louder, more desperate, and her face twisted with pure carnal pleasure. She was the most beautiful sight he'd ever seen. Soon she was gasping his name, and he took her mouth again, his tongue thrusting hard and deep as he stole every wonderful sound rising from her throat. When her orgasm finally rippled through her body, he swallowed that too.

She wrapped herself around him and clung tightly, and he held her and planted soft kisses on her hair and neck until her breathing evened out and her heart stopped slamming against his chest. Then she pulled away and ran her fingers over his beard, his ear, and into his hair. "Wow. Just … wow." He felt his smile broaden under her deep blue gaze because she was looking at him with unabashed awe, like he was some fucking sex superhero.

"Wow yourself," he whispered.

"I think I like you being in charge."

"Well, that's good because I'm not done yet."

She rolled onto her back, her fingers still dancing over his skin. Her peaked pink nipples were there for the taking, and he lowered his head and licked. "Can't get enough of you, Ellie." He closed his mouth over one, flicking it with his tongue, and she sank her teeth into his shoulder. His plan to make her come at least twice more before he entered her sailed right out the window. Soon he was on her, his hands splayed over her thighs as he pushed them wide, the tip of his cock sliding along the length of her entrance, inching into her welcoming wetness.

"Dave!" she gasped and reached for one of the packets on the nightstand. She thrust it at him. "You forgot."

No, he didn't forget. His mind had simply gone missing for a moment, filled with an ache to feel her without any barriers, feel himself surrounded by her slick walls, and he'd been about to give in to that ache. He hurriedly rolled the rubber on and sank back into her open arms, back atop her soft body with her pillowy breasts squished against him, back between her parted legs, where he lost himself inside her banked heat with one long, steady thrust. So hot. So wet. So tight.

He pushed up on his hands, his arms carrying his weight so he could study her as he plunged in and pulled out, in and out, over and over and over. He watched her teeth sink into her lower lip, watched her fingers dig into his forearms, her eyes close, her lips part, her chest rise and fall as her breaths shallowed out, her throat move with each moan and mewl, her hips undulate as they rose to meet his thrusts. A thing of beauty. And when she came, he watched her body seize, watched her eyelids flutter open and her eyes dilate, watched as she hissed out his name.

He stopped and caught his breath, reeled in his pleasure while she floated down from her own blissful cloud. Then he started back up, grinding against her, plunging harder, deeper, faster, flexing, driving, slamming, watching her expressions transform as he meted out pleasure on a knife's edge, that fine line between ecstasy and pain. He could feel her stretch around him, feel himself filling her, feel her body quiver as her orgasm built, detonated, and crashed over her. And again he stopped, holding himself back, transfixed by every emotion playing over her beautiful face.

When he started up again, he hooked her thigh over his shoulder and drove deeper, as if he could reach her very center. Her rising yelps, those fractured gasps and desperate mewls and throaty moans surrounded him like music, growing louder, crescendoing as he hammered home, drilling into her, a relentless pile driver pounding over and over and over. White-hot lightning bolted down his spine and exploded low, racing through him, blanking his mind so he only saw bursts of light, flashes of fire. He spent himself inside her in wave after wave. Exquisite, searing, all-consuming.

He collapsed on top of her, and as his lucid mind returned to itself, he realized he'd entwined his fingers with hers. But more than fingers, his soul was entwined, and he understood what it meant to be addicted. If it were possible, she was in his blood, and he was already fixed on when he could have her again. How many times would be enough? He feared he already knew the answer. Never.

The team played a decent game. Not their best effort, but they managed a check mark in the win column, and in the end, that's what counted. But Dave's real reward was waiting. Ellie had been at the game with Finn and

Sonoma, and his eyes had wandered to her more times than they should have. Playing it cool hadn't come as easily as he'd imagined it would, but he'd managed to keep a lid on it. Barely.

Flexing his hand, Dave smiled to himself as he wandered into a fog of thoughts about Ellie and the night before. Not just the sex, which had been fucking phenomenal, but the talking in between. The hanging out and eating popcorn. The cuddling on the couch and Ellie falling asleep curled against his chest. Letting Casper hop up in his lap when Ellie wasn't looking. Waking up at the ass crack of dawn when Ellie stirred in his arms. When she made him breakfast and kissed him good-bye on her way to work, leaving him and Casper to clean up the kitchen.

Sweet. So sweet.

"Hey, your hand okay, Cap?" T.J.'s voice startled Dave from where he stood staring at his name plaque on his stall.

He stopped flexing. "Yeah, all good. Doc just wants me to stretch it now and again." Not the truth, but not exactly a lie either.

"Well, I figured it might still be bothering you when you made that beauty tape-to-tape pass to the other team." T.J. chortled and shook his head. "I was trying to make excuses for you, man."

Dave smirked, hiding the fact T.J.'s innocent tease stung. "I can make my own, thanks."

While most of Dave's teammates gave him a wide berth, Quinn, Viktor, and a few other guys ribbed him good-naturedly, and he gave it right back. He wasn't the only one who'd flubbed tonight. Despite the sore subject, the joking felt good. As they filed out of the dressing room, most of the guys tossed him a "good night"—they always did—but no one invited him to join them for a late meal at one of the local restaurants. Didn't matter, he told himself. He already had plans to eat with Ellie, Sonoma, and Finn, but it would have been nice to be included by the guys like they used to do. Guys had facetiously accused him of "holding court" at those dinners, which was utter bullshit, but the respect had fed his self-confidence nonetheless. He wanted that back, and his inner Han railed at his teammates.

As he strode from the locker room, last man out, his phone pinged. Expecting a text from Ellie, he glanced down and stopped.

Bobby: *How's the hand holding up?*

Dave: *Why do you ask?*

Bobby: *Looked like you were struggling a little tonight. Just remember I'm here.*

Dave stared at the screen. His hand seemed to throb a little more than it had a minute before, and he once again pondered how quickly the recovery would go if he gave in to Bobby's couched offer. *Testing is infrequent and predictable now. I could do it and no one would know. And my hand would feel so much better.*

He dragged a hand over his jaw before tapping in his reply. *Thanks, man. I'm good.*

Bobby: *You know how to find me. Remember, you ain't getting any younger.*

Sliding the phone in his pocket, Dave puffed out a breath. A few more strides and his eyes landed on Ellie waiting with Sonoma and Finn in the family and friends area. *Everything's okay now.* She turned and arched her eyebrows as he approached. *Kiss her? Not kiss her?* Few people still milled around, but he opted for cool and casual and merely offered her a "hey" before greeting Sonoma and Finn.

"Wow! Look at Mr. Reaper all dressed up." Ellie's eyes traveled over him appreciatively.

"They're supposed to dress up whenever they arrive or leave the arena," Sonoma explained.

Finn chuckled. "Dude, if I didn't know better, I'd say you were someone else."

Dave gave him a friendly chin lift while flipping him off. He shrugged his gear bag. "Ready to grab something to eat?"

They all said they were, with Ellie adding, "I imagine you're starved."

"Always." He grinned and grabbed her hand with his good one. "You riding with me?"

She gave him a shy smile. "If that's okay."

"That's perfect." He stopped on the way out to greet a few fans and sign autographs while Ellie stepped into the background and watched.

"I hope you didn't mind about the fans," he said afterward as he led her to the GTO.

"Not at all. It's your job." Her eyes went wide when they landed on the GTO, and he tried not to chuckle. "Even if I did mind, you brought the GTO, so all would be forgiven."

"I brought it just for you."

After he settled her in the passenger seat, he stowed his bag, pulled off his tie, and slid behind the wheel. Her eyes roamed over the interior of the car with obvious reverence, so he fired up the engine and gave it an extra rev. Her fingertips reached toward the dash, then retracted, as if she were afraid to touch anything. He resisted the urge to pull her into his arms and kiss the daylights out of her. Instead, he said, "It's okay to touch. You won't break anything."

She folded her hands in her lap. "No, I'm good. I do think you could use some fuzzy dice, though."

"And a hula girl on the dash."

"One of those spring-loaded jobbies that swivels her hips?"

"No, a *real* hula girl swiveling her hips. Might make driving a little challenging, though." He laughed when she swatted his arm.

On the way to dinner, the *only* subject they discussed was the car, how he'd found it, what he'd done to restore it, and other vintage cars he'd owned or wanted to own. At dinner, the four of them merely glossed over the usual topic—hockey—covering instead subjects ranging from spy planes to growing water lilies. He couldn't remember being so relaxed after a game.

When dinner was cleared away, when they'd agreed he'd take her home, when they'd said good night to Finn and Sonoma, and when they were finally seated in the GTO, he leaned across the bench seat, wrapped his hand around her nape, and pulled her in for a kiss. "I've been thinking about that ever since I laid eyes on you tonight."

She smiled at him. "Well, now you've got it out of your system."

Not a chance.

They reached her house way too soon, and on the short walk up to her door, he tried to come up with an excuse to linger. "Would it be okay if I came in and got my Casper fix?" *Until I can figure out how to finagle my Ellie fix?*

"Sure. I think she needs her Dave fix too," she said on a laugh as she let them inside. Said ghost dog hopped straight up as though she had pogo sticks for legs, then proceeded to wag her way around his pants legs.

Ellie's hands flew to her cheeks. "Oh no! She'll get dog hair all over your suit pants!"

Dave bent to pet the dog. "No worries. I'll just take my pants off." He stood upright with a grin, and Ellie gawked at him before breaking into laughter.

"I thought you were serious!"

He began unbuckling his belt. "I *am* serious." He let the belt and pants drop and pool around his socks and shoes. She laughed louder. "Doing wonders for my ego here," he chuckled.

"It's just that … I mean, you're all dressed up, except for your pants … and then hello! There are your hairy legs."

He waggled his eyebrows. "Give you any ideas?"

"Yeah. Can I get a selfie with you like that? I'm a big fan, you know." She batted her eyelashes at him.

"Haha." He snagged her arm and pulled her in close, tangling a hand in her hair. "What *other* ideas does it give you?"

Her small hands ran under his jacket, radiating heat through his shirt. She pushed the coat off his shoulders. Then her hands cupped his face, pulling him in for a kiss, sucking his bottom lip into her mouth while her eyes searched his. The tip of her tongue danced out and teased his lips. He opened immediately, but she pulled away and moved to his ear, breathing, "I can think of a few things." She nipped his earlobe, then his neck.

His hand tightened in her hair, and he swatted her butt with the other, growling, "No biting until I've got you naked."

She spun from his grasp and raced toward her bedroom. "Gotta catch me first."

"Game on, sweet thing!" He took off after her and immediately thudded to the floor, pants twisted around his ankles. *Shit!* Casper covered his face with licks before he could push her away. Down the hallway drifted Ellie's hysterical laughter, making his own bubble to the surface. In that moment, his wounded hand and wounded pride didn't matter. The only thing that *did* matter was the woman who was going to let him into her bed tonight. He had everything he wanted, and it was easy to silence the voice warning him he was getting in too deep.

"I can't believe you're hungry again," she said behind him an hour later as he stuck his head in her open refrigerator. Her voice held a sleepy smile. He raked his hand through his messy hair—the hair *she'd* messed up—and turned, the sight of her filling him with something he couldn't understand because he'd never felt it before.

Dressed in yoga pants and a tiny tank top under a gaping terry robe, she'd pulled her hair into a ponytail that hadn't quite captured all her strands. Some of them wisped around her face, and others hid one eye. She was sex-rumpled. Breathtaking. Utterly stunning. And he couldn't wait to rumple her again.

She yawned and stretched, and her top rode up and gave him a peek at a stripe of smooth pink skin. "If I'm going to hang out with you much longer," she said, "I'll have to adjust my sleep schedule. Any more of this going to bed at 2:00 a.m. and getting up at six, and I'll be falling asleep at the wheel and crashing into people, like someone I know."

He perched his hands on his boxer-clad hips. They were all he had on, and he felt surprisingly comfortable, even though he wasn't in his own house. "That accident had nothing to do with lack of sleep."

"Oh no? What, then?"

Being distracted about everything and everyone driving me nuts in Denver. Which, interestingly, wasn't holding his attention hostage like it had. "Not watching where I was going, I guess," he lied. He closed the fridge door, scooped her up, and sat on a kitchen chair with her in his lap. An errant thought streaked through his brain, sending him into a near panic. With soft strokes, he ran his fingertips over her hair, her face. "God, I'm so glad I didn't hurt you. I can't imagine—"

"Shh. It all worked out." She kissed him softly.

He cleared his suddenly clogged throat. "Yeah, it did. So maybe you should start adjusting that sleep schedule?"

Chapter 29

Playing House

"Hey, El. Looking a little worse for wear today," Finn greeted her cheerfully as she sped into the office, late again. Except she was the boss, so she wasn't *technically* late, but still, there was a standard to uphold, and if your employees beat you to work every day for the past week? Not a good example.

She dropped her bag on her desk and picked up Casper's water bowl to fill. "Where's Felipe?"

"Off picking up more lights. Where's Casper?"

Ellie stared at the empty water bowl in her hand before setting it gingerly on the floor. "Um, with Dave."

Finn barked out a laugh. "Again? You sure he's not dating you for your dog?"

"Haha. No, I'm not sure, actually. Although he will be dropping her off later this morning when he heads to practice."

"Oh good! Maybe he can help me with my problem."

Ellie plopped into her chair and rubbed her forehead. "What problem is that?"

Finn parked himself on the corner of a desk, his expression bordering on pained. "I don't know what to get Sonoma for Christmas. I want it to be something special, but not *too* special because I don't want to spook her, but it should be *more* special than some generic friend-zone gift, and I just can't come up with … Hey, do you think she'd like a pair of diamond earrings?"

The shock on Ellie's face must have been obvious because Finn's next words were, "Too much, huh? Yeah, I thought so. But I want it to be something—"

"Special. Got it." Fascinated by her stepbrother's transformation, Ellie watched him a few moments. "Have you ever bought a woman you were dating a Christmas gift before? Besides a bottle of wine or some cheap ornament you picked up at the Walgreens checkout, I mean?"

If Ellie doubted Finn was serious before, his next comment sent her across the finish line. "She's just … I don't know. Different from anyone I've ever known. She's funny and smart and pretty and—why are you looking at me like that?"

Because you're gushing like a sixteen-year-old girl? "Lordy, Lordy! I think I'm witnessing history. Unless I'm mistaken, she's hooked the king of bachelors. And that's not to say you're royal, Finn, just that … Jeez, I never thought I'd see the day." Ellie stood and pulled him into a tight hug, then gave him a knuckle-rub on his head. "My baby brother is turning into a man!" She feigned a sob.

"Shut up. You're no help," he chuffed and pushed her away, and she laughed all the way back to her desk. "Glad to see you're happy, El, even if it *is* at my expense." He reached behind himself, picked up a clipboard, and fanned through some sheets of paper. "After Felipe picks up the lights, we should have enough to complete our five remaining jobs, which will be the end of our season. Until after the holidays, when we go back out and take everything down, of course. But I've got that covered already. We start on January fourth with the McKenzies, then the Millers, then …"

She tuned out the rest because she was too busy trying to figure out who this person in front of her was and what he'd done with Finn. She stole a longing glance at the empty coffeepot. "How come no one made coffee yet?"

"You're the only one who drinks it, El."

"Oh. Right." God, she was losing it! Too much sexy time between the sheets and no sleep was making her a little loopy. Thank God Dave was leaving tomorrow on a five-day road trip. A few twelve-hour nights and she'd be back on track. Except she was going to miss him. He'd become a fixture at her house, surprising her with how seamlessly she'd adapted to him taking up her space. Though his place was bigger, he felt more at home at hers, and she had no problem with that because he wasn't a bad roomie.

He took Casper for runs, cooked—even cleaning up after—and left the toilet seat down. In other words, he was housebroken. And so, so hot! *Wonder if I could get him to wear an apron and nothing else when he cooks? That cute man tush right there for the grabbing—*

Finn's whistle startled her. "Hey. Where'd you go, El? Did you hear what I said about the coffee?"

"Um, maybe you should repeat it?"

"I said, I think we should get one of those pod dispensers. We'll cut down on waste that way and have fresh coffee to offer walk-ins. As it is, I think we throw out about three pots a week."

"Right. Coffee." As she stared at Finn, a thought struck her. "Shit, what am I gonna get *Dave* for Christmas?"

He shrugged in answer.

"I mean, what do you get a man who can afford whatever he wants?" *Fuzzy dice and a hula dancer—but not a real one.*

"No idea, El. Never walked in those sneakers before."

She raised a finger to make a point but stopped mid-thought when a man walked through the front door and sent alarms waving through her. Finn stood abruptly, and she shot up from her chair, whacking her knee on her desk. *Suckitup, suckitup, suckitup.* "Agent Clemente," she managed to grit out. "What can we do for you?"

The agent's cologne reached her before he did. In his hands, he held a cardboard tray loaded with Starbucks cups. "You're a busy lady, so I thought I'd bring you and your staff some coffee, then maybe stay and chat a while."

Ellie sat down hard. *What does this man want?* Whatever it was, there was no escaping him now.

Dave checked his phone as soon as they were wheels down in LA, the first city on their West Coast swing. His heart thumped a little harder when he saw Ellie's message, a selfie of her and Casper with the caption, *Have a great game tonight. We'll save you some popcorn.*

He looked around at his teammates, who all had their noses stuck in their phones too, some with shit-eating grins that probably matched the one he was fighting to hold back. While it was great to be back on the road, he missed Ellie already. He couldn't remember missing Nicky this much. *Anyone* this much—as though he'd left a hulking hunk of himself back in Denver. What was different? And another question orbiting inside his brain: If he'd thought of Nicky half as much as he thought of Ellie, would they still be together? How much had their breakup been his fault?

Christ! Don't overthink. Just go with it. He'd been repeating the mantra since the first night he'd talked himself out of following his conscience and into following his dick instead—right into bed with Ellie. But it had gone beyond sleeping with her. Hell, it had already passed that point when he finally *did* sleep with her. He'd had plenty of casual hookups that had remained just that. While some of them had lasted more than a night, a week, or even months, and he looked back on them fondly when he thought to look back at all, they'd never taken possession of him the way this girl did. When he wasn't on the ice and in the game, all he could think about was *her*. Christ, he'd even invited her to his car cave! Because he wanted to see the look on her face when he pulled every last cover off. Not to impress her, but to delight her. He was tuned in to the Ellie Channel twenty-four-seven. And if he thought about it *too* much, it scared the fuck out of him. *Just go with it, dumbass.*

With Christmas right around the corner, teams had gone deep-space dark, even though he'd been playing as if he were at the pinnacle of his game. As if his hand wasn't in constant pain—so much pain that he'd thumbed dozens of texts to Bobby only to delete them.

Truth be told, he was okay with letting his trade demand simmer on a back burner for now. There were no guarantees Herb could find the right opportunity for him anyway, and he could easily wind up staying in Denver. If he kept himself healthy, kept his nose clean, he'd still be tradable. In the meantime, no one needed to know he'd asked for the trade. No harm, no foul.

He looked around at his teammates joking with each other, and envy took a few steely stabs at him. Ellie's words from the other night had been rolling around in his head like rocks in a tumbler. Leaders went into the dirty places, they took their lumps, and they came out of it pulling everyone else along with them. They got the job done. Not by themselves, but by galvanizing those around them into one cohesive force. He'd been that guy once, hadn't he? Or had he just stumbled into it? It had come easily then. As he watched his teammates, he wasn't sure he could dig deep enough to pull it off again.

If Ellie could peep into his thoughts right now, she'd tell him he absolutely could. Her faith in him was one of the reasons he'd fallen in love with her.

Oh shit!

Two nights later, Dave was in Anaheim's visitors' locker room getting ready with the rest of the team when Coach Marty LeBrun sauntered in. "Grimson, see you for a minute?"

"Yeah, Coach." Dave dropped his roll of hockey tape and followed Coach into the office designated for the visiting club's coaching staff.

Coach closed the door and indicated a seat in front of the desk. "Have a seat." Dave did, and Coach sat behind the desk and leaned forward, forearms on the desktop. "So what's this I hear about you looking for a trade?"

Fuck! "What makes you think I'm looking for a trade?"

Coach gave him a mirthless smile. "Word on the street is an elite defenseman with leadership skills is looking to make a move out of Denver."

"We have other defensemen on this team who fit that description," Dave answered smoothly.

"Maybe, though none of them is struggling to fit in with the club right now." Coach gave him a pointed look. "Look, I'm not gonna bullshit you. That's a tight-knit bunch of guys in there, and they play for each other, but they still need a leader they can follow. I know you've been trying to earn back their respect, but it's no secret you're not there yet. It's hard to come back. I get it. You still have some things to figure out, but I believe you can do it, given enough time and effort."

Figure out? Dave bristled. "So what are you saying? Bottom line?"

"I'm saying you've given this organization your all for the past ten years, and you're still a top-six defenseman at the peak of his career. Sometimes change is good, and if you decide a fresh start is what you need, I get that too. I don't see you staying if you're not wearing the *C*—that'd be hard to swallow—but if you want to stay and be this team's leader, you need to step up and take some responsibility for what landed you here in the first place. While I'd rather not lose you, if you're hell-bent on a trade, that might be the best answer."

And just like that, reality smashed Dave in the face like a high stick. Breath stalled in his chest, and the seat seemed to go out from under him. This was the only club he'd ever played for, and he'd bled team colors since the first day he joined.

He looked around the room, trying to get his bearings, his balance. It was one thing to *talk* about a trade; it was another thing altogether when your coach said it might be better if you moved on.

Dave looked squarely at the man across the desk. "Is that it?"

Coach leaned back in his chair and steepled his fingers. "That's it."

Dave rose, rapped the edge of the desk, and gave Coach a head bob. "Duly noted."

As he walked back toward the locker room, his mind was a tilt-a-whirl. Before stepping inside, he pulled his phone from his back pocket, leaned against the wall, and made a call.

"Dave?" came Ellie's voice. His world felt a little less rocked. He closed his eyes and sighed. "Dave, is everything okay?"

He straightened and blinked. "Yeah, I'm good. I just wanted to hear you wish me luck for tonight's game."

She laughed. "Good luck, Captain. Casper and I will be watching."

Wish I were gonna be there, curled up with my favorite girls. "You gonna be eating popcorn?"

"Oh, you know it!"

"Hey, uh, before I let you go, I … Nicole texted me about watching Benny the week between Christmas and New Year's." A few beats passed, and when Ellie didn't speak, he kept going. "But I have an away game, and I wondered—"

"Casper and I would be happy to take care of him while you're gone. Can't wait to meet the little guy."

He laughed, and it helped blow off some of the stale air crowding his lungs. "He's not so little, but thanks. I really appreciate it." An assistant coach walked past Dave and went into the locker room. Once the door closed, Dave said in a hushed tone, "Hey El, I should go. I'll talk to you later, okay?"

"Okay. Have a great game. Smash somebody! And score a goal!"

"Any other demands?" he chuckled.

"That's it."

"Okay, cutie." Corralling an "I love you" fighting to roll off his tongue, he hung up. Any lift he'd gotten from talking to her evaporated when he opened the door and stepped into the locker room.

Dave sucked that night. So did the rest of the team. They redeemed themselves the next night, though, when they finished off their road trip with a win in San Jose. Fatigue seeped into his bones, but he was amped at the same time. Though it was late, he called Ellie. God, he couldn't wait to get home and see her, and he didn't want to wait until tomorrow. Hell, it was *almost* tomorrow now, but he needed his fix. Bad.

Hours later, he stood on her front stoop, poised to unlock it with a key she'd hidden for him, arguing with himself. *It's 2:00 a.m., for fuck's sake. You're going to wake her up. No, no. She said it was okay.* He'd acted like a little pussy, practically begging her to let him come over. *This isn't about sex. I'm too tired anyway. I just want to hold her.*

"Excuses, you make. Leave her alone, you must," Yoda growled at him.

Yoda, have you ever actually had *sex? No need to ask you, Han. Maybe you can explain it to the little green guy while I go cuddle my girl.*

The argument in his head continued as he pushed the door open, dropped his bag, and locked up. A little grunt and the click-clack of claws alerted him Casper, the ferocious guard dog, was headed his way … to lick him to death. Once he got her settled down, he toed off his shoes, shed his jacket, and padded into Ellie's bedroom.

Soft light glowed from the bathroom door she'd left ajar. A sprawl of hair the color of Black Hills gold fanned across her pillow behind her, beckoning him to tangle his hands in it, and he started unbuttoning his shirt with urgency. The covers were pulled up to her chest, one satiny-sleeve-capped shoulder peeking out. Were these the PJs from their first night together? Hard to know since the only thought he usually gave her PJs was how fast he could strip them off. But not tonight. Tonight he just wanted to drift off with the comforting weight and feel of her in his arms.

Finally down to his underwear, he gingerly lifted the covers and eased himself in behind her so he didn't let in cold air. Then he was wrapping her up, cradling her, tension leaving his body in one long, mattress-sinking sigh. She made one of those little mewling noises he loved and nestled against him, her familiar fragrance wreathing him. So soft and warm. She smelled and felt like home, and he melted a little inside. *Home.*

"Dave?" she whispered. With a shift of her hips, she rolled to face him and wound her arms around his shoulders. "I'm so glad you're home," her warm, moist mouth mumbled against his bare chest. Then her leg was over his hip, and she was pulling herself closer. "Mmm. You feel so good." She dropped her hand between them and started a featherlight stroke through his boxer briefs.

Jesuuus!

His dick sprang to life, wide awake, and so did he, all his best non-carnal intentions taking a hike as a low groan unfurled inside him. Suspiciously absent were the aches and pains from a few minutes before. In their place, his nerves were firing in the very best way, primed and ready to go. She had that effect on him.

Her hand continued its soft caress. "I think someone's happy to see me." Her voice was scratchy, full of sleep, and incredibly adorable and sexy at the same time.

He stroked the silky fabric over her shoulder blades with one hand and entwined the other in her hair as he cupped the back of her head. He placed a soft kiss on her forehead. "I didn't mean to wake you up. Just wanted to hold you."

She withdrew her hand, running it up his neck into his hair. "Tired?" As good as her hand felt in his hair—hell, anywhere—he missed it down south.

"I *thought* I was tired," he rasped. "You have this amazing power to re-energize me."

She giggled against him, and his hands were under her top, relishing the sensation of her soft skin, his nose buried in the crook of her neck as he breathed her in. Then he was softly sucking, loving the taste of her. Suddenly, he couldn't get enough. She pressed and molded herself against him with a sighing moan. So welcoming. Trailing kisses up and down her neck, he worked the buttons of her top free. Pulling back, he splayed the fabric wide, his eyes drawn to her plump breasts and taut pink tips. The breath stuttered in his chest. *So fucking gorgeous.* His wood-hard shaft became petrified rock.

He palmed a breast and looked into smoldering blue eyes looking back at him. "I swear you have the most beautiful tits I've ever seen." Reverence laced his voice.

A laugh bubbled out of her, and he stilled. "That's funny?" Confusion quirked one corner of his mouth.

"No, not funny." Her eyes still locked on his, her expression sobered, and she toyed with his hair, shooting chills down his neck, his spine, straight to the fingertips that had started gliding over her flesh again. "Considering the number of tits I expect you've seen in your lifetime, I'll take that as quite the compliment, Captain Reaper."

He stared at her. Nothing moved for a beat. *Oh shit. Did I say that all wrong?* Before he could string together enough thoughts to ponder it further, she breathed, "Show me how beautiful you think they are."

Something primal rose up inside him, and soon he had her on her back, jerking her sleeves off as his mouth took one breast, then the other. Tongue, teeth, lips, he used them all gently at first and then not so gently, fire blazing brighter inside him with every gasp of his name and musical moan that fell from her lips. He worshipped her, then gathered her wrists in one hand and hauled them above her head, worshipping her even more. Beneath him, she bucked and writhed, and it drove him out of his mind knowing he was driving *her* out of *her* mind. Only him. What he was doing alone. And he wanted that feeling to go on forever.

While he sucked and licked and nipped, he kept her hands pinned. His other hand snaked down her body, diving under her teeny-tiny silk shorts, his fingers entering her hot, wet softness hungrily, mimicking what he wanted to do to her with his cock. As he rocked his fingers in and out of her with determined strokes, she arched her back and moaned incoherently, pressing herself deeper into his mouth.

"So fucking hot," he murmured. "So fucking good."

Yeah, she was right. He'd seen more than his fair share of women, but they were a blur from another lifetime. He'd never been with anyone like her, had never experienced anything like this with anyone else, had never felt so alive and powerful and complete before. She was all he could see. Taste. Smell. Feel. What she did to him was off the charts. Out of this solar system. This universe.

"Dave!" she gasped. Her body seized, becoming a hard plank. "I can't hold out much longer."

That's my *line.* He raised his head and looked into her heated eyes, his fingers still curling and pumping inside her. "Then don't hold out. Let yourself fly, Ellie."

Squeezing her eyes shut, she shook her head from side to side. "No. I want to come with you inside me," she panted. "I want to feel you filling me, stretching me beyond my limits."

Holy fuuuuck!

"Now!" she demanded in one breathless rush.

He pulled his fingers from her body and stretched over her, settling between her bent knees, re-cinching his hold on her wrists as his lips and tongue worked their way across her chest, over her collarbones, up her throat to her earlobe in slow, savoring slides. "Someone's being bossy," he mumbled against her heated skin. Truth was he needed to pause and catch his breath, regain control, slow himself down before he was doing what she demanded and blowing his load on the first thrust. If anyone could make him do that, it was this girl. His free hand trailed down her silky side, returning to knead her breast and toy with her tight nipple.

"And someone's being a tease," she huffed beneath him.

"Bossy *and* impatient." He grinned. "You're my dirty little good girl."

She puffed and squirmed halfheartedly, trying to pull her hands from his grasp. His lips landed on her neck. "You want to be fucked gentle or hard, Bossy?"

Cocking her head to the side, she ran a blatantly lust-filled gaze over him. At the same time, her foot skated up and down his bare leg, "As hard and as dirty as you can give it to me."

He stopped breathing for several beats. "Fuck, you are a sexy thing."

"For someone who says 'fuck' so much in my bed, you're doing very little of it." One corner of her mouth twitched. "All dirty talk and no action."

"You like it when I talk dirty to you?"

"Mmm, but I prefer when you *do* dirty things to me."

That did it. What was left of their clothes was in a heap on the floor, and he was straddling her hips, carrying his weight on his knees, sweeping his eyes over the beautiful full curves laid out below him. He might want to believe he could control her body, but she definitely had full control of *his* body, mind, and soul.

Shifting his weight, he planted his forearms on either side of her and wedged his thigh between her knees. "Open for me." He hadn't needed to say it because she was not only opening for him, but she was angling her hips to take him in. Soon he was inside her, surrounded by her warm, wet walls. He nearly lost it. He pulled out and plunged back in, burying himself to the hilt.

Even in his sex-hazed brain, he knew he should *stay* out and sheath himself, but she was so sweet and tight and warm, and he wanted to feel himself encased by her, wanted to feel himself fill her with nothing between them. That annoying little voice whispered there were consequences for careless behavior, ones that arrived nine months later. Another voice answered it didn't care, that if she got pregnant, he could make her his. The first voice reminded him his Denver days were numbered.

She dug her nails into his back. "Oh so good," she moaned, and it silenced the voices in his head. "More. Like. That." Her head was tilted, eyes closed, mouth parted, back bowed as if she were offering herself to him on an altar.

He heard himself say, "Most fucking beautiful thing I've ever seen," but he was too far gone. Fingers digging into her waist to hold her in place, he slammed into her, lost in the sound of her hitching gasps as he drove in and out, his hips flexing and pistoning in a rhythm fine-tuned to her humming body.

She wrapped her legs around his waist and tightened, meeting him thrust for thrust, pulling him farther inside as he rode her. A shudder vibrated her entire body, and she wailed his name. And then heat was streaking down his spine, pooling, expanding, releasing, and he barely had time to pull out before spurting in hot, pulsing jets.

When he drifted back to the conscious world, he felt as though he were made up of floating pieces of confetti that had been fired from a cannon. Panting into the crook of her neck, he was sprawled partway across her, one arm encircling her. Her ragged breathing matched his, and her pretty eyes blinked, seeming to appraise him.

Alarm spiked in him. "Did I hurt you?" Another concern loomed, equally alarming.

She swept his hair off his sweaty forehead. "No, I'm fine. Better than fine. But I'm sleeping on *your* side tonight because that's quite the wet spot." A soft giggle bubbled in her throat, and she threw him for a moment because … well, he had his own *side*. And he liked that.

"I'm sorry. I should have stopped and used a rubber." Jesus, when was the last time he'd been so reckless? Even when past girlfriends had been on the pill, he'd left nothing to chance and had *always* used a condom. "I know it's a little late, but I'm clean."

"I know. I trust you. And it's okay. I'm off-cycle."

He believed her. Had no reason to doubt. "Was that hard enough?" He tucked a few wisps behind her ear.

"It was perfect. *You're* perfect." She placed her hand on his chest, her blue eyes filled with an emotion he couldn't unravel but that touched the center of his heart and rippled outward, steadily swelling until it lapped at his rough outer edges and blanketed them in sublime warmth. Because she trusted him, and she thought he was perfect.

Only in your eyes, he wanted to say. Instead, he said, "No, you're the perfect one." He got up and padded to the bathroom, wet a washcloth in hot water, and returned to clean off her thighs, her abdomen, and what he could of the sheet. When he'd disposed of the rag, he climbed under the covers, rolling to his side, and pulled her against him, away from the wet spot on *her* side of the bed. Smiling to himself, he cradled her in his arms, stroking her hair and kissing the top of her head. She nestled against him, her body seeming to melt in that telltale way she had of drifting off. He was one lucky son of a bitch. As he descended the rest of the way from his euphoric cloud, reality placed its unwelcome, cold grip on him. Coach Lebrun's words spun in his head. How much longer before he couldn't fall into a contented sleep with her? How much longer would this last?

His body glazed in a cold sweat.

Chapter 30

Overthinking Can Lead to Dumbassery

Ellie was long gone by the time Dave roused. She'd taken Casper and left him a note letting him know she'd stocked his favorite morning smoothie fixings, how to run her blender, and to not forget about the Millers' cocktail party tonight. The one he'd reluctantly agreed to escort her to. But he couldn't help the smile kicking up a corner of his mouth—being thought of, taken care of, was a nice feeling. And because Yoda was an anti-good-feels kinda guy, he once again reminded Dave not to get too comfortable.

Dave was on his way to the arena when he placed a call to Herb and filled him on his meeting with Coach LeBrun.

"Well, I wasn't going to call you until I had something more definite," Herb replied, "but the GM from Arizona contacted me yesterday. Seems one of their top defensemen turned up his nose at their proposed contract extension and made noises about testing free agency. And if that doesn't pan out, Ottawa is back, champing at the bit to sign you. Nashville and Boston are perking up too. I don't know if they're hearing about the other teams' interest, but you're suddenly a popular guy, buttercup. You'll have no trouble landing in a new home soon."

Dave hung up and scrubbed his hand over his beard. He should have been all kinds of elated, but instead he was *de*flated. Numb. His mind leapt to living in Ottawa. Boston. Nashville. At least Arizona was closer to Denver, but doing the long-distance thing? Skillfully avoiding the fact that the first leap his mind had taken was to Ellie and *not* his career, he drummed up other reasons the relationship couldn't work. He'd be busy with his new town and his new team. She'd be busy with her business. The fleeting thought of asking her to come along danced through his head before it died a quick death, like a hapless bug in a zapper. They'd only started this *thing*, whatever it was. Shit, it was so new he couldn't even name it. How could you know what you needed to know about someone after a few short months? He and Nicky had been dating ten months when they moved in together, and look how that had turned out. A disaster on so many levels he couldn't even count them all. On a long exhale, he decided to follow Herb's advice and park the dizzying questions in a back corner until after Christmas. No teams would be making any serious moves until the holidays were over anyway.

Which reminded him. Christmas. After he parked his car at the arena, he thumbed a quick text to Sonoma, leading off with, *Help!!! It's Christmas.* As he was composing a follow-up text, her immediate reply chimed: *Cutting it close, aren't you?* To which he answered, *Which is why I need you.* He could practically hear her smirk on the other end as she agreed to go shopping with him. Thank God! Hopefully, she could come up with a gift for Ellie because he had no clue. He'd given it exactly zero thought, which made him a jerk. And, it occurred to him, he'd never bothered to ask Ellie what she was doing for Christmas. Which made him a bigger jerk. Or was it self-preservation? Was doing Christmas together, giving her a gift, sending out the wrong signals if what he really should be doing was pulling back?

Yeah, this relationship was nowhere near the "Want to move to Freeze-My-Balls-Off Ottawa with me?" stage, nor could he see when or how it would be appropriate to even consider asking. *Enjoy it while you can.*

And that was the exact thought caroming around in his head when he texted Ellie later. *How about I take you to dinner tonight?*

Ellie: *Before or after the cocktail party?*

Oh shit. Somehow his memory banks kept ejecting the party looming large.

Dave: *After? If we're still hungry?*

Ellie: *I'm sure you will be.*

"Maybe not," he muttered to himself. His stomach felt like a wrench-happy monkey had overtightened all the lug nuts on his wheels. Yet he was eager—a little *too* eager, a little *too* desperate—to see her, to please her by going. Again and already. Shit, he had it bad. Probably a *good* thing he wouldn't be around much longer, for his sake and hers.

Ellie checked herself in the mirror one last time, smoothing her ivory silk blouse over a pair of fitted black slacks she'd found in the back of her closet. Silver dangles, a silver pendant with a pretty leaf detail, and her red cowboy boots completed the look. She'd meant to do some shopping, but competing with a zillion Christmas shoppers was daunting enough that she easily talked herself out of it. Oh well. Men didn't really notice clothes, did they? Not unless they were Agent Clemente, whose job was to notice *every* detail. He wasn't *Agent* Clemente, though, he'd admonished her. He was *Rick* now that he'd visited her office no less than three times with a non-threatening smile and coffee as a "peace offering." She couldn't decide if he was playing a new game instead of showing up unexpectedly at jobsites, or if he was simply a lonely nice guy showing interest. There had been no mentions of busting her ass or where her money came from. Did he still suspect her of taking part in some smuggling ring, or did he like her? She couldn't read the man, so she played it safe by warily playing along. Between the publicity drummed up by the Habitat project and Paige's clients, the potential for spring business was the most promising it had ever been. Ellie didn't need another ICE debacle derailing it.

The throaty purr of a muscle car at her curb had her smiling to herself and glancing out the window. The GTO was so buffed it caught the reflection of the streetlights and reminded her of a slab of softly twinkling silver. In true form, Dave was out of his door and halfway up the walkway before she'd locked the front door. He bent down and planted a chaste kiss on her cheek before stepping back and leading the way to the car. No reassuring fingers against the small of her back or big hand wrapped around her upper arm. *He's uptight about the party.* A little wave of guilt washed over her, but damn it, if they were becoming a couple, then they'd go to these functions for and with each other, right? Then again, the "if" was a big one. He'd been sending the "we're a couple" vibe for a while, yet he hadn't invited her to the team Christmas get-together earlier in the month. Sarah said he'd come alone and hadn't stayed long, but still, good old self-doubt rose up and posed the question, *What if you're reading the signals all wrong?*

God, she hoped she hadn't because she was pretty damn sure she was falling in love with the guy.

He slid behind the steering wheel and started the car. Elvis's "I Can't Help Falling in Love with You" blared over the speakers. *How appropriate* was the first thought to rocket through her brain, followed by a hopeful, *Did he put this on for me?* A moment later, that thought was annihilated when he jabbed the radio's buttons as if they were about to explode. He landed on a Mexican station and left it there before finally settling on one playing old-time Christmas tunes.

"Sorry," he mumbled. "Wasn't feeling Elvis tonight."

She raised an eyebrow. "Apparently, you're feeling Christmas?"

"Well, 'tis the season and all." He wiped his palm on his dress pants.

Twisting a piece of hair around her finger, she side-eyed him. "Are you feeling all right?"

"Yep." He side-eyed her back. "Why?"

"I don't know. You seem a little … twitchy."

He flicked a finger toward the windshield. "It's all this damn holiday traffic."

"Well, don't get distracted and plow into someone."

The look on his face told her he didn't find her comment amusing in the least, and she murmured a quick apology. He answered with a grunt. She sank into her seat and stared out the window, feeling as chilled as the icicles hanging off the frozen gutters they passed. *I never should have pushed him into coming.* The revelation was far too late.

Ellie's spirits lifted as they approached the Millers' house because Landscaping with Altitude had strung the exterior lights, and she felt a surge of pride. The guys had really outdone themselves, and the house was a spectacular showcase for the Millers *and* for Ellie's company. She'd have to make sure they got pictures.

Paige's green eyes sparkled as she welcomed them inside with hugs. "Ellie, we've gotten so many compliments on the lights! You're going to have to staff up next year because I think you're going to be flooded with clients wanting the same treatment."

Dave shot Ellie a questioning look. "You did their lights?" He seemed astonished.

"Well, Finn, Felipe, and the crew."

"Huh," was his single response.

Paige shut the door and held out her hands. "Let me take your coats. Dave, I hear you're a big car buff. Beckett's in his man cave slash garage with some of the guys—including a few from your hockey club—if you want to head out that way." She pointed down a hallway and grinned. "He's got a full bar set up out there too."

"Maybe later, but thanks."

Ellie looked him up and down as they followed Paige toward a festive burble interwoven with jazzy Christmas music.

"What?" he hissed.

Whoa! Ellie did a quick throat clear and ignored him. "So, Paige, I wanted to thank you for the referrals. I think I've gotten six calls already, with landscaping consultations set up for right after the holidays."

"Oh, that's wonderful!" Paige ran on, though Ellie barely heard a word, too busy wondering what was wrong with her date.

They reached a large great room festooned with fresh boughs and silver bows and tiny lights—also done by Landscaping with Altitude—and the first people she spotted were Lily, Natalie, and Sarah happily chatting in their own cluster. Paige pointed to where the drinks were, and Dave headed in that direction while Ellie made a beeline for her tribe. Maybe Dave taking a few stiff belts would chill out whatever had crawled up his butt. It occurred to her he'd been taking a lot of stiff belts lately, but she pushed the observation to the side.

Soon she was lost in conversation about one project or another with her friends, trying not to think about how elegant they all looked in their shiny cocktail dresses and their pretty nails. *Maybe Dave's embarrassed to be with me.* As happened too frequently, an image of picture-perfect Nicole popped into Ellie's head, bringing with it a list of Ellie's shortcomings. Her eyes wandered the room trying to spot him, but he was nowhere to be seen.

T.J. appeared beside Natalie and gave her a little squeeze. Natalie grinned up at him. "Where have you been?"

"Just checking out Miller's latest acquisition, a sweet Rolls-Royce Dawn. Can I get one?" He waggled his eyebrows at his wife, who just rolled her eyes and muttered something about her impractical husband.

T.J., whom Ellie had met after a game, recognized her. "Hey, Ellie. Where's Grims?"

She didn't hide her surprise. "I figured he'd be in the garage ogling the cars with you guys."

Lily dropped her lashes and sipped her drink. "Gage is out there," she offered apologetically.

After an awkward beat, Ellie excused herself. "I'll go see if I can find him." *And get myself a glass of wine.* It only dawned on her in that moment that Dave had neither offered nor returned with anything for her. Not that he had to wait on her, but it was unusual. He was normally so attentive. She squeezed through the huge crowd, looking for some wine and breathing space on the fringes, ending up by a wall of French doors that opened onto a deck strung with lights. *So classy and beautiful!* Next year, she'd be sure *her* house got equal treatment, by God.

As she was admiring the lights, she noticed a stunning brunette bundled in a coat, talking with a broad-framed figure who was handing her a smile and a glass of red wine. Grumpy Bear, his back to Ellie, didn't look quite so grumpy anymore. An unexpected stab brought stinging tears to her eyes, and she sucked in a huge breath and tried to shake it off. A hand gently encircled her arm. "Ellie?"

Blinking rapidly to stave off the pending waterworks, she turned toward the familiar voice, startled and relieved to see Damian Mencher's smiling face.

"It *is* you!" he exclaimed and pulled her into a one-armed hug. "How have you been? You look fantastic!"

Running a self-conscious hand through her hair, she opened her mouth to spit out her thanks, but before she could, he scanned her and frowned. "You're empty-handed. Let's remedy that situation right now." He took her hand and led her toward the kitchen, cutting through the crowd and creating a seam she could easily navigate.

They found a quiet corner. She'd had one sip of wine and they'd talked for maybe five minutes when someone large and warm loomed behind her.

"Damian, is it?" Dave's deep voice rumbled.

Really? He ignores me, but as soon as a man pays attention to me, he's front and center? What the hell? Talk about mixed signals. She shot him an exasperated look, which he totally ignored, preferring, it seemed, to smirk at Damian. To his credit, Damian didn't show any sign he was intimidated. Amused, perhaps. Either stupid or cocky, the man stuck his hand out. "Damian Mencher, Director of Habitat for Humanity. Nice to see you again, ah … Dave, was it? Ellie looked like she could use a drink." He offered Dave a shrug and a bland smile, so different from the brilliant one he'd bestowed on her.

Dave glanced down at her as if only then realizing she stood beside him. She raised her glass, gave him a fake smile, and slugged down half her wine. *Asshole!*

Paige rescued her from the bizarre man-standoff by tapping her on the shoulder. "Some more clients who'd like to meet you." To the men, she said, "Sorry, gentlemen, but I need to steal Ellie for a little business talk."

"Thanks for the wine, Damian," Ellie said before turning away, grateful she was on Paige's heels and headed, hopefully, to some remote part of the house where she could escape and catch her breath. And while she didn't give Dave a backward glance, she felt his eyes drilling into her nonetheless. The stark possibility she'd once again misjudged a man sobered her. Was she guilty of seeing only what she wanted to see and blanking out warning signs that would cause her to shield her heart? Dave was used to a certain kind of woman, one with whom Ellie shared no similarities. Maybe he was slumming. Maybe she'd been convenient, and he'd taken advantage and was now ready to slide back into a more glamorous world.

Ellie steeled herself. Whatever was going on with him wasn't her problem unless he made it her problem. At least *this* time she could stop herself from falling before it was too late and she was knocked to her knees. That was, if it wasn't too late already.

In the anonymity of the darkened car, they hurtled home through the incongruously merry holiday twinkle show outside the windows. Dave stewed in the misery of his own making. How could he bridge the uncomfortable quiet that hung thick and juicy between him and Ellie? He'd been a total jerk, abandoning her at the earliest opportunity and making an appearance only when Damian Douchenugget started fawning all over her. Yeah, he hadn't wanted to be at the party, but he'd agreed, and it was seeing her with Damian that shook him into remembering that fact. Also shook him into realizing that while *he* didn't want to be there, he didn't want *her* there with anyone else.

Christ, he was screwed up! No wonder she'd turned her back and practically run away from him. Fawning aside, Douchenugget had done her the small courtesy *Dave* should have done. But then again, maybe not. And there was the rub. If Dave left it alone, let her believe he didn't give a rat's ass, letting go would be easier when the time came.

He stole a sidelong glance and winced inside at her body language. Was she hurt? Mad? Practically hugging the car door to stay as far away from him as possible, eyes either cast down or glued to the window, and her fingers continually rubbed her bare collarbones. Something was missing.

"Where's your necklace?"

A tiny shrug. "I lost it. Paige knows, and she'll look for it."

Ah shit. His natural reaction was to ask if there was anything he could do, but he didn't want to give her an opening to tell him to go fuck himself. "I think I owe you an apology for being a dick." *Again.*

Without hesitation, she swiveled her head. He could feel stormy blue eyes burning into him. "You *think* you were being a dick?"

Ouch. Not the reassuring pass he didn't realize he'd been hoping for.

She let out a huff, followed by, "So why *were* you a dick? To drive home the point of how little you wanted to be there? The only time you seemed to notice I was even on the same block was when some other guy—a business acquaintance, no less—was gracious enough to say hello and offer me a drink."

Though he'd totally deserved her brittle words, they left a scorching red welt. And he had yet to stop bristling about Damian slobbering all over her, as if Dave had a right to be possessive in the first place. Confused emotions—guilt, regret, self-pity—congealed in the pit of his stomach. "Just a lot going on right now, I guess. I know it's no excuse, but sometimes I get caught up and sort of blank out."

She let out a sarcastic chuckle. "Kinda selective, isn't it? You didn't seem very blank when you were making sure the pretty brunette on the deck had a glass of wine."

The bite in her tone took him aback, and he found his temper kindling—like it had whenever Nicky accused him of two-timing her. And just like then, he knee-jerked like a guilty man and started pleading his case with annoyance edging his tone. "I didn't get her a glass of wine. She asked me to hold hers while she put on her coat. I was merely handing it back to her. I was being polite." That chiding inner voice reminded him while he'd been *polite* to the brunette—whose face he couldn't even recall—he hadn't given Ellie as much consideration, and his words came out petulant even to his own ears. And really, the petulance was directed at himself. Not her. She hadn't done a damn thing wrong, except be who she was, which was so far above him, he couldn't crane his neck back that far. And seeing her with Damian had been a sharp-toothed reminder that Dave wasn't good enough for her because he couldn't give her what she deserved, which was *all* of him. Not just his money. Not his celebrity. Those were easy to give, and they were all he'd ever given. Soon enough, it wouldn't be an issue because he'd be gone.

He pulled up to her curb and looked longingly at the front door, picturing the cozy space beyond, the one with smells of home, a dog happy to see him, and a ridiculous mound of too-soft cushions he wanted to sink his body into. A girl he could pull into those cushions with him, one he could hold, except he was pretty damn sure she wanted nothing to do with him right now.

As if she'd heard him, said girl abruptly flung open the door and had her heels on the pavement before he'd managed to get a hand on his door latch. She was bent over, hair swinging like a shimmering gold curtain as she looked at him through the gap of her open car door. "Well, you warned me, didn't you? And I should have listened. I'm sorry I put you through that, Dave. Sorry I put us *both* through what I really thought would be a pleasant … Never mind." Her voice, laced with regret, about undid him.

"Ellie, wait. Can we talk?"

"I'm really tired, and all I want right now is to get some sleep."

In a hopeful gesture, his mouth hitched up on one side. "Want me to tuck you in?" He realized too late what a dumbass remark he'd uttered, and if he'd had any doubt, the scowl on her face left no question whatsoever.

A sigh, a shake of her head, and the scowl vanished, but she held up a staying hand. "Not tonight. And I can walk myself to the door." With that, she shut the car door and pivoted, leaving him sitting like an asshat, helplessly torn between running after her and letting the invisible grip that locked him behind the wheel keep him there.

What the fuck was the matter with him? The one woman, the *only* woman, whose opinion counted, and he'd done everything in his power to send her running. He glanced back at her house, but it was dark and still, buttoned up tight, as if nothing and no one stirred inside. With a sigh, he thumbed her a text. *Call you tomorrow?*

He waited long minutes, and her non-answer became his answer. As he pulled away from the curb, an overwhelming sense of loss moldered in his gut.

Chapter 31

Your Signals Are Unreadable in the Fog

Dismal days later, Dave still hadn't spoken to Ellie, but he'd coaxed her into a thaw. They'd exchanged texts, and, bonus, she'd agreed to come to his game tonight and grab dinner afterward. God, he missed her! Sitting in his bare-walled town house these last nights had only added to his misery, and driving it home further was a bubbly Sonoma too busy with her own successful love life to help him grind down some of his pointy edges. All of which made him a total pussy.

It was in this funked-up frame of mind he took the ice that night, glad for the distraction. His anger and aggravation blended with the excitement of seeing Ellie, becoming a concoction that rapid-boiled inside him. Harnessing the seething brew, he unleashed it on their rival, Detroit. And by God, it was working because the Blizzard was winning, and Detroit's frustration showed in the number of cheap shots they resorted to and the fights they picked.

"We're getting under their skins, boys," Dave declared to his teammates while he sat on the bench between shifts, eyes studying every move their opponents made on the ice. "Watch yourselves out there. Play smart, and don't take any penalties. That's what they want." He hadn't expected any responses, so when a few sailed his way in the form of "Okay, Cap," or "We got this," he was pleasantly surprised.

More surprises came later when he took up his position beside the chute leading to the locker room, giving each teammate who filed past his usual, “Great job tonight,” or “Awesome game.” In return, he got a few extra stick taps, nods, and fist bumps. After getting cleaned up, he stood in front of his stall knotting his tie. T.J. nudged him. “Good game tonight, Grims. Hand must be feeling better.”

On instinct, Dave flexed it, biting back a wince.

T.J. gave him an approving nod. “Hey, you joining us at the ChopHouse?”

The invite caught Dave off guard, and a smile tugged a corner of his mouth before he could stop himself. “Can’t, man. Got dinner plans with Ellie.”

“Bring her. We’ll do our best not to scare her off. Besides, Nat and Sarah will be there, and those girls are *thick* when they get together.” T.J. gave him a light punch in the arm. “C’mon. It’ll be fun.”

Dave snorted, belying his spirits lifting like a helium balloon escaping a kid’s hand. Drifting up into the atmosphere. Not at jolting speed, but floating leisurely as it climbed higher.

How Dave had won a reprieve with Ellie, he had no fucking clue, but he was so damn relieved when he spotted her forgiving smile that he decided to put away the opposing battalions warring inside him and soak up the sweet feel of *that* victory. His eyes flew to her—and fixed there—as she stood waiting for him in a cluster with Natalie, Sarah, and a few other wives and girlfriends.

Awkwardly at first, they tiptoed around each other as though they picked their way barefoot over shattered glass. Soon the uneasiness gave way to the comfortable familiarity he hadn’t realized was between them before, and his spirits lifted a little higher. At dinner, he slid into the seat beside her, proud he was there with *her*, especially when he caught the looks other men gave her—looks she was utterly oblivious to. An unruffled air of confident sweetness surrounded her like a full-body halo, drawing those appreciative glances and him closer to her. This woman beside him was rare beauty personified, inside and out, so much a part of her essence that she didn’t even see it herself, and he pondered how long he’d been aware of it.

They laughed long into the night among his teammates and their SOs. Like the old days. And much later, when he had her alone in her bedroom, the same desperation that had been gunning through him thrummed inside her, and any remaining differences between them dissolved after two rounds of torrid makeup sex. He was left panting and spent and unable to recall what fears and doubts had been spinning in his head. Maybe staying in Denver wasn't the worst fate ever.

As he fell asleep with Ellie curled naked against him, he thought fuzzily that she was downy insulation he could wrap around himself, muffling out the rest of the noise. Nothing in that moment felt more right than this. He'd slid all thoughts of injuries and trades and uprooting onto the back burner, instead eating up the way having her in his arms made him feel. Needed, worthy, significant. And damn, he loved seeing her smile, making her happy—which was amazingly easy to do when he didn't act like a douchenugget.

He could have remained suspended in his little cocoon well into the morning, but Ellie was out of bed before he roused and could reach for her. Casper, however, was a different matter entirely when she wriggled her way beside him and licked his chin. He pushed the dog's face away. "Does your mom know you're up here? Pretty sure that's a no."

"Most definitely a no," came Ellie's voice from the bathroom doorway, where she leaned against the frame. He looked up at her and grinned. She was fresh out of the shower, all dewy and soft, and to his delight she wore nothing but low-cut panties and one of those half-cupped bras, both pieces embellished with dainty yellow flowers against white. With a fake glare fastened on the dog, she smirked. Her arms were folded across her chest, drawing his eye to the creamy skin cresting over the bra. His dick raised itself to full attention and saluted all that smooth curvature. He gave her a languid head-to-toe sweep and licked his lips, calculating the quickest way to entice her back to bed. Honestly, even *he* was surprised by his overachieving libido. He was outdoing his nineteen-year-old self. Then again, he was constantly inspired by the woman before him.

"You'd better get Casper off the bed," he said.

Ellie shot him a quizzical look, but when she reached for the dog, *he* lifted the covers and reached for Ellie, yanking her under the sheets alongside him. Casper scampered from the room while Ellie bucked and squirmed, giggled and squealed. "What are you doing?"

He wasted no time corralling her hands and getting his lips on the sensitive spot at the base of her neck. "What does it *look* like I'm doing? Someone wants to show you how happy he is to see you again." Now he worked his way up to her ear, spending extra time on the other sensitive spots he was becoming so intimately acquainted with. Her body turned pliant in his arms, and she let out a breathless sigh as she gave herself over to him.

"Better call your boss and tell her you'll be late," he murmured as he teased her skin with his tongue. She smelled and tasted so fucking good, and he couldn't get enough.

He unclasped the bra. "So pretty. But it has to come off." Then he slid the panties down her legs, off her ankles. "These too." Now his mouth and hands were all over her.

A husky laugh rose in her throat. "You're going to undo the shower I just took."

"I'll help you get squeaky clean again. Promise. Least I can do."

Her mock protests faded, replaced by breathy mewls and pants that fired his blood and strangled all conscious thought. Before he knew what he was doing, he was inside her, plowing into her, his balls constricting.

Her nails dug into his arms. "Dave!" she rasped. "Condom?"

Shit! He'd lost his mind again. While thoughts of why this had happened with only her mingled with thoughts of asking her to go on the pill and how selfish that was, he swiped a condom from the nightstand, tore it open, rolled it on, and sank back inside her with an extended guttural grunt.

Heaven.

Home.

Dave was as good as his word, getting Ellie thoroughly clean in her tiny, barely maneuverable shower after their wild morning lovemaking session. That session rekindled in said shower, no doubt because of its very cramped space. She wasn't complaining; far from it. She loved the feel of his hard-angled body against hers, all that touchable skin stretched over layers of solidly packed muscle. Strength and power, barely leashed when he held himself back for her, then completely unleashed when he let himself go. Roughness tempered by the exquisite gentleness of his giving, moist mouth and his inquisitive fingers that made her stomach dance and her blood sing. She grew light-headed and a little hot just thinking about it.

Part of her wondered—but didn't want to know—if he was this voracious with all his bed partners … and if he normally forgot protection. If they were going to keep seeing each other, maybe she should consider going on the pill. *No, El, you're getting way ahead of yourself.*

After she got dressed, completely this time, she followed her nose to the smell of breakfast wafting from her kitchen. Dave was coaxing poached eggs onto buttered wheat toast beside strips of bacon. His eyes flicked up, and he smiled. "Hungry?" *No growly Wookiees today.* "I hope you don't mind that I raided your fridge." One-handed, he pulled out a chair for her while adoring Casper sat oh-so-properly and oh-so-hopeful at his feet.

"I don't mind. Especially not if it's to fix me breakfast."

"Yeah, well, I think I just about wiped you out. We need to get you more food."

Planning on staying? The thought had her tummy executing somersaults.

He attacked his breakfast like he'd attacked her in bed—with single purpose and primal abandon. It was kinda sexy. Halfway through the meal, he pulled his nose out of his food, glanced at her half-full plate, then at her. "No like?"

She shook herself back to breakfast. "No, I like. Just lost in thought, I guess."

His head dipped back down. "About?" He shoveled another forkful of toast and gooey egg in his mouth.

"Just wondering about … Are you usually like this with …?" *Shit, El! Really? Just blurt it out there.*

He straightened and put his fork down. "Like what with what?"

She felt a hot flush creep up her neck and engulf her face. No doubt she was covered in bright pink splotches. "Do you normally make breakfast for the women you sleep with?"

He rocked backward, looking utterly stunned, before seeming to compose himself and pick up his fork. One eyebrow lowered, and he pointed the fork at her. "Exactly how many women do you think I'm sleeping with?"

Shoving her hands under her thighs, she looked around the room. *Damn spiderwebs! Where do the little buggers hang out? Maybe this weekend—*

"Ellie?" Dave's intense stare bored into her.

Her attempt at a shoulder shrug came out as a jerk. "You're a single, professional athlete who can get whomever he wants." This she said as if it explained everything.

A squall seemed to brew in his hazel eyes. "Therefore I screw anything and everything that moves?" He dropped his fork again and sat back with a sigh. "If I were that guy, why would you even date me? You're better than that. Besides, I definitely *do not* get whomever I want." He fired her a pointed look.

She bit down on her lower lip.

"Not all professional athletes"—he used air quotes on the last two words—"are the same. And frankly, when I'm around you, I forget what I do for a living. Which is one of the reasons I like being around you."

She raised her eyes to his. "So you haven't been with anyone since you and Nicole broke up?"

"I didn't say that."

Lancets to the heart. Why did it bother her? "Oh." Before she could stop herself, she said, "How many?"

He arched a thick eyebrow. "Why do you want to know? *I* don't want to know how many *you've* been with. That's why I'm not asking. I'm happy to stay in my ignorant bubble."

Jealousy? A tiny thrill shimmied up her spine, but it couldn't counterbalance the question she'd put out there. "More than six?" She cringed inside. *Please say no, please say no.*

He chuffed out a laugh. "Wow. No. Way less than six."

She held up all five fingers on her right hand. "How many less than six?" Stubborn, her dad called her. Yeah, a chip off the old engine block.

"I don't even tell my *cousin* this shit." Dave darted his eyes to the ceiling, sighed, then slid them back to her. "One. Way too much alcohol and someone I already … knew. Happy?"

"A fuck buddy, then." Her casual tone belied the roiling in her gut.

"Not exactly a fuck buddy, no. I think to qualify as a fuck buddy, you have sex on some kind of regular basis. 'Momentary weakness' or 'lapse in judgment' would be the more appropriate label." He stared at her for a beat. Yeah, she was an idiot. "How did we get here, and can we please be done with this very uncomfortable conversation?"

For some unfathomable reason, she grew bolder—or stupider—still. "Did you have many 'lapses in judgment' when you were with Nicole?"

Now he looked offended. "Of course not! I'm not that guy. I had zilch. Zero. Nada." He made an O out of his hand. "I date one at a time."

"Is that what we're doing? Dating?" She let her curiosity bubble up in her voice. "I guess I'm just wondering what you expect from this. From me. If anything."

"I'm not expecting a damn thing. I *hope* we enjoy any time we spend together. So far, that's been the case."

Not the most reassuring words he could have used, which told her what her heart needed to know: she could tread where she dared but should not get any lofty hopes this relationship would advance beyond the casual phase. "I do like hanging out with you," she said almost as an afterthought as she tried to sort his muddled signals and her muddled emotions.

Now the hazel storm subsided into something akin to calm waters with mischief sparkling in them. "You like hanging with me even when I'm a certifiable asshole?"

More than you'll ever know. God, she wished he didn't make her feel the way he did. Like she was special and beautiful and desirable. A temptation he couldn't resist. Like she had the power to lure the softhearted, playful guy out of the irascible bear whenever she wanted. But instead of telling him so, she gave him an eye-roll. "Good point. That's not your most charming side."

"Well, that's encouraging. At least you think I *have* a charming side." He fingered the edge of his paper napkin. "Now that I think about it, I haven't taken you out on a real date, have I?"

Relieved to be out of the quicksand she'd shuttled them into, she grinned. "Box socials don't count? Or dinners after Habitat projects or games?"

He leaned forward and lowered his voice to a sexy growl. "No, they don't. When I say *date*, I mean you and me alone, not surrounded by twenty of our closest friends."

"Kind of like in the bedroom?" Her eyebrows bounced in what she hoped was a seductive manner.

He chuckled. God, she loved that dark, delicious sound drumming in his chest. "While that may be an end game, I'm talking about the part beforehand where we talk over good food we don't cook and a great bottle of wine we don't open or pour. And no, I'm not doing that with anyone but you at the moment."

At the moment. Why did the qualification unsettle her? She nodded and dipped her gaze to her eggs, hating that rubber-band snap of insecurity. *Shields up.* She needed to know the score so she didn't sink too far in the deep end, alone. And one more burning question needed answering because things still didn't add up.

Tilting his head, he peered at her. "Why do I feel like I'm missing something?"

She cleared her throat and hurled herself at that question. "The last few times, we've started without protection, and the one time you almost—"

He startled her when he stood, came to her, and pulled her out of her seat and into his arms. "I'm sorry, Ellie. That's me being selfish. I love how you feel, how you fit around me." *Oh. Totally throwing me off again here.* He pulled back and gathered her hair into a loose ponytail at the back of her neck. Ooh, that felt good. "That's no excuse, I know," he continued. "It shouldn't have happened. I guess you make me lose my mind. I've *never* done that with anyone else. I promise I'll be more careful, okay?"

She gave him a dazed look. *So confusing. At least there's more great sex in my near future.* Yeah, that. Kind of addictive stuff. Would she ever find another man who did to her in bed what this man did? Damn. She was already *in* the deep end with weights attached to her ankles.

He pressed her back to his hard chest, and she rested her hand and cheek against it, relishing the solid thumping of his heart. *Focus on the good stuff. He's never done that with anyone else.* A pleased blush swarmed her cheeks, and she felt her own pulse evening out after its turbulent pace during their conversation. What had gotten into her anyway, going down the treacherous road she'd just traveled? Self-protection, plain and simple.

No more stupid questions, El. Just don't get too close. Breathe him in and enjoy him while it lasts, whatever "it" turns out to be.

Chapter 32

The Skating Santa

Dave was running late when he pulled up to Sonoma's apartment building and killed the Mercedes's engine. Consequently, he didn't check the caller ID when his phone rang, or he would have let it go to voicemail.

"Hello?"

"Dave! I can't believe I caught you!" Nicky gushed.

Shit, was she drunk? He pinched the bridge of his nose between his thumb and forefinger. "What's going on?"

"Nothing. I just wanted to call and see what you were doing for Christmas."

"Uh, hanging with friends." *One friend.* Though he could have been hanging with more because, lo and behold, he'd gotten invites from Quinn and T.J., or rather their wives, who wanted Ellie to join them. Never ones to shy away from saying what they thought, both Natalie and Sarah had told him how much more they "liked" him when Ellie was around. Apparently, his curmudgeon-o-meter settled into tolerable levels when he was with her. No surprise there. But he wasn't about to share. No, having Ellie and Casper to himself was all the Christmas he wanted.

"Oh really? Which friends?"

Dave bristled. Why did she think this was her business? "Nobody you know. Why?"

She paused, and he expected her to press further, but she hmphed instead. "I have a gift for you I wanted to bring by."

A gift? Oh shit. "That's nice, Nick, but you don't need to—"

"I want to, Dave. Please. Don't be a Grinch and take away my fun." He could hear the pout in her voice.

He blew out a breath. "All right." *Shit. Now I need to get her and Isaac something.*

"I know what you're thinking, and I won't complain if you get *me* something, but I don't want you getting anything for Isaac."

Huh? "Not even a video game?"

"It just confuses him. You're not in his life right now, and he's been doing so well with his dad. Let's leave it that way."

Dave wasn't sure whether or not to be offended, but then he realized it wasn't about him. And if Isaac did better *without* Dave in his life, he had no business upsetting the family dynamic. "I'll be home until about eleven on Christmas Eve," he finally said. "But I've got a game the night before and—"

"I know, Dave. I used to live with you, remember? I won't wake you up before nine. Although I remember a time you didn't mind me waking you up early." Her voice had gone all husky, and a few shivers clawed down his spine.

Long time ago, Nicky. "Yeah, okay. But text first."

"Why? Afraid I'll catch you in a compromising position?"

"Oh, for fuck's—"

"Just teasing! Lighten up." She giggled. "See you in a few days, handsome."

Handsome? What the actual fuck? he grumbled to himself after she hung up.

A half hour later, he and Sonoma were dodging shoppers in front of the boutiques at Cherry Creek North—one more reason he hated Christmas shopping. Usually, he just bought family everything on their Amazon wish lists and skipped the congestion, but not this year.

"So you're taking Ellie on a date *where*? And on Christmas?" Sonoma's questions had his prickliness on the rise because she reminded him what a lame idea it was. How lame *he* was.

"Christmas Eve and Christmas are the only days I have free, and since you were busy with Finn and I promised to take Ellie on a date …"

The classic Sonoma eye-roll. "So you're taking her to your *garage*, then out for dim sum? That's it?"

"And a movie, Nome. Don't forget the movie." He wagged a playful finger at her right before he opened the door to Oster Jewelers. Once inside, he took in the crowd of customers—mostly frantic men like him—clustered around display cases. "And why are we here, exactly?"

She waved a queenly hand. "Because I'm brilliant, that's why." Then her blue eyes got that crazy gleam that always had him looking for the nearest exit. "Why not replace the necklace Ellie lost the other night? She said it didn't cost much, so you can get her something personal without going overboard. Keeps you in that safe 'I like you' zone."

Huh? "She wants a new necklace?"

Sonoma unwound her scarf and huffed. "Men. Honestly. Why is it we have to bash you guys over the head to notice the important things?" She continued in an exasperated voice. "The pendant she was wearing was a graduation gift from Finn and her other steps. No one found it, and Finn says she's really upset about it."

Why did he not know this? Because Finn was Ellie's closest friend, not Dave. Oh, and because Dave had been in dick mode that night, which didn't help him make it to the top of her friends' list. But this was a problem he could solve, and all of him perked up at the prospect of redemption. Soon they were looking at a collection of necklaces, with Sonoma steering him clear of the ones *he* liked.

Her bright burgundy curls bobbed as she argued. "First of all, twenty thousand dollars is way too much to spend. Save the spendy ones for when you're married and you've royally screwed up and need a makeup present to get yourself out of the doghouse."

Married? Yeah, right.

"Ellie's classy," Sonoma prattled on. "She likes simple, not gaudy. Something that fits *her*. She's small-boned, feminine, not like Nicky, who always had you buying that expensive chunky crap. You don't hang a five-pound necklace on a dainty woman."

Dave bit back his aggravation. The saleslady's eyes darted between him and Sonoma, and he swore the woman fought a smile. *Dainty?* Yeah, okay, Sonoma had a point. While she inspected trays in a display case, his eye caught on a delicate chain whose color reminded him of Ellie's hair. The saleslady noticed, retrieved it, and arranged it on a piece of black velvet. The chain, which was decorated with tiny lustrous beads, looked as though it were tied in a knot, and each of the twin tails ended in a small leaf surrounded by the same beads.

"Oh, excellent choice," the clerk cooed. "You say the lady lost something with a leaf motif? This lariat necklace would be a lovely replacement. It's made of eighteen-carat rose gold and is decorated with seed pearls. Understated yet very elegant."

"Ooh, I like that one, Dave." Sonoma held it up to her neck.

He nodded his approval. When she laid it back down on the velvet, a picture of Ellie wearing that and nothing else popped into his brain, and his cock sprang to action, on the hunt for Ellie. "I'll take it," he near-croaked as he shifted his stance. Now the image made a return appearance, but this time Ellie also wore dangly earrings. "Do you have earrings to go with it?"

"Yes, as a matter of fact we do." The lady pulled those out of a different case.

Dangly! "Yep, I want those too." He began sliding his wallet from his pocket.

"Oh, and uh, how much is that bracelet?" He pointed to a thick silver bangle with a fat black gemstone, and Sonoma raised a questioning eyebrow he ignored.

"Seventy-five dollars," the lady said.

"Add that too."

"For Nicky," he said to Sonoma when the saleslady left.

Blue eyes widened. "*What?* Why?" she practically shrieked.

"Shh! Because she got *me* something."

"Seriously, Dave? Jewelry? If you and Nicky are truly over, you are sending the *wrong* message. Just get her a poinsettia and be done with it already."

"She likes jewelry, I'm here, and it's inexpensive. Why would she get the wrong idea?"

Sonoma mimed throttling him. "I give up." When she turned away to look at other glittery things under glass, he sidled away and ended up by a different display case that happened to feature diamond rings. *Dainty, feminine* repeated in his head, and a number of choices leapt out at him. He pictured them on Ellie's slender ring finger, except Ellie didn't wear rings. Did she not like them, or was that her being unfussy? Assuming Will had given her a ring, what size rock had he bought? What size was the right size? Some of his teammates, like Quinn, had gone way overboard, but he couldn't imagine Ellie wanting something huge and flashy. Which made him smile inside. Then his mind wandered to what it would be like to propose and the novel ways some of his buddies had popped the question. He'd never considered doing it before, not that he was considering it *now*. Nonetheless, what would it take to outdo *them*? Who would his best man be? Ellie would make a beautiful bride … white dress, red cowboy boots. Maybe the bachelor party could be in Las Vegas … except he didn't like Vegas. A guys' golfing weekend in Scottsdale instead? Something relaxing, tame. What kind of house would he, Ellie, and Casper live in? Would she want a bachelorette party with hot stripper dudes, and how could he stop that train if she did? *No ripped naked guys are putting the moves on my—*

He practically jumped when Sonoma touched his sleeve. She gave him a coy smile. "Hmm. Engagement rings? For Nicky or Ellie?"

Shit! Where the hell had his mind gone, and had Sonoma read his projection into the Land of Domestic Bliss? He blew out the breath he'd locked in his lungs. "Haha." Turning her around, he marched them both toward the saleslady, who held up a small bag for him.

After leaving the jewelry store and his hallucinations behind, they passed a few ladies' clothing shops, and he came to a grinding halt in front of a window that displayed a shimmering pale blue robe with lace sleeves. Recalling Ellie's tattered wrap, he tapped Sonoma's arm. "Ellie could use a new robe. Think she'd like that?" He lifted his chin at the window display.

"Is that for her or for you?"

His eyes lingered on the robe, and he grinned. "Yes."

"Not to rain on your Santa parade, but you just dropped three grand on a necklace and earrings, and now you're looking at a La Perla robe that easily costs fifteen hundred. And if you step into that store, they'll get you salivating over some wispy little nothing to match, and before you know it you'll have dropped another three grand."

"Too much?" He continued eyeballing the robe, picturing Ellie in it. And out of it. Wearing the necklace and earrings.

"Let me ask you something first. Are you thinking seriously long-term? Do you plan on getting engaged anytime soon?"

He swiveled his head toward his cousin and scoffed a little too loudly. "Of course not."

She hooked her arm through his and tugged. "Then trust me and step *away* from the pretty lingerie, or you'll be sending *two* women the wrong message."

"Seems to me giving Ellie lingerie sends the *right* message." He waggled his eyebrows.

"No, dummy. I'm talking about the spend. Blowing six grand signals *way* more than 'just friends.' Besides, you might make her feel bad because, honestly, how could she ever reciprocate?"

"But I don't want anything from her." *And I like buying her stuff.* She'd been so cute about the dress and boots, and he just wanted to make her smile like she had the night of the square dance. Buying for her was fun, not the chore it had been with past girlfriends who had practically inspected his offerings with a jeweler's magnifying lens.

His mind segued to how he'd always thought Ellie was pretty, but she just seemed to grow more beautiful every time he laid eyes on her. Whether she was in her work clothes or relaxing clothes or dress-up clothes, it didn't matter. That same inner glow, that same smile that lit everything around her was always there. Same pretty blue eyes and strawberry-blond waves. Same laugh that did something to him deep inside.

"That may be, but just like you felt obligated to get Nicole a gift, Ellie will feel obligated to get *you* one. And she'll want to match you dollar-for-dollar, but no way can she do that. See where I'm going with this?" Sonoma raised an eyebrow for emphasis, and he sighed in defeat. "C'mon," she laughed. "You owe me a dinner at La Merise."

After they'd been seated and their wine had been poured, they looked over their menus in silence. *Wonder if Ellie would like this place? It's quiet, romantic. What would she order?* His eyes skimmed the choices as he tried to guess, completely forgetting he needed to select dishes for himself.

When their orders were placed, he raised his glass. "Thanks for your help, Nome."

"Anytime."

"God, I hope she likes what I got her."

Sonoma smirked.

He frowned in reply. "Why are you looking at me like that?"

"Nothing. Just enjoying seeing this squishy side of you that seems to come out whenever you're around Ellie, or talking about Ellie, or thinking about Ellie. I haven't seen it before. Not even with Nicole."

"Don't read too much into it," he grumbled.

"No?"

A server deposited a basket of bread, and Dave slathered a piece in butter. "It's not serious. We're just … spending time together."

Sonoma scrutinized him over her wineglass. "She's a keeper, Dave. You're smart enough to know this."

"Maybe." He shrugged it off. "What happens if I get traded, Nome?"

"So what? A trade doesn't mean you have to cut everyone you know out of your life, does it? You gonna stop talking to me 'cause you're in a new city?"

"Of course not."

"My point exactly." Sonoma gave him a saccharine smile. "So what's the problem?"

"It won't last." He stuffed another bite of bread in his mouth. Despite the butter, it tasted like dust.

Sonoma speared a piece of lettuce and pointed her fork at him. "A bit defeatist, aren't you? You planning on sabotage?"

He speared his own greens. "She can do better than a broken-down hockey player with a shit ton of baggage." Damian Douchebag flashed in his head, he of sleek manners and buffed nails. Dave recoiled inside.

"What baggage, specifically?"

"A team that doesn't want me, a not-so-great track record, a history of doping, for starters." Bobby's latest text popped into Dave's head. *I've got something that'll fix that hand right up.* No lie, the texts were getting harder to ignore.

"So yes, you are planning on sabotaging the relationship. And who says you're broken down? You're selling yourself short, Cuz. Just ask the Mandys of the world," Sonoma snorted.

No thanks. "Things still good between you and Finn?"

Sonoma's face broke out in a girlish grin. "Yeah, they're great."

"I'm happy for you, Nome. He seems like a decent dude." Finn wasn't Dave's first choice for her, but he couldn't argue with how the guy took care of his cousin or how happy she was.

"*Despite* his 'baggage,'" she air-quoted.

"What kind of 'baggage'?" he air-quoted back. Ellie had hinted at Finn's checkered past, but she'd been tight-lipped whenever Dave had pressed.

"Suffice it to say I'm smart enough to see past it and realize he's a rare one … just like Ellie's the rare one, and you need to figure out a way to hang on to her, even if you have to face-off against yourself to do it."

He shook his head. "I have no business getting in deep, especially when there's a chance I'll get shipped off somewhere." He cringed a little at his own deceptiveness. He *still* hadn't told Sonoma about the trade he had asked for.

Sonoma looked him over thoughtfully, her expression telling him she *knew* he was holding something back. "The whole time you and Nicky were together there was a 'chance' you'd get shipped off, but that didn't stop you. Know what I think?"

"No, but you're going to tell me."

"Damn straight. Someone has to. I think you're already so gone for Ellie that it scares the shit out of you, and you're throwing up one excuse after another so you don't get too close. Your man logic is telling you if you're not close, you can't get burned. But I've seen how you look at her, how you act around her. You're different than you've ever been with anyone else—more relaxed, more *you*. And when she looks at *you*, I don't see dollar signs in her eyes. I see something meaningful."

Despite the warning bells constantly clanging in his head, Sonoma's words warmed him, and he uttered one telling word. "Yeah?"

"Yeah. And the sooner you admit how *deep* you're in already, the better."

Better for whom?

Minutes before Nicole arrived on Christmas Eve, Dave hustled home from Ellie's, where he'd spent the night after his game. He was bagging up some foodie items to take to Ellie's when Nicky's knock sounded. In true Nicole fashion, she just let herself in through the door from the garage and walked upstairs, trilling his name. He should have closed the garage door, damn it. Or kept the door between the house and garage locked.

"Right here, Nick." He lifted his eyes and tried not to let his astonishment show. She was decked out in skin-tight black leather pants, stilettos, and a gray sweater with a neckline that plunged to where it crisscrossed at her waist. One tug of that dangerous neckline and the goods would be completely exposed. *Holy shit!*

Her makeup was flawless, her lips done up in shimmering gloss that accentuated their poutiness, and her hair was a perfect arrangement of tousled white-blond curls. Before he could get his mouth working, she was in front of him, her spicy perfume overpowering him. With those sky-high heels, she was nearly eye-to-eye. "Merry Christmas," she breathed and laid a parted-lip kiss on his mouth.

Wiping gloss from his lips, he took a step back and smacked into the counter. "Aren't you a little cold?" he blurted, keeping his eyes trained on her face. *Go, me!*

Scanning him from his sweater to his boots, she smirked. "Aren't you a little warm?" She thrust a package at him that was as done up as she was.

He took a few more steps back until he was anchored to one side of the kitchen island. "I've got something for you too." The Oster Jewelers bag sat on the bottom step leading to his bedroom, and he snatched it, extracted a small wrapped box, and placed the bag back on the step.

She strutted over and glanced inside the bag with a huff. "Hmm. Guess I'm not the only one you went to Oster's for."

Ignoring the comment, he handed her the gift and began tearing the paper off the one she'd given him, anxious to get through this gift exchange ordeal.

She squealed and launched herself against him. "Oh, Dave, I love it!" Then her lips were on his cheek, his neck, leaving sticky gloss on his skin. He caught her as she lunged for his mouth and set her apart from him.

She slid the bracelet on and cooed, "Oh, you knew exactly what I wanted!"

Huh? His Yoda voice echoed Sonoma, grunting about the stupidity of giving Nicky a gift in the first place. She hugged his arm to her chest as he tried to free a flat box marked "Brunello Cucinelli" from its wrapping.

"Do you like it?" she pressed.

"I don't know. You need to let go so I can open it."

With another huff, she released him but stayed inside his personal bubble, hooking an arm around his shoulders. From layers of tissue, he pulled out a soft cream-colored beanie.

"It's cashmere," she gushed. "It cost six hundred dollars."

Way to pull a crushing guilt blanket over him. "Thank you."

She raked her nails through his hair. "Put it on!" He created distance between them and pulled on the hat, and she closed that gap and straightened the beanie with a triumphant "There!" Then she rubbed her hands up and down his arms. "Ooh, I miss these muscles."

What the hell? He peeled her hands away. "Nicky, I've got somewhere else to be and a few things to do before I get there, so …"

Her face fell, and she blinked rapidly. Her brown eyes glossed over. "I thought we might spend the day together."

He began scouring his memory banks to figure out how the hell she'd gotten that idea into her head. "I don't recall us planning to do that."

"Well, we didn't exactly, but I hoped … Isaac's with his dad, and I'm all alone."

"You have Benny," he tossed out.

"I brought him with me. I thought we'd all cozy up on the couch together like we used to." Her eyes shimmered with fresh tears.

"What? Where is he?"

"In the car."

For fuck's sake! "It's cold out there. I'll walk you down so I can say hi to him."

"Well, actually, I was hoping to leave him here with you since I'm taking off day after tomorrow."

WTF? His annoyance was approaching detonation. "Nick, what's going on?"

And the dam burst. While tears spilled down her cheeks, she hiccupped and spluttered through her speech. "I miss you, Dave. I want us to be together."

The irritation that had been rising inside him went into a free fall. "Nick," he said softly, "that ship sailed a long time ago. And you're the one that launched it."

"I made a terrible mistake. It can't be too late." She closed the distance between them, wound her arms around his neck, and leaned in to kiss him, pressing her bra-less breasts to his chest. "Tell me you don't miss this."

Before she could kiss him, he grasped her arms and broke free of her grip. *I don't miss this.* But he couldn't bring himself to tell her, not with her crying and looking so pathetic. "Nicky, don't do this."

His phone rang on the counter, giving him a much-needed breather. "Get Benny. I need to take this."

Something hard flickered in her eyes, and she grabbed her coat. He looked at the caller ID and picked up, moving farther out of earshot. "Hey."

"Merry Almost Christmas," came Ellie's cheery voice. "Again."

Nicky's heels clicked on the stairs, and he let out a gust of air. "Merry Almost Christmas to you too, again." He grinned inside, remembering the "Almost Christmas present" she'd given him that morning in bed.

"If you haven't gone to the store yet, could you grab a string of lights?"

"You mean you don't have boxes and boxes lying around?"

"Not since someone destroyed them a few months ago," she laughed. "Seriously, I just tested my only string, and it's dead." She'd bought a little tree the day before that she wanted help trimming.

"Sure." Downstairs, the door opened and a collar jingled. He needed to end the call.

"Oh, and I thought of something else for breakfast tomorrow," Ellie said.

"Uh, maybe text that to me so I don't forget?"

"It's just two things."

Benny lurched up the steps, followed by a crown of platinum hair. *Shit!*

"Text is best. That it?" Benny was beside him now, dancing and panting, and Dave reached down to scratch his head and calm him down.

"Is that jingling I hear?"

Nicky stood a few feet away, her mouth opening to say something, and he panicked. "Santa on TV. See you soon." He clicked off with Ellie's confused-sounding "Okay" in his ear.

Nicky removed her coat and crossed her arms in a way that pushed her tits to the spilling point.

"What are you doing?" His alarms began raising again.

"You told me to get Benny so he didn't freeze while I hang with you." She looked crestfallen again, and a pang of guilt hit him.

At least she wasn't crying anymore. "Nick, I said I need to go. You can't hang with me."

Her arms banded a little tighter, accentuating the swell of her breasts, and she dropped her voice to a husky low. "I could stay here until you get back." Her sweater slid off her shoulder. "Get naked and wait for you in bed—"

"No! Jesus, Nick, I'm trying to be nice here, but you're not getting the message." *Which is not just a pass, but a hard pass.* "I'm leaving in five minutes—I'll take Benny—and I'm not spending the night here tonight. Or tomorrow night." Frustration surged once more and manifested itself in a ticking jaw muscle.

She yanked the sweater back up and jerked her coat on. "Oh, I get it. You don't have to paint me a picture." She paused to glare at the Oster's bag. "You have to *deliver* the rest of the jewelry." The breathiness was gone, replaced by icy sarcasm. "Did you get her something nicer than what you got me? I sure hope so if you expect to fuck her because this cheap piece of shit"—she held up her wrist, exposing the bracelet—"*might* get you a blow job, but she won't—"

"Okay. You just made this a hell of a lot easier. Get the fuck out."

"Or what, Dave? You gonna *throw* me out?"

"I've never laid a hand on you, so why would I start now?" he gritted out.

She tapped her chin dramatically. "Hmm. Oh, I know. Because you're back doing drugs, and you've lost your mind again?"

I was never "doing drugs," and I never lost control! Not that way. But he didn't bother arguing with her. Lost cause. Instead, he made a pushing motion with his hands. "Do us both a favor. Cut the drama and go." Benny whined at his feet. Nicole's expression, her entire demeanor, grated. Her mouth was a thin, hard line, her eyes small and unspectacular, her hair stiff and brassy. *Jesus, was I really so blind before? Nicky's first priority will only ever be Nicky.*

She stormed off, and the slam of the downstairs door had him dropping his shoulders a few inches. He glanced down at the dog. "Christ, Ben. At least I have a choice about putting up with that bullshit. But hey, let's forget her and get our Christmas on. I have a real treat for you because you're gonna love Ellie and Casper." *Just like I do.*

Chapter 33

GUILT AND GIFTS

Ellie juggled a scorching-hot cookie sheet in unwieldy oven mitts when the knock came. "It's open," she yelled. Casper, who'd been licking her chops since the aromatic cookies had been freed from the oven, whimpered, obviously torn. Continue in her sit-squirm, hoping for a treat to hit the floor, or run to the door and put major licks on Dave?

"If I were you," Ellie whispered to the dog, "I'd go for the licks. Much more satisfying."

"I brought company," his deep voice boomed. This made up Casper's mind, and she bolted for the front door. Yips and yaps ensued.

Ellie set the tray down on a rack and tossed the mitts to the counter on her way out of the kitchen. Dave stood framed by the closed front door, bags in hand, a beanie on his head, and a grin on his face as he watched Casper cavort with a black-and-white Australian shepherd mix. Though she'd spent the night and morning with Dave, her heart bumped a little harder and a whole lot faster at the sight of him. *Hubba hubba! Merry Christmas to me!*

"Is this Benny?" It dawned on her that with Benny came Nicole. Her pulse jumped for an entirely different reason.

The dog looked up at her and grinned, its pink tongue lolling, before turning back to Casper's persistent nose.

"Yeah, and I think I'm jealous. My girl Casper's totally ignoring me."

Ellie sidestepped the pretzel-twisting sniffing dogs and threw her arms around his square shoulders, rising on tiptoe to kiss him. "Well, *I* won't ignore you." A spicy floral scent jammed her nostrils, and she reared back.

He cinched his arms around her, but with his hands full, she easily eluded his hold. "Hey," he protested. "You just said you wouldn't ignore me!"

"No, but you smell like a perfume counter, and I don't want any of it on me."

His eyebrows shot to his forehead, and he seemed to freeze up.

Damn, that's a guilty look. She crossed her arms, like shields folding over her vulnerable heart. "If you've got Benny, I can only assume Nicole came by."

"Uh, can I put some of this stuff down?"

"Sure." She shrugged and pivoted back toward the kitchen, feeling foolish for reacting the way she did. She rubbed her sternum as if it would drive the hurt from her heart. *You have no claim, so knock it off already. Easy, breezy, remember? Besides, this is Christmas, so lighten up.*

It was one thing to give herself little speeches, but quite another to believe them. She braced herself against the counter as he deposited bags on her breakfast table.

He gave her a tentative smile. "I think I got here just in time. Those cookies smell fan-fucking-tastic."

Her eyes were drawn to the beanie. It looked especially soft. "Nice beanie."

He snatched it off his head so fast he nearly gave her whiplash. "Forgot I was wearing it," he grunted.

Weird reaction. Why is he acting like a groom with his hand up a bridesmaid's dress? Reality struck her like a thunderclap. *A gift from Charlize's double—the ex. Or is she really an ex?*

Something Sonoma said about Dave being susceptible to Nicky reeling him back in poked Ellie's raw spots. Was he still in love with Nicole? Had she realized her mistake and was now making a play to get him back? Not that Ellie could blame her. Invisible steely ropes wound around her chest, her throat, making it suddenly hard to breathe.

Spinning the beanie on one finger, he studied her as if he was calculating how to frame what he would say next. "Yes, as you guessed, Nicky did stop by."

Ellie mustered as neutral a voice as she could, happy that it didn't quaver. "I thought she wasn't bringing Benny over for a few more days?"

He flung the beanie on the table and scratched the back of his head. "I guess her plans changed. Maybe she was letting me have him a little longer as a Christmas present." A snort left him.

"Is that beanie"—Ellie pointed at the offending hat—"also a Christmas present?"

Hazel eyes drilled hers. "Yes. I meant to leave it behind, but I totally spaced it was on my head."

"Looks soft."

"Cashmere, apparently."

Ellie drew in a quiet breath. "So what did you give her?" God, she sounded like a shrew conducting a cross-examination.

He shrugged a shoulder. "Nothing much. Just a cheap bracelet I saw when Sonoma and I were out shopping. I had to get her something, and she always liked jewelry, so …"

Ellie ignored how his words caused a rip inside. "And the perfume? Did you spray that on, or did she?"

He heaved out a breath. "She hugged me."

Ellie's eyebrows crawled up her forehead. "That must have been quite the hug to leave a scent that strong behind."

"Well, shit. I probably should've taken a shower before I came over, but I was already running late."

Not the reassurance Ellie had hoped for, and her heart thudded while her mind leapt to the reasons he might need a shower. Even as she fought the urge to disintegrate a little inside, she questioned if she had a right to expect reassurance from him in the first place.

When she didn't respond, he waggled his eyebrows. "I could take a shower now and have you scrub the smell off me."

She clamped her mouth shut to keep it from dropping open. While she didn't believe he'd actually screwed Nicole—he would have definitely taken that shower *before* coming over—she couldn't stop from wondering if he'd wanted to. Or how much he wanted to succumb to whatever hold Nicky had on him … because how hot would a hug have to be to smear that much scent on him? Her head spun in a vortex of emotions.

"Okay, so no couple's shower," he said. "I'm gonna check on the dogs." He took one of the bags with him.

No sooner had she puffed out a breath than he was back without the bag, but with both dogs in tow. "They're getting along great. So who are the cookies for?"

Her eyes darted to the cookie sheet she needed to unload. "Um, I was gonna pack some up for my neighbors."

"None for me?"

"Maybe a few, depending on how nice you are."

He leaned forward, grabbed her hand, and pulled her close. Twining his fingers with hers, he anchored her in front of him, and his other hand tugged her ponytail loose. "How about this?" His voice was sinfully low, seductive, like his fingers working through her hair, stroking her neck. "Is this nice enough?"

The cloying perfume invaded her senses, and her stomach revolted. She turned her head to keep from inhaling it.

He placed a knuckle under her chin and turned her head so she had to look at him—which was when she noticed a smudge of shiny pink below his jaw. She reached out and traced it with her fingertips. *Sticky.* "What've you got on your neck?" *Please tell me it's not lip gloss.*

"Hmm?" He craned his head and looked at her fingers. "I don't see anything." He tried to tug her closer, but she pressed her hands on his chest. A half-smile played on his face. "Do I smell that bad?"

"It's just … the perfume's really strong."

"Ah shit. Sorry. Nose blind. I don't even smell it. I'll hop in the shower and be right back."

Her eyes followed him as he walked away. *He doesn't smell it because he's used to it.* Benny watched him forlornly, and she crouched down to comfort the dog, putting her disconcerting thoughts on hold.

Ellie managed to keep those thoughts at bay the rest of that afternoon, aided by sappy Christmas music, trimming the tree, two silly dogs, cookie baking, and her hunky baking assistant slash taste tester who smelled shower-fresh and kissed her stupid every chance he got. Stupid was a welcome state of mind.

"Ready for our date?" he asked after she returned from delivering her cookies next door.

"I think so. Will the dogs be okay alone, do you think?"

"Are you kidding? Look at those two."

Sure enough, they were curled up beside each other, their backs butted together as though they were lifelong littermates. She smiled wistfully at the scene. Benny was such a sweet dog, and her heart ached for him and for Dave. *Nicole is a piece of work.* Ah, but it was Christmas Eve, a time to be charitable. Besides, Ellie reminded herself, there was no room for thoughts of Nicole.

Though it was only 5:30 when Dave pulled up to a gate, darkness shrouded the starless sky. He fiddled with his phone, the gate opened, and he guided his truck toward a line of storage units with garage doors built into them. They passed a building displaying a sign that read, "Sterling Luxury Garage Condos."

Ellie grinned. "You keep your cars in a condo?"

Eyes focused ahead, he replied, "I think they call them that because you actually buy the garage, just like you buy a condo to live in."

She cocked an eyebrow as he slowed. "Is your cars' condo heated, like a regular condo?"

A glance at his phone, and he thumbed something. A tall, double-wide garage door set among others rolled up. "Not only is it heated, but it has a work area with a lift where I can tinker, a kitchenette, a TV, couch, and a bathroom with a shower." As if on cue, light flooded a huge garage, and he pulled into an empty slot, coming nose to nose with a covered vehicle. The garage door rolled back down and closed behind them.

A laugh burst from her. "Oh Lordy, it's a luxury, off-site man cave! Entertain here much?"

With a wide grin, he killed the engine and opened the door. "That's *exactly* what it is, and no, you're the first person I've ever brought here."

A frisson of delight traveled through her bloodstream.

He scrolled through his phone again, and Elvis demanded a little more action and a lot less conversation through speakers suspended from the ceiling. One corner of Dave's mouth tipped up. "C'mon. I have something I want to show you."

She stepped out of the truck, surprised at how warm the air around her was, and her eyes widened as they swept the cavernous garage. License plates, fine art featuring cars, and vintage neon signs amidst an assortment of hockey memorabilia covered walls that weren't otherwise stacked with gleaming red metal cabinets. The floor, done in black and gray checkerboard with a red border, was pristine. The space was the polar opposite of his sterile town house, and she drank in the details steeped in Essence of Dave.

"Have you ever lived here?" She strolled past a section that resembled a studio apartment, complete with small kitchen, man-sized leather couch, recliners, tables, area rug, a huge wall-mounted TV, and a gaming system.

He pulled the cover off a turquoise-and-white Chevrolet Nomad with chrome details. "I've been known to spend a night or two here." He bent to buff a strip of chrome with the sleeve of his flannel shirt. "What do you think?"

"It's beautiful!"

"It's a project car, but it's drivable now." He hefted the hood and wedged a rod in place to hold it up.

She peered inside, standing close enough to feel the heat coming off his body. "Looks like the original engine. Two-sixty-five?"

"Yep."

"Three-speed manual? Four?" She moved to the driver's side door and scanned the interior. "Oh wow! Not a manual at all. A Power Glide transmission. How cool is that? And God, I love the old gauges." Now she was back at the hood, and she stuck her head in a little deeper while he held up his phone with a flashlight app shining into the engine compartment.

She glanced over her shoulder at him. "Are you planning to restore it to its original configuration? Do all the serial numbers match?"

He grinned. "They all match, but I'm toying with turning it into a hot rod."

She withdrew and dusted off her hands. "I'm guessing you'd drop in a three-fifty crate motor?"

"That's my thought. Do you have any better suggestions?"

She ambled around the car. "God, no. The exterior does need some love, though, doesn't it? Were you planning to do all the work yourself?"

"I'd like to, but it takes a lot of time. Maybe it'd go faster if you helped me." He removed the rod and lowered the hood.

Her eyes flew to his, and her insides turned warm and gooey with the signal *that* comment broadcast. "I don't know enough about restorations to be much help." Now she stood beside him again.

"You could hold my wrench."

She gave him a playful shove. "You did *not* just say that."

He let out a laugh and tugged her to the back where he lifted the window and lowered the tailgate. Crawling inside, he beckoned her in after him.

She crawled in and settled against him. "What are we doing?"

"Checking out the best feature of this car." His lips were on her neck, warm breath stroking her skin into a landscape of goose bumps.

She tried not to gasp. "Which is?"

"A big cargo space for watching drive-in movies and necking."

A laugh escaped her. "Necking?"

"Necking," he repeated, his mouth continuing a thorough assault on her throat and ear. She tilted her head and closed her eyes with a low moan. His hands glided over her sides, her back, under her sweater. "Do you know how hot it is when you talk cars?" he whispered against her skin.

He proceeded to show her just how hot he thought it was, and soon they agreed to skip the movie, grab the dim sum to go, and head for the privacy and comfort of home.

As they drove in contented silence, she contemplated that being in love with a man like him wasn't for the faint of heart. An athlete who made big paychecks, who was sought out by adoring fans, many of them beautiful women who wouldn't be easily discouraged from going after what they wanted.

A moment of clarity struck her. In spite of the doubts that dragged her down, despite the fact that a robust self-image wasn't part of her makeup and that she'd rather fall for someone who flew *way* under the radar, Dave Grimson was worth the risk. And if he asked her to take that risk and be with him, she wouldn't say no.

For a guy who was supposed to be distancing himself, who was supposed to be bracing himself *against* falling deeper, he was doing a shitty job of it, and he tried not to ponder chickens coming home to roost. He stole a side glance at Ellie, who stared out the window at Christmas lights with a dreamy little smile on her face. A smile he loved. Christ, he couldn't help himself because everything about her was *easy* to love. Couldn't stay away from her. Didn't *want* to stay away. He'd never felt like this before, and it scared him and made him feel invincible at the same time.

Taking her to the garage had made him edgier than a skate blade, but as soon as he had driven inside, he was glad he had. He'd thought about inviting a teammate or two when he first bought the space, but then things went to hell, and he hadn't felt like sharing that part of his life with anyone—too close, too personal, too exposed. He'd never considered taking Nicky there—not that she'd have been interested—and he'd kept it his secret. Sonoma had a vague idea about a garage somewhere, but he hadn't revealed it even to her. Hadn't wanted to. Not until Ellie. Why was that? Besides the fact she could talk cars—fuck, he'd been harder than hickory from the moment she'd first asked about the Nomad's engine—it felt oddly safe to open up with her, and he found himself wanting to do more of that. With her, he forgot he was a hockey player with an image to uphold. He was just plain old Dave, and he got the distinct impression she preferred him that way.

Yoda growled in his head about everything he was doing wrong, but he didn't care. It was Christmas, damn it, and he deserved some happiness, no matter how fleeting. And being with Ellie made him happy. Being with her was like tearing off a dull film that grayed everything out and replacing it with a blindingly bright kaleidoscope of color.

Her hands rested in her lap, and he reached over and covered one with his. It felt so right. She turned and smiled at him.

"Do you want to drive around and look at more Christmas lights?" he offered.

She shook her head. "I'm getting my fill right now. Besides, my mouth is watering for that dim sum."

"Your wish is my command."

Back in her house, they gated the dogs in the kitchen and spread a quilt in front of a cozy fire. The only light came from the flames and the white lights on the little Christmas tree, but it was enough to eat by.

Ellie handed him a Christmas plate and chopsticks. "A Chinese picnic on Christmas Eve," she laughed.

He grinned back and held up his beer bottle. "To new traditions."

She gave him a curious look before distributing the boxes filled with their supper. "I like it this way. It's fun and different."

"Special," he agreed.

As they ate, they shared stories about their family traditions and past Christmases.

She topped off her red wine and handed him a cold brew from a little cooler. "How long has it been since you spent the holidays with your family?"

"Probably about four years since I spent it with my mom in Florida." He studied her for a beat as she munched away, then blurted, "It'd be fun to get together with all of them again. They'd *love* you."

She stopped chewing and blinked at him. *Shit. That's not anything she wants to hear. Way to scare the crap out of her.* Her half-smile a moment later put him somewhat at ease—apparently, he hadn't totally blown it—and they went back to casual talk about their childhoods. Soon she piled their empty plates and set them to one side, and he did the same with the empty food cartons.

"So you think you'll still be okay watching Benny when I go on the road?" he said.

"Absolutely! He's such a sweet boy. Although I'm afraid to say Casper might have found a new favorite guy."

"Figures. Another fickle female."

"Be careful, or I might not give you your present."

"You got me a present?" He shouldn't have been surprised, especially after his conversation with Sonoma, but he'd been so focused on his gift for Ellie that he'd forgotten she might reciprocate, whether he wanted her to or not.

Ellie laughed. "Don't get excited. It's pretty lame. Just something to open."

With Christmas tunes in the background and the dogs nestled in the kitchen, he pulled the little bag from under the tree and handed it to her. "Open this."

She took it from him. "Now?"

"Yes, now." Along with his building excitement, he fought the smile threatening to break out.

Her teeth sank into her bottom lip, and her eyes sparkled as she pulled the box out of the bag and carefully untied the satin bow. "What is it?"

"Open it!" he laughed. The look on her face made this as much a gift for him as for her—like a little kid getting his first hockey stick.

"Oster? What's that?" She pulled off the pretty foil wrapping and carefully removed the lid. Then she stared at the tissue paper.

"There's more in there," he goaded. "It's not just tissue paper."

"I know." With nimble fingers, she peeled back one flap of tissue, and he held his breath. Now the other flap, and her blue eyes went wide and … Shit! Shimmered with tears as she looked up at him. "This is beautiful!" she whispered. "Are you sure it's for me?"

He swallowed, fighting down whatever was going on in his chest. "Of course it's for you. See the leaves? It's to replace the necklace you lost at Paige's party."

She brushed her fingertips reverently over the pieces. "Oh, I love them. They're so pretty. And so, so delicate."

Delicate, Sonoma had called it. Yeah, he owed his cousin big-time.

Ellie pulled out the necklace and draped it over her slight wrist. He held out his hand. "Want me to help you put it on?"

One tear slid down her cheek. "Oh, now the present I got you is even more lame."

"Doesn't matter." *You just gave me all the present I need.* He took the necklace from her, and she lifted her hair and presented him the back of her neck. He clasped it on and smoothed it. "There."

She turned and opened the top buttons of her sweater, her face lit with a smile. "How does it look?"

"Beautiful."

After swapping the earrings he'd given her for the ones she was wearing, she swiped at her eyes and snatched a gift from under the tree. Cringing, she handed it to him. "I'm embarrassed."

He chuckled and tore into it. "Don't be." A shoebox, and when he lifted the lid, he pulled out a pair of red fuzzy dice and a package with a hula girl holding a ukulele. "Perfect!" he laughed.

Ellie dropped her forehead in her hand and shook her head. When she raised her face to his, her cheeks glowed pink. "At least I got the girl whose hips swivel the most."

He leaned forward, pulled her hand from her face, and kissed her. "I love these. They're awesome."

A sigh left her. "I got you something else. It's at the bottom of the box."

When he spotted an envelope, he opened it, confused about what he read.

"It's an adoption certificate for a dog of your choice at the Dumb Friends League," she explained before running on, a frantic quality to her voice. "I might have overstepped, but I just felt so bad about Benny. With the way you love on Casper, I thought you might like a pup of your own. And I've already spoken to Natalie; she's totally down for pet-sitting when you're on the road." Now she *really* accelerated. "And if you don't want a dog, I understand. The certificate can be donated back to the shelter so someone else can adopt one." Bright, anxious eyes fixed on his, and that funny feeling that had been tightening in his chest moved to his throat and wedged there.

They sat facing each other, cross-legged. "Come here." He wrapped his hand around her nape and pulled her to him so her forehead rested against his. "This is the nicest damn gift anyone's ever given me," he rasped. And he wasn't lying.

He kissed her again, lingering this time. She opened, inviting him in, and he didn't hesitate. The kiss deepened, and his tongue plunged in, tasting her while she tasted him, claiming her mouth as their arms wound around each other. *So fucking sweet.* Soon her fingers were tunneling in his hair, and she was tugging in that way that turned his blood into ribbons of heat.

She pulled back, her chest rising and falling with shallow breaths that mirrored his own. "Are we back to necking?" she teased.

More than necking, I hope. He drilled into her deep blue pools. "So I have this fantasy."

One eyebrow, along with one side of her mouth, cocked. "Oh? Sounds interesting."

"I got the necklace and earrings because they reminded me of you." He paused to clear his throat. "But then I imagined you wearing them …"

Now the second eyebrow joined the first one near her hairline.

"… without anything else on."

A knowing smile slowly spread over her face, and she rose up on her knees. "In this fantasy of yours, do I take my clothes off, or do you?"

Hell yes! "Oh, I think *I* do."

Her hands fluttered down her sides and extended outward by her hips, as if she were presenting herself to him. Which, in fact, she was. "All yours."

He rose to match her stance and began fumbling with the buttons of her sweater. Moments later, she was naked, the firelight and Christmas lights bathing her in a warm glow. The real Ellie in nothing but jewelry blew his fantasy girl to dust.

Merry Christmas to me.

She gave him that same knowing smile and stood boldly while his eyes took their time feasting on every inch of her. His hands followed, gliding over her, his heart galloping as her skin rose beneath his touch.

No one had ever affected him the way she did. She took his breath away, and he wasn't sure he'd ever pull air into his lungs again.

Chapter 34

On the Road Again

Three days later, Dave was still riding a Christmas high when he woke up in his St. Paul, Minnesota, hotel room. In the other bed, Hadley was a snoozing lump. A morning skate, followed by a meal and a nap, and Dave would be ready for tonight's game. The days off at Christmas had been welcome for so many reasons—the ache in his hand was nearly gone now—and he was raring for tonight's game.

His phone blinked, and he picked it up and grinned. The other reasons he'd enjoyed the best Christmas he could remember since he was a kid had everything to do with the girl whose text he was reading. *Casper, Benny, and me on the couch with popcorn tonight. Go, Grim Reaper!*

Morning wood stirred, growing harder as his mind lingered on gorgeous, sexy Ellie.

Dave: *What will you be wearing?*

Ellie: *Your necklace and earrings.*

Now his cock was fully awake, and morning wood became morning rock. *Naked?*

Ellie: *Lol. Might get a little cold.*

Dave: *Tell me you'll wear the Xmas Eve outfit. That way if I get hit by a 100 mph slapshot, I'll die happy.*

Ellie: *OK. I'll be wearing your jewelry and nothing else.*

Shit! Why exactly was he torturing himself? Because they were flying home after the game, and he'd be with her late tonight.

Dave: *Send pix.*

Ellie: *No way!*

Dave: *I'm not a perv.*

Ellie: *Could've fooled me. Lol. How about I wear your fav outfit to bed? That way you get to see it when you wake me up.*

Dave: *Can't wait. Might have to wake you up with my tongue.* He added a few crazy-eyed, tongue-hanging-out emojis.

She replied with a string of puckered lips.

Stifling an inner groan, he glanced over at Quinn, who was still sound sleep. *Thank fuck!* If Dave hurried, he could commandeer the shower for a while, and God, did he need to commandeer the shower! As he went to put his phone down, he realized he'd missed another text. An urgent text. From Herb. He rose and made his way to the bathroom, skipping the shower and pulling on some gym clothes so he could find a private corner outside his room.

Minutes later, on the business level in a different part of the hotel, he hit Herb's number.

After exchanging niceties about their Christmas celebrations, Herb began with, "Sorry to get you up so early, but I thought you might enjoy some good news. And I need something from you."

"What's the good news?"

"Arizona contacted me, and they are *very* interested. They want a call back from me within the hour with either a thumbs-up or a thumbs-down. Do you want to pursue a spot on their roster?"

Dave's heart plummeted to his knees, which caught him completely off guard. "Why the hurry?"

"Rumor is you're their top choice, but they have their eye on another defenseman if you pass, and they don't want to miss the opportunity."

Out of habit, Dave looked down at his hand. "Uh …"

"Oh, that's not a good sound. It's do-or-die time, buttercup."

Shit!

Shit, shit, shit! This was *Arizona*, a club built to make repeat appearances in the finals for years to come, poised to win it all, maybe become a dynasty. For months, he'd imagined playing there, pictured how sweet it would be to hoist the Cup over his head and kiss it at the end of *this* season. Besides the team, there was the allure of the warm desert climate for his muscle cars, fantastic golf courses, a fresh start.

But no Ellie.

Wasn't having Ellie long-term just a pipe dream he'd indulged this past week, though? She'd never move to Arizona. Hell, the best he had to offer a woman was his bank account and a slice of celebrity, and that hadn't even been enough to hold Nicky. How the hell would it be enough for Ellie, whose soul ran as deep as the roots she planted in the ground? Besides, he liked being with her—okay, loved—and couldn't get enough of her, but that was how he felt in casual mode. Enjoy-it-while-it-lasts mode. Han mode. What would happen if they shifted into something more permanent?

"Dave? You there?"

"Uh, yeah, Herb. Just a little shocked."

"Understandable. Want to take five minutes and call me back?"

"No." Dave swallowed. "No, I'm good. First, tell them thank you. Second, tell them … I'm in."

"Will do. Make sure that hand's a hundred percent."

The call ended, and Dave ran his hand over his face, then parked his elbows on his thighs. Leaning forward, he hung his head and dragged cleansing breaths through his lungs. Shit, he could use a double shot of *something* right now. For a guy whose big dream was on the verge of coming true, why did he feel like he'd just sliced himself open?

The game was a bitch. Minnesota took it to them with whacks and cheap shots all night long, and they got away with them because the refs either weren't looking or had swallowed their whistles.

Halfway through the third period, T.J. had just left the ice and Dave had just come back on when Minnesota's enforcer, a big, ugly motherfucker, cross-checked Nelson in the mouth. The bastard had been harassing the Blizzard's first-line center—and their other skilled players—all night. Dave wasn't normally a hothead who stirred the pot. He also wasn't a fighter—that was T.J.'s job—but he could fight, though his size usually deterred opponents from testing him.

Tonight, though, the sight of blood spewing from Nelson's mouth—combined with the wasps buzzing in his stomach over the Arizona trade—flipped a switch inside Dave, and the gladiator took over.

Guys had come together, and the douchebag who'd hit Nelson was taunting him, even though Nelson was bent at the waist, his blood painting red circles on the ice like an ugly Rorschach test. Dave skated into the scrum to get the asshole away from his teammate and give him a nice little face wash with his stinky glove.

Douche shoved Dave across the chest with his stick and laughed. "Wanna taste of the lumber too, you big pussy?"

In a blink, Dave shook off his gloves and took hold of the guy's jersey. Power surged. He was Thor in fucking *Ragnarok*, with lightning coursing through his body, shooting out of his eyes. He connected with a few quick punches and pulled Douche around like the sack of shit he was before throwing him to the ice and landing on him. Words were pouring out of his mouth, but he couldn't remember what he said as he manhandled Douche—only the gratifying *Holy shit!* look in Douche's eyes and the linesman pulling him off.

Douche never got the chance to take his gloves off—which should have cost Dave extra in penalty minutes if the refs' whistles had been active—and as he and Douche skated to their respective penalty boxes, Dave taunted him with a jerk of his chin. "Afraid to ruin your manicure, *you big pussy*?"

Once he took a seat in the sin bin, Dave sobered. Shit. A five-minute major for fighting meant he was off the ice for half of the remaining period. That wouldn't help his team one damn bit. The adrenalin ebbed, and his hand throbbed, screaming at him for throwing punches into meat and bone. *Not totally healed here, dumbass*, it seemed to say. Then everything around him sharpened, and he registered his teammates thumping their sticks against the boards in appreciation. Suddenly, his hand didn't ache as much.

Neither team scored during the penalty, and when he finally made it back to his own bench, he looked around for Nelson, but he wasn't there. The trainer shot Dave's hand a concerned glance, but Dave shrugged it off. "How's Nelsy?"

"Don't know yet. They took him to the hospital to check him out."

"Shit," Dave muttered and took a seat, averting his gaze from the trainer. No way was he going to let anyone think he'd re-injured his hand, even if he had to grind his molars to dust if the trainers decided to manipulate it after the game. Nothing mattered but what was before him on the ice. His club was up by one, and he could smell sweet victory. His club *deserved* this win.

In the end, they earned it, beating their opponent by two goals when Minnesota pulled their goalie and Quinn fired in an empty-netter.

Back in the locker room, guys slapped him on the back of the head or fist-bumped him, which made him wince inside until he switched to his left. The right was a pulsing balloon, and he kept it tucked against himself as much as he could without anyone noticing.

"All right, boys," he warned when they began cutting up. "Your alternate captain's still getting his squash scanned. Yeah, it was a sweet win, but our boy made a huge sacrifice to help us earn that win. Don't forget that."

"Reaper's right," one of his teammates said.

"Listen to your captain," another said.

And still more gave him nods or an "Okay, Grims."

It dawned on him that they were circling around him—metaphorically speaking—giving him the respect they hadn't shown in a long time, and Christ, did it feel good! It *also* dawned on him that he'd invited them in by not being such a pissed-off jackass every time one of them looked at him. Had it been that way all along and he'd simply been blind?

In front of his stall, he glanced down at his scuffed hand. Shit. If he'd done something more than aggravate the hand and Arizona found out, he was done.

Beside him, T.J. said in a low voice, "Nice fight. Better get some ice on that."

Dave flexed the hand—or tried to—and whatever didn't hurt like a mother was numb. "As soon as the medical staff is out of sight."

"Did you re-injure it?"

"Nah. Just hurts a little, but you know what fucking ladies they are about this shit. 'Ooh, did you hurt your poor little hand?'" Dave falsettoed.

T.J. chuckled. "They *are* looking out for you."

True, damn it, but it's not enough. A younger man's body and a steady source of HGH, catabolic corticosteroids, and hydrocodone would have taken care of the nagging injury, keeping his pain tolerable, slashing his healing time by …

He pulled out his phone. After weeks of fence-sitting, he texted Bobby.

Ellie awoke, cold and alone, and blinked. The digital clock told her it was 6:11 a.m. Rolling to her side, she ran her hand over the cool, unruffled sheets beside her. The other pillow was undisturbed. Where was Dave? Panic welling inside her, she sat up and shivered, then shrugged her robe over her bare shoulders and grabbed her phone from the nightstand.

One text at 3:48 a.m.: *Wind delayed our flight. Heading to town house to sleep. Catch up with you later.*

She stared at the screen. Not that long ago, he'd told her he slept better *with* her than without her. Add to that the fact she had Benny *and* her house was closer to the arena than his, and her mind began puzzling over the real reason he hadn't come over.

"Stop it!" she grumbled to herself. "You're reading too much into it."

She swung her legs out of bed and stuffed her feet into fuzzy slippers. Off came the necklace and one earring—the other had fallen out during the night—and she hugged the robe around herself and stepped into the bathroom. Forty minutes later, she'd showered, dressed, eaten, and taken the dogs out for a brisk walk, but her phone remained devoid of new Dave messages. *He's exhausted. He's sleeping.* Then her mind leapt to the fight. *He got hurt! That's why he didn't come over.*

She had a morning meeting with Paige she needed to prepare for, so she tucked the phone away and headed for the office. She'd text Dave later to be sure he was okay.

"I'm leaving you two here in case Dave comes by, so stay out of trouble," she warned the dogs. They wagged and smiled as if they couldn't wait for her to leave.

Alone in her office, she was reviewing a landscape plan at her desk when a knock came at the front door. Too late to hide, she sucked in a breath, took slow steps to the front door, and unlocked it.

"Good morning." Agent Rick Clemente raised one hand in greeting. In his other hand, he held a cardboard tray with two drinks. One, she knew, would be a skinny blonde vanilla latte—her favorite.

She held the door open. "Good morning, Agent. Come in."

"Rick," he admonished as he breezed past her. In his wake, he left a strong, spicy scent that tickled her nose and had her suppressing a sneeze. He deposited the tray on her desk and flashed her a white-toothed smile. "Did you have a nice Christmas?"

Crossing her arms, she took wary steps toward her desk and him. "I did. You?"

"Fantastic." He cast his eyes on her plan. "Working on something new?"

"Yes, and as a matter of fact, I need to meet with my client in about thirty minutes." She looked at her watch, though she was oblivious to the numbers on its face. Her nerve endings rippled with apprehension, and her stomach lurched. What did this man want?

"I won't keep you. I was in the area and wanted to stop by, see how your holiday was, and wish you a Happy New Year."

"Um, thank you. That was—"

A big man in an ivory beanie threw open the front door and pulled up short, his face puckered in a frown as his eyes bounced between them. She nearly dropped her jaw. "Dave?"

Rick held out his hand for a shake. "Don't think we've officially met. I'm Agent Rick Clemente. And you're Dave Grimson, I assume?"

Dave's frown morphed into a question mark, then returned to a scowl as recognition seemed to dawn. "You're the guy who gave Ellie a bad time about her van." His hands remained firmly stuffed in his jacket pockets.

To his credit, Rick looked unruffled while he retracted the hand. "Yeah, an unfortunate misunderstanding. I've been trying to make it up to her ever since." He slid Ellie a wink, and Dave's scowl deepened.

"Agent Clemente was in the area and was nice enough to bring me a coffee." *No way am I going to call him "Rick" in front of Dave.* "Which is perfect," she babbled on, "because I needed another shot of caffeine for my meeting with Paige Miller, and if I don't get going, I'll be late. Not good to be late when someone's about to turn over a boatload of business." Both men stared at her as if she'd sprouted cat whiskers.

Now the back door whooshed open, and in stepped Felipe. Wide with surprise, his eyes scanned the three of them before landing on Agent Clemente. The two men, she could have sworn, exchanged a look.

Ellie began gathering up her things. "Gentlemen, I need to go. Felipe, you'll lock up? Rick, thanks for the coffee." *Oh shit! So much for not calling him Rick.*

Rick gave her an especially dazzling smile. "Anytime, Ellie."

"I'll walk you out," Dave growled and placed a possessive hand on the small of her back while he threw another glower Rick's way.

Ellie executed an inner eye-roll and headed out the back door for the Sienna.

"Here." Dave slid the fob from her hand, opened the side door, and disencumbered her of her load, stowing it on the backseat—which was when she noticed his taped right hand.

"Are you all right?" she blurted. "When I didn't hear—"

He took her jaw in his rough hands and kissed her hard. He ended the kiss as abruptly as he'd started it, his breaths shallowing, then kissed her all over again, more slowly this time and with a whole lot of heat, hunger, and tongue, as if he were laying claim to every inch of her mouth. When he broke the kiss, she opened her eyes slowly, a little dazed. He scanned her face and released her. "Why's that guy in there?"

Huh? "I … He … I don't know. He's been coming around with coffees. Maybe he's trying to figure out if I'm harboring undocumented workers or running some kind of smuggling ring. Or maybe he's just being nice. What are you doing *here*? I thought you were home sleeping."

He dragged his untaped hand over his beard and glanced away. "I was, but I have to be at the arena. I stopped by Sonoma's and saw your van. Didn't expect you to be here."

"What's going on with your hand? Did you hurt it again?"

His eyes remained focused elsewhere, his pulse twitched erratically in his neck, and he looked as though he were hundreds of miles away. Zoned out. *Why is he acting so pissed off? For that matter, why is he acting so* off? His injury and his past with PEDs suddenly collided in her brain, and her heart bottomed out. *Is he using that crap again?*

His gaze swung back to hers. "No, it's fine," he gritted out. "Will you be around later?"

She nodded. "I'm heading home after my meeting with Paige. Will I see you then?"

He gave her a quick head bob. "Better get going."

As she drove away, she kept her eyes on the rearview mirror and the man she wasn't sure she recognized. *What the hell happened?*

Chapter 35

Tug of War

Dave had been surprised to see Ellie's van at her office when he'd stopped by Sonoma's. Even more surprised when he walked into Ellie's office and found the muscle-bound dude staring at her as though he wanted her for breakfast. And she was smiling back. *What the fuck?*

"Waiting for Sonoma?" a feminine voice asked, rattling him from his wallow. He hadn't noticed Mandy approach as he stood beside Shear Indulgence's back door, waiting for his cousin to arrive.

"Uh, yeah."

She winked at him. "Well, come on in out of the cold. I'm sure she'll be along any minute."

Not knowing what else to say, he watched as she punched in a code and followed her inside, keeping his distance, before settling himself in Sonoma's chair. Mandy deposited her stuff at her station, opened the front door, and threw him a salacious grin as she tied on her apron. "Nice fight last night."

"Thanks." He stifled the urge to wince because just the reminder made his hand throb that much more. It had grown steadily worse on the flight home, and by the time they'd landed, he hadn't had the energy to deal with the concern he knew he'd find in Ellie's eyes. So he'd headed to the town house instead, where it would be easier—more private—to hook up with Bobby. Bad idea. Had he been with Ellie, at least he'd have been able to put the pain aside and sleep. As it was, he was sleep-deprived on top of being pissed off because Bobby had postponed. *Just a few more hours.*

Mandy leaned a hip against the chair beside his. "I'd still like to buy you that drink sometime."

Fuck! "Thanks. Uh, wish I could, but I'm seeing someone." *I think.*

Her eyes narrowed. "Is it serious?"

Was it serious? *No, it's casual. No strings, no commitments. Which'll make it easier to let her go once she finds out.*

Mandy smirked. "If you have to think about it *that* hard, I'd say the answer's no. And even if it isn't, if you're ever in the mood for something different, you know where to find me." She wiggled dark, perfectly plucked eyebrows at him and smiled, reminding him of a sleek wolf.

"Sorry I'm late!" Thank God Sonoma burst through the door and saved his ass from having to come up with a comeback. Maybe she had the power to pick him up while she was at it and make him believe he was worthier than the pond scum he felt like.

Hours later, he sat on Ellie's couch while she flitted around the living room. Flitted over eggshells because of *him*, most likely. He was battling the urge to push Ellie about Clemente. Deep down, he admitted she'd done nothing wrong. More to the point, he had no right.

Besides being all kinds of pissed off about the douchebag agent, Dave had spent the better part of the morning convincing his club and his agent that his hand was fine, and thankfully they'd bought his story. For now. It was up to him to keep up the façade until it healed. Worse than his hand, though, was the fact they'd kept Nelson behind in Minnesota last night for "observation." And no one was talking about when he'd come home. Shit, that was bad!

He needed to call Nelson's wife and see if she needed anything, but after the last twenty-four hours, he was fucking tired and wanted to go to sleep. In Ellie's bed, not his own. But his own was where he was hoisting his mind to be when Finn showed up at Ellie's front door.

"Hey!" A fist bump made Dave flinch, though Finn didn't seem to notice. Soon the guy was parked in a chair across from him. "That fight last night? That was fucking amazing! The way you horsed that asshole and took him down was awesome!" Finn enthused. "How's the hand?"

Glancing at said hand, Dave gave it a tiny flex and gritted his teeth. "Fine."

"I heard the douchebag might've broken Nelson's jaw when he chopped him in the kisser. Looks like my favorite center might've also spit a chiclet or two."

"My favorite center too," Dave sighed. What Dave *did* know was they'd managed to re-plant Nelson's tooth. He just hoped Nelson wasn't out of the lineup long because the club needed him. Bad.

"Damn shame you didn't knock out *that* fucker's teeth when you hit him," Finn lamented.

Dave didn't bother telling him Douche didn't have any front teeth to knock out.

Ellie appeared in the living room with sports drinks. "Will you be checking in with Gage today, Dave?"

The question made him bristle. "Why?"

A small crease divided her eyebrows. "Because he got hurt and he's your teammate?" She paused a moment, seeming to organize her thoughts. "I can always call Lily and find out if you're too uncomf—I had wanted to call her but didn't want to step on your skates, as it were, since I'm not really part of … since it's *your* team, *your* tribe."

Finn's eyes darted between them, and he took a quick swallow of his drink. He seemed to squirm where he sat.

Ellie's innocent words, spoken haltingly as she obviously tried to navigate the murky waters of their whatever-it-was, had Dave pondering how hard this relationship shit was. Better if he could be left alone to lick his wounds. Literally. He wrestled these thoughts while simultaneously banishing the pain radiating from his hand and thinking about what waited for him back at the town house. Sweet relief, that's what. In the meantime, he asked Ellie for a shot of whiskey, and she gave him a double and a questioning eyebrow.

A half hour later, he still hadn't stirred, but Finn was gone. Why Dave was welded in place was beyond him. Ellie worked in the kitchen, and the TV in front of him flickered, though he had no clue what was on. A text chimed, and he relaxed a little when he read Nelson was on his way home. Broken jaw, grade-two concussion, uncertain return, but he was coming home, where his wife could take care of him, and family and friends would form a safety barrier around them all.

When Dave next became aware of his surroundings, he was prone on the couch, a pillow bunched under his head, a blanket thrown over him, and Casper licking his hand. The TV was still on, its volume a low buzz, and it was dark outside Ellie's windows. Shit! How long had he been asleep? He sat up, and Casper's entire back end wagged as if he were the best thing since dog treats. His neck was on fire, and he rolled it, popping it.

Small, strong hands were suddenly on him from behind, massaging his tight neck muscles. "Just relax," Ellie whispered behind him.

"Where did you come from?" he asked.

"I was lurking in the shadows, of course," she chuckled. "No, I was reading in the other room with Benny, and I heard Casper's tail cleaning the carpet, so I surmised you were awake."

"How long was I out?"

"Four or five hours." Now her fingers were in his scalp, and he let out a low groan. *Fuuuuck!*

"Feel good?" Ellie asked.

"God, yes."

"If you're hungry, I have a batch of homemade black bean soup on the stove. Or I can whip up something else."

Did I die and I'm in heaven now with my very own personal angel? As he relished the feel of her fingers digging into his tight knots, warmth flared and spread through him. A question bobbed and broke the surface of his mind. Did he really need to solve *all* his problems now? Couldn't they wait until he was back on the road in a few days?

Dave managed to put what gnawed at him aside for at least that night in Ellie's bed. And it wasn't solely the mind-blanking effects of the lovemaking that had done it. When he'd fallen asleep, it was the comfort of holding her that had made it easy to drift. When he'd wakened several times during the night, it was her reassuring weight nestled against him that had allowed him to sink back into sweet sleep.

Driving through town the next day, he was contemplating getting a dog of his own with Ellie's certificate when his phone rang. Herb's name popped up, and he immediately answered. "Hey, Herb."

"Are you sitting down, buttercup?"

Dave couldn't decide whether to be excited or terrified. He drew in a sharp breath. "I'm driving, so yeah, I'm sitting."

"If you're driving, you'd better pull over. Colorado and Arizona have started their trade talks."

Whoa. This is really happening. Dave pulled into a parking lot while Herb went on.

"Arizona has made it clear to *me* that if they get you, they'll extend your contract another four years and add a no-trade clause. And they're willing to pay forty-five mil." He paused to sip something. "Since you're driving, I'll do the math for you. That's eleven million, two hundred and fifty thousand a year."

Holy shit! No wonder Herb had asked if he was seated. "Why would they do that? I'm thirty-two."

"And an elite defenseman. Also a franchise player and a team captain. Guys like you aren't on the market very often, and teams will pay. Look at the seven-year, sixty-one mil contract Vegas gave Petriangelo."

By the time they hung up, Herb had Dave practically dancing in his seat. The first person he wanted to call and share the news with was Ellie. A mere moment later, he realized he couldn't. Not only was it not a done deal, but he'd have to figure out how best to frame it. His inner dancing feet stuttered to a stop as though he were dragging on a one-ton sled.

As he looked around the parking lot where he sat idling his engine, he realized he was on the outskirts of Nelson's neighborhood—lots of his teammates lived there—and his heart sank. He *should* call, but Nelson wouldn't want to hear from him. Maybe he could get an update from someone on the medical staff, not that he wanted to go anywhere near them and have them probing about his hand more than they had been.

Would management fill him in if he asked? A big negative there too. Quinn, then.

"What would I do if I were just a straight-up teammate who wasn't carrying around all this damn baggage?" he thought aloud.

"You wouldn't hesitate to call him," Yoda replied. Only it sounded more like, "Call him, you would. Right thing to do, it is. Hmph."

"Shut the fuck up, Yoda."

Dave stewed on it a few beats before expelling a big sigh. Yoda was right, damn it. Dave punched a button on his steering wheel and held his breath.

"Hello?" a feminine voice answered.

"Lily?"

"Hi, Dave. I'm answering Gage's calls because he's hard to understand with his jaw wired shut. I still have a long way to go before I can interpret his grunts myself," she laughed lightly.

Thank fuck! Not that the guy's jaw was wired shut, but that Dave didn't have to talk to his surly ass. Lily was the much more pleasant Nelson. "So how long do the doctors think it'll take for the jaw to heal?"

"Months before it's fully healed, though the wires will come off in a few weeks and he'll probably be able to play before that, depending on how things go with the concussion."

"Jesus, what a cluster-fuck. And now with you pregnant. Congratulations, by the way." Dave had heard—from Ellie, who'd heard from Sarah—that Lily had just passed the three-month mark, and they were going public with the news. "Can I do anything for you?" he added.

"No. Except …"

"Except what?"

"He hasn't been home that long, but I think Gage is already climbing the walls. Could you maybe stop by? Doesn't have to be for long."

Fuck. Dave pondered how uncomfortable that visit would be as he rummaged around his brain for an excuse to decline. "Has anyone from the team been to see him yet?"

"Not yet, but Quinn and T.J. promised to drop in before you guys go on the road again."

Damn it. "If captain, you are," Yoda grumped in his head, "responsibility you must take."

Before he could stop him, Yoda was telling Lily, "Sure. I happen to be about ten minutes away. Is now a good time?"

"That would be great!" She practically sang out her answer, she sounded so relieved.

"Can I bring him anything? Smoothies? Protein drinks?" What else could Nelson consume? "Booze? Warm Jell-O?"

"No, thanks. I think we're squared away in the food and drink department."

"All right. Call me if you think of anything." He made a right turn and took his time heading toward Nelson's place. Yeah, uncomfortable didn't begin to cover what loomed.

Dave trailed Lily through a big-ass entry decked out in Christmas decorations into a wood-paneled room she called the "library." *More like a man cave for an ascot-wearing asshole from the hoity-toity set.* Of which Nelson was neither. There were books and a desk but also a hell of a lot of hockey memorabilia. Perpendicular to the doorway where Lily and Dave stood, Gage sat on a cushy leather couch, his back to them as he faced a flat panel TV showing a car commercial. Daisy sat close by, reading to him from a book. Sounded like … *Grimms' Fairy Tales*? On an opposite wall stood a stone fireplace flanked by floor-to-ceiling windows that looked out on a backyard that could have doubled as a park. As luxurious as the place was, it had that unmistakable feel of home. The Christmas decorations, the daughter, the pregnant wife. Nice life.

"Gage? Someone's here to see you." Lily's soft voice had Nelson craning his head toward her with a smile lighting his eyes. The smile disappeared when those eyes landed on Dave.

Dave held up his hand in a clumsy wave. "How's it going?"

Nelson grunted out a greeting between clenched teeth and turned back to the TV.

"Hi, Mr. Dave," Daisy called.

"Hey, Daisy girl." *Such a cute kid.*

Lily's gaze bounced between Dave and Nelson. "Daisy sweetie, why don't you come with me so the men can spend some time alone? Dave, if you want something to drink, there's a stocked mini fridge built into that cabinet. Help yourself." Lily pointed it out as Daisy joined her. The two pivoted, and the glass double doors closed behind them.

All alone. Great. Now what?

Smoothing his beard, Dave ambled over to an armchair. When the commercials gave way to a hockey game, he sat down gingerly. *Ten minutes, and I'm out.* "Who's playing?"

Nelson side-eyed him and frowned.

Dave slapped himself on the forehead. "Stupid question. It's right there. Montreal and Tampa Bay. Whoa! And Tampa Bay is smoking them." Did he really sound as ridiculous as he thought he did? He could feel Nelson's eyes on him, and he glanced over at him. "How's the jaw?"

Some muffled noises Dave interpreted as, "Hurts like hell." Beside Nelson on a side table stood a half-full cup with a straw. "Need a refill of whatever that is?" Dave offered.

Nelson shook his head, then jabbed his thumb over his shoulder toward the mini fridge. Dave didn't know if he wanted to stay long enough to drink anything, but he was twitchy, and raiding the mini fridge was something to do. The sucker was well-stocked, and he bypassed the beer and canned cocktails to pluck out a water.

Behind him, Nelson grunted loudly and slapped the leather seat beside him. *What the hell is going on?* Dave turned in time to see a Tampa Bay player score a mind-bending between-the-legs goal.

"Shit! How did he do that?" Dave laughed as he dropped back into the seat and unscrewed the water. They watched the replays showing the goal from every possible angle. "Unbelievable! That's even prettier than the one Hads scored against LA."

Nelson grunted agreement, his mouth tipping up at the corners.

They watched the rest of the game together, with Dave providing sparse commentary which Nelson answered with grunts and barely understandable words. Occasionally, Nelson texted him when he had an important point to get across, like the turnover that led to a goal or a diving call the ref missed. A few hours passed before Dave realized how late it was.

"Shit. I should go." He rose from his seat and looked at Nelson. "Take care of yourself and feel better, buddy. We need you back on the ice." The words simply slipped out of his mouth as natural as you please. After a beat, he added, "I hope it's okay if I stop by to check on you, see how you're doing, see if you or Lily need anything."

Nelson gave him a slow nod and blink, then picked up his phone and tapped a text. Dave's phone pinged, and he looked at the screen. *Thanks for stopping by, and thanks for beating the shit out of that mofo. Hope your hand's OK.*

Dave let out a laugh, loosening a wad of tension that had been balled up in his chest. "You're welcome, but I think it was more me throwing him around the ice than beating the shit out of him."

Nelson's thumbs flew. *Even better. You muscled him like he was a kid's rag doll. I've seen the replays. Fucking awesome.*

Heat rose up Dave's neck, and he shuffled from foot to foot. He coughed. "Well, ah … see ya soon. Text me if you need anything. I mean it."

Lily walked him to the door and looked up at him, a tear threatening to spill from one corner of her eye. She rose on tiptoe and planted a kiss on his cheek, then squeezed his arm. "You're a good guy, Dave," she whispered. "Thank you."

He drove to his town house with a single purpose, but Lily's words and the look of gratitude in her eyes were doing funny things to him. When he locked himself inside and pulled out Bobby's bag of goodies, he did the same damn thing he'd done since he'd traded Bobby money for the stuff. Stared at it. Argued with himself. Back and forth. How simple it would be to cave and *do* it. Make his hand stop hurting.

But then what? He'd fought hard—was still fighting—to earn back his teammates' respect, and even if they never found out, *he'd* know.

He'd been envious of Nelson today despite the broken jaw. The guy had it all, but it hadn't been handed to him. No, he'd fought and clawed and earned every damn bit of what he had. So had Dave. So why were their lives so different?

Dave huffed out a breath.

As he laid out the syringes and pills, it struck him that no fucking way would Nelson entertain what Dave was contemplating. And that was the difference. Nelson lived and breathed integrity, no matter how hard it was to stick to his guns.

For ten agonizing minutes, Dave stared at the PEDs in front of him. The neat arrangement represented salvation for his injury but devastation for his soul. If he got caught, how could he look his teammates in the eye, knowing he'd let each and every one of them down? That he hadn't cared enough to tough it out? Disgust and disappointment would be reflected in their faces, and rightfully so. And what about Ellie? She might not run out on him, but could he stand to see regret in her beautiful blues instead of that look he loved, the one that told him he was her fucking superhero?

Everything crystallized all at once. He had one chance—one—to not blow it all again, which left only one answer. Before he could talk himself out of it, he destroyed everything he'd bought off Bobby and sent him a text saying he wasn't in the market anymore before deleting him from his contacts. And though his hand hurt like a son of a bitch, he felt better than he had in days because he wasn't the muck stuck on the sole of someone's shoe anymore. Maybe Yoda had been right all along.

Dave stood staring at the stall in the visitors' locker room. One more stall, one more locker room, one more road game. What city was he in? What would it feel like when he was dressing in a completely different home locker room? *Not playing anywhere if my fucking hand doesn't get better.* Not only was it not getting better, it was so swollen he was having a hard time putting on his glove despite the tape job. He washed down another four ibuprofen while no one was watching.

Tomorrow was New Year's Eve. He'd focus on celebrating with Ellie before his next game New Year's Day—the anticipation would help him grind it out tonight. *Sixty minutes. You can do this.*

"Grimson?" Dave turned and faced Coach LeBrun. Coach gave Dave's hand a pointed look and, with a jerk of his head, motioned for him to follow. *Shit, shit, shit!*

Chapter 36

The Wicked Witch Carries Prada

Flanked by Benny on one side and Casper on the other, Ellie stared at the TV. Why wasn't Dave playing in tonight's game against Dallas? The announcer said something about an injury, but what injury? Dave hadn't uttered a word when he'd left this morning.

Though he wouldn't see the text until later, she started composing one anyway, asking what was going on and if he was all right. Was it his hand? He'd been so weird lately, so moody and twitchy—

The knock on the front door had Casper barking and Ellie jumping. Benny trotted after Casper, who growled and yipped ferociously at the door until Ellie nudged her aside with her foot. Ellie looked through the peephole. She pulled in a sharp breath and looked again. *What is* she *doing here?*

Ellie opened the door and peeked through the gap. Standing on her front stoop, stomping her booted foot and blowing on her hands, Nicole looked beautiful even under the harsh bright-white light cast by the carriage lamp.

Ellie swallowed. "Yes?"

Nicole flashed her a brilliant smile; she could have been auditioning for a toothpaste commercial. "Ellie, right? Can I come in? I'm here to pick up Benny."

What the hell? Ellie opened the door and let Nicole inside. "I wasn't, um, expecting you."

"No?" The tall, gorgeous blond's gaze took a quick trip around the interior of Ellie's house before sweeping Ellie from head to toe. Ellie tugged at her yoga pants and her baggy sweatshirt, as if doing so would transform them to something as stylish as what Nicole wore. Skinny jeans showing off skinny legs tucked into black knee-high boots. Wide leather belt sitting on a skin-tight white top over lean hips, topped with a luxurious gray shawl cardigan sweater. In the crook of her elbow, a black designer purse with a triangle displaying "Prada." Expensive, sleek, everything perfectly in place, from her Swedish-white blond hair to her pink lip gloss to her glittering diamond jewelry. She looked as though she'd just stepped out of the pages of *Vogue*. Smelled like it too. In fact, it was the same cloying fragrance that had clung to Dave on Christmas Eve, and Ellie's stomach flipped over. She could never be Nicole—didn't *want* to be Nicole—but there was no denying the stun factor of the entire glamor package. No wonder Dave had fallen for her.

Nicole gave Ellie a half-smile. Or was that a smirk? "Nice place." Benny yipped a doggy hello. Nicole looked down and took a step to the side, as though afraid he might leave a spot of drool on her perfect ensemble. Casper, on the other hand, had backed up and sat sloppily on Ellie's foot, as if to say, "We slovenly types gotta stick together."

Ellie straightened her shoulders. "How did you know who I am or where Benny was staying?"

Now the smirk transformed to a "Duh, really? How stupid can you be?" look. "Because Dave told me, of course. He and I talk nearly every day." She waved a hand carelessly, and the sparkle of a sapphire-and-diamond-encrusted tennis bracelet caught Ellie's eye.

Is she telling the truth?

"Can we close the front door?" Nicole asked. "It's freezing."

Guess she's staying more than one nanosecond. "Um, yes. Of course." Ellie was unnerved by having this woman see her private spaces. Hell, about having this woman under the same roof! Ellie switched off the TV and snatched up her phone, scrolling through her recent conversations with Dave. Nothing about Nicole picking up Benny. She slid the phone into a sweatshirt pocket.

"I'm still a little confused," Ellie began. "Dave never mentioned you coming to get Benny."

Nicky shrugged. "Typical Dave, though I can see him forgetting to tell you, given how busy he's been. On the other hand, there's a lot Dave *won't* tell you. He's big on 'need to know,' except *he's* the one who decides what *you* need to know. Like most pro athletes, he's a different breed and not for mere mortal women."

No, only for goddesses like you, apparently.

Nicky gave her a sympathetic look. "Look, Dave and I go way back, so it's natural we have an understanding. Did he tell you why we broke up?"

What the hell does "an understanding" mean? "You mean the sort of understanding where you turned your back on him over the doping?"

Nicole snorted. "Who told you that?"

"Dave. I guess it was 'need to know.'"

"*That's* what he told you?" Nicole shook her head. "Unbelievable. Well, I shouldn't be surprised. That's easier than the truth, which was that he cheated on me on the road. Every. Single. Time. Have you ever been around a group of hockey players when the puck bunnies come hopping around? A little alcohol, throw in some hot chicks in skimpy clothing willing to do anything, and I mean *anything*, and Dave doesn't hesitate to leave good intentions on the floor with his clothes. Disgusting." Nicole twirled the bracelet again. "No, of course he wouldn't tell you all about that."

"If it's true, why on earth would you want to be with someone like that?"

"Who says I want to be with him?"

Ellie was caught in a weird nightmare she couldn't wake from. That *had* to explain why she was trapped in her own house experiencing whiplash because of this snotty, terrible woman. In an attempt to buy herself time so she could maintain some sort of equilibrium, Ellie said, "That's a beautiful bracelet."

Nicole turned her wrist and regarded it with a dazzlingly dreamy smile. "It is, isn't it? I told Dave we didn't need to exchange Christmas gifts this year, but he insisted. He's so generous." She gave Ellie a pointed look. "And speaking of generosity, did he tell you what *I* gave him for Christmas?"

"He showed me the beanie, and—"

"Oh, but that wasn't *all* I gave him. Guess he's keeping that intimate little detail in his 'need to know' bucket." She licked her glossy lips like a dog about to tear into a juicy bone.

She's lying. Don't let her bait you. Ellie wasn't a hater, but in this moment she hated this woman. "I guess he is. As for the uselessly extravagant beanie, what you should've given him was his dog back instead of holding Benny over his head like a weapon," Ellie gritted out.

Nicole raised a tinted, well-plucked eyebrow. "He *told* you that?"

"No, but I've been around him long enough to know."

"What did he get *you* for Christmas?" She shook the bracelet yet another time, and Ellie bit back the urge to rip it off her wrist and stuff it down her lily-white throat.

"Something I've been wanting for a while," Ellie lied. Sort of. While she *loved* the set Dave gave her, she hadn't been pining for it. She was no jewelry hound, but she knew enough to recognize the bracelet Nicole wore wasn't just some "cheap" trinket that had required little thought on Dave's part. Ellie didn't care about jewelry, but knowing Dave had dropped a small fortune on Nicole when they weren't together anymore tore a gash inside. That ugly, worn-out question about him and his former flame danced through Ellie's mind: Were they, or weren't they?

"Well, isn't that nice? Whatever he got you, I'm sure it was special," Nicole crooned.

Ellie crossed her arms. "Nicole, as fascinating as this conversation is, I need to get back to work, so if we can just—"

"Doing what? Scrubbing toilets?" Nicole swept another disdainful gaze over her. "I don't get what he sees in you. Dave likes his women … polished." She tapped a long nail against her cheek. "But that would explain so much, like why he's not quite ready to end *our* ongoing, um, relationship."

"Your *what*?" Ellie nearly kicked herself for letting this woman goad her into a reaction, no matter how egregious the cause.

Nicole covered her mouth with graceful, manicured fingertips. "Whoops! Guess that's a 'need to know' he kept to himself too," she tsked.

"Or there's nothing to tell." Ellie clenched her jaw. "Did you ever consider the only reason he has an 'ongoing relationship' with you is because he wants to see Benny?"

Nicole jutted a bony hip and chortled. "*He* insisted *I* keep Benny so he has an excuse to see me." An evil gleam lit her eyes. "While we might've broken up, we didn't stop sleeping together. Ask him about it sometime."

Anger. Confusion. Disbelief. Contempt. These all detonated inside Ellie at once, and she dug her nails into her palms while she silently counted to ten.

Another drippingly sympathetic smile. "You seem nice, but like I said, athletes are a different breed. They like trophies on their shelves and trophies on their arms. And Dave's no different. In fact, he still tells me I'm the most beautiful woman he's ever seen. The physical attraction between us has always been off the charts, and some habits are simply unbreakable. It's not your fault."

Ellie made another silent count, only making it to five this time. "I'll get Benny's stuff together so you can get the hell out of my house."

"Oh, I'm so sorry. Did I strike a nerve?" Nicole checked a nail. "You know, I can send you my stylist and my personal shopper's contact information. I mean, no offense, but you're not exactly burning up the fashion scene," Nicole snarked and blatantly eyeballed Ellie's shabby attire.

Ellie turned to gather Benny's toys, trying not to squirm inside. Her heart about broke when he followed her into the kitchen with a plea in his eyes. *Don't send me home with that awful woman.* Ellie ruffled his neck and fought the stinging tears overwhelming her eyes. "I'd keep you if I could, sweetheart," she whispered, stuffing the toys, his bowl, and his food into a bag.

When she returned to the living room, the sneer was still frozen on Nicole's face, and something hit Ellie between the eyes. She handed her Benny's bag. "I feel sorry for you, Nicole. You live and breathe for your looks, for how beautiful men tell you you are, but that's not forever. And what will you be left with when they fade?"

"At least I *have* looks. You might have just enough to hold Dave's interest for a little while," the evil woman continued, squeezing one eye shut, pinching her thumb and index finger together. "But soon he'll get bored, and you won't be enough."

Did this woman share a home with the same man I know? "That may be. From what I know about Dave, he goes way deeper than that. But frankly, if I'm wrong, it's better I find out now because I don't want to be with a man who only cares about what's on the surface anyway."

Without another word, Ellie opened the front door and made a pushing motion with her hands. Nicole and Benny walked out, and as Nicole turned with a finger raised and her wicked mouth open, Ellie slammed the door in her face and locked it. She shuffled to the couch and flopped down, face first, and let the dam of tears burst.

Casper stood vigil beside her, and when Ellie had cried herself dry, she rolled over and stroked her little dog's head. "I didn't do so well keeping it casual, huh, girl? Well, at least it explains his schizophrenic behavior lately. Maybe he's been trying to find a way to break it off so he can be with her. If that's the case, I'll make it easy on him. As for what Naughty Nicky said, if it isn't all a bunch of BS, at least Dave and Benny will have each other again."

She pulled herself upright, slid the phone from her pocket, and read her unsent text to Dave. After deleting it, she shut the phone off and curled up on the sofa with Casper.

Dave checked his phone one last time before takeoff. Nothing from Ellie. Not one reply to any of his seven texts. He'd called when they first boarded the charter, but it had gone straight to voicemail, and he hadn't left a message because he wasn't sure he could without sounding surly as hell. Should he try and tap out one more text left-handed? His right hand throbbed mercilessly, and even *without* the shiny new splint, it would have been totally useless. Correction: *fractured* right hand. A fracture discovered when Coach and the medical staff had insisted on X-rays before the game. And surprise, surprise, not just one fracture but two—a fresh one and the old one re-injured, though he suspected the old one had never fully healed to begin with. Now the docs were talking over the possibility of surgery.

That stellar news had shredded his fledgling hopes and sent them crashing to the ground. He hadn't spoken to Herb yet, but there was no doubt going to Arizona was off the table. As for Colorado, they'd either ship him off to God-knew-where or buy out his contract.

Fuck! Can this get any better?

Instead of texting Ellie, Dave sent a short one to Finn, who replied immediately that he'd heard from Ellie earlier and she seemed fine. Dave blew out a sigh of relief. He'd try to reach her once they landed. For now, he closed his eyes and focused on locking out the pain while the plane climbed.

Once they'd leveled out, guys started milling around. Across the aisle, Quinn juggled his damn beanbags. "Interested in a game of poker, Cap?"

"No. Think I'll watch some *NHL Tonight* and see what's happening around the league. Besides, it's a little tough to play one-handed."

In the seat ahead of him, Wyatt laughed. "Which is exactly *why* Hads asked. He figures he can finally beat you if you can't handle all your cards."

Quinn threw a beanbag at Wyatt's head. A few more guys drifted back to ask about Dave's hand, and soon he was surrounded by a half dozen or more teammates who ribbed him about his injury. They accused him of doing it on purpose to get out of spending New Year's playing in St. Louis, or because he was going for a permanent "pinky-up" look. The more good-natured shit they gave him, the more his sour mood lightened.

Much later, when guys had gone back to their seats or fallen asleep, Coach LeBrun ambled to Dave's row and leaned against the seat. "Hey, Coach."

"How's the hand, Grims?"

"Hurts."

Coach nodded. "I expect that's not the only thing hurting."

Dave simply nodded.

"I know it sucks, but try not to let it get you down. Things have a funny way of working out."

Huh? "I'll keep that in mind, Coach."

Dave was still trying to puzzle that one out hours later as he stood on Ellie's stoop. It was late. Really late. She hadn't exactly invited him over, but she hadn't said *not* to come over either. Because she hadn't talked to him. The key wasn't where she'd left it before, which any smart man would have taken as a sign she didn't want to see him tonight. But damn it, he wasn't smart. He was still worried about her, and besides, she had his dog. Plus, he was tired from pain meds and lack of sleep, and it was damn cold; seeing her would warm him up.

Breath steamed the air in front of him, and he knocked, gently at first, then louder.

The first sound he heard was a dog snuffling. Then the front door cracked open a few inches, and long strawberry-blond hair glinted in the light. Ellie peered at him with one eye. "What, Dave?"

"Can I come in? It's cold."

"Suit yourself," she grumped, adorably sleep-tousled, wrapped up in her robe.

As soon as he closed the door behind him, he reached for her. "Aw, I'm sorry. I woke my girl up and made her all grumpy. I'll get Benny and go."

She sidestepped him and folded her arms over her chest. "Benny's not here, and I'm not your girl." Her eyes darted to his splinted hand, but she said nothing.

"Am I in the wrong house?" He chuckled mildly.

"As a matter of fact, yes, so please leave. You'll find Benny with Nicole, wherever that is," she bit out.

"Wait. *What?*"

Even in the dim light, he could make out the daggers in her eyes. "I said, Benny is with *your girl*, Nicole. She picked him up this evening."

Questions bombarded his brain all at once, and alarm rose inside him like bile clawing its way to his throat. He held up his hands, palms out. "Whoa, whoa, whoa. Back up. How did she know where you lived? Or that Benny was with you?"

"She said you told her. She had a lot of other things to say too."

Shit! I'll bet she did. His mind whirring, he dragged his hand over his jaw. How much damage control was he facing? "Like what?" He cringed inwardly, imagining the crap Nicky might have filled Ellie's head with.

"How about we start with the ten-thousand-dollar bracelet you gave a woman you supposedly don't care about?"

"What are you talking about?"

"I saw the bracelet you gave her for Christmas, Dave. I don't consider five carats' worth of diamonds and sapphires a 'piece of crap.' And it's not that I give a damn about you giving her extravagant gifts. Just don't lie about it."

"Ellie, I gave her no such thing," he sighed. "The bracelet I gave her was silver with an onyx stone or some crap like that. You can even ask Sonoma because she was with me when I got it." *Should have listened and gotten Nicky the poinsettia … although it wouldn't have stopped her from coming over here and pulling her stunt.* Goddamn Nicky.

They stood, facing-off at opposite ends of the living room. Casper was leaning against Ellie's leg like a marble sentinel. Something told Dave they wouldn't be sitting anytime soon.

He pulled in a lungful of air. "Forget about what Nicky said. She's a manipulator and a liar and—"

"Then why is this woman still in your life? You say things about her like that, yet she seems to have control over what you do. You take her calls, you cater to her, you put up with her bullshit. I don't get it. Can you explain it to me?"

He'd been asking himself the same thing, but he had yet to come up with an answer. "It's because of Isaac."

"A boy who's not yours and who's not in your life anymore? No, that one doesn't fly. How about this for a reason: you're hoping to get back together with her. She said you've slept together since you broke up."

Fuck! He hadn't seen this coming—because he'd never *imagined* Nicky confronting Ellie—and he wasn't prepared to deal with it tonight. He pinched the bridge of his nose.

"Oh my God, you mean it's true?" Ellie's voice pitched high, and she laughed mirthlessly. "And here I was, giving you the benefit of the doubt. My mistake. I seem to make a lot of those."

A slow simmer started inside him. "You're putting words in my mouth. Look, what happened between her and me was just that. Between her and me. It was never about *you* and me. You didn't need to know about something that happened in the past for this *very reason.* I didn't want it getting blown up into something it's not."

"Excuse me?" One fist went to her hip, and she held up her index finger. "Wait a minute, wait a minute. You're telling me it's *okay* that you've been sleeping with her, and I didn't need to know?"

"That's not what I said."

"Pretty damn close. Want me to repeat it to you?"

"No, damn it, and I haven't been sleeping with her! You make it sound like this is recent, but it's not." A few times over the course of several months not long after they'd split, and he'd been lonely and stupid and drunk. And it had been a mistake every time, but he couldn't turn back the clock no matter how much he wanted to.

"So she's the woman you had the 'lapse in judgment' with because of 'too much alcohol'? You made it sound like once with a random hookup, but obviously that was a bendy truth. Guess you not only had a lapse, but you had some *re*lapses too."

"This is why I didn't want to be in a relationship," he muttered, never thinking she'd hear him. Yeah, definitely *not* a smart man.

"Excuse me?"

"You sound like that woman in *Holes*," he huffed. "I said I didn't want to be in a relationship with you. Wait. That didn't come out right. I meant I hadn't planned it." He shook his head. "Ellie, I'm tired and things aren't coming out the right way. Can we please talk about this in the morning after we've both had some sleep?"

"I don't know about you, Dave, but I haven't slept so far, and I doubt I'll get any sleep the rest of tonight." Her jaw clenched as she spoke, and a little muscle jumped. "I don't want to drag this out until tomorrow. I want it all out now, and I want to get it over with."

Over with? He gaped at her.

Her eyes blazed, and she stood straight and beautiful and completely untouchable. "Actually, I have my answer. I *do* get it." The angry quaver in her voice was gone, replaced by something calm and chilling.

"Get what?"

"Why you've been blowing hot and cold. One day you act like we're in a relationship and you're talking about things we might do in the future, and the next day you pull away—it's because you *are* getting back with Nicole. You used me to make her jealous, and it worked! Well, leave me the hell out of it. I don't want to play this game anymore."

"Jesus fucking Christ, Ellie! You don't understand! This isn't about getting back with Nicky. I've been trying to get traded to Arizona. *If* I've been swinging back and forth, *that's* the reason." He held up his splinted hand. "And now my chances are shot to hell."

Now *she* gaped at *him*. "Since when have you been trying to get traded?"

"Since before I met you. Now do you believe me?" *Christ, please let this be the end of the argument.*

Instead of the end, he got Car-Crash Ellie, and she ate up the distance between them and smacked his chest with both palms. "You mean you've been planning to get traded this whole time, and you never said a damn thing to me? Instead, you strung me along and let me believe … Was this some kind of game to you? 'Oh, I'll just buy the landscaper a new van and watch her fall all over herself.' You were just biding your time. At *my* expense, asshole!"

He lifted his hands to reach for her, but she evaded him again. "Ellie, you've got to believe me. It wasn't like that." *I never meant to fall in love with you.* That's what he *should* have said—because it was the truth, but it also left him wholly, painfully exposed.

"Then what *was* it like, Dave? Please explain because I'm having a real tough time understanding how this wasn't all about you having some fun before you moved on to the next city and the next idiot." Her blue eyes were dark and stormy, her mouth firmed in a hard line he didn't like.

"I can't win." He clapped his hands on top of his head and blew out a frustrated breath. "You're reading more into it than there is."

"You mean like reading you actually gave a shit?" She yanked at her hair. "God, I am *such* a sap! Why did I let myself … I thought you were different, that *I* was different. I thought I was smarter now, but no, I guess some things never change. Fool me once … At least I found out who you *really* are before it was too late."

"If you're comparing me to Will, then you're *way* off base," he snapped. The slow simmer was rolling into a slow boil.

"You know what, Dave? Just … I am sick of worrying about being all things to all people. I haven't been fair to myself. Well, I'm over it, and I'm going to take care of number one from now on. You'll be much better off with someone flashy who's more your speed. That girl is definitely *not* me."

"Ellie, for fuck's sake! I don't want someone flashy." *I want you.* "You're being ridiculous."

"Well gee, thanks for confirming my looks aren't on par with Nicole's." He opened his mouth to argue—God, he couldn't say the right thing!—but she held up her hand. "But you know what? I'm good with that. What I'm *not* good with is people who slip and slide around the truth and blame everyone else when things don't turn out their way." She marched to the front door and opened it. "We're done here. You can leave now."

"Wait. That's it?" He was stunned. Frozen. Suddenly, he wanted the argument back—didn't matter what it was about anymore, only that they argued because it meant they weren't giving up. But this—

"Yep, that's it. Have a great life, Dave."

Chapter 37

When Chickens Come Home to Roost

We need to talk.

Those were the first words Dave tapped after a sleepless night.

When? Nicky texted back.

An hour, Griffin Coffee at Sloan's Lake.

He didn't wait for her reply. Just rolled out of a bed tangled from restless tossing and downed his first cup of coffee, though he couldn't chase the sand from his eyes or the dull weight sitting in his chest. Part of him was still pissed, part of him still stung, and another part was suspended in disbelief. How the hell could this have happened?

He stared at his reflection in the mirror. "You let it happen, dumbass. That's how. Just like you let the doping take over, and like you let your team slip away." *And Ellie.*

That last admission, losing Ellie, hurt far more than the other two combined.

It was time to pull his head out of his ass and own his life, starting with putting his toxic relationship with Nicky in the dump, where it belonged.

Tossing and turning all night had shaken loose a few other realizations. Like how he'd wasted too much time, energy, and heartache on a woman who was all wrong for the future he wanted—had always been all wrong, but he'd either been too blind or too stupid to understand exactly what he truly *had* wanted. In the past year, his fuck-ups had come home to roost, and he'd spent last night reconciling his shortcomings, re-evaluating. For the first time in a long time, everything was as clear as a Rocky Mountain winter sky.

Because of Ellie. She'd given him an appetite for that life he wanted, and it had woken him up. Now he couldn't imagine living without it, and he was lining it up in his sights.

Nicole waltzed into the coffee shop, her camera-ready smile plastered on her face. He nodded in return and pointed at the counter, indicating she could get her own drink. Yeah, he should have hopped right up and gotten it for her, but he wasn't feeling that generous. Though she seemed surprised at first, she got her frothy coffee-that-wasn't-really-coffee drink and joined him at the table. When she leaned in for a kiss, he turned so her lips landed on his cheek.

She settled into her chair with a perturbed purse of her lips. "How have you been?"

"I was great until I got home last night and talked to Ellie."

Nicky lifted her nose a little higher. "So this is how you're going to play it? Right out of the gate, you're going to take her side and accuse me of God knows what?"

"I'm not accusing you of anything—yet. Let's look at the facts first. You obviously figured out where she lives—I can only guess you followed me at some point—and you showed up on her doorstep while I was on the road and she had Benny. You timed your little visit well. My game had started; I was unavailable."

Nicky sipped her drink and didn't look at him.

"Would you agree those are the facts?" he pressed.

"Maybe," she said.

"Then you had the unmitigated gall to barge in and *lie*, telling her I'd told you to get Benny. You weren't even supposed to be in town, so either your plans fell through or you had your little showdown planned all along." She opened her mouth, but he held up his hand. "At this point, it doesn't matter. What matters is you showed up when you weren't welcome, you pushed your way in, and you lied some more—about your damn bracelet, saying I bought you something far more valuable for Christmas than what I *actually* got you, which cost less than a hundred bucks."

"I knew it was cheap." Her tone was icy; he didn't give a shit. "But I didn't lie because you *did* buy the expensive one for me, Dave. Don't you remember that weekend in San Francisco—"

"That was years ago, Nicky, and as I recall, you pulled out all the stops to get me to buy it," he gritted out. The bracelet hadn't been a gift; it had been a way to shut her up. Another manipulation—he was seeing them all so clearly now—and he'd played right into it because it had been easier to maintain the "status quo." Suddenly, he was exhausted. "I'm so tired of your games. Tired of how you twist the truth and use people and hurt them without a thought for anyone but yourself."

"How dare … You can't talk to me like this!" Her voice was a hiss.

"I can, and I am. It's long overdue."

"If that's true, then why didn't you do it sooner?" she huffed.

"I've given that a lot of thought. I've been in denial for a long time, and your stunt woke me the hell up. The reason I've been hanging in there is because I didn't want to pull out on Isaac. But irony of ironies, you'd *already* pulled me out of his life. I was clinging to an impossible commitment. He's a good kid, and I wanted him to understand he's worth something to me. That I wouldn't just walk away from him. I hope he remembers that and that someday he realizes it was beyond my control." He sighed. "I also realized I've been letting you use Benny against me, just like you used Isaac against his dad when we were together." He paused to gather his words and swallow the lump in his throat. "Benny's yours, Nick. I gave him to you. That means the next time you need someone to watch him, you call a dog sitter. The next time you let him get into rat poison, you call the vet, and the bill's on you. I'm not your fix-it guy anymore. I'm not your bottomless bank account. In fact, the next time you want something from me, you call my attorney."

Her eyes popped. "Are you nuts? Have the drugs fried your brain?"

He shrugged off her worn accusation. "I've let you walk all over my boundaries, but it ends now." A mirthless chuckle rumbled inside him. "You know, you did me a huge favor when you dumped me. I would have hung in there, taking the abuse, letting you work me. But you made the decision for me, and God, am I grateful you did."

She sat back as though she'd been slapped. Her eyes turned stormy. "Dave—"

Ellie's words, fresh and raw, had dug a hole deep inside him. He stood and used them on Nicky. "Have a great life, Nick." He walked away without a backward glance.

A week later, Dave hadn't gotten so much as a "Happy New Year" from Ellie, and he was still numb. The holiday had come and gone, with him keeping his own miserable company in his stark town house. He'd meant to check out the dogs at the Dumb Friends League, but every time he so much as pulled up the website, he talked himself out of it. A few saving graces had been his teammates inviting him to parties he didn't attend and him visiting the only guy he knew who was almost as miserable as he was: Nelson. The two of them watched hockey or attempted playing poker, which looked more like a comedy routine, what with Dave forever spilling his cards and Nelson grunting at him. Sonoma had texted him too, wishing him a happy New Year, but mostly she'd gushed about what she and Finn were doing to celebrate.

His mind, as always, circled back to Ellie. He'd sent her texts she hadn't bothered to answer. He'd even tried pumping Lily for information, but Lily hadn't spoken to her since Christmas. They were planning some Paige Miller girls' spa day get-together, and Lily asked if there was a message he wanted to pass along. Since the only message he could think of would make him sound like a total pansy-ass, he declined.

No matter how many times he told himself it was for the best, that not having ties would make a move easier, he couldn't swallow it all the way. It felt like cramming a fully spiked sea urchin down his throat because he couldn't move past the simple fact he missed her. Like he missed taking his next pull of air.

And Jesus Christ, it hurt.

He was reclining in front of the TV when his phone buzzed, and he blew out a breath and picked up. "Happy New Year, Herb."

"Same to you, buttercup."

"Don't tell me. Let me guess. Every team that expressed interest has said, 'Don't call us, we'll call you,' and you're pretty damn sure that's the last you'll hear from any of them."

Herb chuckled. "Ah, ye of so little faith. While *some* teams appear to have taken their ball and gone home, Arizona isn't one of them."

Dave sat forward with a thump of the recliner. "Are you shitting me?"

"Would I do that?"

"No, not when it comes to something as important as this. But seriously? I can't believe they're still interested."

"Now that doesn't mean they're willing to offer the same compensation package, so if you've still got your heart set on playing there, you might have to lower your expectations where salary's concerned."

"I'll keep an open mind."

"Good. Now do what the doctors and trainers tell you, and I'll be back in touch once I have an update."

When they hung up, Dave sat back with a "huh." Arizona still wanted him, even though he was damaged goods? Surprise—and something strangely akin to dismay—twisted inside him, at odds, dark and light, like a vanilla-and-chocolate swirl cone.

Mid-January, and the all-star break loomed. Dave wasn't going this year, which was disappointing because he could have used the distraction. Today he found himself doing skating drills alongside his teammates, a number of whom *were* going. No hand stuff for him yet—just legs—unlike Nelson, who was back on the ice, going nearly full-tilt, a full face shield the only sign his jaw had been broken a few weeks ago. At least the dude wasn't all wired up anymore.

A small audience watched from the stands, including the team owner's asshole son, Travis, surrounded by a gaggle of hotties. In typical Travis fashion, he was shamelessly leveraging his association with the players to puff up his importance. What the guy lacked in looks and charm, his daddy's bank account more than made up for, which explained why his ugly ass was surrounded by these attractive girls.

Dave shook his head as he skated by, which proved a mistake because Travis yelled, "Come on over and meet some of my new friends." Yeah, the guy was planning to apply some holier-than-thou vise grips for Dave's sin. With an inner eye-roll, Dave headed toward the group—he knew better than to say no to the owner's son.

Travis introduced Dave to his companions with flourish. It was a scene straight out of a gladiator movie: the emperor showing off to his fawning harem, displaying the meat whose sole purpose in life was to entertain said emperor. And to look good in these girls' eyes, Travis was primed to one-up the gladiator with his supremeness. Tear down the other guy to build himself up.

Practice was winding down, and some of the guys joined Dave—either to check out Travis's "new friends" or because they wanted to satisfy their curiosity about the ongoing conversation.

"Girls, this is Dave 'the Grim Reaper' Grimson, our team captain," Travis pontificated. "We go way back. Dave recently flattened a guy but hurt his hand in the process, which is why you don't see him practicing with the puck today."

"I know Dave," one of the girls said in a honeyed voice, surprising the hell out of Dave. He glanced up and recognized Mandy from Sonoma's shop, and she flashed him a toothy smile and waved a little finger.

His shock at seeing her had him nearly busting out with a laugh. Travis's mouth swung open, and his beady eyes darted from Mandy to Dave and back again. "How do you two know each other?"

"Oh, we go way back," Dave couldn't stop himself saying. He winked at Mandy.

"It's true," she giggled right on cue.

Travis stammered but quickly regained his composure. "Anyway, as I was saying about Dave's unfortunate injury, age isn't your friend in this sport. At thirty-two, his best playing days are behind him, but he's good for our club, so we like having him around." A self-satisfied chuckle followed.

Da fuck? Fat little asswipe!

Travis droned on. "I've told him hand-to-eye is the first thing to go." He yuk-yukked at his own joke.

"So, Travis," came a voice behind Dave. "I've always wondered. Where did you used to play?"

Dave turned slowly, and warmth surged inside him when his eyes landed on Nelson.

Travis went bug-eyed. "Excuse me?"

"Hockey. Where did you play?" Nelson persisted in that California-laid-back way he had of putting people on the spot without them knowing it was intentional. In that moment, Dave could have hugged the snot out of him.

"You're obviously a man who's done more than just grow up around the game," Nelson drawled. "You walk the walk, so I assume you played at some elite level once. Minors? College?"

By now, a bigger clog of teammates had joined the fun.

"Uh, a little here and there."

"Yeah? What league?" Nelson pressed, wonder in his eyes and a guileless smile plastered on his face. Dave had known Nelson long enough to know the smile was anything but guileless. Travis was on the hot seat, but Nelson was doing it so *nicely* that all Travis could do was squirm.

"Not a league you'd recognize. You know, overseas."

Now Nelson rested his gloved hand on his stick blade and raised his eyebrows. "Really! Wow! Like Slovakia? Finland? Kenya?"

A few suppressed snorts rippled through their teammates.

Travis flipped his hand. "Yeah, in there."

Nelson nodded approvingly. "What position?"

Dave could have sworn sweat beaded along Travis's receding hairline. His bug eyes got a little buggier. "I moved around."

Now Nelson feigned confusion; dude should have been an actor. "Forward or defense? You weren't in the net, were you?"

Travis suddenly whipped out his phone. "Oh hey, totally forgot this meeting. Been great talking to you guys, as always. Ladies?" He scurried away so fast the women had to run up the stairs to catch him.

Dave and the guys kept their laughter in check until the entourage was out of earshot. "That was fun," one of them said.

Nelson shook his head. "If you're gonna shoot your mouth off—"

"Better know what the hell you're talking about," Dave finished for him.

"Ain't that the truth!" Nelson grinned and held up his fist for a bump, setting off a chain reaction of emotions Dave held in. Surprise. Excitement. Gratitude. A shit ton of relief. It was the first genuine smile he'd gotten from his alternate captain in over a year, and Jesus Christ, was it a gift!

Dave bumped his fist with his good hand. "Hey, thanks, man. Appreciate it."

Nelson gripped his stick and tapped Dave's shin. "Yeah, no problem." Then he skated toward the chute.

One simple act, and bands that had been cinched around Dave's chest gave way.

Another surprise awaited him when he piled into his car and noticed a text from his attorney. He called the guy right away. "Hey, Tom. You said it was important?"

"Yeah, Grims. I got this weird call from your ex."

"Nicole?" Emergency warning lights started flashing in Dave's head. This couldn't be good.

"Yes. That's the one. She said something about giving you full custody of a dog you guys used to share?"

Dave's heart jumped into his throat. "Benny?"

"She said for me to arrange a time and place for you to meet a friend of hers who will hand over the dog and whatnot. I asked, but she swore there are no strings. Then I asked why, and she said something about her kid spending more time with his dad, who's allergic. She thought the dog would be better off with you."

Dave threw himself back in his seat. Tears blurred his vision as he stared out the car window.

Chapter 38

No Pining Allowed

Another gray mid-January day. Ellie parked the van in the alley and checked her mirrors. No muscle cars, no shiny red Mercedes SUVs, no bright white trucks. Not that she suspected Dave was the stalking type, but if he just happened to be visiting his cousin and he just happened to park in back and he just happened to get in his vehicle … Ellie wanted to be prepared. She quickly hopped out of the van and scrambled through the back door into her office.

"C'mon, Casper," she urged the dog, whose head was forever on a swivel these days, on the alert for her favorite Wookiee since that awful night weeks ago. "He's not here." Ellie's heart squeezed. Her anger had dissipated long ago, but the disappointment and hurt left a bone-deep ache inside her. In time, that would go away too, she reminded herself—again.

"Hey, El," Finn greeted her as she dumped her load on her desk.

"Hey."

"We're all done with the Christmas light takedown, and next up …" He went on, and Ellie's attention floated in and out, snatching a key word or phrase here and there. She'd been in a sort of fog the last few weeks and wrote it off to a Dave hangover. God, getting your heart snapped in half sucked. It wasn't just mental—it was physical. And she couldn't even get a Dave fix because he wasn't playing. She'd caught one glimpse of him on camera before a game, all dolled up and waving at the crowd from the team suite, where he and other injured players were relegated during home games. And oh, he'd looked good. She didn't dare ask Finn or Sonoma how he was or what he was doing because she didn't want anyone knowing how affected she was by the split—as if they didn't already know, judging by the big sympathy eyes they continually gave her.

No word about a possible trade, and she couldn't probe about that either because Dave had told her it was top secret until it was a done deal.

"El? Did you hear a fucking word I said?" Finn's voice jolted her back to the present.

"Um, yeah. Mostly."

He put down his clipboard and pen, then leaned forward on his desk. "There's something I've been meaning to talk to you about for a while."

Her eyebrows crawled up her forehead. Was he going to lecture her about how *non*-present she'd been of late?

He pulled in a big breath. "I've been thinking about going out on my own—"

"Finn, you can't do that!" she howled, panic shooting through her like a wave of electricity.

He chuckled. "Hold up and hear what I have to say first, okay? Nice to be needed, by the way."

She did need him, didn't she? When had *that* role reversal happened? She chugged water and took a calming breath. "Okay. Better now."

"Like I said, I was thinking about running my own show, which got me thinking how much I've always admired the way you run your business and how you've taken it from life support to a brand the community associates with quality again. I've also been thinking about how hard you work and how unhealthy that is, El." Light blue eyes pierced hers. "What if I were to buy in for a fifty-fifty share and we split the load?"

She blinked. "You want to buy in? And you've got money to do it?"

He wagged his head side to side. "I've put a little aside. Why do you think I've been living in that shithole all this time? I wouldn't be able to pay for it all up front, though, and I was hoping we could work out an arrangement, like maybe you carry a note for the rest or something like that. We'd need an attorney to hammer out the details, but what are your initial thoughts?"

"I don't know. I'm a little stunned, to tell you the truth."

"That's not a no."

"It's not a no. It's a 'Wow! Never considered that.' Although I gotta say, on the surface, it holds some appeal."

He smacked his palms against his thighs. "Good! That's a start."

Movement outside the front window caught Ellie's eye, and her tummy went into hummingbird flight mode. Just as quickly, it stopped fluttering when she recognized the motion was caused by Agent—er, Rick—Clemente and Felipe. Together. Weird, but neither of them was Dave, so her stomach calmed down to a manageable clench.

Felipe opened the door, and Rick breezed through with his usual coffee offering and a wide grin. "Morning, Ellie."

"Hi, Rick. Just happened to be in the neighborhood again?" He stopped by once a week, sometimes more, always with a smile and a coffee, and she couldn't decide whether it annoyed or unnerved her. Nor had she figured out what, if anything, he was up to.

Today Felipe was grinning too as he parked his butt on the corner of the desk beside Ellie's. She looked from one man to the other, then back to Finn, who shrugged.

"What's going on with you two anyway?" she said. *May as well put it out there.*

Rick handed her the tall vanilla latte from a local coffee shop he'd found a block away, claiming he preferred supporting local business over mega Starbucks. "Well," he began, "I'll tell you. Because I can now."

She straightened and wrapped her hands around the cup. "Tell me what?"

"For the past few months, Felipe has been helping me out with an especially thorny problem."

Ellie and Finn both raised their eyebrows at the same time. Felipe nodded in silence.

"What kind of problem?" Ellie asked.

"Thorny," Rick repeated with a chuckle. "I'm not at liberty to disclose, but let me ask you this. Did you read about the human-trafficking ring that just got busted?"

Finn crossed his arms over his chest. "About a week ago, right? They were bringing people in from Central America and Mexico?"

"That's the one. Well, my team was part of that bust, and Felipe here"—Rick nodded his way—"was very helpful."

"What?" Ellie gawked at mild-mannered, so-seemingly-average Felipe. "But how? Why? I thought you were dogging us because you wanted to arrest him or *me*."

Rick laughed. "Like I said, I can't go into specifics. Let's just say he and I came to an agreement that worked out very well for us both … and more importantly, for the people that were rescued."

Ellie sat back hard. "Oh. My. God!"

Finn stood and clapped Felipe on the shoulder. "Super-secret spy, huh?" Felipe grinned wider in response.

Ellie pointed at her coffee and said to Rick, "The coffees were a cover so you could come in here and talk to Felipe."

Rick leaned in and dropped his voice. "And they gave me an excuse to see *you*. Now that this is over, I was wondering if I could take you out to dinner?"

Finn frowned, but one side of his mouth quirked. "I heard that, Agent. Hitting on my sister when you think no one can hear?"

Rick straightened and put his hands up in surrender. "My bad. Should I ask for your permission first?"

"Damn straight."

"Please, sir, may I take your lovely sister out?"

"That's entirely up to her." Finn shot Ellie a pointed look while Rick gave her a questioning one. Felipe's eyebrows bounced mischievously.

A blush rose and heated Ellie's cheeks. *Nothing like being on display.* "I'm, uh, sort of coming off a breakup, and—"

Rick barreled ahead. "Then it'll be good for you to get out and have some fun. I promise I don't bite. My job doesn't allow it." He beamed a boyish grin. "You can't shoot me down in front of an audience now."

She had to hand it to him: he was persistent *and* charming. But going out with him? The invite soothed her abused ego, but *no one* appealed right now. "Can I think about it?"

"Absolutely. I'll be back in a few days with another coffee."

Shit! Nothing like a little pressure.

Days later, Ellie had put aside the uncomfortable question of how to turn Rick down nicely as she got a mani-pedi alongside Natalie. Paige had booked the entire spa at Four Seasons for herself and her crew, which consisted of her contractor's wife and daughter, her assistant, Katie, Natalie, Lily, Sarah, and Ellie. They'd been pampered and soaked, buffed and massaged, fed and champagned. Ellie was reduced to a polished, boneless, fleshy mass that smelled really good.

Natalie and Sarah were going for the royal treatment because they would soon be on their way to the all-star weekend with their men. Ellie learned that Dave, a perennial fan favorite, had to sit this one out because of his broken hand, and her mind once again detoured to how he was doing.

"Paige thought of everything, didn't she?" Natalie inspected her blue-gray fingernails on one hand while the manicurist applied polish to her other hand. "Even a limo to bring us here and take us home."

"Mm-hmm," Ellie sighed. "I think I could get used to this. Although the nails don't hold up so well when I'm playing in the dirt." She gave her own silky-pearl polished nails another appreciative once-over.

"I hear ya. Same with watching dogs all day. I think Lily's got the right idea with social media management. Those nails can tippy-tap away and stay perfect all day."

Lily protested from a styling chair. "Are you kidding? Between my seven-year-old hockey player slash ballerina daughter, my broken-jawed hockey player husband, and lugging this melon in my belly around, I don't have time to keep up my nails!"

"Okay, Lil. You get a pass," Sarah declared. "Nat, how many dogs are you watching now?"

"Since adding Dave Grimson's dog, I have five."

Ellie swiveled her head toward Natalie. "He got a dog? What dog?" Her heart did a little tap dance. Had he actually cashed in her certificate? God, she hoped so.

"The same one he had before. Cute black-and-white pup named Benny. Did you ever meet him when you guys were dating, El?"

Ellie swallowed the hard knot wedged in her throat. *Dave's back with Nicole.* "Yeah. Um, he's super sweet."

"What?" Katie piped up. "You guys aren't dating anymore? No one ever tells me anything!"

"Are you seeing anyone else right now, Ellie?" Paige asked sweetly.

"Why? Does Beckett have any brothers?" Ellie tried to make it sound light, she really did.

"He does, but he's taken."

The manicurist added her own two cents. "All the good ones are. Even some of the bad ones."

Natalie got a wild gleam in her eyes. "Not all of the good ones are. My brother, Drew, is available. You should let me set you up with him, Ellie. Sarah dated him. Ask her what he's like."

I need to corral these matchmakers. "Guys, thanks, but I really don't—"

"I only dated him the one time," Sarah added helpfully. "He's super smart, a gentleman, and really, really hot. But don't tell Quinn I said that!"

"How about it, El?" Natalie wiggled her freshly waxed eyebrows.

"No, I, um, I just started seeing someone."

"You did?" Lily didn't mask her surprise. "What does he do?"

"He's in law enforcement." Ellie wasn't really lying. She *was* seeing Rick—every time he sauntered into her office—and he *was* in law enforcement.

The girls began discussing the merits of dating law-enforcement officers versus hockey players. The thought of Dave and Nicole back together made Ellie's heart and head hurt, so she faded into the background while the conversation ping-ponged around her. Suddenly, she couldn't wait for what had been a pleasant spa day to be over.

Chapter 39

Can't See the Ice for the Hockey Sticks

Sonoma bounced up and down, clasping her hands together. "Guess what? Finn and I are moving in together!"

Dave glanced at her from where he sat in her chair, trying to muster excitement. "You sure that's a good idea, Nome?"

Her scowl made him backpedal—he really needed to watch his mouth when she held sharp instruments.

"I mean, you haven't known each other that long," he added lamely.

"Just because you fell off Mount Dumbass doesn't mean *I* can't recognize a good thing when I see it. In fact, I noticed *your* good thing long before you did. I just never thought you'd—"

"Fall off Mount Dumbass. Haha. I get it, Nome." God, she was irritating!

He sat in stony silence. It had been several days since Nelson had schooled Travis at the rink, and the guys—minus Dave—were back on the road. Even Nelson. Sonoma was way too happy to be a good drinking buddy—she was her own damn Hallmark Channel—which left Dave with no one to drown his troubles with. Not that he was drowning his troubles anymore. No, he was owning that bad habit too.

But why the hell was he here getting trimmed? It wasn't like he had anyone to impress. As if she'd read his mind, Mandy breezed by and tossed him a wink. "That was fun the other day, huh?"

He replied with a quick head bob.

Sonoma's eyebrows knotted together, and she hissed under her breath. "Is that what you want? Another shiny bauble?"

"It's not what you think."

"Talked to Ellie lately?" Sonoma practically growled.

"No." But he wished he had so he could return her latest check. The damn woman was *still* trying to pay him back for the damn van.

Quiet minutes ticked by, and he couldn't take it. "Is she doing all right?"

Sonoma gave a nonchalant shrug. "She's fine. Just lots going on with that girl right now."

"Like what?"

"Like she's selling part of her business to Finn."

What? "Why?"

"So she can take more time off."

"Why does she need more time off?" he near-barked. Not that he disagreed, but Jesus Christ, he hated that Sonoma knew what Ellie was doing while he was relegated to fishing for info.

Another shrug and a snip. "Who knows? Maybe she needs to clear her calendar so she can keep up with the demands on her social life," Sonoma chortled. "Finn says that ICE guy's been hanging around—or is he FBI? Anyway, I guess he's been trying to get her to go out with him, and Finn says he's wearing her down. Oh. And some guy from her Habitat project. Even a few guys from your team are sniffing around." Sonoma whacked his shoulder with her comb. "Don't you guys have some sort of bro code about women you date?"

"What?" Was it fucking Viktor or fucking Wyatt? Nothing but horndogs, both of them. All of him wanted to bellow, then go find the assholes and have a few words with them. Those douchebags were only after one thing. That he felt protective wasn't new—just the degree to which he felt it. The ferocity was on a completely different scale, and he had to rein himself in. Ellie wasn't his to protect.

Sonoma smirked at him in the mirror—of course she did because, with his little outburst, he'd just spoken volumes. "I liked you better with her," she said to his reflection.

"And now you like me less?"

Her expression softened. "Honestly? Yes. Plus, I think *you* like you less."

Nope, he wasn't going to dignify her armchair psychology with so much as a huff. He went for the deflect instead. "So what makes Finn so 'special'?" Air quotes on the last word.

She spoke while she snipped. "He's cut from the same cloth as Ellie, which makes him different from the clueless guys I usually meet. He put himself through the school of hard knocks, and now he knows what he wants and has a plan to go after it. He doesn't give a shit if people like him; he's unapologetic about who he is." A dreamy look drifted over her. "And who he is is pretty terrific."

Dave faked a retch. "More than just a pretty face?"

"Way more." She crouched down to eyeball Dave's ear. "His looks sort of put me off at first—he was a little *too* perfect—but he's really smart, takes care of those he loves, and he makes me laugh. Which is amazing, considering what he's gone through."

Dave's interest sharpened. Maybe now he'd finally get the skinny on Finn. "Such as?"

Sonoma lifted the hair on his crown with a comb and trimmed. "Years ago, Finn got himself into a bunch of trouble doing drugs."

Say what? "Did he get caught?"

"Oh yeah. With his pants down."

Dave turned partway in the chair, and Sonoma smacked him over the head with her comb. "Ow! And this is a guy you want to live with?"

She shot him a few daggers. "Some of us make bigger mistakes than others, but it doesn't make us irredeemable. Would you agree?"

Touché. He put his hands up in surrender. "My bad."

"Yes, it is. Anyway, he got caught not once, but several times. And who do you suppose he turned to each time?"

"Ellie?"

"She was front and center, bailing out his ass, no questions asked. She'd bring him home, give him a place to sleep, try to get him squared away. I guess it caused problems in her marriage."

Dave slid Sonoma a look. "Nome, I think her marriage had bigger problems than her stepbrother's drug use."

"True. According to Finn, Ellie tried to be all things to her ex, but for obvious reasons, she couldn't be the one thing he needed. Finn thought the guy was a bit of a douchebag, and he was glad when they broke up."

"Well, duh. If he hadn't been a douchebag, he wouldn't have fucked their employee in their office and he wouldn't have trashed their business and dumped the mess in *her* lap." Overwhelming protectiveness surged in Dave—again. He could be the guy to make sure crap like that never happened to Ellie again; he *wanted* to be that guy. But she wouldn't let him. He was also struck with the uncharitable thought that he was happy Ellie's ex came out, or she might still be with him, trying to fix everything because she was loyal to the extreme. She deserved way better. She deserved to be treated like a queen. Her loyalty, though, was one of the things he loved best about her.

Oh shit. The L word again.

Sonoma tilted his head. "Finn's kinda bullheaded, like you, so he didn't learn his lesson."

Dave snorted. "Gee, thanks, Nome. But let me guess. He got busted again."

"Yep, but for dealing this time, and the charges were way more serious. Again, it was Ellie to the rescue."

"Where was the rest of the family while this was going on? Why didn't one of them step up to the plate and help out?"

"No one else in the family knew. They still don't know. She kept his secret. Long story short, he helped send away the guy higher up the food chain, and in exchange they reduced his felony charges to misdemeanors. He did jail time, and it was rough. If it hadn't been for Ellie coming to visit him and making sure he was okay, he might not have made it.

"She also gave him a job when he got out—being employed was one of the conditions of his probation. Who else was gonna give the guy a chance?"

"Ellie," Dave muttered. *Because she's also forgiving.*

"You might say she's her stepbrother's keeper. Or was."

A little stunned, Dave met Sonoma's gaze in the mirror. "She never said a word to me." *Why didn't she trust me? Because I didn't earn it. Why does she have to shoulder this stuff on her own? Because she may be soft and delicately beautiful on the outside, but she's tough as nails inside. And damn stubborn.*

"Of course not, numbnuts. It wasn't her secret to tell. Apparently, you haven't figured this out yet—though I've said it over and over—but Ellie's one of a kind. I thought you were wise enough to realize this and finally break your old patterns." She leaned to his ear and whispered, "You know, the Mandys of the world." Then she straightened and sighed. "I hoped you'd finally graduated to an Ellie-grade person."

"What else did you think?"

"You really want to know?"

In the past, he would have been affronted by her comments. Instead, he said, "Yeah, I do," then shut his mouth.

"I look at how you acted around Ellie compared to other girlfriends. Even though you weren't together long, you were … I don't know, different."

"How was I different?"

She plugged in the clippers, and her eyes traveled to the ceiling. "You were relaxed. You acted like the Dave *I* know, the one you keep from the rest of the world. I compare that to how you were with Nicky. You were always uptight around her, like you walked on eggshells. You knocked yourself out trying to please her, but it was never enough, and I think it made you feel like you weren't enough. And that broke my heart. *She* was the one who was inadequate. I never saw her go out of her way to make *you* happy. And honestly? I don't think you *could've* made her happy. She just kept raising the bar."

The clippers whined at his nape, and he turned over Sonoma's words. She was right about one thing: Ellie came from a completely different end of the spectrum than Dave had expected. And the part about Nicky? Sonoma wasn't wrong about that either. With Ellie, all he had to do was show up, and she gave him a look that told him that was all she needed to make her happy. Correction: all he had *had* to do. Past tense.

Sonoma dusted off his neck and turned his chair so he faced her. "Ellie's not into all the glitz and glitter, like Nicole was." Sonoma paused to laugh. "I mean, Ellie's box dinner sums it up, don't you think? It's so quintessentially *Ellie.* Substantial yet simple and incredibly beautiful at the same time. She's … understated. Also, she's more like you than you realize. She doesn't size people up from the standpoint of 'What's in it for me?' She takes them at face value. She likes to do for those she cares about, and she doesn't mind wading in and getting dirty to do it.

"I've thought about why you went for her, even though she's not your 'type.' Unlike the others, where you were attracted to their looks, you got to know Ellie first—who she is, what's in her heart. You were attracted to *her*, not her face or her body or her hair. Although …" Sonoma wiggled her hands in the air. "Bonus! She's the prettiest of the bunch, in my opinion, and it's all natural."

Can't argue that. He could get lost in those Delta Blue eyes for days, never get tired of plunging his fingers in those spirals of silky golden hair, and kiss that plump, strawberry mouth of hers for the rest of his life. Physically, she was perfection. She was also a craving he couldn't satisfy. God, he was practically addicted to her. He'd never felt that way before, and he couldn't see himself feeling that way about anyone else. He didn't want to even try with anyone else. And it wasn't about the sex, although it had been off the charts from the beginning. He couldn't have imagined it going higher from there, but it had. Rockets and fireworks. Every. Single. Time. She'd brought out desires and emotions in him beyond anything he'd ever experienced, touching him on so many levels he never knew existed; he'd nearly overflowed with it.

And he wanted that back.

Sonoma released him from the cape, and he stood and kissed her cheek. "Thanks, Nome."

He'd parked in back, and when he headed out, his eyes immediately strafed the alley. The burgundy van sat outside Ellie's door, and his insides rippled. Unfortunately, Mandy followed him out, a huge grin plastered on her face.

Shit. What does she want? I knew I shouldn't have winked at her the other day. He crossed his arms. "So how do you know Travis?"

She shrugged. "A friend of mine met him at a club and invited me along for some fun."

As she talked, Dave blanked out what she said because he was too busy realizing everything Sonoma uttered was true. Mandy was a brunette version of Nicky. *This, my friend, is the type of woman you'll end up with if you continue being an idiot.* Was *this* what he wanted for the rest of his life? A revolving door of high maintenance, shallow women? *No.* He wanted a woman he could build a home with. A life with. A family with. A woman he could make smile. And there was only one for him, but she happened to be unobtainable.

"Unobtainable?" Yoda chortled inside his head. "If true you believe it to be, then true it is."

I have so much to lose.

"But to gain, much more," Yoda hmphed. "Stopped you before, this has not." Okay, so Yoda had his good points.

"Dave?" Mandy was smiling and frowning at the same time, and he shook himself back to the present. What had she been saying? Her eyes darted over his shoulder. "Oh, someone's dog is loose."

He turned. Casper was streaking toward him like a bolt of lightning. He dropped into a crouch to wrangle her, and when he looked up, Ellie stood by her back door, dressed in slacks and a sweater that showed off her slim lines and mouthwatering curves. His pulse launched into hyperspeed. She started toward him, stopped, and started again, her eyes furtively sliding between him and her door. Yeah, she wanted nothing to do with him. The girl was stupid-stubborn, but so was he. Could he out-stubborn her? In that moment, determination crystallized. If she was willing to give Finn chance after chance, then why not him? All he needed was one more shot. No waffling. He. Would. Not. Screw. It. Up.

"You know Ellie?" Mandy was asking.

"Yeah, I know her," he said absentmindedly, his eyes locked on his prize. Leaving Mandy behind, he scooped Casper up and loped toward Ellie, who grew more frantic the closer he got. "This your dog, miss? I think she's in love with me." *And I want her owner to be too.* Casper wiggled and licked, trying to reach any part of him she could.

Ellie hung her head with a defeated sigh, her loose hair folding around her face like a golden curtain. He dropped Casper at his feet, stuffing his good hand in his front pocket, while the dog snuffled the scent from his shoes.

"How have you been, Ellie?"

She lifted her face, her skin creamy and smooth as ivory, her big blue eyes flickering. God, he missed looking at her!

"I've been"—she swiped the back of her hand across her forehead—"a little out of it lately. Probably the weather."

Tingles riffled through him, and his heart swelled. "Are you pregnant?" he blurted.

First her mouth dropped open. Then her eyes got about as wide as a pair of headlights. Finally, her nose and her eyebrows scrunched together, and she took a step back, looking at him as if he'd lost his ever-loving mind.

"Pregnant?" she squeaked. "Where did you get *that* idea? Why would I be pregnant?"

He shrugged. "I've been thinking about those couple of times we, you know, and I didn't, you know, and I wondered. You can get pregnant that way."

"No, I am most definitely *not* pregnant."

An odd disappointment sliced through him. "You sure?" *Would you like to be?*

One corner of her mouth twitched. "Yes, Dave, I'm sure." Thoughts streamed behind her eyes as she surveyed his face, but he couldn't read her. "I need to be somewhere, and I'm late." In a reverse déjà vu, her eyes lifted and zeroed in on something over his shoulder. "I think Mandy's waiting for you."

He didn't bother to turn around. Just jabbed his thumb over his shoulder. "You know her?"

"Well, yeah. She works in Sonoma's shop. Obviously, *you* know her." Her arms folded over her chest, and he noticed for the first time she was wearing makeup *and* his jewelry. Where was she going all dressed up?

"Uh, yeah. From Sonoma's." He barreled ahead. "I haven't been out with her, if that's what you're wondering. Pretty sure she'd *like* to go out, but I'm not interested." *Oh great, dumbass! Don't think you could sound much stupider.*

"Um, okay. Not sure I needed to know that, but … thanks?"

"Just trying to be as open and honest as I can here. And speaking of being honest … you look beautiful." His eyes roamed over the necklace, and he tried to lock out the image of her in muted golden light with nothing on *but* the necklace and earrings. "Going on a date?" He held up his hand. "Sorry. I shouldn't have asked."

"No, you shouldn't have. And honestly, why do you care now that you're back with Nicole?"

Now it was his turn to go slack-jawed. "I'm not back with Nicole. Who told you that?"

"Benny."

He couldn't hide his amusement. "Benny told you?"

She gave him an eye-roll, and that pretty blush of hers pinked her cheeks. "No, Natalie says she watched Benny for you a few times."

He nodded. "So you assumed …"

Ellie slid her eyes to the side as though she were embarrassed. "Natalie said you had him for keeps, and I couldn't see any other way of that happening."

"I was a little shocked myself when I got a call from my attorney—"

She tilted her head. "Your attorney?"

"Yeah." He blew out a breath. "I finally did what I should have done a long time ago. I told Nicky there was no place in my life for her anymore, and that if she wanted to get word to me, she had to do it through my lawyer." Her gaze held his without wavering, and he wanted to drown in it. "I was beyond pissed about what she did to you. That *never* should have happened, and it was my fault because I ignored it until it reached the boiling point. I never, never intended for you to get hurt."

She nodded.

"Hey," he ran on, "I haven't used your certificate yet, but I was thinking, I don't know, a friend for Benny? Look, can we go grab a coffee, a drink, go somewhere and talk?"

"Can't. Like I said, I have an appointment."

"A date?" he repeated, his gut clenching at the thought.

"Dave, I really have to go." She pivoted, and Casper followed in her wake.

Stuck where he stood, he watched helplessly as she climbed into her van and shut the door. The sound tolled a bell of finality and shook something loose deep inside him. All of him sprang into action, and he ran for his car, nearly toppling Mandy as he climbed behind the wheel.

Let her go out with another guy? Oh hell no.

Chapter 40

Grim Redemption

Ellie's heart thundered like a runaway locomotive in her chest, threatening to break free and hurtle over a precipice. Her hands shook so badly she couldn't stab at the ignition button.

"Get yourself under control, for God's sake!"

Finally, she got the van started. Her only mission was to floor the accelerator and get away from Dave as quickly as possible. If she looked into those intense hazel pools any longer, she might embarrass herself. Rattled to the core, she didn't pay attention as she pulled away from her back door. The alley wasn't wide, so when a car swerved around her and pulled in front of her, she had no room to maneuver. It skidded to a hard stop at an angle, and she stomped on her brake, narrowly avoiding plowing into the moron. Now her exit was blocked.

What the hell?

Emotions already whipping around inside her like a summer twister, anger joined the mix and she jumped out, determined arms and legs pumping as she made for the car. *Asshole! Jerk!* The driver got out at the same time she registered the deep blue Aston Martin DBX.

Six-foot-three of towering, hard-packed muscle drew up to meet her. Casper had jumped from the van and now capered around the tower's ankles, adding a touch of ridiculous whimsy to the scene.

"What the hell are you doing, Dave?" Ellie screamed. Then, stupidly, she said, "When did you get the Aston back?" She shook the idiotic thought away. "Never mind. What the hell are you doing?" she repeated.

Hands on his hips, he shrugged unapologetically. "It worked for me once before. Thought I'd try it again."

"Crashing into me?"

"Well, technically, you would've T-boned *me* this time, but bottom line is whatever it takes to get you to stop running and listen to me. To give me another chance. To look under car hoods with me. To square-dance with me." He narrowed his eyes. "Exactly *why* were you running anyway?"

Why *had* she been running? Her muddled mind hadn't a clue. But give him a second chance? Or would that be a fifth? Not that she was counting. "There's too much Nicole said that I can't un-hear."

"Then lay it out there, no holds barred. Let's talk it through."

"Here? In the alley?" she squeaked. Casper yapped.

One corner of Dave's mouth twitched. "If that's how you want to play it. Like I said, whatever it takes."

Intense eyes locked on hers, and she could have sworn he saw straight into her soul. Every emotion seemed to shimmer in those hazel depths: sadness, heat, hunger, overwhelming determination, and so much tenderness it nearly stole her breath.

"I feel like a puck."

He quirked an eyebrow. "A puck?"

Yes, and you're skating for me. "Never mind."

A two-second standoff ended when he said, "Aren't you going to come over here and push me around?"

"Pretty sure that's impossible."

"Pretty sure that didn't stop you the first time." His eyes suddenly lit with a smile. "I'm also pretty sure that's when I first fell in love with you. So damn bossy, so full of spirit and fight, and you didn't give a shit who I was or that I was twice your size … or that I was scary. You rocked me, Ellie. Literally."

"What did you say?" She pulled in a few shallow breaths—it was all her lungs were capable of—marshaling her thoughts, corralling her emotions, willing her jelly knees to hold her up.

"You want to hear it again? Good, because I want to say it again. It's something else I should have done a long time ago." His stance softened, and his arms fell to his sides. "Ellie Hendricks, I love you. So damn much, it physically hurts. And I need you in my life to help me be less Wookiee and more human."

Oh. My. God. In that moment, she realized how much she'd longed to hear him say he loved her, and here he was saying that and more, baring himself to her. And Lordy, he was making mincemeat out of her insides in the process; she could only stare at him.

He bent to scratch Casper's head. When he stood upright, he puffed his cheeks and blew out a breath. "I understand if you don't want anything to do with me. I've had a lot of time to think, and I realize how wishy-washy I've been, jerking away one minute, then coming back because I can't stay away from you, then pulling away again because you're so out of my league. But I don't care if you're out of my league because I know right here"—he beat his fist against his heart—"that I'm the best man for you. If I thought there was somebody better, I'd find him and introduce you."

"I'm out of *your* league?" How was that even possible? She of short stature, skinny knees, and questionable fashion tastes. In other words, *nothing* like the Nicoles of the world.

"Yeah." He visibly swallowed. Then he tucked his good hand in his armpit and dropped it again, as if he didn't know what to do with the appendage. Was this big hunk of a man *nervous*? "You are more beautiful than any woman I've ever known, and I'm not talking about just the outside, but the whole picture, through and through. Plus, you're so damn smart and independent and giving and loyal. Jesus, so loyal! And so, so sweet." Melancholy shone in his eyes, and it gripped her heart.

A beat passed, and she recovered herself and cocked her head. "I thought I was bossy."

He cast his eyes down and quickly swung them back up to hers. His lips tipped up. "Incredibly bossy. And did I say sexy? Because you are *really* sexy, especially when you boss me around in bed."

She felt a heated flush race up her neck and engulf her cheeks. Her heart kicked up a few beats and began slamming against her rib cage again. "You mean, when you let me *think* I'm bossing you around in bed."

He shrugged. God, he so was damn cute! She wanted to plant her hands on those square shoulders and rise up on tiptoe and nibble that full bottom lip of his. She had missed him like summer without sun. Could they get back to where they'd been? Maybe … if …

"I want to come clean about something," he said. Casper sprawled in a sloppy sit across his foot. "I don't know what all Nicole said, but she lied about the bracelet. I gave it to her years ago, and it was more a matter of giving *in* to her than actually giving her something. But I did not give it to her this past Christmas. I got her exactly what I said. Something that was in a display case that took little thought and little money. And it's no excuse, but I bought it because she had just told me she'd gotten me something. Now. Am I missing anything else that has to do with her? Because I don't want to talk about her anymore. I want to talk about us."

Did Ellie want to bring up the bit about the "most beautiful woman in the world"? No. Didn't need to. He'd more than answered that question without her having to ask, and she could bury that doubt.

"What about us?" she challenged. "And by the way, you can't block me in an alley and tell me you love me and expect everything to go back to where it was."

"I don't *want* it to go back to where it was. And by the way? Your dog's really smart, and she loves me."

"You're confusing me again."

"Then let me be very clear because I want something much, much more than what we had before."

A ringtone echoed off the alley walls, and Dave slid his phone from his pocket. He held up a finger. "I gotta take this."

She blew an exasperated breath out of her nose. *Great way to show how important this relationship is, Dave.* But he crooked that same finger at her and began a slow walk toward her while he put the phone on speaker, Casper dogging his heels.

"Herb? What's happening?" Dave covered the phone's mic and whispered, "My agent."

His agent? Ellie drew a little closer.

"Just calling my favorite Blizzard captain with some more good news," a smoky voice said.

"I'm your *only* Blizzard captain." Dave slid Ellie a look and winked.

The gravelly voice on the other end chuckled. "True, but you're still one of my favorites. How's the rehab coming?"

Dave glanced down at his bad hand. "Good. The doctors are happy with how it's healing, and they've already started me on PT."

"Excellent. Just what I want to hear, and I'm sure Arizona's management will feel the same. I just got off the phone with them, and they're willing to keep the offer the same as long as you pass their medical evaluations."

"Gotta admit I'm still a little surprised."

"Don't question the hockey gods," Herb said. "Arizona's a solid Cup contender, and you'll make an impact the day you join their club."

"That's, uh, great news, Herb." Dave's tone had Ellie craning her head to look up at him; he was looking right back at her, a frown puckering his face. "Herb, what if I stayed in Colorado? Is it possible the club wants to keep me after all?"

"It's not April Fool's yet, Dave." Herb's voice held no amusement whatsoever.

"And I'm not joking."

Herb blew out a long, slow breath. "Why?"

"Colorado holds a whole lot more appeal than it did before. I'd even entertain a pay cut to stay if that's what it takes."

The phone call ended with Herb grumbling about clients who couldn't make up their minds.

Ellie blinked wide eyes. "Why would you do that?"

"Because someone I know has a business here, and I figured she wouldn't want to move to Arizona."

What? "No one ever asked her," she sputtered.

He picked up her hand in his good one and enveloped it with his strength, his warmth. "The truth is I'm not the easiest guy to get along with, and I've fucked up so much in my life that I couldn't imagine you wanting to be with me for the long haul. I was afraid that if I asked, you'd say no."

"As the great Wayne Gretzky once said, 'You miss a hundred percent of the shots you never take,' or something sage like that."

His eyebrows kissed his hairline. "You're quoting Gretzy now? You *are* a hockey fan."

"I'm a Dave Grimson fan."

Still holding her hand, he brushed a rough thumb over her knuckles. Chills—the good kind—raced through her body, numbing the toes she wanted so desperately to bounce on. "So about this move. You'd actually pass up a chance to make more and have a shot at the Cup with Arizona to stay in Colorado?"

"I would … for you. Not for anybody else or for any other reason," he said softly. The intensity and heat that shone in his eyes left her with no doubt he was serious, and fresh shivers rippled through her.

"I'm speechless. I don't know what to say." Tears flooded her eyes and spilled over, taking her by surprise.

"Well, you need to say something soon because you have to help me make an important decision. Do I stay in Colorado, or do I go to Arizona?"

"You want *me* to wade in on something that … earth-quaking?" Her voice warbled with emotion she fought to hold in.

"Of course I do. It's what families do. They make big decisions together. I'm not going anywhere you won't be happy, so …"

"We're not exactly family."

"Not yet, but I'm just stupid enough and determined enough to believe you'll sign on." He squeezed her hand. "Would you like us to be? I sure as hell would."

"Meaning?"

"I want you to marry me."

"Wait."

"Am I confusing you again?"

A laugh broke free from her chest, and she was part-crying, part-laughing. "I haven't even told you I love you yet."

"Then what the hell are you waiting for? Here I am proposing, you're accepting, so get with the program already."

Up on tiptoe she rose, and she wrapped her arms around his neck and kissed him. It wasn't one of those wild, out-of-control kisses they'd shared so many times before, but it was filled with love and promise and something so bottomless she couldn't fathom it, and it spread like a wildfire from her heart to the tips of her toes. It lit every lamp in her arena and had her melting against him. She pulled back to catch her breath. Her eyes dove into his. "I missed you so much. I love you, Dave. With all my heart."

He cupped her face with his good hand. "I love you too, Ellie. With all my hearts."

"Hearts?"

"Wookiees probably have more than one. They also mate for life. Marry me, Ellie."

She started laughing and couldn't stop. Tears flowed down her face for an entirely different reason, and she thought she might actually lift off the ground.

"That was funny? Shit. I need to work on my proposals."

She caught her breath just long enough to gasp, "Planning more than one?"

"No way. Although when I imagined *this* one, it was way cooler than asking you in a back alley."

Laughter burst from her again.

He chuckled along with her. "See? Now that's what I want to see the rest of my life, and I'm going to do everything in my power to make you laugh like that every single day."

She straightened and swiped moisture from her cheeks. "Ooh, I like the sound of that. So what do we do now?"

"We go to Oster's. I saw some rings there I need to show you."

"Oh shit! I totally forgot I have to be somewhere."

Dave's face turned dark and growly. "Not on a date with an ICE guy? Or a Habitat guy? Or one of my damn teammates?"

"No!" She burst out with another laugh. "At the lawyer's office. Finn and I were going to lay the groundwork for him buying into Landscaping with Altitude."

"I'm an off-duty paramedic," a breathless voice came from behind them, startling them both. "Does anyone need help?" They turned to see a guy with concern etched on his face. Beyond him, to their surprise, a few cars and a small audience had gathered, including Finn and Sonoma.

"El," Finn yelled, "I canceled the appointment. This is more important."

"Guess we were in our own little world here," Dave mumbled to Ellie. To the paramedic, he said, "We're good, dude. We didn't crash … this time. I just had to block her in to get her to agree to marry me." He smiled down at Ellie. "Of course, I still haven't heard the *yes* it's going to take for me to let her out of this alley."

Casper added a few yips as if to say, "Go, Dave!"

Before Ellie could answer, Dave had his hand up and was addressing the crowd. "What does everyone think? Should she marry me? Yes or no?" He pointed at them. "If you say yes, I'll buy each one of you a pair of tickets to a Blizzard game. If you say no, you're dead to me."

"Yes!" the crowd yelled, and Casper yapped at his feet. Then people began chanting, "Say yes! Say yes! Say yes!"

"You're bribing them!" Ellie squealed.

"Damn straight. Whatever it takes. So? What'll it be? Speaking from experience, it's always a good idea to give the crowd what they want."

The chanting grew louder, amplified by clapping.

"Then I guess I'd better say yes!" she practically yelled to be heard above the noise.

He cupped an ear. "What was that?"

"Yes!" she shouted.

He gave the crowd two thumbs-up, and they broke into wild cheers. He swooped her up in his arms and twirled her, and she wrapped her legs around his waist. "I love you, Ellie Hendricks, for the rest of my life."

Tears threatened to flow again. "I love you too, Dave Grimson," she choked out.

"That's all I need to know." He kissed her long and deep.

Breathless, she pulled away. Behind them, the crowd had quieted to a dull roar. "How about we take this someplace more private?"

He rubbed her nose with his. "Let's go get that ring first—I don't want you getting away. And maybe we should go on that real date we still haven't had. Considering we just got engaged, don't you think it's overdue?" He waggled his eyebrows. Ooh, she'd get to see him do that over and over and over … and she'd get to kiss him over and over and over … and …

"What, exactly, did you have in mind for a date?"

"There's this little honky-tonk I've been hearing about that has great ribs, a live band, and dancing."

"Line dancing?"

"Yes, ma'am."

"What if I stomp on your feet?"

He gave her a wide grin. "Don't care. Stomp away."

"I have a dress I could wear."

"Yeah, you do, and red boots that make my knees weak when you're in 'em. Or out of 'em. Come to think of it, maybe the date can wait."

"Mmm … better bring your cowboy hat."

Chapter 41

Only the Beginning

Five months later

Sweat dripped down Dave's face as he leaned forward, his stick ready, every muscle taut, waiting for the puck drop in their defensive zone … waiting for the final seconds to tick down … waiting for—

The whistle blew, the linesman dropped the puck, and Nelson's stick blade swept it back. Hadley corralled it and made a quick pass back to Dave in the corner. Dave skated it around the back of the net, looking for the outlet pass, but they were outnumbered six-to-five and he didn't have an open man. He found that extra gear he'd been finding all night and skated hard, fast, took a hit against the boards that had the other guy losing his balance and going down. Dave tapped the puck out of his zone. Nothing fancy. No icing. He didn't dare look up at the clock, didn't dare take his eyes off the puck.

C'mon, c'mon, c'mon!

And then it happened.

The horn sounded, and all hell broke loose. Sticks hit the ice, gloves flew in the air, helmets spun where they were dumped, leaving a yard sale of gear strewn over the rink as he and his teammates yelled, skated at each other, mobbed one another, becoming one big tangle of sweat-drenched players jumping, tackling, shouting, cheering.

"We won!" he roared from within a clog of guys. "We fucking won!"

They'd won it all! They'd won Lord Stanley's Cup!

His eyes lifted to the stands, to the sweetest sight in the whole goddamn world. Ellie, in *his* jersey, tears streaming down her face, jumping up and down, hugging the other women, blowing him kisses, mouthing I-love-yous. His heart was so damn overfull he wasn't sure it could take any more before it burst. The exuberant noise faded into the background as he held her gaze, sharing this pinnacle with her, savoring the frozen seconds, engraving this sweetest of all moments in his heart, locking it in his memory vault forever.

The clamor thundered back in his ears, and the arena was a blur of screaming fans and pulsing pompoms. Next came a whirlwind of victory: the traditional handshake with the opposing team, followed by cramming on ball caps declaring the Blizzard this year's Stanley Cup champs, the team picture with the Cup at center ice, and the awarding of the Conn Smythe trophy to Gage Nelson for most valuable player during the playoffs. The entire time, Dave's eyes traveled to Ellie, and every time she met and held his gaze, her face lit as though a Roman candle blazed inside her.

Then the best moment of all, after he'd posed for pictures with the commissioner and the commissioner finally relinquished the Cup to Dave. He hoisted it over his head amid his teammates' cheers and skated a small circle before lowering it and kissing it. Another pump of the gleaming silver trophy toward Ellie and he handed it off to Nelson. And so it went, guys lifting the Cup, kissing it, passing it on. When the families finally made their way to the ice, he spotted Ellie and skated right at her, hoisting *her* above his shoulders, lowering her to kiss her, and twirling her in his arms on the ice.

Tears trailing over her cheeks, she told him how much she loved him, how much he deserved this, how happy she was for him.

"This is you and me, El. No way could I have done it without you." He buried his face in her neck. "I love you."

Without a doubt, *she* was the best prize he'd ever won. How the hell had he gotten so damn lucky?

"Created your own luck, you did, yes," Yoda said approvingly.

After myriad on-ice interviews and congratulations, it was finally time to head to the locker room. As captain, Dave held the Cup aloft and walked it down the hallway through a gauntlet of cameramen, reporters, and cheering staff. When he stepped over the threshold into the locker room, his teammates greeted him with deafening shouts of their own. His eyes quickly took in plastic sheeting and stainless tubs filled with iced champagne and beer bottles. The boys each had a bottle of something they were shaking up, and a beat later, fountains of foam spewed at him, at the Cup, and anyone caught in the middle. Drenched, he handed the Cup off to T.J., who took a solid spray-down of his own.

Dave and his teammates yanked off their jerseys and gear, pulling on T-shirts that also declared them the winners. All around him was joyful chaos as guys hugged, sang "We are the Champions" way off-key, and poured beer and champagne on the coaches and each other. Coach LeBrun stepped up on one of the stall benches and let fly a piercing whistle, and the noise dropped a decibel. A huge mic suspended on a pole hovered by his head.

"Yeah, Coach!" someone yelled.

He patted the air in front of him, and the racket slid another decibel. "What a ride, huh, boys?" They hollered and cheered in answer. He perched his hands on his hips. "It was long and it was grueling, but I had no doubt we'd get here because you are true warriors. You battled your way through, and you persevered … through injuries, through the toughest, the best teams in the league, through sacrifices at home. There's not one selfish guy among you. You believed in each other, took care of each other, and you played your hearts out. For each other. With courage and strength." Then he bellowed, "You are truly the. Champions. Of. The. World!"

Whoops went up, together with a few more sprays.

His voice dropped. "Every winning team needs guys who step up to the plate, who put aside their egos, who overcome their own struggles, who put other guys on their backs and carry them across the finish line. And every winning team needs a leader." Coach swiveled his head, and his eyes landed on Dave. "You had a damn fine example of what I'm talking about right here in your captain."

The room roared around Dave, and emotions that had been dancing in his bloodstream suddenly fused, shot up, and lodged in his throat. He swallowed hard. In that moment, he was damn glad he was covered in champagne because tears were spilling into his beard.

Coach pointed at him. "This man had a battle of his own going on, but you didn't see that because he put everything aside for his team, and he overcame those struggles so he could be everything this team needed him to be. That's the mark of a true leader."

Dave glanced at Ellie, who stood on one of the benches against a far wall with other WAGs, out of the champagne-and-beer rain, her wet eyes mirroring his. His tears came harder, and there was no hiding them. He pressed a knuckle to his eye while guys clapped him on the back, pulled him in for hugs, and cheered, "Rea-per! Rea-per!"

Nelson, hoisting his Conn Smythe hardware, made his way to Dave with a shit-eating grin. "This should have been yours." He tried to hand it off to Dave, but Dave shook his head.

"Nah. That's all you, man." Dave cleared his throat and raised his voice. "It's every damn one of you in this room. I am so in awe of all of you, of us, and so damn proud to be your captain."

Thank fuck they threw out more deafening cheers and drowned him out because he was too choked up to say more. Coach hopped off the bench and threw his arm around his shoulders. "Glad you didn't go anywhere," he said so only Dave could hear.

Dave swiped at his eyes. "Yeah, me too." *It was all worth it.*

"All right," Coach yelled. "Enough speeches from me. Party on! You've earned it!"

And party they did.

Later that night, after a rowdy team dinner, Dave was still on a high as Ellie drove them home. Jesus! Would his feet ever touch the ground again? His face hurt from smiling so much. At every red light, he leaned over and kissed her. He had no idea what time it was when she pulled into the driveway beside the house they'd bought months before, but the whole damn block had turned out, and another party was under way. Lots of familiar faces: neighbors, teammates and their wives, Finn and Sonoma, Dave's and Sonoma's moms, Felipe and his family, Ellie's family.

It was a warm June night, and grills were going, coolers of beer and every other drink imaginable filling the cul-de-sac along with tables loaded with food. Music thumped around them, and sugared-up kids tore through yards. People congratulated him, and he got lost in the noise and the crowd.

When he went looking for Ellie, he found her in their front yard, sitting in a lawn chair beside Sonoma, surrounded by Casper, Benny, and their new dog, Rico. Sonoma stood and patted him on the chest. "Sit with your girl."

He slid into Sonoma's chair and offered Ellie his beer, which she declined with a "No, thanks."

He chuckled. "You're off DD duty for tonight. You can party too. Do you want me to grab you some wine?"

She shook her head. "No, I'm good."

He suddenly noticed her face was drawn and pale. A few alarm bells went off inside him. "You tired? What time is it? Do you need to go to bed?"

She smiled her special smile at him. "Yes, I'm tired, it's around 3:30 a.m., and not a chance I'm going to bed. Not on a memorable night like this."

He leaned over and nuzzled her neck. God, she smelled good. "No? What if *I* need to go to bed?"

"To bed or to sleep?"

He fiddled with the strap of her sundress. "Oh, I'm not sleeping for at least another twenty-four hours."

She giggled and gave his playoff beard a tug. "Maybe we can take this off now?"

"I thought you liked the way it tickles your—"

Someone shrieked behind them. A teammate's wife, being thrown over his shoulder and taken for a jog around the cul-de-sac. Which gave Dave a great idea.

"What do you say we duck into our bedroom for an hour so you can congratulate me the right way?" He waggled his eyebrows.

Her small hand pressed against his heart. "People might miss you."

He traced her jawline before covering her hand with his. "Nah. They'll never notice."

"But you're the captain of the team."

"Captaincies come and go." He shrugged.

"Meaning what? You won't be team captain next season?"

"Probably will be, assuming the boys still want me, but I'll need to earn it."

"I'm sure you will. And if you don't, well, you're about to become the captain of a new squad. A permanent one."

He cocked his head. "Huh?"

"You've been too consumed by playoffs to notice, but it's not only tonight I've stayed away from alcohol. I've been doing it for the last several weeks."

Though he was buzzed, he felt the full impact of the jolt that went through him. "El? What are you trying to tell me?"

"That maybe we should move the wedding up a little sooner?"

He dropped his beer can, and his impossibly wide smile grew wider. "Shit! Ellie! Seriously? Are you pregnant?" They'd gotten a little careless lately. Okay, a lot careless, considering the rhythm method wasn't exactly foolproof to begin with.

Tears filling her eyes, she nodded. "Is that okay?"

"Are you fucking kidding me?" he yelled. "Jesus, it's more than okay! C'mere, sweetheart." He pulled her out of her chair and into his lap, where he kissed her and locked her in a bear hug. "Oh shit! I shouldn't do that."

She laughed. "I'm not a piece of glass, and keep your voice down! I'm not ready to announce it to the world yet."

"When are we … when …" Suddenly overcome by emotions on a night already overripe with them, he couldn't make his tongue work. He stared into her glossy blue eyes and felt tears welling in his own again. "Aw Jesus, El. I love you so damn much." The tears spilled over, and suddenly they were forehead-to-forehead, crying and grinning together. "We're going to be parents," he whispered.

"We're going to be parents," she repeated. "In mid-February. Not great timing for the hockey calendar."

"I don't care about the hockey calendar, El. All I care about is right here"—he cradled her cheek, then moved his hand to her flat belly—"and here. You and the baby are my whole world. That's all I want. Ever. It doesn't get any better than this."

He pulled her to his chest, tucking her close. She nestled against him, and he wrapped his arms around her and nuzzled her silky hair. "When my career's over, let's buy a nice spread where our ten kids can run around."

"Ten?" she coughed.

He chuckled. "Okay. Nine. And we'll hold box socials and square dances."

She looked up at him. "Except for the nine kids, that sounds perfect."

"Yeah, it does."

Less than a year ago, his life had been a cesspool. He could hardly fathom the man he'd been back then. This man right here, the whole one cuddling the love of his life … who carried his child. *Their* child. This was the man he had always wanted to be. Would always be. For her, for their new family.

His family to love, to cherish, to protect. Forever.

The End

MAC IS A SINGLE DAD UPROOTING his children, and Mia's struggling under the weight of her own chaos. Neither has happily-ever-after in their sights. Here's an excerpt from *No Touch Zone*, Book 6:

> They discussed hockey for how long, Mia had no clue, but they kept it up through an order of appetizers and more cocktails. She was grateful, getting lost in a different world, and her mood lifted. Mac knew his stuff, and the longer she talked to him, the cuter he got. Or was that because Alli kept the drinks coming … especially his? No, *him* consuming alcohol wouldn't make him cuter. It should make *Mia* cuter, more appealing despite her bedraggled business clothes and frazzled façade anyway.
>
> The bar had grown crowded and a little rowdy. During a lull in their conversation, he leaned in to be heard above the din. "So what do you do?" A musky sandalwood fragrance wafted off of him. Subtle and really, really nice.
>
> "I thought you knew. I'm a bedbug wrangler, of course." She giggled, actually giggled, not missing her big sister's eye-roll.
>
> He guffawed. "No, seriously. What do you do?"
>
> Something—maybe the scotch—made her say, "How about we don't trade personal information? No names, no jobs."
>
> A slow grin spread, highlighting a very square jaw under scruff. "That's not exactly fair because you already know *my* name."
>
> "Do I? Sounds more like a nickname to me."

"Well, I need to call you something besides 'hey you sitting next to me.' What's *your* nickname?"

Before Mia could deflect, Alli butted in—of course she did. Where had she come from, and how could she hear above the din? Big sister radar. "Fruit Loops. Loops for short," Alli blabbermouthed.

"Traitor!" Mia growled as Allison speed-walked away.

Mr. Blue Eyes's grin broadened. "Fruit Loops?"

Mia glared at him. "I used to love Fruit Loops, okay? Lots of kids do."

"Yeah, but most kids don't get stuck with the nickname."

No one had called her that in years, not even her mom. Suddenly, the very thing she'd been trying to escape all night came rushing back and whomped her like the bad-tempered willow in *Harry Potter*. Mac was talking, and she reminded herself to get it together and tune in.

"… crowded in here. Can I take you to dinner? In the restaurant here or somewhere else or …"

She blinked. "You bought me dinner."

"Only appetizers." He suddenly shoved a hand through his wavy locks, looking all kinds of cute and nervous, and Mia's mind detoured to whether he had a hotel room upstairs. From there, it was a short hop to imagining the warm weight of his big body on top of her in a fluffy bed.

Staring at him for a beat, she tuned into the silent signals thrumming between them, running through possibilities in her head. A one-night stand with a good-looking guy who wasn't local, who wouldn't want more than she could give. *Oh, so tempting.* She considered it for a hot second before her responsible self stepped in, though not soon enough because Mac was talking again.

"Then maybe we could order you dessert—or more scotch—while *I* eat dinner?" Hope danced in his eyes, and the cockeyed grin returned.

While she might be happily lubed, she was neither so lubed nor so happy that she would cross her sane self. Though Mia had never been in love before—she'd been close once—she recognized that a guy with eyes like his was dangerous, whether he was an out-of-towner or not. Something about him set off all kinds of sirens, complete with bullhorns shouting, "Run the hell away!" because with a snap of her fairy godmother's fingers, Prince Possible-Dream-Come-True could morph into Asshat Supreme. Mia had heartache in spades as it was and couldn't afford to heap on more.

Urgency to leave surging inside her, she gathered up her purse. "That's really sweet, but I have an incredibly busy day tomorrow. In fact, I should get going."

Disappointment transformed his features. He cleared his throat. "Don't go yet."

Seeing the lonely plea in his eyes twisted emotions inside her, and warring factions tugged at her to stay, tugged at her to flee. Reminding herself that lonely guys often transformed into clingy ones, she slipped into her saleswoman persona. "I really enjoyed spending time with you. It was fun, and you kept my mind off … well, off my troubles, and I can't tell you how much I appreciate that. And tempting as staying sounds, I really need to go." She patted his surprisingly steely bicep, and electricity raced through her fingers, up her arm, her chest, her shoulder. Nothing like that had ever happened to her before, and it rocked her, making her reconsider for another hot second.

Get your copy of *No Touch Zone* at Amazon and find out how fate steps in with plans of its own, putting two hearts on the line.

SEVEN PLAYMAKERS COUPLES unite for a winter wedding getaway, but there's trouble in Paradise. Claim your free copy of *Puck the Halls* at www.gkbrady.com and see if they can find the spirit of Christmas—and each other—before it's too late.

Author's Note

Thank you so much for reading *Defending the Reaper*! Despite his scary Wookiee exterior, Dave has a huge heart. He had some issues to work through, and I wanted to pair him with someone who could see the good guy hiding beneath the gruffness. Ellie came to life as I wrote, and she ended up being Dave's perfect match!

If you enjoyed Dave and Ellie's story, I would love it if you would leave a review on Amazon, BookBub, or Goodreads to help readers like you find the story. And if you do leave a review, I would love to read it! Email me the link at gkbrady@griffin-brady.com.

Be the first to know about upcoming releases, bonus content, giveaways, and discount deals by joining my newsletter. Simply go to: https://www.gkbrady.com.

Trouble is brewing. Disaster strikes. Can they conjure a mistletoe miracle? Claim your free copy of *Puck the Halls* (Book 7.5), a Playmakers novella, when you join. Download it at https://gkbrady.com/bonus-content/pth/ or scan this code:

The playlist for *Defending the Reaper* can be found on Spotify.

Acknowledgments

To Cryssa, a wonderful author, ARC reader, and friend who first planted the seed for giving the Grim Reaper a story of his own. He thanks you, as do I.

To the country and western music aficionados among my readers who so generously helped me with the playlist.

To Jodi, for once again helping me suss out these crazy characters and what they get up to.

To Stephanie, for your artistry and your endless stream of great ideas.

To Jenny Q, my editor and cover designer. I'm running out of ways to say thank you!

To Word Servings (aka Persnickety), for your astute catches, as always, and for keeping my inconsistencies from being consistent. I'm so glad you're versed in Yoda-speak.

And always, to my husband, Tim, my own Rock of Gibraltar. It's been one hell of a year, and I'm so glad you were there to hold me up when I couldn't do it myself.

Books by This Author

The Playmakers Series®

Book 0 - *Line Change*
Book 1 - *Taming Beckett*
Book 2 - *Third Man In*
Book 3 - *Gauging the Player*
Book 4 - *The Winning Score*
Book 5 - *Defending the Reaper*
Book 6 - *No Touch Zone*
Book 7 - *Twisted Wrister*
Book 8 - *Besting the Blueliner*
Book 9 - *Guarding the Crease*
Fall Novella - *Love Rinkside*
Winter Novella (Book 7.5) - *Puck the Halls*
Spring Novella - *Deking at Love*
Summer Novella - *Slapshot Summer*

The Fall River Series

Book 1 - *The Keeper*
Book 2 - *The Fixer*
Book 3 - *The Rescuer*
Book 4 - *The Harborer*

About the Author

Since childhood, all sorts of stories and characters have lived in G.K. Brady's imagination, elbowing one another for attention, so she's thrilled (as are they) to be giving them their voice on the written page.

An award-winning writer of contemporary romance and historical fiction, she loves telling tales of the less-than-perfect hero or heroine who transforms with each turn of a page.

G.K. is a wife and the proud mom of three grown sons. She also writes historical fiction under the pen name Griffin Brady. She currently resides in Colorado with her very patient husband.

Connect with her on these platforms:

 www.amazon.com/author/gkbrady

 www.twitter.com/GKBrady_Writes

 www.facebook.com/AuthorG.K.Brady/

www.bookbub.com/authors/g-k-brady

 www.goodreads.com/author/show/19488321.G_K_Brady

 www.instagram.com/authorg.k.brady

 www.youtube.com/watch?v=a7b48cfYQuE

 www.pinterest.com/gkbrady0993/

www.ingramcontent.com/pod-product-compliance
Lightning Source LLC
LaVergne TN
LVHW010559100826
845148LV00014B/2778
9781735455891